CAMERON WALKER

DREAM LORD

THE PRODIGAL

I0563810

SILVERSMITH
PRESS

Published by Silversmith Press—Houston, Texas
www.silversmithpress.com

ISBN 978-1-961093-53-9 (Softcover Book)
ISBN 978-1-961093-54-6 (eBook)

CONTENTS

THE DOOR

Clavin shoved the massive blackwood doors back and stalked into the chamber, prepared to kill anyone who got between him and the two he'd come for. As the forty-foot-tall, inky, black panels continued their slow opening traverse, he quick-scanned the massive throne room to gauge the reaction of the denizens who thronged the two-hundred-foot table. The great doors boomed to a halt behind him as hundreds of stupefied faces glanced up to stare.

Clavin tensed as he prepared to dole out a lesson in swordsmanship.

The boom echoed back down from above; all the faces turned upward for a moment and then angled back to the food-laden table before them.

Clavin gave a quick glance up at the ceiling, cloaked in distant shadows. He focused back on his goal and took long, purposeful strides toward the far end where he could see a man sat at the head of the table. His guide, the beautiful witch-princess, rushed to catch up. He felt as if lightning charged his muscles and forced his fingers to dance on the hilt of his sword. Clavin was halfway through the room when a scowl twisted his face. But, recalling the first encounter, he forced it to a semblance of a smile.

Where are they? All this work for nothing? Nothing?

The woman beside him looked over. "What brings the turns of happiness to your face, Sir Knight?"

He recalled the same line from before, so he returned the same reply. "Naught," he snarled, but caught himself and sweetened his voice, "but the thought of meeting your blessed father."

She inclined her head in return. "Right this way then."

Clavin approached the seated king, with the two dogs beside him. He stopped and nodded.

"Why have you come here?" asked the king.

To exorcise my demons.

"Great King, I have come here to meet the Knights Rige and Garner."

"Rige and Garner," ruminated the king with an expression more smirk than smile. "I am afraid your mission is failed. There are no such knights here."

Clavin's eyes widened a hair as his pulse increased while his hand clamped down on the hilt of his sword and ground the pommel into his palm. He took a breath. *Calm. Be calm. Could be different names.* "Rumors of you and your kingdom have come to me. I was told that two mighty knights stood always behind you, and two dogs sat at your sides. I see the dogs but not the knights."

"No, I am sorry. I have no such warriors at this present

time. Please sit." The king waved to the chair next to him and his hounds.

As the princess slid the chair back for him, he stood still as a rock, and his jaw tightened. "No. If the knights are not here, then I must be going."

The princess beside him lay her hand on his arm. "Oh, but you cannot go."

"And why, pray tell, is that?" he growled.

"The castle is burdened with magic. Only a great warrior can remove it, thus freeing us all. We must have your strength."

Clavin smiled in return. *I don't think so.*

She smiled and reached for his hand.

He saw her do so and replied with his thought. "I don't think so."

The princess dropped her hand and stepped back as a stern look crossed her face. "Father," she spat to the king at the table.

The king stood to his feet with a red-faced scowl as wine sloshed from the cup he slammed down on the table. "You *shall* help us. Oh, yes, indeed, you most certainly shall, or my wrath will fall hard."

Deep down inside, a stream of invective roared through Clavin's head as he fought a red tide of rage. He took a deep breath and stilled the tremble in his sword arm.

"And if I should help you?" asked Clavin in a mild voice.

"Hmph," snorted the king as he nodded in triumph. "Then, sir, you may go on your way."

"Last time your offer was far better." Clavin's mouth smiled, but his eyes refused to follow the lead.

"What?" demanded the king.

"Your daughter in marriage and your throne as my own."

"I think not!" growled the king. "Get thee to thy duty, or thy head shall be forfeit."

Something inside Clavin Roth broke, and he laughed in a near hysterical pitch before responding. "I think not, *old bean.*" He reached out, grabbed the princess, yanked her up to him ...

And kissed her.

The king screamed, "TO ARMS, TO ARMS ALL."

Clavin released her and stepped over to the king while his enhanced strength launched an open palm that slammed into the king's chest and lifted the man completely off his feet.

The king flew backward as robes flapped like flags in a storm and crashed back down onto his great chair. The massive guard dogs leaped; the one on the right directly at Clavin and the other on the left up onto the table which separated them.

Clavin pivoted and bent his legs as his right arm jacked out to catch the first dog on its chest. He thrust upward from his waist and twisted as he threw the beast like a snarling sack of teeth at the men now approaching from behind.

The second dog had landed in the plates to the right of the king's seat, and dishes flew everywhere as it scrabbled back to its feet, slipping in the food and the wine. It rushed across the massive table to launch itself at Clavin as he, in turn, flipped in a backward somersault. He landed beside the throne even as the dog flew through the air where Clavin had stood a moment before.

As both dogs gathered themselves for a rematch, Clavin drew out two knives and threw; they sank hilt deep into the dogs and they sank to the floor. Clavin spun back to the king, and in unthinking, red rage, whipped out his hand, snatched the king's goblet off the table, and drained it in a single gulp. Clavin tossed the cup away and ignored the sound as it bounced on the table while he stepped forward and yanked the king's crown from his head. "I'll be taking her and your crown with me."

The king, however, relaxed in his chair as a strange calm overtook him and a true smile lit his face. "Oh no, now it is *my* turn to *think not*." He then called out in a louder voice, "Stand down, stand down all."

Clavin had no time to wonder at the strange shift in the king's mood as a wave of lethargy passed through him and replaced the electric energy that had pervaded him moments before. A strange mist covered his eyes, and things began to move slowly.

The witch-princess laughed behind him.

His eyes blew wide open as understanding hit him. *THE WINE! You fool. You stupid fool.* He scrambled to reach for his pouch, but his hand would not move.

"So," said the king, who rose from his throne and recovered his crown. "I think perhaps you *will* be helping us out after all. However, in your present condition, you won't be terribly useful. We must fix you up a bit."

With a snap of his fingers, another set of doors opened and in came two men, obviously twins, huge in size, who carried between them a sack that clattered like a stack of teapots. They stopped before Clavin's motionless body and began to draw forth the contents within.

Clavin screamed in his mind as they dressed him in the armor. The king took the Hand of Fate, Garner took his pouch, and Rige took Peccavi.

When they finished, the king stepped before him and laughed in his face. "Now, *old bean*, you shall accompany these two worthies down into the dungeon and aid them in a small matter." The king studied the Hand of Fate for a moment. "Oh, is this some charm against magic?" He tsked. "Can't have that now, can we?" The king took his flagon and smashed the amulet into bits on the tabletop.

Clavin groaned inside.

The king grinned. "Well, that's that, then. Now, when these nobles are done with you, you shall come straight back here. I have a nice spot for you behind my chair." He glanced at the two dead hounds. "My *new* dog."

Carried by the laughter, Clavin was forced to watch through his own horrified eyes as his body responded to the orders given to him. They marched off to the first stairwell and began the long trek down. Stair after stair, flight after flight, landing after landing. As they passed below ground, the passage grew dank, dark, and dirty. But still they descended. The Dark Castle was vast, both above and below.

Down they traveled. Man, Clavin, man, as the squeak of Clavin's new armor assaulted his ears. After a while, one of the men stopped and declared he had a potion that would further strengthen Clavin's armor.

"Shall I apply it?" the man asked of Clavin.

Clavin was forced to agree.

Onward they went while a desperate Clavin struggled for some control to no avail. By the time he stepped off the final stairwell, he didn't even fight the unbidden words from his mouth.

"Bottom floor."

Events replayed much as they had when the roles had been reversed. The twins discussed various methods for dealing with the troll, and Clavin listened in deepening despair. Soon the troll would charge down this hall, into this room and, magicked as he now was to attract attacks, he would be killed by the beast soon thereafter.

They settled in to wait.

Clavin's mind spun over his life. The grand adventures he'd lived and his greatest moments. His thoughts turned back to his mom and dad who, though not always agreeing with him, had clearly always loved him. He stopped on his childhood memories and was surprised to realize that, with all of his adventures, some of his best recollections related to his youth.

Clavin glanced over at the two dead men who now sat on the far side of the room; one yawned as he looked backed and raised his head. Clavin looked away. "I couldn't have known."

7

His supposed companions both looked up at these muttered words, and he returned a baleful glare. Rige grinned and went back to his nap. Clavin paced the damp room, back and forth, like the caged tiger he was, waiting for death.

He came within an arm's length of the doorway and tried to take one final step and escape through it. The magic that ruled him clamped down on his muscles, turned him around, and marched him back to the far wall.

Like a goose, I'm cooked. Waiting for the troll to show up and stick in the fork.

The great Ranger of Samlin-Cordis had come to the end of his tricks. Every strategy, every clever move, every magic, tactic, and potion; he reviewed them all yet again. There was nothing. The magic had trapped him like a bug in a double-thick web. Now, here he was; hundreds of feet under the Dark Castle, five thousand miles from Cordis ahead and the same from Samlin behind, with two days left to get to one of them and exit the Dream before it collapsed.

If I could just break free of this spell. I could make it.

But he couldn't. He had crossed into the Vast Desert yesterday to reach the Dark Castle. He had found it, of course; he had forced it. A bad idea, but he'd run out of the good ones. Even as dread wrapped him in a stifling blanket, anticipation had built for a final showdown to end this nightmare, one way or *another*. It was clear now that it was going to be *another* in a twisted end that made him the butt of his own villainy.

THE DOOR

He stared at the door which yawned back at him. Lintel stones marched like gray teeth and mocked at him to try for the door yet again. Clavin leaned back against the wall and felt the cold stone of the dungeon seep through the unaccustomed armor. His eyes fell to the dirty stone floor and found a crack which he followed to where Garner sat quiet on the floor.

Garner opened his eyes, looked back at him, and raised an eyebrow.

Clavin looked away. *You killed them; now they're going to kill you. That's only fair.* He nodded. The image of his parents flashed through his head, and he envisaged the scene, in days to come, as they received the news and his letter. He sighed. *Mom, I'm sorry. I'm so sorry.* He thought of the last fight with his dad. *And that too. At least I didn't kick them out of the house. I left them that.*

Thoughts of his youth flashed. There he was with his mom, after he fell from the tree. She held him close, stroked his hair, and sang to him as they waited for the doctor. When he broke her prize vase and he'd felt so bad she'd hugged him and said ...

"I love you, Buster," he whispered the final words of his memory aloud. He recalled other words burned into his mind from a treasure house of memories formed long ago by a master craftswoman expert in the language and tools of love.

I love you more than this vase, more than this house, and more than the whole world. Do you know that, my little man? Do you?

He imagined her opening the letter he had written long before. "I hope you like it." *What was the first line again?* It came to him in an instant. *Right. Take me to an Alpine Valley and there let me lie.* He remembered playing ball with his dad, fishing on the river. *Thanks, Dad.* He recollected fights with his sister and the many races they'd had. He'd been fourteen the first time he beat her in a race. He had whooped like a warrior who'd just defeated an army. Clavin gave a wan smile at the memory. *You were a great sister, Aline.*

Clavin's gaze traveled back to the door, and he imagined the door of his parents' house in its place. *What I'd give to see that just one final time.* A tear threatened to run, but he stopped it. *No. You brought this on yourself.* "So suck it up," he ordered. *In a few hours, back in real-world, the sleepers will wake, the Dream will collapse, and I'll disappear, like a bubble in a wash stand. Like Meri.* "And Steel." *How did it come to this? How did I let it go so far? How did a Ranger end up bound and trussed by magic, waiting for death?*

Clavin cast his mind back. *Right. Let's start there.*

ANTIK Y'THERA

A young Michael stood on the bank of the river Satus, a stone's throw from his uncle. Solidly between the age of toy soldiers and the discovery of young girls, he struggled to understand one of the great hows. He glanced over at his Uncle and down at the basket next to him where lay three captured fish, and he considered his own, empty, basket.

He shook his head and began to spool in his line onto the crude box attached to the base of his pole. Done, he dropped the pole and stomped over toward the older man.

The man saw him coming and pointed his chin toward him. "Hey, Buster, packing it in?"

Michael, who'd long answered to the nickname of Buster, shook his head. "Uncle Antik, how? Three fish? How?"

His uncle's face opened with a broad smile at the question. "Oh, dear. Something wrong? How's your basket doing over there, Buster?"

Michael's lips pressed together, causing Antik to laugh.

Michael felt the emergence of a smile but fought it

down as he pretended to be angry. He took off at a run and launched himself at Antik's stomach.

For his part, Antik was no newcomer to Michael's unpredictability, and he responded in a flash. In less than a minute, he stood holding the boy by the ankles upside down as he continued to struggle. "Well, say it. Antik is the best fisherman ever. Go on."

Michael barked out the word, "No," even as he laughed at his situation.

"Okay," the man replied. "We'll do it the hard way." He stepped forward and waded down into the river till the boy's hair trailed off in the water due to the current. "Now, who's the best?"

Michael continued to struggle. "I am. I'm the best ever."

"What was that?"

"I said, I am ..."

But Michael's sentence was cut off by the cold water as his head dunked down into river.

"Sorry," Antik replied, "I didn't quite catch that?"

Michael had sputtered out the water already and began to reply. "I said ..." As he felt himself being lowered again, he quickly changed his tune. "Wait, wait, wait. I meant that you're the best. Uncle Antik is the best."

The man hoisted him back up again. "You know, I like what I'm hearing. I'm not sure though, you might recant if I let you go. Maybe one more dunk to be sure."

"No, no, no," yelped out Michael. "You're the best. I mean it." Michael laughed out loud. "Really, you are the king of the fishermen."

Antik walked back up onto the bank and let him down.

Michael squeezed the water from his hair and then plopped down beside his uncle who, was now seated beside the basket. "I don't get it, Uncle Antik. What am I doing wrong?"

"Buster, is it time for you to begin to learn the dark arts of that most wondrous activity; fishing. You know how to hook a line to a pole and throw it into the water. But, down the ages, from thousands of years past and many frustrated hours of fruitless angling, the knowledge that different types of fish respond to different types of lures has come to us. An expert fisher understands that his vocation is ancient, complex, and mysterious."

The man spooled up his line, drew his lure into his hand, and then presented it for the boy to look at. "What do you see?"

"Well, you've bound a few small, silver, spoons together and attached feathers to them. Is that your lure? Where's the worm? Did it fall off in the water?"

"Nope, not at all. There is no worm on this lure. No cricket, no fish, just this. This lure, which I call Spoon Baby, attracts Culan Bal such as the ones I've caught today. The Satus is full of these fellows, and believe me, they are good eating. So, that's what I'm fishing for. You see the results."

"The lure? That's it?"

"Well, you still have to know how to fish, where to drop the lure, how to snake it across the water as you draw it back to you. And, of course, there are days when even

I still don't catch anything." He shrugged. "Part of the mystery, part of the challenge."

"Okay," Michael replied doubtfully. "So, where do I get a lure like that one?"

"You don't, you make it."

"Make it? You made that lure? Yourself?"

"I am Antik y'Thera, the great lure maker and fisherman."

"Where'd you learn to make lures like that?"

"In Stowling City. A friend I met there taught it to me."

"Stowling? Where is that?"

Antik looked down at the boy and paused for a moment. "I'm not certain we should go down that path, Buster. Your dad might not approve."

"What? Dad wouldn't approve of learning how to make a fishing lure? You're putting me on."

The man plucked up a piece of grass and chewed on it for a moment before tossing it away. He gave a shrug and turned back to the boy. "You know what I do for a living, right?"

"Uh, well, Dad says you travel a lot. I don't know how you make money doing that though. You haul stuff around, I suppose."

The man nodded as his head cocked sideways. "Well, that's actually an apt explanation. I Travel, and I haul goods. But the Traveling I do probably isn't the traveling you are thinking of. I'm part of the community of people known as Dream Walkers. You've surely heard of those, right?"

Michael nodded. "Sure. The other guys talk about it. They talk about fighting dragons and doing magic. Dad doesn't talk about it at all. I sort of thought it was all a joke. Sort of like Snipe hunting."

"And that, Buster, is why I'm hesitant to talk about it. Your dad is a good man. One of the best I've ever known. But he doesn't like what I do." Antik shrugged. "At least, I don't think he does. He avoids talking about it with me. It's one of the things I like about him. Too many people hound me to talk about my trips between the worlds, and Hollen just talks about real life. It's stabilizing."

The boy stared at him. "Between worlds? So, you're saying that the stories are true? You have been to other worlds?"

Antik nodded. "That I have. Actually, to one other: Stowling."

"I thought you said that was a city?"

"It is. It's a bit complex but, in short, nearly every world has a city named the same as the world. They are endpoints of the journeys. People like me, Travelers, we end up getting assigned a route—or a Path as we usually call them—named using the two endpoints. Our world is named Cordis. So, since I Travel to Stowling, my Path is named Cordis-Stowling or Stowling-Cordis, as one prefers."

"Are there many other worlds then?"

Antik nodded. "Oh, yes. Thousands. Some say there could be millions, but we only have access to a few thousand. I'm not sure about that. No one really is, I don't think."

A wonderous thought passed through Michael's mind. He sat up and focused on his uncle. "Uncle Antik, have you ever fought a dragon? Seriously?"

The man stared out over the flowing river for a moment before replying. "I think, in deference to your dad, I better not get into the details of any of my Crossings. That might be a bridge too far. This conversation might already be. I hope not."

Michael was disappointed but not defeated. "So, how do you get paid doing that? It sounds like fun. Why would someone pay you to have fun?"

Antik smiled. "That's a great question, Buster. It turns out to be pretty simple. There are things on our world that people on Stowling will pay good money for. There are things on theirs that people here will pay for. There are Merchants who pay people like me to carry them between. Straightforward."

"Okay, but you seem to be pretty well off. They pay that well for you to just take a trip? Why doesn't everybody do that?"

The man sighed and wobbled his head back and forth. "So, Buster, the thing is, without going into the details of *the thing*, these Crossings, while usually safe, can turn deadly, and they can do it faster than a bird can change direction in a dive. People die. Often. So, what we're really getting paid for is the danger. And the dangers are real. Probably a third of the people who begin don't survive their first ten Crossings."

Michael's eyes popped open wide at this revelation. "How many trips have you made then, Uncle Antik?"

"Sixty-two. I'm forty-eight from Runner."

"Runner? What is that?"

"We have rankings in our society based on how many Crossings you've made. They can be modified by the general danger of the Path and the length. Plus, some people can call out the number of notable Charks they have survived. It gets complex."

"Wait. What is a Chark? I've never heard that word before."

"Of course not. But, in a sense, you've experienced it before." The man rolled to his feet and swatted his pants to knock off the dust and grass.

Michael followed suit and replied, "I don't understand."

"I presume you've had bad dreams, right Buster?"

"Yeah, of course. Had a full-on nightmare last week."

"Well, in your dreams, you probably don't enter the situation with some monster about to kill you, right? Things start out normally and then turn bad. At least that's how it works for me."

"Right. I remember one time I was walking through the fields picking corn and suddenly the corn all developed poisonous stickers. I was too terrified to move."

"So, just before the corn turned, do you recall the mood changing? Did things seem to get darker even though the sun still shone just as brightly as it had the moment before? Do you recall anything like that?"

Michael focused down at his feet as he recalled the faded memory of the nightmare. He shook his head. "Not in that one, no, but I have had dreams like that. Everything would seem fine, and then it would feel like it had gotten colder and dimmer but, as far as I could tell, nothing had really changed. It just got creepy, for no reason. And then the reason would show up later."

Antik nodded. "That's it exactly. You can feel a chill that isn't real, you can see a darkness that isn't there. Chilly dark is what they called it, and it long ago got shortened to a single word: Chark. That, in turn, required another word, Feening, to describe how we register a Chark. It is the act of feeling the chill in our souls and seeing the dark that doesn't exist. We Feen it. So, two made up words that mostly only make sense to Dream Travelers."

"Chark. Huh. Chilly dark. Okay. So, the Chark sort of notifies you when things are about to get dangerous then? Sort of warning signal, right?"

"Close. Charks always tell you that things are about to become more dangerous, that is true. But, even on a normal Crossing, there is danger." Antik pointed at the river. "It's a lovely day today, but if you go swimming in the wrong parts of the river, it could still kill you. Same for the Paths. There are still dangers, and you still need to avoid or deal with them. You just pray a Chark doesn't blow up while dealing with a normal danger. Suddenly, crossing a beautifully-made hanging bridge can turn deadly with blowing winds and fraying ropes." The man shuddered as if recalling a memory.

"So, we could be standing here, and suddenly a whale could jump out of the river to try and kill us? Like that?"

The man nodded. "Yep. Almost anything. And magnified

in a Chark. If bad enough, you pretty much have no chance. Flowers on an empty grave."

Michael considered what he had heard and pondered his uncle, who seemed to have turned somber, unlike his normal magnetic personality. After a while, he probed again.

"How is it possible? It's magic, right? But I thought magic didn't exist."

His uncle nodded. "So far as we know, there is no such thing as magic, with the exception of DreamStone."

"DreamStone?"

"Under the right conditions, people who are sleeping in the close vicinity of DreamStone somehow give it the ability to open the portals that enable us to pass between the worlds. No one knows how it works, it just does. No one knows how the Inn was created or what enforces the rules inside of it. We know it has been around for tens of thousands of years, it is complex beyond our ability to comprehend, and mysterious as to who or what formed it all."

"You think someone formed it?"

"Well, I'm a simple man, but yes, I don't see any way something so complex and enormous could have been an accident."

"Do you think he is good or bad?"

Antik looked over and focused on him. "Who?"

"Whoever created it all."

"Ah." Antik rubbed his chin as he considered it. "Well, he could have set it up to give us access to things normally beyond us. That would be good. But why didn't he make it safer? That seems like the work of someone bad, doing it for their own amusement."

Michael added, "Maybe it was the only way he could make it? You couldn't get one without the other?"

Antik nodded. "So, a choice between leaving us all separate from each other or letting us take the risks if we want to. Hmm. You might be onto something there, Buster. Then, it's not him causing pain, it's ourselves. It's up to us. A choice."

Emboldened by his uncle's approval Michael added, "And that sounds like the work of someone good, at least to me."

"I agree. But it does seem like a lot of people die who might not have needed to." He shrugged.

"Uncle Antik, why do you keep doing it? Is it really that dangerous?"

Antik released a great sigh and turned to face the boy. "Buster, I started Traveling in order to earn a little more money. And I've made more than I ever imagined I would. I could stop. I should stop. But ..." He shook his head and chewed his lip.

"But what?"

Antik's gaze fell onto his caught fish. "Michael."

Hearing him use his given name focused the boy on the words that followed.

"Look at those fish. They saw something they couldn't turn away from. If I were to have released them back into the water, given some time, I could catch those same fish again with the same lure I used before. They couldn't resist their natural urges. Do you see that?"

"Well, yeah, I suppose."

"Try this then. You haven't spent time in Cordis City. It is a place of enormous wealth because that is where the Dream Gates and the Sanctum lies. But if you travel about, you'll find that there are beggars in alleys desperate, not for food—for there are jobs everywhere in Cordis City—but for certain plant extracts that cause them to feel wonderful for short time periods. They live from one day to the next, begging money to buy more of their favorite plant. Most of them know it is bad for them, that they will die early, but so strong is the desire that they can't stop themselves. They're trapped by it."

Michael's forehead scrunched as he considered the words. He looked up into the man's eyes. "You're trapped by your job? By Traveling?"

Antik nodded. "It's addictive. Michael, if you ever have a thought to take up Traveling, think long and hard about what I've said. And then, when you are done, think about it again. There are dangers beyond just the Crossings, and they aren't obvious until it's too late."

Sobered, Michael replied, "I will, Uncle Antik." He paused for a moment to feel the wind on his face. He spoke, a little shyly, "Uncle Antik, you know, you're not just the best fisherman, you're my favorite uncle too."

Antik smiled. "And you, Buster, are my favorite nephew. Now, let's head home."

Months passed, and Michael worked beside his father on their farm. The fields and farms turned into verdant green lakes of tasseled corn that rippled in the cooling winds as farm dogs ran the borders to keep out the unwelcome and the barn cats kept them free of mice and rats.

He sat by a wagon, washing the corn and pulling the tassels while he savored the smell of freshly baked bread along with the beans his mother was cooking inside the house. His sister, Aline, came out from the home and sidled up beside him to help him out.

"Is this all you've done?" she jibed at him. "Been out here sleeping again?"

He replied by cramming the tassels in his hand against her cheek.

She slapped his hand away and yelped, "Hey, I came out here to help you. Try that again, I dare you."

At eleven, she was two years older and a lot bigger. Michael knew better than to try it.

He sighed.

And then he tried to cram another wad of tassels into her face.

Aline grabbed his arm and twisted it up behind him. Once he cried out in pain, she grabbed her own wad, reached around, and shoved it into his mouth. "Don't do that again."

"Okay, okay," he promised, spitting to clear his mouth out.

She let him go and watched him warily for a moment before going back to work.

"What you been doing in there?" he asked.

"Churning butter, helping Mom shell peas, and learning how to make a pie crust."

His eyes lit up. "We having pie tonight?"

"Yep. Cherry."

"Ohhh," he gushed. "I love cherry pie. Not as good as her apple, but still." He closed his eyes and imagined the taste to come. "Soooo good."

An ear of corn smacked him on the forehead. His eyes popped open as he watched Aline get to work detasseling the weapon she'd just used on him.

"Keep working," she ordered.

Eventually his dad, Hollen, came back from the barn, followed by their two dogs, Shuch and Harwick. "Okay, kids, I'll push this into the barn. Take the dogs and go wash up. Time to get in for the night."

They were more than ready and hungry as the dogs who ran circles around them on the way to the house. Aline went in and helped their mother, Gantiel, get the table set while Michael saw to feeding the dogs and getting them settled for the night.

Their dad came in and settled. He said a prayer of thanksgiving, as he always did, and they began to eat. They talked about the small things of the day as they ate, taking their time to savor the meal. Just as they were finishing the main course, the dogs began to bark out front.

Their father, Hollen, rose and went out onto the front porch, taking a large, heavy walking staff with him as he went. Michael and Aline crept into the front room to peek out the window. A somber-looking man stood there murmuring to their dad and, after a minute, handed Hollen an envelope, nodded, and turned to go back to the coach that was waiting for him in the distance.

Their dad stood holding the envelope down by his thigh even as his head dipped forward and down. A long moment of time passed.

"What's Dad doing?" Michael asked Aline.

She looked over at him, worried. "I don't know, Buster, but it's bad, whatever it is. Dad just got some bad news."

Michael wondered how she could tell, but then he studied his dad for a moment and nodded. "Yeah."

Hollen straightened up and turned back to the house. Aline and Michael waited for him to come back in. Hollen saw them.

"Dad, what is it?" Aline asked.

He gave a great sigh before answering. "I have a letter here from Uncle Antik. Let's go back to the table, and I'll read it aloud."

A stab of fear shot though Michael's heart. "A letter from Uncle Antik? Why didn't he just come himself and tell us what he needed to say?"

Hollen reached out a hand and gently gripped his son's shoulder. "Come on, son."

Michael followed woodenly and took a seat along with his mother and sister.

Hollen opened the envelope, pulled out the letter, and began to read.

ANTIK Y'THERA

Hey, buddy, it's me, Antick.

Well if you're reading this, I guess things didn't work out so well for me as a Traveler. I know you weren't thrilled when I told you I was going to give this a try. You know me, I had to give it a turn. And, who knows, maybe I had a really long run and did some good. I hope I was able to leave you something.

I know we aren't strictly family, but we may as well be. Making me godfather to your kids, I took that as a great honor. I was lucky to have a friend like you from a young man on. You're a good man, and I think I was made better by knowing you.

Those kids of yours are absolutely first rate. Both of them smart, honest, hardworking, and tough. Stubborn too. I like that. Not quitters. You tell them I was proud of them both. Just as I was proud to know you.

If I didn't get married first, then I'll have left you something on account. Make sure you get it. Hope it amounts to something.

Well, there's not much left to say. I hope this doesn't hit you too hard, old friend.

Soldier on and, who knows, maybe we'll meet again one day.

Antik y'Thera
Friend of Hollen and Gantiel
Godfather to Michael and Aline

Michael could see the mist in his father's eyes and felt it in his own. His jaw clenched, and he jumped up and ran from the table, out into the night and into the barn. Shuch and

Harwick followed him in and bedded down beside him in a pile of hay where he curled up and bit down hard on his fingers to well the tide that threatened to erupt.

A little while passed before the barn door opened. Through closed eyes, he heard steps approach and then felt the hay move as someone settled down next to him. A heavy arm wrapped around Michael, and he knew his father's touch.

They said not a word, and the boy reached over to hug his father.

His dad released many a deep sigh as he stroked his son's hair.

Michael woke the next day in his bed, clothes on, and hay stuck into shirt and hair. He came down to breakfast and found a warmed pie waiting for him. He stared at the desert, so delicious, that he'd been anxious to get at last night. Before. He turned for the door.

"Buster," his mother called. "Aren't you going to eat?"

"I will, Mom, just not now. Thanks though."

"Okay," she replied softly. "You let me know when you're hungry."

Michael went out and began tasseling corn. He worked for hours until Aline came out.

"Hey, Buster, you've done a ton of work here. Go on in and let me finish it up, okay?"

He grabbed another ear in reply.

"I know you're hurting, but how is working your hands bloody going to change things?"

He paused, opened his hands to look at them, and replied, "Hurt hands ease hurt." He grabbed another ear.

Aline wrapped her arms around him in a strong hug and forced him to stop.

He struggled. "Let me go. Let me go."

"No," she murmured. "Much as I want to kill you sometimes, I love you."

Michael replied bitterly, "So did Uncle Antik."

"Well, I'm still here. So are Mom and Dad. Do we count for anything?"

Michael stopped struggling and nodded.

She released him, turned him around, and pointed him back to the house. "Go eat, Buster. I'm your big sister. That's an order."

He caught her eye and replied, "Thanks, sis," before marching off.

The funeral was four days later. Antik was a beloved figure, and the ceremony was large. Many people came to say goodbye to the man. Michael's family returned home, and he asked his sister for a pen and some paper.

"What for? Who are you writing to?"

"It's ... well, for Uncle Antik," confessed an embarrassed Michael. "I have to say something, but I don't want to say it out loud. Okay? Can I have it now?"

Aline's features softened. She retrieved the items and handed them over without a word.

He nodded his thanks and turned to leave. He stopped at the door when she spoke.

"Good for you, Buster. He'd have liked that."

He nodded again and left.

A few days later, Michael entered the graveyard accompanied by Harwick. He stopped by a fresh tombstone where he laid flowers and a note upon the stone and then left immediately as tears poured down his face. A wind blew up and sent the note sailing. It landed not far from the home of a nearby family. The mother retrieved the note and read it.

You were the best of all fishermen and the greatest creators of lures. But you were a better uncle. I miss you and feel like someone has augured out a hole in my heart. I pray you are in a better place. I now understand those words you spoke at the river. While there are many others laid here already, I've come today to lay my own flowers on your empty grave. I love you, Uncle Antik. Goodbye.

The note eventually made its way back to Gantiel, who kept it always as a reminder that her tough, little boy had a soft heart.

And that made her glad.

WARRIOR

A dark forest of light-sucking trees welcomed Clavin's sight as he crested the ridge. "Dark Forest indeed." *What did they say back at the Inn?* He murmured the words, "Deadly in day, but beautiful night, stay on the Path, Traveler's delight." He absently chewed his bottom lip for a moment. *Let's have a look.*

He dismounted and led his horse forward down the trail to the edge of the wood. He stopped to study the leaves of a tree from close up, stretched out a hand to touch one of them, and halted. "Nope." *Let's not do that.* He drew his belt knife and used it to shift the leaf, about to view it from different angles. *Getting pretty dark. Can't tell much. Cut one off for later?* He squinted at the leaves. "And maybe the trees wouldn't like that." He re-sheathed his blade. *How dark does it need to get? Pitch?*

He shrugged and stepped back to pet his horse. As he did so, something akin to a sigh poured from the trees, and the smell of cut grass sweetened the air. He turned and noticed that the leaves, so black before, were now changed.

Are they regular leaves now? Hard to tell in the gloom. He stepped back to the nearest tree and reached out again. His hand hesitated and hovered close to the leaves without touching them. *Lot of things could go wrong here.* He nodded and shrugged. *But the trees are normal now. Normal trees don't kill people who touch them.* "Point." *It doesn't pay to go looking for trouble.* "But, no risk, no reward." *There's that, of course.*

He sighed, reached out, and plucked the leaf off of the tree. *Probably should have checked for magic first.* He considered his supply of potions and shrugged. "Limited supplies. Anyway, nothing happened." *Still.* "Shut it."

He tried to study the leaf, but the dark was too thick upon him. *Regular torch or a potion?* The crackling noise of a thousand fires swept through the air, breathed out from the forest. The night receded from the glow of a million leaves that danced in cool flame, emitting warmth rather than absorbing it.

Nice. He looked down at the leaf in his hand, but it remained a leaf. *The power flows out from the trees themselves then.* With the practiced motion of a thousand rides, he mounted and headed into the woods. *Ten miles.* "Easy."

He rode for half an hour when the sound of a song accompanied by cellos and flutes drew his attention through the trees to his left and into a meadow of some sort. Three women, beautiful, willowy with hair of green and skin of brown, danced there and sang. The smell of honeyed roses halted him.

The women ceased and turned to look at him through

the intervening trees. "Come and stay with us, traveler. Tell us about your journey. So little news comes to us here." Lips red as ripe berries, eyes blue as deep pond water, their hair rustled in a wind that he did not detect and whose strength did not touch the trees about them.

Clavin's mouth grew dry as his pulse hammered a song of desire inside his veins. He opened his senses to feel for any Chark. Nothing. He adjusted his collar to release the sudden heat as he focused on the women.

Girls on the path, bring sudden wrath. Girls in the bed, you wind up dead. He clinched on his reins and gave his head a shake. "No, ladies. I have a pressing engagement. I thank you, but I must be moving along." He kicked his horse, trotted away, and ignored the offers called out from the women. Once they were entirely behind him, he reached down into the pouch and thought of *silence*. He pulled out two balls of a waxy substance and placed them into his ears.

He considered what he had just given up and shook his head. *Might have been innocent, and might have been death.* "Half the fresh Walkers would have jumped right into that." *And that's why I'm headed for Ranger status, and half of them die on their first ten trips.* "Bad to the bone."

He moved along and reveled in the beauty of the glowing forest. After another half hour, the woodland trail took him over a hill and down again to spill out into a large glade. In the very center sat a fire pit, surrounded by cut stones and filled with blazing logs. Five large, wooden benches surrounded it and, on one of them, sat a man with a knife whittling away, flicking chips into the flames before him.

Where's the exit? He scanned the glade and didn't see where the trail left the meadow again. He looked back at the man and sighed. *Here we go.* Clavin reached into his pouch and concentrated on *see magic.* He pulled out a vial, flicked it open, and rubbed a drop of oil onto his left eyelid. Clavin replaced the vial and next focused on *disperse magic.* He pulled forth a different vial and sprinkled some of the contents onto himself. He returned the vials and earplugs to the pouch, dismounted, and walked up to the fire.

"Hello there. I'm passing through. The path seems to stop here. Can you help me?"

The man ceased his carving and looked up at Clavin. His eyes burned bright as the sun and startled Clavin, who stiffened at the sight. The man replied in a musical voice.

"The way runs out before you,
based on where you seat.
If you stay upon your path,
fear not who you meet.
But even on a path,
though pleasure you may find,
time is not your friend.
You must keep that in mind."

Clavin pondered the words. "I understand. One thing only is not clear to me. There are five benches here, including the one you sit on. I am heading for Cordis, and I am not sure which bench would send me in that direction. Would you be so kind as to suggest the correct one?"

"Seasons come the trees do grow,
benches to the kingdoms go,
but benches change from man to man,
depending on the person's plan."

Crap. Riddle time. Clavin smiled and gave the whittler a small nod. He closed his left eye and, from the magic drop placed on it before, looked through the closed lid and scanned about him. Sure enough, the man, the fire, and all five benches were magic. Clavin began to study each bench, front and back. Nothing presented itself. He got down on his back and explored the bottoms of the benches to no effect. *Of course, it's hard to be sure of the backs and bottom in the shadows.* Clavin concentrated on *light,* pulled a glowing stone from his pouch, and re-examined the benches. He chewed his lip, got back to his feet, and leaned onto a bench as he focused on the fire before him.

Okay, is there anything out of place here? What do we have? "Five benches, all magic." *Choosing one by sitting on it must cause a path to appear. That's their reason for being here and why they need to be magic. Got it.* "A direction giver," he murmured with a glance at the man. *Which could have just as easily been a sign but, hey, this is the Dream.* "And the fire." *Why does the fire need to be magic?* "Why is the fire magic?" He focused back on the whittler and called out to him in a louder voice. "Why is the fire magic? What does it do?"

"A clue you've found
to this riddle.
Take that thought
and with it, fiddle."

Fiddle; instrument? Music? No, surely not. Just a rhyming way to tell me to work with the idea. Music. What is he carving? Could it be a flute? "May I ask what you are carving?"

"The wood I carve the fire feeds
no answer here is what you need."

Clavin nodded. *Okay. But that would have been clever.* He sighed again. *Back to it.* He stepped around and prepared to sit down on a bench to ponder the situation but caught himself halfway with a hand and addressed his companion again. "If I sit down, is that making a final choice, or can I choose another later?"

"Once you seat your way is set.
A wrong choice here you won't forget."

Whew. Almost a disaster. Clavin pushed back up to his feet, paced around the fire, studied it, and focused on the cut stones. *Maybe a clue is hidden there.*

But the stones were only stones.

Fire burns, and light reveals. He shook his head. "But nothing is revealed by this light." *Well, this light doesn't fall on the shadowed places.* "But I used my own light on those." *That's a different light.* "Ah. This light is magic. Maybe ..."

Clavin grabbed a bench and shoved to see if it could be moved. It spun around, grating like a giant's pestle. There, in the firelight, the word *Arndal* shone. Clavin grinned. The third bench he spun blazed the word *Cordis*. "Bad to the bone," he chuckled. He checked the other two on general principle with the whittler's agreement to change benches. Clavin sat down on the Cordis bench, and a path rippled through the grass of the glade out to the tree line. The trees shifted and formed a clear exit. The whittler stood as the other benches disappeared, and Clavin addressed him one last time.

"Thank you, sir, for your words. Have a good evening. I'm off for Cordis."

The man nodded without a reply.

Clavin mounted his horse and rode out of the clearing.

Another hour passed as he flowed through the magical woods. A chill rippled through him, and a subliminal feeling of dread interrupted his mood. The forest seemed to emit a low groan, and his horse jerked to the left as if startled by the wind. *Showtime.* Clavin dismounted and walked ahead of his horse. *Better check him.* He turned and stared into the eyes of the stallion. He checked the teeth and hooves too. Satisfied, he led the horse forward. *I should be over halfway through the wood now.* He considered the possibility that the forest was now much more than ten miles thick and shook his head. *Don't borrow trouble, and don't say that out loud.* Clavin looked up into the sky and spoke in a stentorian voice. "Physical dimensions don't change once set. Less than five miles to go."

The forest grew both brighter and warmer. What had been so charming and cozy turned harsh and sweltering as the light of the leaves blazed brighter. In a few minutes more, Clavin squinted against the light as sweat poured off him.

At full gallop, we'd be clear in minutes. "We might not have minutes." Clavin's hand stroked over the amulet that hung around his neck, but he shook his head and yanked his hand away. *That would kill you.* "Focus." *What can I do?* "Fire burns, but water cools." *But these trees aren't on fire; they're just emitting heat.* "Let's fix that." *And then what? Where will you avoid the flames?*

Clavin scanned about till he saw a depression in the ground nearby. He rushed over to it even as his hand pulled out a large flask from the smaller pouch. He hesitated a moment. *It won't empty fast enough.* He grimaced and then shouted, "Burst all in thirty." Clavin tossed the flask down into the depression and reached into the pouch again. This time, he drew out a large, glass flask filled with red liquid and stoppered with a nozzle attachment. He twisted it open, and a gout of flame streaked out. He sprayed fire up into the leaves of the trees about him, and an inferno erupted.

The horse screamed and bolted.

Clavin brushed off a momentary pang of conscience.

It's not real, idiot. The heat of the flames scorched him. He backstepped, tripped, and fell onto his back into the hollow where he gasped for relief. *Thirty was too long.*

Clavin concentrated on counting. *One, two, three.* When he reached ten, water exploded and enfolded him in a cooling deluge. From under the surface, he saw the trees all around him burning, like wooden giants with blazing hair, circling about his small pond, angered by his presence, and forming a roaring furnace. Able to think of something other than being cooked alive, he reached into his pouch and pulled out a different vial. He wrapped his lips around its mouth, twisted the cork off with his teeth, and managed to take a swig as he concentrated to keep the cork securely crushed between his teeth.

A new tingle ran through him. He opened his mouth to let the water run in, and he breathed like a fish. Clavin smiled and lay back to enjoy the show above him. After a half-hour, the strange feeling of dread and disquiet dispersed, and the nearby trees burned out. Clavin rose from his watery refuge and trod along the path to the nearest unburnt trees.

The leaves had returned to their normal warming glow.

He thought about the horse and shrugged. *Guess I'm walking.*

He reached the end of the wood before midnight and camped just beyond the final trees, where he made use of the light. Still soggy from his drenching, he lay out his clothes. *Might as well study the forest while waiting on the morning.* He approached the nearest tree and cut off entire branches. He found that a branch the size of a staff continued to energize the leaves to give off their light. *Nice.* From some of the branches, he cut off individual leaves and practiced touching the cut leaves back to the branches. As soon as they touched, the leaves began to glow again. *Light sticks.* He shrugged. *Not as convenient as the potion though.*

"But these also absorb energy during the day." *Might be handy someday.* He opened his pouch. "Hmmm. What to call these? Light sticks?" *No.* "Glow sticks?" *No. I don't care about its lighting properties. I have potions for that.* "Absorbers?" His face scrunched in disdain for the word, but after a moment, he nodded. "Okay. For now." He concentrated on his pouch again. "Add item absorber." He then proceeded to add ten of the long branches into the small pouch.

As the dawn approached, the forest returned to green, and then, minutes later, shifted into the light-sucking darkness for which it was known. Clavin pulled on his clothing, now dry and stiff, and headed off in the morning rays.

The following two days passed with no new complications, and he approached a small cottage with the word *Cordis* carved large and deep into its lintel. Clavin stopped to study it. "What? A cottage?" *About the right distance. But it's pretty much always a town or city. A cottage?* He shook his head. "But that forest was odd too." *Must have a new Dreamer in the mix.* "Or someone has been reading stories." He shrugged the thought away and delved into his private store of wisdom. *Things that are new and stand in your way, approach them with care if you'd be okay.* "Right."

Clavin pulled out a couple of vials and anointed himself. He walked around the cottage and finally, satisfied, strode up to the door and knocked. When no one answered, he leaned in to inspect the latch, then reached out and opened it. A white mist, like a captured cloud, filled the frame such that he could not see beyond it. He stepped in, walked a few paces, and the mist disappeared. In front of him ran a short hallway, maybe 10 feet long, which ended in a heavy, metal door. He pushed open the door, walked through and entered into a large room, more like a cavern, perhaps three hundred yards on each side. The room was formed of an unusual stone, a blueish gray with slight silver flecks embeedded in it. He glanced back and watched as the door he'd just come through, and the number above it, 92, disappeared, leaving a blank space on the wall.

Tables filled the center of the massive chamber with floating numbers that glowed above them suspended in mid-air. Clavin headed for table 92. As he walked, people in the hall greeted him. "Hello, Warrior Roth. Safe trip?"

"Yep. No sweat." He chuckled. *Actually, there was sweat and lots of it.*

As he arrived at 92, three men and one woman, all stunning, sat talking. One of the men stood.

"Warrior Roth. So glad to see you. No problems, I presume?"

"Nope. But I was hot to get out of there." Clavin grinned.

"Oh? Ready to get home then?"

"Yes, you could say that. So, here's your load."

Clavin pulled off his pack and handed it to the man. He exchanged papers with the Merchant, and both signed. "Thanks again, Merchant Coinmar. Have a great evening."

TRAVELER'S INN

Clavin exited Cordis Hall into a wayfair composed of subtle magic, striking men, and beautiful women. People flowed in both directions, some of whom he knew, and all of whom knew him. Clavin turned left and strolled along with the traffic. Every single person he saw was an exemplar of humanity. The men averaged six and a half feet tall, the women six inches shorter. Muscles bulged on the men; the lithe women bore the features of stylized paintings by masters of the craft.

Everyone emitted a discernible glow, making them out to be angels or ghosts depending on their outfits and general demeanor. A large crowd jammed the passage ahead, but he didn't bother to slow. He focused on a clump of people and walked straight at them. They looked over at him, stiffened for a moment, and then relaxed.

Clavin moved right up against a stunningly beautiful woman with bright green hair. She made a kissing motion with her lips. He winked just before passing through her and walked on. He forged through them for another ten steps before he broke free of the glut and could walk around the ghosts instead of through them. Seeing a doorway denoted Kerginshore, he turned in. Before him lay a room subdivided into a hundred sections, each fenced off with different materials and marked with differing signs. Clavin made his way over to the Night Star and paused.

Marcus stood, as always, and watched the entrance. "Ah, Warrior Roth, back early as usual. Go right on in, and glad you're back safely."

"Thanks."

Clavin strode to a table with a sign marked 400-1300. He sat down, kicked his feet up on a chair, and relaxed. He spoke to the many people who came by and shook a dozen hands. About an hour passed before a man of broad shoulders and a ghostly glow arrived. He kicked Clavin's chair out from his feet.

"Stave," Clavin protested, "I'm using that, man. You in a mood?"

Staven Drath laughed and claimed the chair. "Oh, sorry, I forgot to ask permission, mighty one."

Clavin smiled and pulled up to the table. "You had a good one, I suppose? You look to be in a cocky way tonight."

Staven lay his palms flat on the table as he leaned in closer. "Clave, I flew a Wyvern tonight. A freaking Wyvern. What a trip. I want to go back and do that again. Soaring in the clouds. Nothing like it."

Clavin felt a jealous pang. "Seriously? You lucky dog. I never get to fly. Not real flying, not like that. I ought to trade you Dreamer groups."

Staven sniffed. "Yup, some of us got it, others don't. And uh," he paused to give Clavin a mock look of arrogance, "you're the don't. Sorry."

Clavin slumped back in his chair as if wounded. "To the quick." With that, he dropped his head and exhaled a huge breath.

"Okay, enough of that," Staven ordered. "You? Anything this trip?"

Clavin reanimated and replied, "Three Chark, maybe four if I'm lucky."

"Tell me."

"Wait, let's get an order in."

Staven motioned for the waitress, who bustled over. She took their order and sashayed away.

Staven watched her go.

Clavin watched him. "Guess you're going to try and get to know her better?"

Staven sighed. "I'd like to but, you know."

"Glad to hear you say that. Inn entanglements can lead to entanglements easier to get in than out of."

"That was almost clever."

"I'm an almost clever guy." Clavin smiled.

"Boy, this place is tempting."

"It's tempting only if you're a boy," Clavin replied glibly.

"Now, see, that's straining it right there. Boy or man, we're all tempted by beautiful women. You've got a clever line, but it's not actually correct. See?"

Clavin shrugged. "Sometimes you win."

"Right. So, your trip?"

"Let's wait for Meri."

"Sure. So, what should we talk about then?"

"Real-world?" suggested Clavin.

"Nah." Staven shook his head. "What's the fun in that?"

"Well, we do actually exist there, boring though it might be. And if things aren't good back home, so to speak, we know that can affect us here."

"Okay, fine. I bought a really nice bed two weeks ago. Thought it might help me sleep better. Carved headboard, silver inlays, finest bedding, all that."

After a pause, Clavin prodded his friend. "And? So?"

"So, that's what makes real-world so boring to talk about."

Clavin threw up his hands in exasperation. "Work with me here, Stave. Did you sleep any better? Do blue fairies dance in your dreams now? Is it something I should try?"

Staven sighed and proceeded to engage in a lengthy discussion about beds, pillows, sheets, and the general care and feeding of the body. Finally, to their mutual relief, Merinda Swift arrived, sat down, and interrupted their conversation. She was the sort of beauty that should have knocked them out: twenty-eight, six feet tall, muscled but not masculine, fire-red hair, and eyes with the color of blue flame.

Clavin spoke first. "Meri, we've been waiting for you."

She grimaced at that. "You and your nicknames. Maybe I should call you two Tweedledum and Tweedledee? Catch me up."

"Who'd be dum?" Staven asked.

Merinda gave him a pointed look.

"Well don't get snippy, we were just talking about beds, and here you are wanting to get in on it. Convenient."

She proceeded to snap her fingers in front of his face a few times. "Focus, dream boy; this is reality."

Both Staven and Clavin laughed.

Staven replied. "Okay, I had a pretty smooth Crossing but—and this is what Clave is drooling over—I got to fly on a Wyvern tonight. One of my best Crossings ever."

She raised an eyebrow. "I'm with Clavin. Color me jealous. Details?"

Staven proceeded to talk about the events leading up to mounting the Wyvern and the flight itself. Staven finished. "I landed not two miles from my exit. I strolled in with time to spare. Uneventful but a whole lot of fun."

"I've never heard you talk of Wyverns before," she replied. "Is this new?"

"I've seen them before and fought them before, but they've never been tamed like this. So yes and no."

"Nice for you." Merinda turned to focus on Clavin. "What about you?"

"Not quite as nice as Staven's trip. It was all pretty smooth till near the end. I spend the night someplace, and they warn me about the Night Forest ahead on the trip. Deadly in day, lovely at night."

Staven squinted. "Huh. Kind of the reverse of the normal shtick. Okay."

"Right. So, I reach it at twilight. Basically, the forest sucks in light, warmth, and maybe even life during the day.

So, in bright sunlight, it's a cold, dark place. But, at night, it emits all that. The leaves light the entire thing up."

"Sweet. So, things changed, I suppose?"

"Yep. I avoided the calling maidens in the wood easily."

Staven pointed his finger at him as he nodded. "No entanglements."

"'Zactly. I move on, and I'm probably just a couple miles from being out when the Chark began. No mistaking it, not a barely perceptible throb."

"So, a three or four."

"Righto," Clavin agreed.

"And it manifested how?" Merinda asked.

"The leaves that had been putting out a pleasant light and warmth cranked up. I realized they were going to toast me."

Staven threw out a guess. "Water?"

Clavin cocked his head sideways a hair as he gestured back with a finger. "Partly. I couldn't be sure how long it would last or how hot it might get. I thought if I could find a clearing, I could get far enough away from the trees to be safe."

Staven squinted in thought. "You found a pond?"

"Close, very close. I made a pond. You put that together fast."

Merinda broke in. "You told us water was involved and then mentioned a clearing. It was obviously a stream or pond. Pond made more sense."

Staven looked a bit offended. "Mer, you're sucking the life out of it."

She gave him a stern look, which melted after a moment. "Sorry, Staven. You did put it together quickly. I'm getting used to how you two think is all. Sorry." She looked back at Clavin. "So, you made a pond and jumped in."

A now deflated Clavin replied, "Now you're ruining it for me."

Staven laughed and leaned back. "Go on. Give us the details."

"Uh, uh. No, not now. The moment's passed."

Staven just smiled and stared at him.

Merinda half rose and leaned in exaggerated movements across the table to stare into his face.

Staven gave an appreciative growl at his view from the side. "Whoa. You know, Meri, we could ..."

She lifted her right hand off the table, shoved it in front of his face, and snapped her fingers multiple times without a glance at him.

Clavin laughed out loud. "Okay." He leaned back in while Merinda settled back into her chair. "So, I knew I'd have to be able to breathe while remaining immersed. Think about it. Stick a breathing tube up into hot air, and you're cooking your lungs. Did you think about that smart guy?"

Staven's face took on a wry aspect as he gave a small head bow to his friend.

"So, I had to drink some potion to handle that. Next, I couldn't be sure how much heat the trees would put out or for how long. So, before creating my pond and taking my potion, I set all the trees around me on fire."

"Wait, you what? But that would have created an enormous amount of heat, and that's what you were trying to avoid."

"Sure. But the leaves are what emit the heat. I knew they'd burn off quickly, and then the area would have to start to cool. Once that happened, everything near me was defanged, so to speak."

"You know," mused Merinda, "if that Chark had cranked up right then, those trees might have fallen down on you."

Clavin opened his mouth to respond and closed it again. *Yeah, she's right.* He caught her gaze and nodded. "You're right. That might not have been the best move there."

"Well," Staven shrugged, "it worked, and no one has better instincts than you do."

"What else could I have done?"

"Found a cave or a hole. Or made one if you have some magic for that."

"Good point. But I don't have any hole digging magic. What else?"

"Your carpet," suggested Merinda.

Clavin shook his head. "Nope. It's strictly an up or down thing. Besides, I'd have had to deal with the forest canopy. Those hot leaves might have set me and the carpet on fire while I was trying to cut a hole through."

There was a pause before Staven spoke again. "So, a three or a four." After a moment, he picked up again. "So, Ranger, you're getting close. How long has it been since anyone has been this close?"

"Thirty-two years. A woman named Silver Dawn. She fell on an eight Chark, forty short."

Staven whistled. "Eight Chark. Man. What a trip. No one survives an eight."

"Well, a few have," Merinda countered.

"Sure. If they were close to the entrance or exit, but that's almost cheating."

"Different sides to that argument." Clavin shrugged. "The other times are just that the Dreamer causing it woke up and cut it off. I've been through an eight once. It lasted maybe ten minutes; so about half a minute for the Dreamer powering it. He woke up, and things went back to normal. That's typically what's going to happen with the full-on nightmares. Now, I've been through twelve sevens, and two nearly killed me. I think the longer lived Charks are more dangerous, overall, than the really bad ones."

"The Binders say that many fall in an eight even when very close to an exit," stressed Merinda.

"Sure. You can be close to the exit but prevented from getting to it. Then you're dead. Again, mostly the Dreamer just needs to wake up."

Staven raised his mug. "Here's to five Charks."

Clavin clinked his mug against Staven's. "Like hot peppers."

Merinda paused, and they gave her an expectant glance back. "How so?"

Staven answered, "They spice up your life."

"But they don't kill you," finished Clavin.

A second passed as she mulled it over. She shrugged,

raised her mug, and clinked it against theirs. They all drank.

"But," she said, "you could have died tonight, and by your own estimation, it was only a three or a four."

Staven clapped Clavin on the back. "Not Clave. Not our boy."

"Why?" she demanded. "I know Clavin is excellent. So are you, Staven. So am I. But I don't take Charks of any level lightly. Maybe I'm too fearful, though."

The laughter cleared from Clavin's face as he shook his head. "No, Merinda. We can never take a Chark lightly. Fear is useful. It keeps us alive. Only a fool has no fear. But—and I don't mean this to sound like it's going to sound—but ..."

"But," she broke in, "you're about to make Ranger, and you've been through a lot of five Charks, so you feel very confident in your ability to handle them now."

He half shrugged. "Basically, yes. I don't take them for granted, though."

"And that," said Staven, "is why you're going to make Ranger and history in the next month or so." He raised his mug again. "Soon to be Ranger Clavin Roth."

They all drank again.

"Go ahead and say it, Clavin." Merinda smiled.

"What?"

"Your little phrase."

"Phrase?"

"When you're really pleased with yourself and how good you are."

A light dawned on his face. "Ah. Well, no, it's not the right place in the conversation for it."

Merinda looked over at Staven, who smiled back.

Staven started to pound the table in rhythm with a single word.

Merinda joined in.

"Speak, speak, speak, speak ..."

"Okay, okay." Clavin laughed. "Fine. I'll say it. Give me an intro, Stave."

"Clavin Roth," Staven cried out and then pointed at him.

Clavin rolled his eyes but grinned anyway before he finished it up. "Bad to the bone."

MICHAEL

Clavin left the Sanctum an hour after Merinda and became his real-world self again, Michael Envine. Light pink, blue-ish gray slabs of marble, along with slate-brown rock and stone formed the halls of the Cordis Sanctum. He stepped outside under the large portico lit by dozens of burning lamps. The rain played the sound of a million crickets, and the near edge of the darkness beyond the lamps reflected from falling drops of water.

Eight coaches, fully covered, waited under the roof, and a line stood farther out in the rain for their turn under the portico. A few of the drivers had taken cover under the porch and stood talking while they waited. He strode over to the coach-master who sat in a high chair to conduct the operations. The man nodded as he walked up.

"Michael—"

"Envine," the man cut in. "Yes, sir. I know you. No need to check the register." He turned and gestured at the first coach in the line before returning to Michael. "I trust you had a good Crossing tonight, Master Envine?"

52

Michael smiled as he recalled the man's name. "I did. Thank you, Perin. Ready to get home and get some rest now. I feel like I've been up for a week."

Perin returned a repressed smile and lifted his chin. "A week on the Path for one night in real-world, correct?"

Michael affirmed Perin's guess with a pointed finger. "Exactly so."

The coach pulled up. Michael didn't wait for Perin but swung open the door and bounded in. He leaned around the window to catch the driver's ear. "The Meadows, Balmede road."

As the coach pulled out, the soothing castanets of the continuous rain played music on the roof, and he soon fell into a deep slumber. He woke to the sound of his driver at the open door calling out to him.

Michael exited the coach and enjoyed the sting of the chilled raindrops on his skin. He walked along a wide lane bracketed by white fences that stood like wet, watchful soldiers, vigilant to guard their charges within. Every six hundred feet, a gate broke the line to cover an offshoot of the main road that broke away and ran into the grounds of a country estate. Water ran from the puddles that danced to the tune of falling droplets and into the channels alongside the road.

He passed six of the gates, taking time to geyser the pools with a rake of his boots, until he came to a gate formed of stone. He turned in, worked the latch, and waded through the puddles. The house stood a long arrow shot down the path. It was the grandest home on Balmede road, two stories with four-story towers on each side, formed from wood and stone with a marble entry and a green-slate roof. Water sluiced from angel-carved downspouts into waiting barrels beneath.

He walked up and worked the large knocker. After a minute, he heard the bolt slide back, and the heavy, walnut door swung open with a small squeak.

A woman near fifty stood there in an apron. "Buster, you're soaked. Get in here, boy."

Michael smiled as he stepped in and pulled off his cloak and boots. "Hey, Mom. What's for breakfast?"

She pointed with her head. "Go on and see. I'll be right in."

He moved to obey but stopped when a young boy of seven charged toward him down the hallway. "Uncle Michael!"

The boy crashed into his legs, and Michael gave him a big hug. "Jase, good to see you. You want to hide and seek later?"

"You bet. Did you just come off a Path? Did you? Did you kill a dragon? Fight a troll? An ogre? Did you? What happened?"

"Okay, tell you what, let me eat something and get a nap, and we'll get down to the fun stuff. Can you wait that long, buddy?"

Jase grimaced and replied, "Yeah, I can. Come on."

"Wait," Michael said. "Nana wanted you a second ago. Better find out."

Jase turned and looked back down the hallway

where his grandmother stood with another woman who held a mop. He took a step and called out, "Nana, you wanted me?"

Michael grinned and took off at a dead run for the kitchen.

Jase spun and rocketed after him, yelling, "Cheater."

Michael pulled up at the doorway into the kitchen and cried out, "Beat yuh."

Jase shot past him, into the kitchen, and crashed into his mother, Michael's sister, passing by at that moment, knocking her off-balance and into the table. One plate and two glasses smashed onto the floor, a pitcher fell over, and milk poured across the table.

"Jase!" Aline cried out as she righted herself and grabbed for a towel. "What are you doing? Look at this mess."

"Uncle Michael started it, Mom."

"Michael, you walk in the door and set him off?"

Michael's father, Hollen, at the end of the table, spoke softly. "Glad you're home safe, Michael. You want to lend a hand with this mess now?"

Michael nodded. "Sure. Hey, Jase, get a dustbin and broom, okay? Let's get the broken stuff off the floor first. I'll help your mom clean up the table."

Jase rushed to comply.

Aline expelled a sigh of frustration. "Why doesn't he mind me like that? I'm only his mother, after all."

"Because I'm a lot more fun than you are, sis."

"And Buster has stories that appeal to a young man,"

Hollen said. "You have to be a parent, and Michael doesn't. He's a lot like a grandparent. We can have fun with Jase and spoil him, but you're the one who has to do the parenting. Your mom and I weren't always fun, were we?"

"No. You sure weren't." Aline paused from moving dishes around and sopping up milk to focus on Michael. "When exactly are you planning to get married, Mr. Dream Walker? I'm ready to return some of this fun with your own kids."

"Dream Warrior, actually. Runner, Walker, Warrior."

"Fo! Cus!"

He grinned. "Sis, I don't meet anyone. How am I going to get married?"

"Maybe you spend more time here, on Cordis," Hollen suggested, "and less fighting dragons. Then you could meet a woman and get married. You already have quite a reputation. There'd be a line of women interested in marrying you, I suspect."

An image of women from the Inn flashed through his mind, counterpointed by the mediocre ones in real-world. He opened his mouth and stopped. *Nope. Don't you dare.*

"What? Cat got your tongue?" Aline asked.

He stopped to look at Jase as he finished the last of sweeping. "Awesome, buddy. Now, get a mop, and we'll get this taken care of, okay?"

Jase nodded and rushed to comply.

Michael's mother, Gantiel, stepped into the kitchen. "What in the tarnation is going on now? We just got the foyer cleaned up. Did you do this, Buster?"

"Well, actually Mom ..."

Aliene barked out, "Yes."

"You're a grown man, Michael," Gantiel said, "you know better than to run into a room like that."

"I didn't run into the kitchen," he protested.

"He just tricked Jase into doing it instead," Aline said sourly.

"Why would you do that?" Gantiel asked.

"I didn't plan it that way. I stopped at the door. I thought Jase would too."

Jase inserted himself into the conversation. "I'm sorry, Nanna. It was my fault. I'm sorry."

Three voices spoke at once in reply.

"No, buddy, it wasn't your fault," Michael soothed.

Gantiel held her arms open. "Give Nana a hug."

"It was Uncle Michael's fault, Jase," Aline insisted.

"It was both of their faults," said Hollen. "But what do we do in this family when we make a mistake?"

"Own it and fix it," replied both Aline and Michael, in unison, from years of practice.

"But Michael is grown, and Jase is seven," said Aline.

Hollen gave his daughter a long look.

"Fine, I forgive you, Buster." She called over to Jase, who had released his hug on his grandmother, who, in turn, held onto him like a smiling wrestler. "And where is my hug, young man?"

Jase ran over and squished her.

"Okay," Hollen said, "looks like we've got this place put back together."

"Except for the broken dishes," Aline muttered.

Hollen held up a hand.

"Sorry," Aline apologized. "Buster, have a seat, and let's eat."

"So, we were talking about women," Hollen noted.

"Excuse me?" said Gantiel.

"I mean marriage," Hollen was quick to add, seeing the look on his wife's face. "Nothing vulgar. We were talking about Michael getting married before you walked in."

Gantiel's eye's widened like the sun breaking through an overcast sky. "What? My boy is getting married?" Her eyes began to water.

Michael gave a quiet groan. "No, no, Mom, hold up. I'm not getting married."

"Gantiel," began Hollen, "we were talking about the need for him to meet real women in real-world so that one day he might get married. That's all."

The light went out, and she settled back with a small frown into her chair. "Oh. Okay. So?"

"Uh, well ..."

"And this is where the cat comes in," Aline said.

Michael's face shot a silent look at his sister, but she cut him off with an answer to the unasked question.

"Tongue."

He shook his head. "What?" A moment passed before he nodded. "Oh. Clever."

His mother reiterated. "So, Buster?"

Everyone at the table focused on him. He squirmed in his chair. No one broke the silence this time to rescue him.

"Okay, look, there might be a girl on Samlin. We're not actually serious. I don't want to get you worked up over nothing."

"How wonderful," Hollen said with slightly raised eyebrows. "Tell me, Buster, what's her favorite story of you fighting a dragon?"

"What?"

"Her favorite story from one of your Path adventures, your Crossings as you call them; which one?"

Both Gantiel and Aliene stared at Hollen, puzzled by the question.

Jase chimed in. "Yeah. Which one? The story of the Acid Devil is my favorite. Did you tell her that one?"

Michael's head swiveled about taking in everyone. "Why would I tell her a Path story? That's the reason I spend so much time on Samlin. No one knows me. I'm just a wealthy kid."

"Mmmmfh," Hollen replied, proceeding to cut off some sausage speared on his fork.

Aline took up the lead. "You're telling me that you've begun a serious relationship with a girl on Samlin and not mentioned that you're the mighty Dream Warrior Clavin Roth?" She scrunched her nose and sniffed.

"You asked me if—"

Gantiel jumped in. "Buster, you can't go marry a Samlin girl. How are we ever going to meet her? And my grandkids. You can't haul them through the Dream for a visit." She shook her head. "No. You wouldn't do that to your mother."

He turned to her. "Mom, don't worry. It'll—"

"He doesn't have a girlfriend," Aline barked. "Or, if he does, he's not serious with her. I just hope you haven't fallen into bad habits over there on Samlin," she finished, making quote marks with her fingers.

Gantiel reached over and took his hand. "Buster wouldn't do that. He has more respect for women than that, don't you, Michael?"

He looked at his mother's serious expression and glanced at Aline. "Can I answer Mom without an inter-ruption this time?"

In reply, she forked up a large helping of eggs and shoved them into her mouth while holding his gaze.

Michael blew out a breath and turned back to his mother. "No, Mom, I would never take up with a woman of ill-repute. I would never dishonor you or Dad. Not only did you train me better than that, but it can have deadly effects on the Paths. That's one of the reasons I've, well, that I'm so successful."

"Good for you, son," Hollen said as he drew his napkin across his mouth. "Whether Path or real-world, you can get in a lot of trouble down that road."

"So," Aline began, "tomorrow's meeting day. I pre-sume you'll show Jase proper manners and go with us?"

Both body and eyes rocked backward as his mouth opened, and he took an audible breath.

"If Uncle Michael doesn't go, I don't want to either," Jase declared.

Hollen lay his knife and fork down against his plate with an audible clink and captured his son's gaze.

Michael paused and released a long breath. He nodded and turned entirely around to face Jase. "Then you're going to the meeting, buddy, 'cause that's where I'll be."

He looked back to his father, who returned to his food, and then at his sister, who quirked the corner of her mouth and nodded at him.

Michael finished his food and climbed up to his room, where he settled in for a long nap. Aline's husband, Kildain, came in and took him around the farmstead as he usually did. Jase shadowed Michael and demanded stories which Michael supplied, changing details for dramatic emphasis.

The next day, the entire family dressed up in very nice clothes, hopped into a large coach, and went to the first-day meeting. Michael found his celebrity had grown since his last visit. Dozens of people seemed to want to talk to him about his Traveling. The children all wanted stories, but he dared not invoke his parents' wrath telling stories of slaying ogres just before the meeting.

He looked up and saw a beautiful, dark-haired woman on the other side of a group of boys who surrounded him. He squinted his eyes, then they opened as recognition dawned. *Meredith Borfeather.* Memories from a decade past flashed. School days fantasizing over the most beautiful girl around. *You were more beautiful than rainbows. So I thought then. And now.* He shook his head in surprise. *Average. Still beautiful, but just average beautiful. Has Dreaming ruined real women for me? Am I destined to be alone because of this?* Michael shook off the thoughts and returned to telling stories until the meeting bell rang. He sighed, went in, and sat with his parents and Jase.

Late the following afternoon, Kildain and Jase hooked up a coach and drove Michael back to the entrance of the Sanctum.

"You know, you don't have to drive me all the way back. I could arrange for a carriage to pick me up at the house."

Kildain waved it off. "It's not a problem. It's the least I can do. We'd not have such a place to stay if it weren't for you."

"I appreciate it, Kil. But it's a half-day of work every time I come in. I'm sure it puts a bind on things."

"I'll pick up the slack over the next few days. Jase loves these visits. You should make them more often, you know."

Michael glanced back at his nephew. "Maybe. But I'm not sure how my influence might be accepted by some."

Kildain's head bobbed. "She's always glad you've come, you know. Usually, after you've gone but, trust me, she's glad."

"Well ... I'll trust you then."

"The women made us a basket. Break it out. I know you're not going to cart it across the Path tonight."

"Now that," Michael replied, "is what I call a plan."

MERINDA SWIFT

Clavin's thoughts returned to the present as Rige's doppelganger rose to his feet. Clavin's heart pounded as he listened for the hammering claws of death coming for him. But it was quiet, and, after a minute, Rige stretched and returned to his seat.

If only Merinda hadn't been so clever. If she hadn't figured out the Hand, I wouldn't be here now. He was beyond self-deception though, and the truth washed the lie out. "No. Not true." *Meri had her own demons, but she didn't push this on me. Merinda Swift, you were the smartest of us. I'm glad you wrote so much down. At least I know your story. And the end of it?* He shrugged. *I can guess. What a shame, a tragedy of birth.* "I remember you," he whispered low enough to avoid drawing attention from his companions.

He closed his eyes again.

"That fresh Walker," began Staven. "Quick Flash? He's not going to make twenty. I've got a gold on it. You want in?"

63

Clavin studied his friend and shook his head. "Stave, sorry, but that's just not my thing. It's, I don't know ..."

"Blood money," Merinda supplied. "You're probably right, but why bet on something like that, Staven? It's like, like ..."

"Like you're jinxing the guy," Clavin finished.

"Awww, come on. I'm not jinxing him; I don't wish him bad. He's an okay guy. I've talked to him. But, well, he's an idiot, and he's going to kill himself. Why shouldn't I make something on him?"

"You talked to him?" Merinda challenged. "Did you let him know who you are and give him some advice?"

Staven shrugged. "They all get the same advice in training. He'd just think I was preaching at him."

"Not ten minutes ago, you were checking me out pretty thoroughly," she said, obviously soured. "Maybe you need some of that advice too."

Staven rocked backward. "Mer, if you didn't want guys checking you out, why'd you pick that bod? Hmmm? And face, hair, eyes? You want to be noticed, to have men chasing after you. Admit it."

She settled back into her chair and chewed her lip for a moment as she examined her perfect, manicured, slender fingers. She looked back up. "Yes, you're right. I never stood out and wanted to know how it felt. But men and women are different. There's a reason there are a lot more women here than men. Maybe some role models could improve the odds for male Walkers?"

"Yep, you're right, Meri," Clavin joined in. "But the

toll isn't only on them. I don't even talk to the Walkers anymore. You know that?"

She answered a little slower as she focused down at the table. "People say you've gotten arrogant." She tensed as she glanced back up at him to see how her comment was received.

Clavin ran a finger around the rim of his mug and stared at it while giving a nod.

"You don't strike me as arrogant—well, not in that way—so why?"

Staven chimed in, "Steel Morning."

Clavin's lips thinned.

"Okay," she prodded, "I'm listening."

"Shortly after Clavin made Warrior, this fresh Walker came into the Inn called Steel Morning. I was pushing up on Runner and remember him well. He was a freakin' character. He had the best stories, and not Path stories either, stories from real life, his family and friends, his church. He'd have us laughing our heads off in ten minutes. He and Clave hit it off. We all did. I got to know Clave because of Steel Morning."

"And?"

"And?" Clavin snapped. "Add it up, Meri."

"I see. I'm sorry, Clavin. But you don't seem like the type to take that sort of thing so hard. I'm surprised—surprised and sad."

"He was the third friend I lost that week. That week!"

"So, after that, you decided not to be sad anymore."

Clavin shrugged.

"But we're here. Aren't we friends?"

"You and Staven have proved yourselves. Not only by making it this far, but by having the right attitude. At least in my opinion."

"So, you ignore the Walkers in self-defense." She looked out across the vast room at the people milling about. "I get it. That actually sounds like good advice."

"Sadness is a Path millstone. The only baggage you want to be carrying is on your back."

She turned back to Staven. "You talk to them, though."

He shrugged. "I guess that really does make me cold-blooded."

"Ruthless. But I bet that helps on the Path?"

"Just like any of us, right? We do what we must to survive and don't worry about the ghosts."

"I suppose. Well, I got an early start today, so I'm heading out. Back down to real-world now. See you two in a couple?"

They agreed.

Merinda rose and headed back to Trailing Hall. Just like the others, the room was immense. Most of the people here had no glow on them and were known to her. She greeted many of these as she passed on the way to the two large, green archways on the far side of the room where the words *Up* and *Down* floated above them. She chose *Down*, passed through, and became her real-world self, Jennifer Davis, once again.

Beautiful white and gray marble formed the room she stepped into. Twenty guards stood relaxed but ready for action. An official stood at a podium nearby, and she stepped over.

"Miss Davis, so glad to see you back safe and sound. A pleasant journey, I hope?"

"Very smooth, Kruthen, thank you."

He nodded and smiled as he proceeded to flip through some papers. He scribbled something. "You're all set. Till next time, Miss Davis."

She moved off and through the exit on the far side of the chamber. A wide tunnel, well-lit and carpeted, angled upward. She strode along and made her way back to the surface. The tunnel disgorged into a larger room, where another group of guards watched the entrance. Here, fountains and food-laden tables were interspersed with each other. An orchestral ensemble played while ordinary people stood about talking.

There were no mirrors or shiny, silver platters to be found in the chamber.

Jennifer Davis moved across the anteroom, eschewing eye contact and exchanging bare nods with the few she could not avoid. From there, the outer hall exited onto a large, covered portico where carriages waited in the lamp-lit darkness.

She took the first one in line.

The driver turned back to face her. "Where to, miss?"

"Hargothen Manor on Little Scurling in the Larsens."

"Yes, miss." He turned back to his duty, and they set off.

"Pleasant journey, I hope?" he called back.

"Yes, thank you. I'm going to nap now. Wake me when we arrive, please."

She saw his head bounce as he called back, "Yes, miss."

Jennifer didn't nap right away but watched as they passed across the wide plaza between the Sanctum and the outer wall. She looked over to the line of carts at the Merchant's gate and the crowd of men verifying contents. In the other direction was a smaller set of gates for the Dreamers and Binders to use, quiet now as they waited for the future outflow of people going back to their normal lives.

They passed out of the Sanctum grounds and into the darkness.

This street was well maintained, lit by oil-fed lanterns that marched along it like sentries against the night. Charming shops and homes lined it on both sides with alleys that ran off the sides like wild dogs. The sound of clopping hoofs magnified in the silence. Here and there, dogs howled in the night, warding off vagrant squirrels that dared disturb their slumber.

Her grainy eyes popped open in response to a voice.

"Miss, miss, we're here."

She stared out at the beautiful, four-story apartment carved like a decorated cake adorned with white marble and trimmed out in black onyx. "Yes, this is it." Jennifer walked up the steps to her door on the second floor. It opened as she approached. A woman stood there.

"Miss Jennifer, so glad you're home. We have a hot bath ready for you."

"Thank you, Magdelene. I'm glad to be back."

Jennifer walked on up another flight of stairs. The home had a strong equestrian motif. A saddle hung from a wall with paintings of horses on others. Bridles and horse-whips were displayed along with silver horseshoes. She walked down the hall into her marble bathroom. A large tub filled with steaming bathwater set into the floor waited for her. Vials of various-colored liquids sat about the rim and promised joys they could not manage to deliver.

She disrobed, entered the bath, and soaked for an hour. Eventually, she exited the bathroom wrapped in a luxurious robe and made her way up the stairs to an engraved door of leaves and columns adorned with a heavy handle. She twisted the handle and slid the door sideways into the pocket that received it. Straight ahead was a massive, four-poster, canopy bed with light blue colors in an alternating stripe underneath a blue and white cover. Four posters, carved as if a herd of horses ran up and around them, supported the canopy. From the corner of her eye, she saw the glint of something silver to her left, matching her height, waiting, silent and still. She pivoted to the right and saw a polished mahogany table laden with a platter of cheeses, bread, and liquors lit by the open window behind it.

She poured out some wine from a red decanter and took a long, slow drink while she stared out the window and watched the receding shadows painted by the rising sun. She poured another. Finally, she took a breath, straightened her back, and turned around. Her lips thinned as she plodded across the room and halted before it.

She sagged as a sad look crossed her face.

The full-length, silver-framed mirror reflected the true image of Jennifer Davis back to her. She frowned and turned to look at the picture that hung over her fireplace. The stunning image of Merinda Swift looked back and, thus bolstered, she straightened her shoulders and turned away from the mirror. "Two days of this." She took off her robe and tossed it over the mirror. Moving to the windows, she drew the curtains closed and then slipped into her bed.

If I could just sleep for two days.

She sighed and soon fell into the darkness that she craved.

CLESTERAL

Jennifer returned to the Sanctum two days later. She marched through the anteroom down to the gates, received her permission and stepped through the portal. Jennifer paused, looked down at her hands, and noted their abrupt change in appearance. She smiled and relaxed. Homely Jennifer was gone, replaced by the radiant Merinda Swift.

Her shoulders squared and posture straightened. Chin raised, she scanned Trailing Hall spread out before her in a way that suggested ownership. She made her way through the farrago of tables and tents to the exit on the far side of the vast chamber. Before leaving, she grabbed a green-capped Caller.

"Warrior Merinda Swift. I'll be in the Night Star in Kerginshore."

The man repeated it back to her, and she left.

Merinda made her way out of Trailing Hall to Kerginshore. Neither Clavin nor Staven was in the Night Star yet, so she walked behind the key bar to a stone railing that encircled a massive gap in the floor.

Men and women made their greetings to her, and she responded professionally but without a great deal of warmth. She leaned against the stone balustrade and watched the activity forty feet below without concern for any of the actual details. From the corner of her eye, she saw a man step up to the rail a few feet away.

"What are they doing down there?"

Merinda's eyes flicked up to focus on the distant wall without turning to look at him. "First run?"

"Almost. Third. And you?"

"This will be six hundred and twelve tonight."

"Wow. So that makes you a, well, let's see."

"Warrior. Four to fourteen hundred is Warrior." Merinda fingered a medallion pinned to her left shoulder of a figure brandishing a sword and a shield. "All of us wear this medallion."

She caught a flash of movement as he gestured to the chaos below. "You must know what this is all about then."

She straightened and turned to face him. His raised eyebrows showed appreciation for her image. "That's where the loads come in from real-world, and the smashers do their work. That's why we're all here."

He turned and leaned over the railing and scanned beneath them. "How does that work? How is it that they can do magic in the Inn and the rest of us can't?"

Merinda allowed a bit of her coldness to thaw. "Now that's an excellent question, especially for a fresh Walker. No one actually knows. If you think about it, no one really understands how any of this works. The Inn is effectively magic and has been here forever, so far as we know."

"But someone had to have set this up."

"True. But who or what that was, we have no idea. We come in through our own gate set apart for us Travelers, but not far from our gates, is another, much wider one. That's the wagon gate. The Merchants have men who haul an entire wagon through that gate, and they appear in the room below us." She turned back to point down at a clump of workers. "They use those cranes to offload an entire cargo bed off a wagon and get it moved out quickly. Then that fellow right there casts the smashing spell. Watch, he's about to do one now."

The man below walked around the pile of boxes strapped together, multiple times, in a tight stack, waving his arms and chanting some words. On the third circuit, the pile began to shrink as he continued his circling. After his seventh round, he stopped. Another man stepped over with a backpack. The small pile that used to be a large wagonload of goods was placed into the pack. Some papers were signed, and the backpack carrier left the room.

"And those are the backpacks we carry across the Dream."

"Commerce between the worlds. That's where the money to pay for everything comes from."

"I'm uh ... I'm Quick Lime," he stumbled on his name. "Thanks for the answer. They said no one would talk to us till we've done five."

"Sure. Free advice, Quick. Don't approach people

unless someone is simply loitering like this. After five, you'll be okay to approach others in the lounges."

"Sure. So, is it okay to ask you to share a drink?"

Merinda gave a small sigh. Though she knew better, she couldn't help but feel a sense of satisfaction. But she *did* know better and repressed the smile that might appear to open a door. "Quick, I suppose you're knocked over by all the women here." She caught his eye and held it. "No, Quick, we're not sharing a drink. And, on that same note, remember this: On the path, don't get involved with women. Stay focused on your mission. You'll live longer."

"How do you know that?"

She waved a hand that swept in an arc around the room. "Look around, Quick. Notice anything? How many women do you see and how many men?"

Quick's lips quivered as he scanned. "Well, right around here, probably sixty women and thirty men."

"That's normal. The only reason there are so many men is because of the Merchants and staff. If you could eliminate them, it would be more like thirty women and ten men. Three to one. Men die here a lot faster than women do."

He stiffened a hair as he focused on her. "Because?"

Merinda shrugged. "It's hard to be definite about it because, after all, when someone dies, there's not an observer to bring back a report. But men are far more likely to do something stupid regarding a beautiful woman than women are when enticed by a handsome man."

A half-frown accompanied a sideways nod. "Yeah,

I can see that. I'm surprised they don't just limit it to women then."

She raised an eyebrow. "You're a thinker, aren't you? That's good. Quick may fit you well. Female Walkers live longer than men but, past that, men gain the upper hand. There are more male Runners and Warriors than there are women."

He rubbed his chin as his head bobbed. "Good to know."

"I'm off, Quick. Safe Crossing tonight."

"See you again?"

She gave a small shake of her head and left him by the rail. Back in the Night Star, she went to the table marked *Warriors 400-700* and settled into a chair. Thirty minutes later, Clavin arrived.

"Hey, Meri, come on."

She rose and followed him to the table marked *Warriors 1000-1300*, and they dropped into chairs.

"How's Trailing?" he asked.

"I don't really know. My house is nice, and the neighborhood is good. I don't get out much anymore. You?"

"I spent some time with my family. I have a nephew, Jase, who's a great kid. Lots of fun."

"And the rest?"

"All healthy. Body and *soul*," he stressed the last word in a descending octave.

"Meaning?"

"Dad was a teacher of the word. They're all believers. They insist on dragging me to weekly meetings when I'm home. So, I don't usually go out to the farm when I'm back on Cordis. I stay in an apartment just outside the Sanctum. It's easier on everyone."

"Well, at least you still have people who care for you—the real you."

"Yeah. I love em, but they drive me nuts."

"Preaching at you the whole time?"

"That. Or my sister is on me, or she and Mom are pressing me to get married."

"Married to who?"

He leaned into the table. "See, that's what I'm saying to them. I don't spend time with real-world women anymore. Who am I going to meet?"

"Don't you have any friends from the past? If you spent some time with them, I bet you'd get fixed up quick."

"I'm pretty well known back on Cordis-real now. Getting fixed up would be easy. Finding someone I want to get fixed up with, well, that's a different animal. And what about you, Meri? Have you found someone there on Trailing?"

She glanced away and then back. He was focused on her. "No."

There was a pause.

"Okay. Sore subject. What do you do for fun when you're in real-world?"

She leaned back as her forefinger ran circles on the table. "I wait to come back here. I'll listen to some musicians, and I sample the best foods. But I live to come back here and be me, the real me, again."

"I get that. Clavin Roth is so much better than the real me. I'm glad for the time spent on the Path. I suspect you are too."

"I am. One day there for one hour here. One night here, and we experience a week in the Dream. Then home for two days. Merinda Swift is more real than my real-world self is now. At least to me."

Clavin looked around. "Guess Staven's late tonight."

"Probably out making a bet on someone."

"Yeah," Clavin replied with a shake of his head. "I don't get that. Well, I do, and I don't. I'm not going to judge."

"I was talking to a fresh Walker just before I came in here. I reiterated the advice about relationships on the Paths. He asked a couple of good questions. He seems smart. I'm hoping for the best."

"Well, I hope so too. You don't look like it though."

Her red hair swished back and forth with the shake of her head. "Even after telling him, he was trying to ask me out."

Clavin exhaled through pursed lips as he agreed to an unspoken statement. Memories of his first months in the Inn flashed through his mind, the extreme temptations. "Yep. Men are simple creatures."

"And the Paths aren't a place for simple creatures."

"What's his run?"

"Are you planning to put a bet down against him?"

"No, no, not me. Not my thing."

"But Staven might be interested, right?"

Clavin shrugged and laughed as he looked away from her. "That's why I like you, Merinda. Quick and smart. Okay, I won't tell him a word about this. Deal?"

"Good. In any case, I don't know. I didn't ask. He was here watching over the Smasher's pit, so I'm guessing this is one end."

"Name?"

"No. Think of this as helping you to avoid temptation."

He grinned in reply.

A man in a green cap walked into the Night Star and called out to the twelve people seated there. "Warrior Merinda Swift, thirty-two."

"Say hey to Staven if he shows before your call." She left the room to sign for her load and step into the Veil.

Merinda had been on the Path for six days. She rode a beautiful, sky-blue horse with enormous hooves like white marble, a tail like a captured trail of smoke, a silver mane, and diamond eyes. She rode up to the outskirts of a town nestled in the steep foothills, hard against the towering peaks of the Teeth of Heaven, and paused to read the posted signage.

Welcome to Stone's Mist, Territory Sir Egmunson of Stone's Throw.

"Well, Clessy, looks like this is our stop for tonight. One more day together, boy."

The horse bobbed its head and nickered happily.

Merinda made her way through the village until she found the Inn that bore the image of a chef's hat on its front. She checked in and went out to the attached stable.

"Excuse me," she called out to capture the stable-man's attention. "I wanted to check on my horse before I turn in."

"Odd-looking fellow, he is. Beautiful, but I've never seen one like it."

"Is that a problem?"

"Oh, no. Not at all, my lady. Just that I've never seen a horse like him before."

"No doubt. Winder horses are hard to come by."

At this, the man did a double-take and appraised the horse far more intently. "A Winder horse?"

"Yes. You can see why he is quite valuable to me?"

"Of course," replied the man in a near-whisper. "A Winder horse. Amazing."

"What is not obvious is that he is doubly valuable to me because he is my friend and companion. If any-thing happened to him, I would become quite upset. You understand?"

"Yes, lady. It would be like losing my own child."

"Good. I shall be leaving early in the morning. Have him ready for me, will you?"

"I do not work in the mornings, but I shall see that the message is conveyed."

"Thank you."

"Goodnight, lady."

Merinda rose early, ate, paid her bill, and strolled out to the stable. She pushed the stall door open to behold an empty stable. Her stomach and hands tightened in unison.

She spun and stormed off to grab the first stable hand she could find.

"You," she growled, "where's my horse?"

"'Scuse me?"

"My horse. Big creature with four hooves—carries people, eats oats, and, last night was stabled right here. Where in this world is he?"

"When'd you arrive?"

"What in the bloody creation difference does that make? I came in last night, stabled my horse, and now, this morning, he is gone. Where's my horse?"

"I don't work at night, miss. I don't know you or your horse. Without talking with someone who was here last night, I couldn't even verify that you ever left a horse with us. Afraid you'll have to wait."

"Wait?" she said in a voice that rose with her pulse. "I don't have time to wait. I need to be going. And besides, the man last night said the morning shift would be informed."

"Hold on," he replied with a bit of disgust.

Merinda's anger ratcheted up, and her hand dropped down to the hilt of her sword.

It didn't register with him. "I'll go in and see what's going on."

Merinda stood and drummed her fingers on the cross-guard, lips pressed tight together. Just when she was about to go find the stableman, a flood of light from the rear of the stable heralded the opening and closing of another door. She focused on the back of the stable and soon saw the stableman return.

"Well?" she demanded.

"Alright, Miss," replied the man, who dropped his chin with a worried tone. "The man last night did leave a note, but it was never delivered to me. I am sorry about that. As to your horse, I was told that Sir Egmunson borrowed it last night with a promise to return it by eight this morning."

The color rose in her cheeks.

He hurried on. "Sir Egmunson is very reliable. A man of his word. He'll be here in just minutes, no doubt."

"Borrowed. My. Horse?" she spat out each syllable.

"I'm afraid so, my lady."

"And now I am supposed to ride my horse after he's been kept up all night? Tell me," her knuckles whitened around the sword hilt, "what would you guess I'm thinking right now?"

"My lady, I was not here. I do not work the night shift. Sir Egmunson is a very great man around here. It is difficult to say no to his requests."

Her jaw tightened. "Does he live close by?"

"Yes and no, lady. He lives at the top of the cliff, next to the mouth of the waterfall."

"If he's not here in twenty minutes, I'll burn this place down. Do you understand?"

The man dared not speak and merely nodded.

"Then," she whispered, "you'd better go tell that to the owner of this place, don't you think?"

"Yes, my lady." He bowed, backed out of the stable in slow, precise steps, then turned and ran off.

Ten minutes passed. Merinda turned to face another opening door.

"Ah," said a very cultured voice, "the lady grows impatient, I think."

A tall man dressed in gray and green with the emblem of an eagle embroidered into his robe entered the stable, leading her horse, who nickered for more of the snow-colored treats being held out to him.

"And you are?" she demanded.

"Sir Egmunson of Stone's Throw at your service, my lady."

"Before I throw you back underneath the stone that you evidently crawled out from under, I'm going to give you a very short time to explain yourself."

"Oh, very good. Nice play on words, that."

Merinda slid her sword an inch from its sheath.

He ignored her action and explained, "I needed to get up to my castle last night. When I heard that a Winder horse was stabled here, I chose to stop by and borrow him. A six-hour trip made in ten minutes was too much to pass up."

"And?"

"And? And what? That is what happened, and now I have told you."

Merinda took a deep breath and blew it out through tight lips even as she worked through a muscle relaxation routine, starting with her hands. After a few seconds, she replied. "What, exactly, gave you the right?"

"I gave myself the right," he replied with a small grin. "I am the overlord of this area, and this town is in my primary control. As such, any who live here do so at my express pleasure. Any who visit, owe me one service should I desire to require one of them. You clearly fall into that category, and now you can consider your service paid. You may go now."

Merinda ground her teeth. She nodded and stepped forward to take the reins of her horse. Instead of mounting, her weapon sang as it slid from its rest, the point halted just shy of his neck.

Egmunson attempted to back up but found the sword point never moved back from his throat as she followed him.

"Stop right there. Stop, or I'll kill you where you stand."

He halted and looked back at her with a mixture of fear and respect. "Very impressive."

"Glad you like it."

They stood there for a moment, silent as if bound by a polished, metal bar that extended from her hand to his neck.

"So?" he asked, as he regained his smile.

Why am I doing this? 'Cause he's a jerk. "I think that now I am the master, and you are the subject."

He cocked an eyebrow and appraised her from the neck down. "So?"

"So, you arrogant, overdressed windbag, now it is your turn to do me a service."

"Gladly." He smirked.

She gave her sword a short flick and him a cut on the neck.

His smile disappeared. "Very well. What do you want?"

"Something to help me on my way."

"To where are you bound?"

"The Wassel Uptake. You'd be wise to tell me something of value and do it quickly."

"Very well. Listen closely."

> "Budda, cudda, dudda, du,
> effie, feffie, geffie, gu.
> Hikki, ikki, jikki, ju,
> kelly, lelly, melly, mu.
>
> The first is good and takes you home.
> The next is bad and takes your breath.
> The third is worse and rots the bone.
> The fourth's a bear and leads to death.
> The fifth will bring you healing water.
> The sixth will age and make you old.
> The seventh will make you weep and totter.
> And now my rhyme is done and told."

Merinda stared at him like the idiot she took him for. "Do you *want* me to cut your head off?"

"Why? I did what you asked. Now, be on your way, and bother me no more."

"I hold the power."

"No. Actually, now that I have done you the service you asked of me, I hold the power."

"I told you to give me something useful, and you gave me gibberish. That's not useful at all."

"It may be gibberish, but it's not at all useless," he replied in a calm voice. "To cross the Uptake Bridge, you'll need these words and, without them, you shan't be crossing it at all."

"Bridge?" She retracted her sword a little.

He noticed. "Yes. Bridge. A construction spanning an obstacle of some sort and designed for the conveyance of people and or animals safely over said impediment. Bridge."

Merinda restrained herself from thrusting the blade through his throat. "And why, exactly, do I need to cross this bridge?"

"To get to the Wassel Uptake, of course. You are going there, I believe?"

"There's no bridge between here and the Wassel Uptake," she snapped.

"Oh, but there is. I should know. I put it there."

Merinda blinked. *Not impossible.* She lowered her sword. "Oh. Sorry. I think we got off on the wrong foot. Can we start over?" she said with her best smile.

"No. I think not. It is time for you to be going. Please shake the dust from your feet on the way out of town. We don't want you to steal anything from us as you leave."

He turned on his heel and strode from the stable, leaving her open-mouthed. A flood of rage roared back over her. She took off after him. *You're dead.*

Six other men, armored and equipped with various pointed objects, waited outside for her. She leapt back into the stable and slammed the door in their faces. That done, she rattled off various syllabic structures as she wove her hands about her. All told, it took less than twenty seconds. Moments later, the doors crashed open.

"Can I help you?" she asked sweetly as her sword danced about her.

"Drop the blade, Missy, and there'll be no trouble," the leader replied. "Or at least not too much."

"Well," she said with a widening smile, "if you insist."

She jumped high and struck down hard with a twist to the left. A quick snap of her wrist brought the sword back to the right and caught the man just under the chin and sliced his head half off his neck.

"Oh, I'm sorry. I guess he meant *my* blade, didn't he?"

"Shoot her," yelled a soldier.

Two arrows flew from behind them and straight at her heart. The shooters never moved a muscle as their arrows disappeared into the dim of the stable and, unseen by them, arced around Merinda and sped straight back at the men who had fired them.

They fell with separate thuds.

"She's a wizardess," barked another soldier.

"Well," she picked up on the thought, "now that you mention it ..."

She leapt forward and engaged the three remaining men. One turned and ran, and the other two, shortly, were unable to run anywhere at all.

"I'm more of a warrior who knows a few tricks," she said, completing her earlier sentence.

Merinda strode out from the stable, saddled her horse, and mounted up for a ride.

"Let's be on our way, Clesteral," she said as she stroked his silken mane. "We've dallied enough with these ignorant fools."

With a quick "Hah!" Clesteral leaped up and into the air. Hooves gripped onto surfaces unseen, and puffs of white smoke kicked back from every stroke. They mounted into the sky, higher and higher, until the town shrunk into miniature and the people into ants. Anyone looking up would have struggled to make out her horse, leaving her, to all appearances, riding through the sky on naught but a breeze.

The cold winds bit, but Merinda laughed as they pushed into them. *One hour to the Uptake.* A morose twinge flashed through her at the thought of leaving her horse behind. He was her best friend, real-world or Dream. She threw it off and basked in the sunlight and the panorama beneath her.

She saw the Wassel Uptake long before arriving; an enormous shaft of light blazed down from above to rest upon the ground like a glass rod that overflowed with glow bugs, emitting golden beams shot through with green.

As she descended, she noticed a short, wooden bridge which sat by itself and spanned nothing of importance. With a slight lurch, they touched back down to the earth and cantered forward to the mouth of the Wassel Uptake and journey's end. A hundred feet from the mouth of the Uptake, it disappeared. *Uh, oh.* She reined Clesteral to a halt. *I bet I really do have to cross that silly bridge.* Turning about, she galloped back to the bridge and stopped to read the sign posted before it.

Choose a stone and cast it on if up away you'd be.
But choose you carefully, my friend, for only one is set apart for thee.
Five are deadly dangerous, and one's a shot for fun.
Bridge and riddles courtesy of Overlord
Sir Egmunson.

As she finished reading these words, another line appeared beneath them.

Budda, cudda, dudda, du.

Close inspection of the marker revealed seven colored rocks which lay in a row at the base of the sign. With a small sigh, she dismounted and knelt down for a better look. *I should have been easier on those guards. I may have to go back.*
"Budda, cudda, dudda, du?"
With the final word, all of the stones shuffled colors.
"Huh. Budda, cudda, dudda, du."
Again, the stones shuffled.
"What was that poem?" she muttered. "What? Budda, cudda, dudda, du, hickelty, pickelty, dickelty, de," she rattled.
The stones dutifully shuffled after the first stanza but remained constant after the second.

"Well, that's not it."

Over the next half-hour, Merinda tried out various forms to no avail. It was clear she wasn't going to remember what Sir Egmunson had said, neither was she going to stumble upon it.

Maybe I can get someone else to tell me how to cross.

Merinda remounted Clesteral and, with a quick "hah," they were off, back into the sky. They ascended a few thousand feet, and she spied what she had hoped for. Clesteral went into a downward swoop and landed without even a thud near a farmer at work in his field.

The man gaped as she dismounted. "Who are you?"

"Hello, good sir. I am Merinda Swift, and I was wondering if you know how to access the Wassel Uptake?"

"The Uptake? It's just a couple of miles from here. That way." He pointed.

"Yes, sir, I know. However, it appears there is a bridge that must be crossed in order to access it and, in order to cross the bridge, there appears to be some sort of riddle to solve involving colored stones. Do you know it?"

"Yes. I've seen it. Used to not be there, yuh know."

"I've heard that," she replied dryly. "Now, what is the solution?"

"For you?"

"Yes, for me," she snapped. "Who else?"

"Well, I'm afraid I don't know. You'd have to ask Sir Egmunson. He dispenses the solutions."

"Surely he's given it out to someone else around here?" she asked politely.

"Aye. That he has, but no two have the same one. Yers would be diffren from mine, so givin you mine woudden hep you a bit."

Crimeny. "Okay. Tell me, if you would, what is your solution?"

"Don't mind telling you. It goes like this:

One, two, three, time for tea,

four, five, six, magic tricks,

seven, eight, nine, drink some wine,

ten, 'leven, twelve, time to delve."

The farmer finished with, "Then I pick up the red stone, throw it ahead of me, and walk toward it. That's it."

"How do you know to pick up the red stone?"

"Oh. 'Cause that's in the second part. The directions, Sir Egmunson calls it.

Orange, green and blue, death is due.

Stones yellow and black make your skin crack.

The stone of white can help after a fight.

The last is for passing; red gets you through."

"Could you choose a stone for me and let me use it?" she asked.

"Reckon that I could. But I'm thinking Sir Egmunson's on to that trick. I think the result would be bad."

Probably right. Especially now that he's said it.

"Sir, I'm quite busy today on various errands. Could I pay you to go into town and ask Sir Egmunson if you could obtain a solution for another person? I can pay very well, I assure you."

"Don't know if that will work. I'd have to break off my work for the day. Are you going to pay me even if it doesn't?"

"Ten silvers for the effort and twenty more for success," she promised.

"Done."

Two hours passed.

I may have to go into town and beat the answers out of Sir Egmunson. She released a small grunt as the image of fighting everyone in the town flashed through her mind. *If I can.*

Ten minutes later, the question became moot as twenty-two men, one of whom was the farmer and another Sir Egmunson, approached from the town.

Oh crap. Merinda began to chant her magic. She finished long before they arrived.

"Hello, my ladyship," began Sir Egmunson. "It appears that you have been to the bridge and back. This worthy farmer was telling me your story, and I felt that I should come and pay my respects in person. Anything else would be rude, wouldn't you agree?"

Merinda took a breath. "Sir Egmunson, I need to cross your bridge and access the mouth of the Uptake. What can I do to make amends?"

"Well, my dear, that is a bit of a head-scratcher. When last we parted, you took with you the lives of two of my men and left three others in a bad state. Tell me, what can you offer?"

"I don't have anything of equal value other than my own life, and that, you can understand, is not really up for negotiation."

"Well, there is one thing you have," he said with an exaggerated leer.

"And what, pray tell, is that?" she ground out the words.

"Your horse," he said smugly.

Her eyes opened in surprise, and then she looked down at her beloved friend from hundreds of Crossings. "Not in a million years."

"I understand. There are other Uptakes, after all. Of course, none to Wassel."

Her pulse began to hammer a discordant tune in her ears, even as her breath shortened to rapid bursts. *Only one day left. I have to get to Wassel.* Anger raged, face reddened, and nostrils flared. Her sword rang out as she demanded, "How do I pass the bridge?"

Egmunson gave his men a signal, and they surged forward.

Releasing a curse word, she prodded Clesteral. He leaped into the air to gallop up and away from the onrushing troop.

You hot-tempered fool. You're in it now.

"Well, my lady," Sir Egmunson called up to her, "feel free to take me up on my generous offer whenever you are ready. However, I think now that I shall also need you to give me that fine sword of yours in trade for that insult I just accepted. Good day."

He turned his horse and led his men off. They kept careful eyes on her and the prancing airborne stallion while six of them kept bows in hand.

Merinda took ten deep breaths, calmed herself, and re-sheathed her sword as she considered the situation.

They've seen my spell to reverse arrows. So, they're either stupid or ready. Egmunson doesn't appear to be stupid. Rude, but not stupid.

She waved her hands about, spoke some words, and focused on the group below.

"Yep," she quietly mumbled, "they've got some magic."

She rode the wind to a place high above them and called down. "Sir Egmunson," she began and paused to unclench her teeth. She started again. "Sir Egmunson, I have been rude to you and your men. I realize that I have acted improperly in your lands and wish to make amends. My horse, however, has been a friend and companion for many journeys, and I would greatly hate to lose him to my own stupidity. I have much gold and even other magic items that I would gladly trade for the information that I need. Can we not come to another agreement?"

Sir Egmunson reined in his horse and pondered her words.

"Lady, it is precisely because your horse is so valuable to you that I now demand it in payment for the lives of my men and my honor. However, you have finally managed to speak well, and with self-control, therefore I will consider any suggestions."

"The mouth of the Uptake," she began slowly, "is

very far from here on foot. Even if I agreed to your terms, I could not make it there in time for my needs. Unless, of course, you would accept my word that I would leave my horse for you there?"

Sir Egmunson gave a tiny smile and shook his head.

"No, lady, I'm afraid that I cannot accept such a pledge. There is another solution, however."

"Yes?" she asked hollowly.

"I too have some magic items of my own. One of them is a ring that can be used four times each day. This ring enables the wearer to transport himself instantly to any location that he can see. I would give you this ring in trade for your horse. A very fine offer considering that originally you would have received nothing in return, don't you think?"

"If that is so, why didn't you use it last night instead of borrowing my horse?"

"Because it was dark and some low clouds obscured it of course. I couldn't see the lights of the castle hidden, as they were."

"How many uses are left today?"

"All four. I rode your fine animal down this morning in order to return him."

"Then could you please demonstrate for me?"

"Certainly. Can your mount hold two people?"

"Yes. You can transport onto horseback then?"

In reply, she felt him appear behind her even as he disappeared from her sight down below.

"Satisfied?"

Take him hostage? No, he'd just pop away again. She pondered her options. *Clesteral is only real in the Dream. I'll get him back next trip. Quit whining and do it.* Still, she paused and reached down to stroke his neck. *Do it.* She nodded and directed Clesteral down. As they descended, Sir Egmunson spoke into her ear.

He repeated his poem to her and explained the precise steps for how to apply it. She shook her head at the silliness of it but kept her thoughts quiet and her mouth shut. After giving her directions to most efficiently use the ring to reach the bridge, he bid her goodbye and held out his hands for the reins.

Her heart filled with sand. She lay her hand on Clesteral's neck and stroked it. The horse understood something was wrong and nickered as it dropped its huge head down on her neck to nuzzle her. Tears welled as she tilted her head back and looked up at the sky. She blinked her eyes and wiped them. "I'll see you again, boy. I love you."

Merinda patted him and pulled back. She forced a leaden arm to lift and hand over the reins to Egmunson. He dropped the ring into her now empty palm. She staggered away on heavy legs.

Clesteral released a sad neigh.

She burst into tears and ran.

A few hours later, with help from the ring and some high mountain peaks that she was able to jump to, she arrived at the bridge. She followed the instructions, passed over, and walked up to the pillar of golden light. She stepped into it and entered the white fog of the veil.

She left the Inn immediately, skipped her normal visit to the Night Star, and went home to mope about on Wassel. The next night, she picked up a dilapidated book, rarely used but highly cherished, and thumbed to a passage her father had once underlined for his temperamental daughter.

The fool shows his annoyance at once, but a wise man overlooks an insult.

"I wish you were here, Daddy. I'm all alone now." And with that thought, she cried herself to sleep.

The next morning, Jennifer stood before her mirror with a glass of wine and considered herself.

You have no one outside of the Inn. No friends, no family. You are wealthy. You could go out and try to meet people, but they'd either friend you because of the money or, worse, out of pity. She shook her head. *I don't need pity. I am one of the best Travelers in the Inn. I can do things most people only dream of. I do not need ..."*

"You're alone," she whispered. "Stop pretending. You do need pity." She bit her lip as she resisted the urge to throw her glass at the reflection. Jennifer relaxed her muscles and blew out a slow breath. *The only people you know who actually respect you are Inn Travelers.* "Clavin and Staven respect me, and they know me as well as anyone." She imagined meeting them in real-world and visualized the shock and disappointment on their faces.

She shook her head slowly.

"No way. I won't risk that." *Who then?* She went through the short list of not-mere-acquaintances but less-than-friends who were also not men and lived on one of her worlds and came to one name. "Liallen." *Something different about her. Beautiful, but not up to normal Inn standards. I'm curious to know what her story is. I actually would like to meet her in real-world.* The following week, after a conversation with Liallen in the Inn, they set plans to meet in three days.

Three days later, after another round trip through the Dream, Jennifer stood in her room, clothes tossed around over chair and on bed, trying to decide what attire to wear. She didn't want to stand out today, look too poor or too wealthy. Her clothes tended to be beautiful but not elegant, meant to conceal imperfection. She traced the beadwork on the silk dress and then laid it aside with a sigh. She focused instead on a well-made dress of simple flaxen threads dyed in green and brown. Comfortable, brown, leather boots brought the ensemble together. She appraised herself in the mirror. A plain merchant's daughter, neither rich nor poor.

She directed her housemaid to hail a coach and waited in her drawing-room on the first floor until it came. It didn't take long, for her street was one the coaches frequented. She paid the man, and he took her into the town.

Jennifer stopped at three shops before a merchant recognized the name in her inquiry.

"Johan Licour. Yes, yes, I know of him—a superb artist.

I've been to his workshop. I'm considering displaying some of his pieces here. You're interested in some of his work?"

Jennifer returned a bare shake of her head. "Not exactly. A cousin of mine suggested I look this artist up to see if I could commission a special piece for my father's birthday. So I need to talk to him in person, you see."

The man wrote the address down on a piece of paper, and Jennifer made a small purchase to thank him. She asked the next coachman how far it was to the address mentioned and learned it was on the other side of Trailing. It would take a few hours to reach it in the bustle of the great city.

"Glad I left so early," she sighed as she settled in for the long ride.

She stared through the framing pane of the coach window and watched the world flow by like scenes on a stage. Houses and people, horses and wagons slid by in repeated succession. Street vendors appeared, calling out to people, and then both were gone, replaced by another view of life in the real- world. A man slid into the frame of the window carrying a blonde, little girl as another skipped next to him holding his free hand. An old pain drew her out the window to watch them as they faded from view.

Visions of her dad, three years gone, preempted her sight, and for a moment they walked together again. She bit her lip hard and burned back the moisture which threatened her makeup and focused back on the life flowing past her.

Some minutes later, a man and a woman came into

view. He faced her and reached down to take her hands. He lifted them to his lips, and she smiled. Jennifer turned away, drew down the curtain, and closed her eyes.

The long ride finally ended as the coachman knocked on the door, opened it, and let the light pour in. He extended a hand to help her dismount. "Here you are, miss."

Upon entering the shop, she saw sturdy cabinets across the back where finished items were displayed. Workbenches dominated the middle of the room, and over a dozen people roamed about studying everything.

A man in a workman's leather smock sat at one of the benches, intent on some carving. Rough quartz crystals lay next to his hands. Three other men stood on the opposite side of the worker, but they weren't focused on the art being formed by the touch of the master before them.

It was the woman next to the artist who had their attention.

She was stunning by real-world standards. Even in the Inn, she was a beauty, though marred with real-world imperfections. *Liallen Shades.* So, this was her surprise; her Inn aspect was a mirror of her real-world self.

Jennifer imagined walking over and saying hello but couldn't move. Those men who hung on every glance from Liallen—or Lilly as she was called in real life—wouldn't give Jennifer a first glance, let alone a second. They might even show a twist of disdain or release a whispered comment of hurt.

Liallen looked up and scanned about the room, and her eyes settled on Jennifer. Jennifer glanced down at the nearest table and stepped over to finger the items that lay there. She had no idea what Liallen's true intentions had been when she'd suggested this meeting. They could be kind, but really, how could a Jennifer Davis ever expect to be friends with a Liallen Shades? There would always be the others, watching, making jokes behind their hands. *Beauty and the beast.*

Memories of school days flashed. And it could be worse; Liallen could have set this up on purpose to make sport of her, to mock like they had in the past.

Jennifer squared her shoulders, made a circuit of the room, and pretended an interest in the figurines. Her shoulders tensed as she passed behind Liallen with her admirers and dreaded the possible sound of Liallen calling out, "Merinda." Jennifer felt a strange mixture of relief and humiliation at the same time when the salutation never came. Her circuit ended and brought her back around to the exit. She slumped as she fled the building, hailed a cab, and began the long journey home.

Her mind returned to the days of her youth when she'd heard the first taunts. Even now, the memories hurt, and her eyes squeezed shut in a futile effort to block out the sounds. The words of her father echoed, trying to soothe her heart as he brushed her hair, wiped her tears, and hugged her tightly to him. She shook her head as the memory flowed through her. *You lied to me, Daddy, you lied. So did Mom.* Her hand clinched onto the leather seat beneath her as she shook her head and reproved herself. "Don't you dare say a word against him." *I know you did it* out of love. *I miss you. So much. But still.* She forced her mind back to the scene she had just fled from. *Women like Liallen are blessed at birth.* Bitterness dripped from her thoughts if not from her eyes. *Everyone lining up to give her whatever she wants.* Her lips thinned even as her mental frame scanned over the men who had flocked about her. *She could be the devil himself, and they'd still fawn over her.*

"Damn them all."

She resented herself for being born an ugly duckling. She resented her father for telling her how beautiful she was when it wasn't true. She resented herself for resenting the father who loved her. She resented women like Liallen for their beauty, unearned. She resented men who couldn't see past her skin.

But, most of all, she resented God.

"You made me this way," she murmured in the silence of the cab. She looked upward. *Do you hate me? Why? What did I do?*

A thought struck her then.

The only one who really loves me now, in all the worlds, is Clessy.

A hard, resolute kernel of determination crystallized in her soul.

She would bring Clesteral back to her if it was the last thing she ever did.

And to hell with everything else.

RUN UP

Inflexible. That was Clavin's thought concerning his father. Clavin sat in the Night Star and waited for his friends. He leaned on the table, arms crossed before him, and glowered down at the pattern lain into its surface without registering it. His visit home had been less than wonderful.

You think you know everything, but you've never experienced what I have. Memories of battles fought, dragons defeated, dungeons explored, and riddles solved, flashed. *You couldn't handle any of that, but I did. I've talked to people from all over the Hall, and one thing is clear: There is no God.*

His father's arguments rolled over him. *Yes, improbable things do happen, but they're not impossible. Doesn't mean anything.* Stories told in the weekly meetings which had once enthralled him burst fresh in his mind. *Miracles? I've never seen one or met one who has seen one for themselves. Magic only works in the Dream.*

A voice interrupted, "Warrior Roth, ten to go, right?"

Clavin leaned back from the table and looked up at

three men and five women seated two tables over. "Hey, Heart." He nodded. "Yep, ten."

One of the women, Deer Hunter, jumped in. "How's it feel? To be so close to becoming a Hall legend?"

Another of the men, Black Forest, added, "The last one to get this close ..."

"Fell at forty—or rather forty short," Clavin finished. "I know. I won't fall."

"You feel good, then?" Heart queried. "No butterflies?"

Black cut in, "Heart, shut it. Don't jinx the man. He's solid."

"Yeah," seconded Deer, "it's Clavin Roth. Nine hundred ninety Warrior runs. What could happen in the last ten?"

"Well," added the other woman, Sky Watcher, "Silver Dawn fell forty short like he said. Not much different."

Clavin sighed and rose from his table. "Do me a favor—don't talk to me till I hit Ranger, okay?"

The people glanced sideways at each other and nodded. Deer spoke on their behalf. "Sure, Warrior Roth. Sorry."

Clavin left a note with the Night Star's entry man and then exited Kerginshore, lost in his thoughts. He sliced ghosts, uncaring of their privacy, not bothering to avoid them. He drew many angry comments, which he ignored. A few people raised a fist into the air with comments like, "ten to go," "almost there," "soon to be Ranger." Clavin gave them a glance and a nod to express his thanks and moved on.

A few minutes later, he entered The Raven's Stoop,

found a nook in the back, and sat hidden in the deep shadows. A group of musicians played in a pit, providing cover to mask conversations and sounds not meant to be overheard.

Hopefully, Staven shows, or Merinda could get the wrong idea.

Staven strolled in a half-hour later and pulled up a chair. He spoke in a low, conspiratorial voice. "Two hooded men meet under cover of darkness. Together, they plan to rule the Inn and become gods. One is legend and the other ..."

Clavin waited a moment and then prompted him. "Yes?"

Staven grinned. "Clavin Roth."

Clavin returned a huge smile followed by a short laugh. "Yep. That's you. Staven Drath, Inn legend. How can I be of service?"

"What's up with this? This isn't our thing."

"Hey, wait, there's Meri." Clavin waved her over.

Merinda grabbed an empty chair from another table and brought it with her. She spun it in place and dropped onto the seat. "Well, this is unusual. Are we hiding?"

"I think Clave wanted a threesome here in the Stoop," Staven drawled.

Merinda gave a loud sigh and shook her head. "I hope you don't talk near your mother with that mouth."

"Did once," answered Staven as he rubbed his right cheek. "Caught me talking to a girl. I had no idea how hard she could slap. Loosened my teeth, I'll tell you that."

"Good for her."

"And later, Dad softened my rear with a switch." He laughed. "One lesson was enough for me."

Merinda turned and focused on him. "Then why do you talk to me like that now? They raised you right, it sounds like."

He slumped back into his chair. "I don't know. It's like, here in the Inn, I'm not me. Right? You get that. I can do stuff here I'd never think of doing in real-world."

"Well," she ordered, "think of me as real then."

Staven raised an eyebrow as he leaned forward again. "Hey, if you're real, then I ...."

Merinda's fingers snapping in front of his nose cut him off.

"Okay, okay. I'll behave. The great one here was about to explain his summons to this sordid corner of the Inn."

Both of them swiveled to focus on Clavin.

"Thanks, both of you for coming here. I just need a little respite from all the well-wishers on my run-up to Ranger." Clavin went on to relate the scene at the Night Star. "I get the distinct impression that there might be some bets out there against me making Ranger."

Staven shrugged. "I've got a gold against you myself."

He looked back and forth between Merinda and Clavin as they stared at him.

"No, I don't think you're going to fall, man. You're Clavin Roth. But stuff happens and, if it did ..."

"What are the odds?" Clavin demanded.

"A hundred to one."

Clavin relaxed and leaned onto the arm of his chair. "You bet against me on a hundred to one shot? What the heck?"

Merinda jumped in. "Clavin is your best friend in this whole place, you moron. How could you make such a bet?"

"There's these guys called bookies ..." Staven began.

She growled at him. "I know *how* you could, idiot, *why* would you? You *know* what I mean."

"And," added Clavin, "you're going to lose a gold. I know you don't want that."

"I don't care about the gold. If something happened, then I'd get some reputation for having made the bet in the first place."

"You know, you're not helping me here, Staven."

"Look, Clave, it's more of a joke than anything serious. I expect to lose the bet. You're going to be fine. Tell you what, I'll go cancel it. You can come with me if you like. I'm serious. I don't mean to rattle you. I thought you'd laugh."

Shifting back into his chair, Clavin nodded. "Normally I would have. I probably will after this is over. I don't get it, you know. Why am I stressing over it? Thirteen hundred and ninety Crossings, what's ten more? It's not like I'll really be different when I hit Ranger. They'll pay me more, but that's about it."

"First Ranger in a hundred-plus years," replied Staven. "It's a milestone. It says that you, Clavin Roth, are the *man* around here. We all know that you are, but it sort of carves it in stone."

"He knows that," snapped Merinda. "He needs to relax and release the stress of it. It's just mental." She turned back to Clavin. "You need to think about something else. What about your family back in real-world?"

Clavin's eyes rolled up as he shook his head. "I just came back from two days with them. I'd rather be here. Let's skip the life and times of ... of Clavin Roth in real-world, okay? What about you, Meri? Tell me something interesting about your life. Anything?"

"I'm sorry, Clavin, I really don't have anything all that interesting to talk about. I would if I did."

"Well, last time it seemed like you might try and make some friends down in real-world. What happened with that?"

She chewed her lower lip as she draped herself back into the chair and looked away from him. "Ah, yes. That. Well, things didn't work out so well. I realized I'm better off with friends I make here in the Inn."

"Do you hang out with some other folks?" Staven asked, drawing her gaze over. "You've never mentioned them to us. Do you mention us to them?"

"Friendships here are like rapids, rollicking and quickly done. Like now. A lot of people would have broken off with you, Staven, after making that bet against them. But you two go way back. You've got a real friendship. It's a lot of what I like about the two of you."

Staven looked over at his longtime friend. A look of sadness passed over his features, and he held out his arms to Clavin. "I love you, buddy! Bring it in, man."

Merinda whipped her hand in a slap against his shoulder. "I'm just about sick of you."

Clavin covered a smile with a raised hand and suppressed a laugh.

Staven turned back to her. "Okay, Meri. Look, I do apologize. But that joke was more for Clavin than a jab against you. Look at him. You wanted stress relief, right? Come on. Serious-time now. Who are you going to look to for new friends? You don't show up to meet us every night, so clearly we're not it for you. There's got to be something, something more serious, more important that you want to hold onto."

"Meri," began Clavin as he leaned in, "who do you love most in this whole world? Why aren't you hanging out with them? I don't know what you look like, but I do know you're about the smartest and cleverest Traveler I've ever met. That has to count for something even in real-world."

She looked down at her hands, fingers stroking each other. "My mom and dad. My dad most of all. But he died a few years ago. I have no other family I care about or who cares about me. Who do I love most of all now? A magical horse that doesn't really exist. So, what should I do with that?"

Clavin stared at her as she raised her gaze back to him. He shook his head and reached out to touch her hand. "I don't know. You lost it a few weeks back, I recall. It hasn't returned? I'm sorry. I am. But it could come back on another Crossing. Things like that do, you know."

"Maybe you could revisit the places you first met it," suggested Staven.

Her chin waffled back and forth like a slow metronome. "I tried that. More than once. But I'm determined to make it happen." Her hand rose and stroked the hand-shaped locket that hung from her neck as a vacant stare took her far away.

"Whoa," said both men together as their eyes opened wider.

Clavin continued, "Merinda. You cannot be serious. You'd twist the Dream to bring your horse back to you? The success rate on that ..."

"One in twenty, I know. No, I'm not quite that reckless. I'm looking into how I can twist it without breaking it. There's a lot of old Inn lore which you can find if you're serious about the subject, how things were done in the beginning. Things they tried, what worked, what failed."

"Okay. As I said, you're the smartest Traveler I know. Be careful. Let us know before you do it, if you ever do, okay?"

She cocked her head toward Staven. "So he can put a bet down?"

"No, but it wouldn't be a terrible idea for something like that. The whole place would be in on that. But, no, just so I'd know and could be waiting for you on your exit."

"Well, I appreciate that, Clavin, I do. But, in your case, I think you might move to have them stop me out of a sense of friendship. I won't do anything until I've done my research and feel confident, I can promise you that."

"Who knows?" Clavin said. "Maybe you'll discover something that can help others out."

"Maybe even you?"

"Me?" Clavin laughed. "Haven't you heard? I'm ten from making Ranger. I don't need help."

Staven slapped a hand down hard on the table. "Ladies and gentlemen, the one, the only, the soon-to-be Ranger of Samlin-Cordis, Clavin Roth. Bad ..." He gestured at Clavin.

Clavin's face opened with a wide smile. "To the bone."

They both laughed.

Merinda nodded and smiled.

TWINS

He snapped back to the present. A sound in the hallway gripped him, and he noted his companions likewise startled. Garner stood and moved toward the ever-beckoning doorway.

I should check too. He rose and paced toward the exit. *Four more steps. Reach the door and, from there, keep going.* As the thought completed, the magic froze him and turned him around. He returned to his place on the far wall. He groaned. *Trapped. Like a bug in amber.* His gaze traced the lines of the distant door yet again. *Done and buried. This is my mausoleum.*

He glanced over at Rige's doppelganger as he settled back down to the floor and his memories. *I guess it was around that time when you two entered the story. I know a lot of it now. Maybe not all, but enough. Enough to know you were the best of us.*

At the end of a graveled road sat a tiny home surrounded by farmland. Two gables and three windows faced

the road, painted white and edged in gray stone. It shel-
tered a family who sat at their table eating dinner. The
mother and father relaxed in their chairs from their day
of work. A young girl faced a half-empty plate and played
with a doll while two tall young men—evident twins—
heaped more food onto their platters.

"So, boys," their father, Graif asked, "did you get that
fence repaired today?"

"Yes, sir," answered Garth.

Rollen, to Garth's right, added, "Those pigs won't get
out again."

"We don't want to have to round them back up,"
Garth spoke.

"That big one bit me," Rollen complained.

Garth paused to look over at Rollen. "Well, that's fair
enough, right?"

Rollen laughed and nodded. "'Cause I'll bite him
soon enough."

"You two." Their mother, Alona, shook her head even
as a small smile quirked the corner of her mouth up. "Be
respectful of the creatures and be kind to them until the
time comes."

Garth sat back from the table and began to intone,
"You can tell the worth of a man ..."

Rollen lifted his fork into the air. "By how he treats
his household."

"And who makes up the household?" Graif asked.

"The mom and the dad, the kids and the cats,"
replied Garth.

"The fleas on the dogs and even the rats." Rollen grinned.

Alona looked over at her daughter, who sat next to Rollen. "Smack him, Enel."

Enel stood up and swung her little fist against her huge brother's head.

Rollen shoved himself backward and crashed to the floor. "Nice one, Enie," he said as he rubbed the side of his head with a grin.

Garth reached over with his fork and speared a large bite of food off Rollen's plate.

"Hey," yelped Rollen as he scrambled to his feet.

"Okay, you oversized clowns," Graif ordered, "settle down. Now, look, both of you have worked really hard this past week. Why don't you take Enel into the city tomorrow and have some fun? Your mother and I both agree that you've earned it."

Rollen and Garth bumped elbows, and Rollen looked down at Enel. "What do you say, little sis? The wild ones lose in Cordis City."

Enel nodded and held out her arms to him. Rollen wrapped her in a huge hug.

The next morning, the three rode out in a small wagon filled with produce from the farm. The crunch of gravel gave way to cobblestone clunk in less than a mile. The busy road shuttled traffic both directions, and every half-mile, a side road forked off to run along next to them and rejoin later.

Halfway to noon, the traffic diverted onto one of those side roads, and they could see workers replacing stones ahead on the main route.

"They've got it down pat, don't they?" Rollen remarked.

Garth's head bobbed in reply. "Keeping the King's Way running smooth."

"An extra lane for broke down wagons."

"An extra road for broke down roads."

"How long ago," mused Garth, "did they come up with this system?"

Rollen glanced over at him. "Right. It didn't all appear at once. Didn't Dad once say the roads had been here since before he was born?"

Garth nudged Enel who was squeezed in between them. "What do you say, Enie? Who made the roads?"

Enel looked up from her doll and stared out ahead for a little while. She shrugged, looked up at the clouds, and pointed her finger into the sky.

Garth nodded. "You may be right about that, Enie." He stroked her hair as she went back to playing with her doll. He leaned down and kissed the top of her head, sighed, then focused again on the road ahead.

Rollen broke the silence. "All of this design and careful planning. They say the Sanctum itself is a marvel of engineering design."

Garth remained silent for a while, lost in his thoughts, before he rejoined the conversation. "If there is a grand designer, a master creator of the Hall and the Paths, if he did, in fact, create us ..."

Both of them looked down at their little sister and left the words unsaid.

"Some things cannot be fixed in this world," Rollen stated.

They looked up from Enel and locked gazes.

"I've never been to the Sanctuary before," Garth said.

"Mom and Dad would go nuts."

"Yeah. Especially with us in charge of Enie. We don't want to send Dad on a goose chase in Cordis looking for us."

"Only one of us has to go. The other can take Enie back."

Garth's eyes flicked back to the horses drawing them along. After a moment, he spoke. "Are we serious or just talking?"

Rollen looked back down at his sister and stroked her hair. "Serious."

Garth pulled out a copper coin from his pouch. "Flip you for it."

"Heads."

Garth flipped and grimaced at the result. "Heads."

Rollen didn't smile. "Have fun with that, Garth. Sorry."

"We could trade."

"Not that sorry."

Garth nodded. "Well, we still have the city to look forward to."

They rode on in the thickening flow of traffic until they came to the warehouse town of Fralen. Here the road split in two. The oncoming traffic on the left swung out, leaving the traffic flowing only one way. Signs hung from marble pillars every hundred feet along the right side of the road. They paid careful attention to them until they saw the one they wanted.

Josten Couriers, right on Marchmore
Hale Masters, right on Marchmore
Maven Freighters, right on Marchmore
Stelton Games & Sons, right on Marchmore
Borlen Arms, left on Marchmore
Baggins, Baily & Barns, left on Marchmore
Kellor Maine, left on Marchmore
Nantine Stores, left on Marchmore

Garth nodded at the sign. "Right on Marchmore."

"Stelton Games. We've used them forever, haven't we?"

"Yup. I think Dad used them since he was a boy."

"Most of these consolidators have been around for generations."

"Like the roads. Even the side roads here." Garth studied the entrance to Marchmore on their left and right. Both streets, like all the others here, connected to the main road at a steep angle; instead of a hard left, they merely had to turn their team at an angle to enter their street. "Someone was pretty smart. Even the turns are easier for a large wagon. We're down on the right."

They swung the wagon rightward and pulled through

a large archway tinted with green stains and watermarks from age. Rain and pigeon poop adorned with the words, "Stelton Games & Sons" carved across the top. A courtyard one hundred yards square housed at least fifty wagons in various stages of being loaded or unloaded. Cranes were used on the larger loads to speed the effort. A middle-aged man stood behind a podium with a quill pen and paper weighted down against the breezes.

"Ah, Rollen and Garth Lossenfell. Nice to see you lads again. Dropping off?"

"Yes sir, Mr. Calig. Farm produce. Not a full load, but we were coming in anyway."

"Certainly. Okay, stall sixteen. You boys have a good time in the city, and be careful with your sister, right?"

"Don't worry, Mr. Calig," acknowledged Garth.

"We'll treat her like she's our own," Rollen finished with a roguish grin down at her.

Enel gave Rollen a look and stomped on his foot.

Though he barely felt it, Rollen responded as if the horse had flattened his toes and hopped about.

Enel rolled her eyes and shook her head but ended with a small smile.

Mr. Calig laughed. "You three have made my day. Now, get on with you, there's another wagon coming in."

At stall sixteen, another man oversaw the unloading of their wagon. They weighed the goods and paid the boys according to rates marked on a large sign. They took their cart to a large parking area, got a token from the parking masters, and left.

They walked to the other side of town where two aqueducts, each twenty feet wide, floated barges packed with consolidated goods from all the warehouses in Fralen. Every fifth barge was set aside for the movement of people, and they boarded the next one to dock.

The twins sat and stood, laughed, sang, and talked to other passengers while the barge guard briefly questioned the passengers about their business. After a mile, the walls of Cordis appeared in the distance. Enel grabbed their hands and pulled them to the front of the barge to stare and point at the fifty-foot walls. The channel and the barges passed through an opening like a cave entrance in the side of a white hill.

The openings were thirty feet wide, leaving room for the mules that pulled them along from the banks to pass through on either side. As they approached, they could see into the tunnel which ran through the wall. At the far end on a platform, which jutted out from the interior wall, sat a figure ten feet above the water. Behind this person, a large lever jutted out from the wall. Enel tugged Garth's sleeve as she pointed at the sight.

"Oh, right. See, though it's really, really unlikely, it's possible that Cordis could one day be attacked by an invading army. That's why these walls are here. The first of three sets of walls, actually. But these waterways we're riding create large gaps for people to get through the walls. So they have those metal grates that they can drop down to seal these off. Understand?"

Enel nodded.

"Now," Rollen picked up, "imagine that you are an enemy, but before you get here, you want to sneak some soldiers inside the walls before they can drop these down. There's a lot of people riding these barges in here every day. So, every barge has a guard whose job is to question everyone before the barge gets to these walls. Right?"

She nodded.

Garth took over again. "If the barge guard doesn't give the all-clear signal to that man up there, he pulls the big lever, and *crash*, both of those grates will slam down and trap us all in here till they can decide what to do with us."

Enel made a gesture to get their attention, brought her hands down on top of her head, and gave them a worried look.

"Yep, if you were under the grate when it came down, it would probably do just that. I suspect the mules pulling the barge would get it first."

"Don't worry, Enie," Rollen soothed. "Cordis is the capital of the greatest empire on our world. It hasn't been attacked in over two hundred years. We have no credible enemies. These precautions are mostly leftovers from the past; not really needed anymore. These guys are just going through the motions. I doubt a grate has been triggered in a hundred years. It's fine, okay?"

Enel nodded and leaned against his leg as she stared ahead.

"So," Garth picked up, "in a minute, they'll pause to let people off. You and I are going to get off and see the outer city. There's plenty to do out here. Rollen has some business farther in, so he'll be staying on the barge. Okay?"

Enel shook her head and grabbed Rollen's hand.

Rollen knelt. "Enie, it's no problem. Actually, I've never been past here myself, so it's an adventure for me. I'll be fine, and so will you."

She let go of his hand and rummaged about in her pouch for a moment. She pulled out a few copper coins and held them out to him.

Rollen shook his head. "Oh, no, no, those are yours. You need to buy something for yourself. That's why we brought you."

She grabbed his hand, turned it over, and forced the coins into it.

Rollen tried to speak but couldn't. Instead, he gave a hard swallow and cleared his throat. He nodded, took the coins, and hugged her. He stood up and looked away from his brother.

An enormous blow to Rollen's left shoulder knocked him off balance. He spun around to see Garth, eyes shining, staring at him. "Thought you needed that."

Rollen rubbed his shoulder and returned a small smile.

"Besides," Garth shook his head, "you took her money. Bad brother. That's why she loves me most."

Enel kicked Garth in his calf, grabbed their hands, and put them together.

Garth and Enel disembarked while Rollen remained and waved goodbye as he disappeared. The two of them roamed the city for a few hours, in and out of the various shops. Garth made sure to buy her some new toys, and many hours later, they were on their wagon rolling back to their farm as darkness fell.

Rollen, however, was on a mission.

DREAM WALKERS

Rollen returned to the farmhouse the following day. He paused at the gate as his pulse quickened, and he flexed his hands to dry the sweat off his palms. He took a long breath and blew it out slowly. His face twitched a bit as he approached the house. He entered and forced his shoulders to relax. Rollen turned and headed into the kitchen.

His mother, Alona, stood with her back to him. The steady *thunk* of a large knife and the smell of onion revealed her work. His hands closed up involuntarily as he took a deep breath. "Hey, Mom, I'm back."

The *thunking* cut off as she spun. "Rollen! What in the absolute blazes were you thinking? Off on some lark into the city by yourself? If you were ten years younger, I'd beat the dust off your backside right now. Now, you go clean up, and I'm going to call your father in." She stormed out of the kitchen, waving the knife around while muttering dark words about foolish children.

After washing up and changing clothes, he returned to the den where his parents waited by the fireplace. Garth sat in a chair and avoided eye contact, fixated on a knot in the wall, while Enel sat in another playing with a doll. She ran over to hug his legs.

His father, Graif, spoke first. "You had better have a very good explanation, young man."

Rollen looked up from squeezing his sister to glare at his brother. "Didn't you explain anything?"

"No," growled Graif. "He said you went off on your own. Not that I believed a word of that. You two share everything. So, now it seems you were both in on this together."

Rollen turned a baleful eye on his brother and looked back to his father. "Dad, I just thought it would be easier if Garth and I explained this together. Could we talk to you separately for now? There's some things better not heard by others."

Graif followed Rollen's pointed look toward Enel, who had returned to her chair. His eyes squinted half shut before he nodded. "Alona, would you girls mind giving us a few minutes?"

Alona took in the words. "Enie, come on, sweetheart, let's go pull some potatoes from the garden for tonight."

Enel gave a suspicious look in return as she got back to her feet and followed her mother out of the house.

"So you two planned this together," Graif ground out the words. "This had better be good."

"Good? No, Dad, it isn't good by any means. Enie can't speak."

"And we're sick of it," barked Rollen.

123

"So we're going to do whatever we can," insisted Garth. "And go wherever we must."

Graif stared at them. His face changed from a grimace as understanding seeped in and settled on fear as he began to shake his head.

"Dad," Garth said, "we'd never go against your wishes unless it was something for Enie or Mom."

Rollen threw in his two cents. "You know that, right? We love you, Dad. You and Mom are the best. But we've got to give Enie a chance."

"The Dream?" asked Graif.

Rollen shrugged. "Where else? No one here on Cordis has a solution."

Garth added, "But there are uncountable worlds on the other side of the Paths. Anyone of them could have a cure."

Graif shook his head. "I know you love Enel. But losing you both, especially over something that may well have no answer, is too much. No, boys. It's a wonderful thing you want to do, but no, I have to forbid it. You are not becoming Travelers. It's far too dangerous."

"Dad, we're going anyway," said Rollen. "We've already been accepted. That was the purpose of my trip."

"We never thought we'd go against you on anything, but we're determined on this," insisted Garth. "If we have to pull down the moon to find a cure ..."

Rollen nodded. "Then, we will."

Graif's face took on a somber mien. "Your Uncle Telamar died Traveling on his fifth trip. You'd leave us bereft?"

"Not willingly," replied Garth.

"But we won't abandon Enel."

"I need your help here on the farm."

"And you'll have it. They don't Travel every night. We'll be home two days and gone one."

Much of this conversation would be rehashed later with their mother while Enel was busy with Graif. In the end, over tears, frustration, and fear, Alona and Graif acquiesced. Some days later, the boys prepared to journey into the city.

Alona's eyes filled with tears, and Enel, responding to the wrongness of the scene, clutched onto her huge brothers. This brought a tear to their own eyes as they squeezed her.

"We'll be back in a couple of days, Enie. We'll bring you something."

"You take care of Dad, he's getting sort of soft."

Graif picked her up and nodded toward them. He opened and closed his mouth and then spoke through a tight throat. "No greater love has a man than this; that he lay down his life for the needs of another. You come back safe."

They nodded and left.

"Well, we're doing it," said Garth when they were down the road.

"Yep. It went better than expected."

"I think Dad would have done it himself if it weren't for Mom and us."

"So it was easier to accept," agreed Rollen.

"Okay, so you know where we're going? You've got instructions? Do newcomers go straight to the Sanctum?"

"No. They have a short training program. We're going to spend two days learning some things before they send us off."

Garth returned the look of a young girl passing them in the back of a wagon. He angled his head toward her. "Cute."

Rollen scanned over and raised an eyebrow after he spied the girl. "Yep. You know, let's keep a lookout for someone with some wagon space available."

"And catch a ride."

"Maybe he'll have a daughter or two on board."

Garth snorted. "And let two unknown men hop on?"

Rollen shrugged. "Okay, some farmer though."

Eventually, they found a ride and rode back to Fralen where they mounted a barge back into Cordis City. A mile from the Sanctum itself, Rollen took them off the conveyance and into the city. Buildings lined the streets, four and five stories tall, constructed from the various stones and woods available in the near countryside of Cordis. They were artistic, ornate, and inviting with slate roofs of red, green, or blue. Well-dressed men and women made their ways to and fro about business unknown to the brothers.

Carriages, coaches, and wagons clattered every direction over smoothed cobblestone streets on their various rounds. Garth gawked at the beauty of it all and the grand majesty of the sheer scale of construction.

"I spent my first couple hours just walking about and staring," noted Rollen.

"What a place. It's like another world itself."

"Yes. But this is real. The wealth of our world passes through the Sanctum, and Cordis is the center of it all."

"Right. I imagine other large cities aren't this amazing."

"I'm going to take us on a detour. I want to show you the Fountain Court. It'll knock you over. But after that, we're straight to the Walkin dormitory."

Garth looked over at him with scrunched eyebrows. "Walkin dormitory?"

"It's what they call the training facility. Think about it. If you split the word Walkin, what would you get?"

A bare second passed before Garth's head bobbed in understanding. "Walk in. We're walking in like any other new Traveler. So they just made a word out of it."

"And new Travelers are called ..."

"Walkers. Right. It all lines up."

They arrived a half-hour later at a four-story building— sturdy and utilitarian but not as ornate as the buildings around it. A large sign of pink-hued stone arched over the entrance with the word *Walkin* carved into it.

The brothers paused to share a glance then stepped forward where Garth worked the knocker. A butler opened the door and suppressed a yawn. "Yes? Your business?"

"We're Garth and Rollen Lossenfell. We should be on the training list, I believe."

"Come in and wait here." The man let them in, rifled

through some papers in a pigeonholed cabinet, and nodded. "Yes, here you are. Upstairs to the room marked *orientation*. Second on the left. Good luck, young men."

They moved up the broad stairway formed of oak, pine, and mahogany woods polished to a shine and bound with silver bands. They entered a room of similar woods covered with a thick carpet worked with an intricate pattern of vines, leaves, and intersecting circles. Six white, leather recliners sat around an unlit marble firepit underneath a bronze hood enclosed by a fine screen of metal wires.

Garth gave a low whistle.

"Expensive," Rollen agreed as he scanned the room. A large, wooden box with a gold-wrapped keyhole sat on a table against the far wall and captured his eye. "That's sort of out of place for this room."

"Huh. It doesn't really fit, does it?"

Rollen walked over, Garth in tow.

Words appeared on top of the box.

Enjoy the refreshments.

"Hoooo," said a surprised Rollen. "Words."

Beside him, Garth stepped backward a pace. "Gone. Only visible from there." He stepped back up beside his brother. "How?"

Rollen duplicated the experiment. "I don't know. What refreshments?"

Garth leaned down and gave a long sniff. "Do you smell that?"

Rollen gave the box a sniff. "Fresh bread. They've left us some food in this box while we wait."

"Loving that. I'm hungry." Garth reached out to lift the lid. "Locked." He released it and scanned the table. "Guess we're supposed to wait for them to open it."

Rollen's hand stroked his chin as his eyes narrowed. "Food in a box set out for us. A clear invitation to eat, but locked." The side of his mouth quirked up as his hand dropped back down.

"You think this is a test?"

"Sure, if we can't figure out something simple like this ..."

"Then we certainly don't need to be sent out to Travel."

"Let's find that key."

It took them less than a minute to find it under a pillow on one of the recliners. They opened the box and heard a bell ring somewhere outside the room. Inside they found a spread of breads, jams, and juices laid out. They slathered the rolls with butter and jam and proceeded to enjoy their first success.

A minute later, a man entered.

"Hello, gentlemen. That didn't take you very long. Excellent. I'm your instructor, Berrett Stimes. You did well. You displayed some curiosity, but not too much. You determined what needed doing and got it done. Load up your plates and come have a seat."

The two jumped to comply as Berret watched them settle onto the edge of their chairs, plates balanced on their knees.

"Well, well. As I said, I am Berret Stimes, and I'm here to give you your instruction today. You're the only two on the list, so we can get started. First, however, there is the minor matter of a legal document you must sign. I shall read it to you and answer any questions you may have."

They nodded, and Berret began.

According to the terms in the document, they agreed to complete a minimum of five trips in the Dream Lands in return for their training. With five trips completed, they could quit or continue, at which point they would be paid at the base standard Dream Walker rate: thirty silvers per night.

Garth's eyes opened wide. "We'll make thirty silver a night? Not week, but each night?"

Berret shook his head, and Garth relaxed as Berret continued, "No. There are two of you, so you'll make sixty silvers a night."

At this, both Garth and Rollen gaped at the man open-mouthed.

"Why isn't there a line at the door?" asked Rollen.

"Or is that just what people make here in the city?"

Berret raised a hand. "Wages are much higher here in the city, yes. But mostly this is hazard pay. Now, you know—or should know—that the Dream can be perilous. It is for this reason Travelers are well paid. You may consider this the greatest opportunity of your lives. Others may see it as an escape. Some will see it as a chance for glory and adventure unobtainable here in the waking world. All of these things are true."

"But," interjected Rollen, "there are risks."

"Exactly. Many who try never make it through the first five Crossings. Only one in ten Dream Walkers will make it to become a Dream Runner and begin to earn a *very* nice living at this. Once you sign this paper, you are committed. Legally committed. Failure to complete your five runs will land you in a work gang for eight weeks. Be certain—very, very certain—this is what you want to do before signing. I am going to leave you to consider this for one hour and, when I return, we will sign with no more delay."

Berret left.

"That's thirty times what we could earn on the farm," Rollen exclaimed in a high-pitched voice.

"And did you catch what he said about Runners? That's when you begin to make the real money."

Rollen's eyes opened even wider. "Thirty silvers a night would make us rich."

"Why don't they tell people what they pay? They'd have lines around the block."

"I think they don't want people to know for that very reason. This way they get people who are interested in Traveling and willing to ignore the danger we're always told about."

Garth pondered it. "Gotta be. And they probably don't want us telling people about this either."

"Well, the money will be fantastic, of course."

"But we're not here for the money."

Rollen agreed. "Let's get those papers signed."

"So," said Berret, "you are walking along a very pleasant forest trail and, coming to a fork in the road, you notice a sign engraved with letters, but you are too far to make them out. What do you do?"

Rollen shrugged. "I guess I'd walk up until I could see what it says."

"Naturally. That would make sense," replied Berret. "But this is the Dream. In all likelihood, your course of action will cause you no problem whatsoever. It is, however, possible that the sign, in the Dream, is magic and the reading of it engages a spell upon you. The spell could be harmless or not. Almost anything, even slightly out of the ordinary, can be suspect."

"Then what can I do?"

"Often you will just have to trust luck. Until you pick up some magic of your own, on your Trail, you will be at the mercy of a great many random things. However, in this case, it may be that another person will wander by and read the sign for you. In fact, if the sign is dangerous, it is likely that there is some way to determine this and, once determined, to avoid or disarm it."

"Everyone says that anything is possible in the Dream." Rollen shrugged.

"That it is, lad. That it is. Now, let's take a break from hypotheticals for a bit and talk about some Inn details. You've heard the stories, of course?"

"Sure," said Garth. "The place between the worlds. You walk through a gate in the Sanctum, and you appear there."

"From there, you walk through another gate that takes you into a Dreamworld," continued Rollen.

"You exit on the other side back into the Inn and then down to a different world," Garth finished.

Berret agreed. "Right. And you know about the people in the Inn? How they look?"

Rollen and Garth shared a glance. "Yeah. They don't look like they do in real life."

Berret shrugged and nodded in unison. "Well, yes and no. You get to choose what you're going to look like when you enter the Inn, and it is strongly recommended that you look like an actual person."

Garth scratched his chin. "What if we want to change after a while? We may realize we chose poorly."

"You can change later, but that's not recommended. Your Dream Groups are chosen for stability, and having the Traveler change his aspect is considered destabilizing. So, think it over. We have a room on the third floor dedicated to statues and paintings of people. They have gear and equipment too that you can try on. You need to spend some time thinking about who you want to be when you step through. Got it?"

"Sure," answered Rollen. "And we're expected to make up a name for use in the Inn, right? Why is that?"

Berret leaned in as he bobbed his head. "Here's the thing, gentlemen. A lot of people don't want their Inn lives following them down to real-world. So, using a fake name is best. And, oddly enough, it seems to make the transition from a normal person into mystic warrior easier."

"Huh," Garth barked. "Why would you care if your Inn life followed you?"

A small grimace twisted the instructor's face as his eyes darted away from them. "In the Inn, people can meet and have assignations with each other that they don't want known about."

"Assignations?"

"The kind of meetings that a man doesn't want his wife to know about. Understand?"

Garth and Rollen inched backward in their chairs a tad as their eyes widened a little. "Ah. Got it."

"Now, let me warn you right here," Berret said solemnly, "that regardless of what you do in the Inn, you need to avoid those pleasures on the Trail. Men are four times as likely to die before they make Runner as women. We're fairly sure it's due to Travelers who ... well, those who ignore this warning. I'll leave it at that."

Garth shook his head. "Don't worry. Our parents would kill us."

"They won't get the chance," reiterated Berret. "And they won't have a body to bury either."

The twins pursed their lips as they stared down at the floor.

"So, you two should write your loved ones a goodbye letter and arrange for its delivery in the worst case. Okay? Assuming you have loved ones, you don't want them left wondering what happened. It's not kind, and it offers the only closure they'll get. Do that, even before the other. Do. That. Understood?"

They nodded and looked back up at him. "We will."

"Good. Now, on a lighter note. In the Inn, you can only physically touch other people who have come up from the same real-world. Everyone else in the Inn will have a glow around them signifying that they are a ghost."

Rollen squinched his eyes a little more closed. "So, you can talk to them but not touch them?"

"Correct."

"I've heard of something called slicing," added Garth.

Barret settled back into his chair. "When an area becomes too crowded for people to pass, you can walk right through them. It's considered bad form in normal circum-stances, but when you do it, it's called slicing ghosts. Now, let's take a break and go upstairs so you can start thinking about your new *yous*."

They spent two days and one night in Traveler training, and on the second night, a carriage took them to a Traveler's gate at the Sanctum. They handed their papers over and were directed along a walk, into the building, and finally into a room where a five-person orchestra played soothing music. Tables were set around the walls stocked with wine, fruit, nuts, and cheeses. A man greeted them as they entered.

"Hello, Travelers. Papers?"

For the second time, they handed them over.

"Okay, you're both headed to Samlin. A double path. Interesting. We don't get a lot of those, but looking at you, I can see why. And your first trip. Nervous?"

"Bit," Garth admitted.

"Could say that," added Rollen.

With a confident smile, the man answered, "Don't worry about it. They give you all that buildup nonsense to frighten people away early. You're going to be fine. Now, if you can eat, feel free to indulge yourselves. You're here early, so take your time. Or you can go on in. But I wouldn't spend more than an hour here. Up to you."

"I'm ready to get on with it."

"Me too."

"Okay." The man pointed across the room to a doorway on the far side. "That takes you down a hallway to the DreamGate. It's a room about forty feet below us. You'll be asked for your papers one last time. Those boys down there are polite but serious, so take it serious down there. As soon as they validate your papers, you can walk through. Got that?"

They thanked the man and made their way to the exit and down the hallway that angled into the earth. They handed over their papers, answered a couple of questions, and were waved onto the famous Dream gate that stood in the middle of the room with guards about it.

It was blue, with veins of black and specks of silver haloed with light pink. Polished to a smooth finish, encased in a solid gold arch, it stood like the foundations of the world: eternal. Garth tensed as walked up to it, put out a hand, and froze. He took a deep breath, blew it out slowly as he forced himself to relax, and reached out to touch the stone. His hand sank in without resistance. With a quick nod, he focused on the image of his new self.

Rollen followed him through.

They stood in a room a thousand feet on a side and forty high. Doors marched down the left wall of the room with numbers carved into the stone above them. The right wall had a line of metal grates with similar carvings above them. Other than a hundred-foot-wide strip around the edge of the vast cavern, the chamber was festooned with tables, colored and numbered flags, sections cordoned off, and tents standing in a riot of colors.

"Looks like the fair," chuckled Garth.

"Yep. We're supposed ..." Rollen gasped.

"What?" Garth looked over at his brother before his mouth fell open, and he too went silent.

"Wow!"

Both of them started a self-inspection.

"Mom would flip," Garth said.

Rollen agreed. "Well, they told us but, wow, to see ourselves completely changed."

Garth pointed his chin at a group passing by. "And another wow."

"Whew. Those guys are studs, and the women ..."

With a shake of his head, Garth said, "This place is going to be tough if all the women look like that."

They made their way through aisles and noted the stunning people all about them. They arrived at a large, wooden counter where two men stood with a wall of keys behind them.

"Hello," began Rollen, handing over his papers. "We're Roll—wait, no, we're Rige and Garner Sistern. Is this where we check in?"

"First time," Garner called out behind him.

"Glad to have you," the barman replied in an amiable tone. "Yep, you're at the right place. Now, I see you two are headed to Samlin. A double. Huh. Haven't seen a double in a decade." He thumbed through the pages of a large book on the counter before him. "Rige and Garner, door nineteen, Samlin. Yep, you're here." He turned to the wall of keys behind him, retrieved one, and pivoted back. "Okay, you're all set. You'll embark through door nineteen over there. It matches your key. Keep that in mind; the key will always match your door. It's over there." He pointed to the wall. "Now, since you're new, you should be waiting in the kindergarten." He pointed in a different direction.

An area roped off with the sign of babies crawling on the floor and playing with blocks stood at the entrance to a section painted with bright colors.

"Kindergarten?" quizzed Garth.

"Hey, we have to have some fun with the new guys. It's only for your first five. After that, you'll be in with the normal Walkers."

Rige elbowed his brother. "Could'a been worse."

Garner gave a wry grin. "A butcher chopping meat?"

"A grape being crushed."

"A turnip off a cart."

"A man with a giant boot crushing him flat," Rige tossed out.

"What?"

The barman laughed out loud. "You two are going to fit in here like peas in a pod. We wanted to do the butcher sign. They wouldn't have it. No shaking up the first timers unnecessarily. Rige and Garner? I'll remember you two. You're going to have a great night. Now off. I've got other people to attend to."

They did as they were told and found that the kindergarten section was set up with tables for games and chairs. They noted that other sections, labeled for higher ranks, had food laid out, musicians, and people giving massages.

They sat and marveled at the beauty—often outlandish—of both the men and women around them. No one came and talked to them. They took to the dartboard and began to play. Time crawled like thirsty men dying for water.

They watched as a green-capped man walked around to other areas and called out names. After a good half hour, he came over to them. "Rige and Garner, door nineteen for Samlin. Is that you two?"

They agreed and approached the door marked with their number. Two men stood there, one surrounded by a glow.

"Ghost," Garner murmured.

"And the Merchant on the other side," replied Rige.

"Gentlemen," began the non-glowing man. "I need you to sign for your load. Both of you on both pages, if you will."

They complied, and he handed them each a backpack. "Okay, so you know these are important. These are the reason we're all here. Don't lose these, and we'll see you in seven or eight hours in Samlin Hall."

The other man added, "Seven or eight days to you in the Dream, just to be clear."

"Understood. See you there."

Garner gave a wave and then gestured to his brother. "After you."

Rige unlocked the door and paused at the sight of a white mist that filled the doorway. Then he stepped through and disappeared, followed by his brother.

DRAGON WARRIORS

After ten Crossings, Rige and Garner entered the Inn as seasoned Walkers used to the drill. They collected their gate key and strolled down to Kerginshore where most of the local Inn community gathered. They passed some people they knew, and Rige was quick to call out to them.

They made their way to the Jade River. Garth focused on a man squared off with another in sword practice. Shorter than most Inn men, but thicker, he bore massive arms and wore sharp features which painted his jaw and chin in harsh relief. His brownish outfit accentuated his somewhat craggy features, making him a fit for his name.

"Hey, Rock, getting the hang of that thing?" Garner asked, quirking up the corner of his mouth.

A small smile was his only answer as the man continued to parry swings from his opponent.

"Gee, Garner, not sure that'd be fair," Rige pointed out.

Garner glanced over. "Probably right. I mean those arms of his ..."

"Exactly. Too short."

Rock stopped, stepped back, and ended the match. "Okay, Switch. Let's call it for now. Keep working on that sequence. Now, I've got to go spank these kids."

"Thanks, Rock. Give 'em hell."

Rock winked at the taller man before he turned to face the twins. "Okay, who wants to beg first? Rige, you're up. Let's see what those long arms of yours have learned."

Switch Blade moved out to lean on the rail that cordoned off the sparring area as Rige entered.

"You idiots been practicing like I told you?"

"Sure have. And we take a day on the Path too like you suggested."

"Good. By the time you make Runner—"

And Rock attacked.

They battled back and forth, but it soon became apparent that Rock was easily the master as he slapped Rige multiple times with his practice sword, accompanied by comments. "Watch your left. Too slow on the recovery. Footwork. Too fancy. Your left. Your left again, dammit. Footwork." Finally, he called a halt, and they had a discussion about his weaknesses. Rock caught Garner's eye. "This is for you too. You listening?"

"Yes, sir," said a sobered Garner.

"Good. You two help each other when I'm not around. Remind each other. Just concentrate on the basics. Now, you, in here."

Rige smiled. "Thanks, Rock." He rubbed the last spot Rock had struck. "I think."

Rock waved him out. "Arrr. Get on with you."

Garner took his place and fared no better. By the time he was done, two others were lined up for lessons. "Much appreciated, Rock. How long will it take to get good at this?"

"Most take a couple of years. You two are progressing a lot faster. I'd say six months for you."

Rige and Garner puffed up as they looked over at each other.

"Nah," Rock prodded them. "It's not your natural talent. It's your ethic. You show up every time for lessons. You practice when you're not here. You have each other to sharpen your skills. It's perseverance and sweat. You two keep it up, and in six months ..." He shrugged.

"We'll be as good as you?" Garner suggested.

"Hah. Then I'll need *both* arms to give you a beating instead of one."

Rige staggered backward as if he'd been struck, and Garner twisted an arm behind his back while raising his other and flexing his muscles. "Fear the Rock."

The swordmaster stepped toward them, and both fled, laughing.

"Rock's amazing," Rige said.

"And clever. He manages to make a living training the rest of us. What do you think he earns doing that?"

"Well, he doesn't Travel, he just enters the Inn and trains. So, he can come in every night. Six people a night, seven nights a week at a silver each."

"Forty a week and no danger. It's not Traveler pay."

Rige nodded. "But it ain't bad. A month ago, we'd have been thrilled to make that."

"Course, it only works because we can all touch the same objects here in the Inn. Otherwise, we'd just be ghosts flailing away at each other."

"Right. Hard to train people in combat otherwise. Maybe we could take up an Inn job. Be safer."

Garner shrugged. "Rock and a couple others have already tied up the training gigs. You want to be a waiter?"

"I'm thinking entertainers," Rige countered.

Garner snorted. "Doing what?"

Rige did a couple of shuffle steps. "A little song, a little dance."

"Puh-lese."

"Well, there's always a fool and his monkey."

Garner glanced over at his brother's lopsided smile and nodded. "Somehow, I can see you in *both* of those roles."

Rige gave a short laugh. "But there are other Inn jobs here, just saying."

Garner nodded. "You're right. Hmm. I think, though, most all of them traveled for a short bit before getting their gigs. Maybe not the Merchants, but everyone else. Lot less money though."

"Sure. But we didn't start for the money."

Rige looked down as he absorbed the words. "You're right, Garth. Time to get serious about this. Where should we begin?"

"With the old-timers. People who've been around. If there are any rumors of things that can heal, they should have heard it."

"Right. Let's see. Who's the first person we've met whose been here for a while?"

After a moment, Garner responded, "Kayman."

Rige smiled. "Kayman the key man. Still trying to decide if that's clever or stupid."

Garner shrugged. "I like it. You remember it immediately. Fits his job. We used names similar to our real ones. Anyway, let's start there."

They retraced their steps back to Cordis Hall and to the central bar where Kayman gave out keys and registered people.

"Hey, Kayman," Rige called out.

"Oh hey, Rige. Garner. One sec while I finish up with Pale Master."

Garner's face twisted into a question as he looked down the bar at the back of a black-cloaked figure. "'Scuse me. Why Pale Master?"

The figure turned to face them with a smile that sported polished black teeth like obsidian daggers. Hair and eyes were black as oil in the night, but his skin and irises were white as milk. Both of the boys stiffened.

"Got it," said Garner.

"So that doesn't make you stand out on the Path?" Rige wondered.

"Yah," the man's voice replied in a silvery hiss. "But frighten's off more trubble than attraccahs."

Like the twins they were, the boys exchanged a glance, raised their eyebrows, and gave a small nod. Garner looked back at Pale and gave him a thumbs up. "Nice. Works for us."

Rige had a question. "Is that your real voice?"

Pale shook his head. "Nooo. The tonne, ess ahltered."

"Darn. I wish I'd thought of that. Nice. Maybe we should do something like that, Garner?"

"No. They don't like us changing after we're settled. 'Sides, I like my voice."

"Right." He turned back to Pale. "Hey thanks. Safe Crossing tonight, Pale."

"Uhnd you." The man took his key and moved off.

"Interesting fellow, that Pale," Kayman said. "Unique way of thinking. Anyway, what brings you back here tonight?"

"Kayman, we have a sister in need of aid not available on Cordis. We're looking for anyone, any rumor, any story of where we might find help for her. We know you've been here for a while, so we thought we'd start here."

The man walked down the bar and leaned against it toward them. "Are you saying you're looking for magic in the real-world?"

"No," denied Rige. "We're wondering if, somewhere way out in the Inn, there is a world with some healing abilities that we don't have here."

"Are there any rumors of such a thing?" added Garner.

Kayman pushed back and leaned against the keywall behind him. He rubbed his chin in long, slow strokes as his eyes halfway closed. "Well, there's rumors, of course. Basically Inn fairy tales. Special healing properties, like you seem to be looking for, would be in high demand. They'd be transported a very long way to other worlds, if necessary. That's why I doubt something like that could be real. If it existed, even way out, a string of Merchants would have formed a chain to get it distributed."

"How far does this place go?" Garner asked.

"No one really knows. You know there's a world hall entrance every hundred feet down the Travel Hall. So, if you walk one mile, you'll pass fifty world Halls. That's fifty a mile. It's said that an expedition was sent out once. Six men at a jog. Four hours out and four back. Twenty miles. They stopped and talked to the people there for half an hour before returning."

"And?"

"The people there said they'd done the same long ago. The Travel Hall seems to go on forever. And that's just one direction in one of the Travel Halls."

"In all of those worlds, surely there is an answer for us," insisted Rige.

Kayman shrugged. "Maybe. But do you have time to find it? A needle in a haystack, for certain."

Garner slumped as the enormity of the task sank in.

Rige slapped his brother's arm. "We came here for Enel. The Master will help us. Have faith. It may be a needle in a haystack, but he made the hay."

Garner straightened up and nodded. "And he is the flame."

Kayman noted their change of location in his registry before they moved off to stare down into the smasher's pit below and watch the work there. Eventually, the Caller came, and they headed off on their run to Samlin.

They stepped through the Veil and onto a vast plain of rolling hills seemingly covered in snow and punctuated with bright-colored stones and rare streaks of brown. The sky above was a gray shroud with colored shafts of lights which flashed back and forth inside like parts of a rainbow that never touched the ground.

"Winter?" wondered Garner.

"No. Way too warm." Rige knelt to study the white at his feet. "It's grass. White grass."

"Grass. Good thing the sky is gray or ...."

In the distance, a flash of green from the sky cut him off as it struck down to the ground and back up into the sky.

Rige stood back and squinted in that direction.

"I wonder what that feels like?" asked Garner.

"Not sure we want to find out."

"Sure. But how do we avoid that?"

"Maybe it only happens in certain places," suggested Rige.

"Or times, or under certain triggers."

"Or there is a wizard up there casting them down to the ground."

A diapason of sound like a string from a giant's cello engulfed them.

"Whoa," Rige said. "Was that the echo from that strike?"

"Guessing so. We need to get moving."

Garner turned about to look behind him. An arch of black stone stood five feet away, and vines of pure white had grown up its side and across the top to form the word *Cordis*. "I guess we'll be looking for something like that on the other side for Samlin."

Rige turned and agreed. "Which way? No signposts, no clear path."

"Why is this so different? Is this a Chark? Our first real Chark?"

"No. They say it's like in a dream when you get that weird feeling of dread for no reason. You might be looking at a sunflower in the middle of a bright day, and suddenly you'll feel that tingle."

Garner scanned about. "Right. The chill of dread. And then there's the dark part."

Rige stepped closer to the arch to touch it. His hand sank in. "Yep, that's the way back to Cordis alright." He turned back. "The dark part. What did the teacher say?"

"When a sunny day has the aspect of cloudy gloom. Something to be seen and not explained. Chilly dark: Chark. Anyway, we don't see or feel that here. At least, I don't."

"Me either."

"So, what's our plan?"

"One or more of our Dreamers is causing this. Maybe a new guy with a strong dream, maybe a new Binder. We're just Walkers, so we sort of get what we get. Maybe we should bail."

"No. We bail out with no Chark, just due to a radical change in our Path, and we might not get another Crossing. The Merchants wouldn't be happy if these packs don't arrive on Samlin tonight. We go on."

"Okay, which direction then?"

They walked around the Cordis arch looking for something, anything, that might give them a clue. An hour passed during which another twelve shafts of light shot from the sky, bounced off the ground, and back up into the clouds.

Finally, Rige screamed at the sky. "Which way to Samlin?"

Nothing replied.

"This is ridiculous. Which freaking way to Samlin?"

Garner walked back to the black portal and kicked it. "A clue. Which way? Which way to Samlin?"

They heard and felt a rumble in their feet.

Both whipped out their swords and stood back-to-back.

"Garth," Rige whispered. "I mean, Garner. Look there."

Garner turned to see the grass lay down in a visible line leading away, over a hill, and disappearing.

"Well, I'll be a stubborn mule."

"You already are," mumbled Rige.

"Okay," Garner replied, ignoring the barb. "After you."

"Mules first."

Garner set off and gave his brother a shove as he went by.

Their path led them within a few hundred feet of a small, gleaming red boulder. Garner called Rige's attention to it. "Let's check it out. Never know what's important, right?"

"Remember. It's good to be curious but not too curious. You can get into trouble. Could be a trap."

"Look, I'll go. If something happens, you pull me out, okay?"

"Fine. Do it."

Garner walked over to the red stone. It was at least a foot high and set in the midst of one of the brown scars of dirt. He took out a knife and tapped on it. After a moment of study, he reached down and rolled it over. He squatted down, wrapped his arms around it, and let out a grunt as he heaved it off the ground. He could lift it, but it was far too heavy to carry it any distance. It gave a thud as he dropped it. He took off his personal backpack and rummaged around till he extracted a hammer. Smashing off a ten-pound chunk, he picked it up and returned to his brother.

"I saw you pick it up. Idiot. Too risky."

"Rige," he said, pulling out the chunk, "it's a ruby."

Rige's eyes widened as he took it from his brother to study it. "No way. If the reds are rubies, then the blues and greens?"

"Sapphires and emeralds, no doubt. This plain is the treasure house of a god."

"I hope not. If it returns and looks down, we're going to stand out like bugs in a saucer of milk, and it might not be very happy. Especially since we've just taken this."

"Let's get a move on then."

They took their pace to a jog and began eating up distance.

Four hours passed as the strange bolts continued to bounce down and up. They took the opportunity to gather emerald and sapphire samples from massive stones close to their path. The extra weight in their packs was noticeable, but they weren't willing to leave them.

"It's a good thing our Inn bodies have so much stamina. We'd have never made a run like this in real-world," Rige said.

"That's why I skipped that last ruby."

"Shouldn't have," panted Rige. "I'm carrying emerald and sapphire. You've just got the ruby."

"Mines bigger."

"Not."

"Keep. Running."

They both stopped dead in their tracks as they saw a blue bolt flash down a mile to their right without bouncing up again.

"What the heck?" Garner said through a ragged breath.

They focused in the direction the bolt had fallen and both noted the pond-like ripple running through the white grass toward them from a distant center point. They could tell it raced across the plain faster than a bird could fly. They locked eyes even as they closed ranks to stand shoulder to shoulder.

"Hold on, Garth."

They gripped their sword hilts tight as the line ran

under them. All it left was a tingle in their feet. Both of them relaxed and laughed.

"Should we go look?" Garner asked.

"No. That's a good mile away. Too much of a detour. Keep moving."

An hour later, they saw a hill that towered over the others off to their left.

"Let's climb it."

Rige nodded and followed. At the top, they focused out into the distance.

Garner pointed in the direction they'd been traveling. "Is that green in the distance?"

"Yep. We're just a few miles away. The light is fading, so I guess the day is coming to an end, but I think we'll reach the edge of whatever this is by nightfall."

Rige felt Garner's hand clamp tight on his arm and drag him down to the ground as he hissed, "Look over here."

Perhaps a mile from where they crouched, at the base of a hill, lay what was unmistakably a dragon, green as an emerald, curled up with a wing covering its head. By common and silent agreement, they backed down the hill until they could stand and remain hidden. Then they proceeded to rush the rest of the way. They didn't speak until they were down.

"Holy smokes."

"Let's just pray it doesn't have some sort of super hearing."

"Pretty sure it was asleep. It might sleep during the day and hunt at night."

"Then let's hotfoot it out of here."

They started a fast jog, kept to the low areas, and avoided the hilltops.

An hour later, as the fading light washed out the colors, they risked climbing a hill and beheld a stark line where the white grass turned green again, and the trees of a nearby forest beckoned them into the safety of concealment.

Their exhausted legs re-energized as they rocketed toward the distant trees.

They ran up to the edge of the forest where a sign stood hanging from a post, and they halted to gasp for breath.

"What's it say?"

Garner shook his head as he leaned down, heaving for air, using his knees for support.

Rige leaned against the signpost, tossed his head back, and filled his lungs over and over.

In a minute, they both stood again. The pulse in their veins smoothed out, and they managed to get a flame going long enough to read the signs.

Midlin	→	3 days
Northgil	←	4 days
Cordis	v	1 day
Samlin	∧	6 days

They smiled and clasped arms.

"We did the right thing," Rige said.

"It's too dark to make our way through a forest without a torch."

"And we probably don't want to stand out with that dragon just a few miles away."

"Cold night for us then."

"Break out the bedrolls. We'll just lean up against a tree here for now." Rige swung his pack off and pulled it open. Green and blue light poured out.

"Close that," hissed Garner.

Rige snapped it shut and sealed off the light. "What do you bet you've got a red light in your backpack now?"

"Those aren't just regular stones, are they?"

"Magic. But we can traverse the forest now. At least until we can find a nice clearing far enough in that the dragon can't see it."

"Mother of pigs," spit Garner. "Look behind us, in the sky."

Rige turned. In the distance, far above the white lands—as they now called them—glowing dragons of emerald, sapphire, and ruby soared through the night. They stood, transfixed, and watched as the beautiful creatures dove out of sight behind the hills even as others rose from various places. "What in the world are they doing?"

Garner shook his head. "I don't know. But they're not looking this way. Let's be grateful for ..."

Two of the dragons, one red and one blue, blasted like-colored flames at each other and closed to grapple, tooth and claw. They fell from sight and disappeared.

"Let's get out of here," Rige said. A moment later, green and blue light flooded from his now open pack and revealed the now darkened forest. They ran into the woods, hearts in their throats, thunder in their ears. Five minutes, ten. When they felt they'd covered a full mile, they found a small clearing, gathered some wood, and built a fire.

The next day, they continued along the trail, and late in the afternoon, left the forest behind. As they exited the tree line, they looked down on a valley filled with beautiful homes, tall towers, and a ribbon of blue which floated among them like the stolen halo of a sea god.

They descended the path, which soon turned into a paved road. A low wall the height of a man topped with a header of silver and gold ran around the town. Above the entry arch were the words *Spell Haven* emblazoned in white. A guard leaned against the entrance, yawning, and then glanced up. He pushed back, erect, and straightened his posture. "Where are you tall fellows coming from today?"

"We're just travelers from a long way off passing through," replied Rige.

"Garner and Rige Sistern," Garner supplied. "Brothers from Cordis headed to Samlin."

The man cocked his head. "Brothers, I believe. But from Cordis? You saying you came through the Steppes of Magic?"

The boys shared a glance before Rige answered, "Is that what you call the white grasslands by any chance?"

"Yep. White grass with magic gems. You crossed that?"

"We did. We came through the Cordis arch."

"Is that a problem?" asked Garner.

"Noooo," the man replied with widened eyes and a

slow shake of his head. "I don't think I've ever heard of anyone coming all the way across the Steppes. We usually send in an expedition a couple times a year to collect some gems for the wizards, but they stay on the outskirts."

"That's why this village is here," Garner realized.

"The gems." Rige nodded. "So, they're valuable?"

"Valuable?" barked the guard. "Yeah, you might say that. The wizards pay a thousand gold a pound. They use them to make magic items for kings and nobles."

There was an awkward silence as the boys stared at each other. The guard spoke again. "So, you're headed to Samlin? You know the Samlin arch is like Cordis, right? In the middle of its own Steppes? You got lucky once by making it here, but are you sure about this?"

"Pretty sure," Garner replied sardonically.

"Do these Wizards sell magic items here?"

"Not directly. There are shops. People come from everywhere to buy them. I should warn you though—you won't be allowed through their doors unless you can show you have the means to buy. Keeps us gawkers out."

The boys thanked him and moved into the town. They found their way to one of the magical shops. They paused to gape at the sight of a river of clear, blue water that ran far above them, suspended in the sky. People were in the flow, laughing and talking. The river ran into the top story of the building they faced.

"Okay, now that's pretty neat."

"We have *got* to try that before we leave," Garner agreed.

They approached the door where four guards stepped out to block them. "Sorry, no entry unless you can show at least a thousand in gold."

Garner pulled out a gem from his pack. "Will this do?"

The man's eyes popped open wide as he leaned toward it. His entire demeanor shifted dramatically. "Welcome to Trahler's Magiceriem. Have a nice day."

They entered to stand in a hall of lavish decorations, carved statues, glowing lights, and plush carpets. An attractive woman approached them and left an equally handsome man alone off to the side. "Hello, gentlemen. I am Jifaine. I will be your personal attendant today." She appraised them, and her gaze turned stony. "I presume you have coin on credit? Do you have a script to that effect which I could see?"

"No, miss, but we do have this." Garner pulled his gem out and watched as her eyes softened.

"How interesting. Well, that will certainly do. Can we value that for you before we begin?"

Eventually, their gems were weighed and estimated at a worth of seventy-five thousand gold.

Jifaine's stern face melted into a smile, and she took Garner's arm in her own. "So, what are you looking for?" She escorted them upstairs to the higher floors where the magic wares were on display. They looked at all of the available items, wanting to grab everything in sight, but soon learned their expense would soon eat through their new fortune. After some private discussions, they came to a consensus on what to purchase.

They left with cloaks that could change colors, keep them warm or cool, and could reflect dragon fire. They both bore split swords—one side of gold, the other of silver. Boots that could allow them to run four times normal speed for up to an hour a day were snatched up, salves with tremendous healing powers were added, and finally, they purchased a single pack capable of holding one thousand times its apparent size for no extra weight.

Jifaine asked about their purchase choices. "Are you warriors in your own lands, then?"

"Yes," replied Rige. "We were surprised by the existence of the Steppes when we came through the Cordis arch. Now that we know that Samlin is similar, we think this gear will help us make our way there."

"Do you know anything about the dragons?" she asked.

"None," said Garner. "What can you tell us?"

"The Reds are deadly. You must avoid them at all cost. They will kill you on sight for the simple pleasure of killing you."

"And the others are different?" Rige asked.

"Quite. The Greens are temperamental but can be reasoned with. Depending on their mood, they might attack you on sight, or they might feel like helping you out if you have something they want."

"And the Blues?" prompted Garner.

"Unless you are carrying a blue gem, they're friendly and helpful. The Reds and Blues are mortal enemies and will fight on sight. From time to time, a Green will fight one but, usually, the Greens only fight each other."

"Hmmm, so are there are more Greens than the others?"

"Correct. So, it's best to have something to trade with a Green."

"Okay, good to know. So, what do they want?" Rige asked.

She shrugged. "It depends on the dragon. They all want gems, but if you have emeralds, they'll trigger into a rage. Very often, however, they like riddles."

"Wait," said Garner. "The Blues will attack if you have a sapphire, the Greens will attack for emeralds. So, are you saying they won't attack over gems that don't match their own color?"

"Correct again. They only can eat gems of their own color."

"What?" they both replied in unison.

"The dragons *eat* the gems?" asked Garner.

It was her turn to be surprised. "Yes. Where do you think they get *their* magic from?"

"Ahhhh," Rige answered.

"So, why haven't the gems all been eaten up by now?" Garner asked.

Jifaine laughed. "You really don't know anything about them, do you? Your lands must be very different. The gems appear when a blast of light from the clouds strikes brown earth on the ground. That's why the dragons roam the plains and burn off swaths of the grass. Usually, the light blasts bounce off the grasslands and back up into the sky. But from time to time, they strike a burnt off patch, and a gem forms. Later, a lucky dragon of the right color will come along and eat it."

"And that explains why they'll attack over like-colored gems," replied Rige. "It's their food. They don't care about the others except as objects."

"Exactly," Jifaine affirmed.

They thanked her and left. They used some of their residual gold and filled the magic pack with a storehouse of various mundane items. They purchased two fine horses and tack, rode the magic river around the town, spent the night in a local Inn, and the following day rode out of Spell Haven.

Days passed uneventfully until they reached the final grasslands that led to Samlin. On advice from the locals, they sold their horses and entered the Steppes at first light when the dragons were expected to be asleep. They shifted the color of their cloaks to a bright white to match the grass and kept their conversation to a minimum. Two hours passed.

Going around a hill, both of them stumbled and halted.

"What was that?" Garner whispered.

Rige craned his head and looked around. His soul felt chilled, and it was as if he experienced a strange type of double vision. Though the sky was still cloudy with colored shafts of light, the brightness hadn't varied, and yet, in a strange way, the landscape also seemed to have dimmed.

"Chark," he replied in a strained voice. "Has to be."

Garner nodded. "Someone's having a nightmare. Okay,

there's nothing for it. We have to keep moving forward. Let's go."

They rounded a few more hills when their path ran underneath a massive emerald boulder just ahead.

"Grab a piece?" asked Garner.

"No. I don't want to risk the sound. It might attract—"

The ground shuddered, and their eyes bolted open. They spun about, and there, on the path behind them, crouched a green dragon perhaps eighty feet long. It appraised them like a cat with two mice.

"Theeeeves," it hissed. "Thuh gem essss miiiine."

"Oh, crap," murmured Garner. He slowly slid his sword a few inches from the sheath.

Rige raised both hands in a surrender gesture. "Mighty dragon, we are simply trying to pass through on our way to Samlin. We just came around the last hill and saw your gem moments ago. We did not know it was there. We have no desire to take what is yours."

"Whell spoken, whiiite warrior. Yet the other drahs blade even nhow." The lids of the scaled monster half closed as they focused on Garner. "And not merely steel, but a split sword, no lehss. You may goh, but he is mhine."

Rige looked over at Garner, gave him a nod, and grasped his sword.

The dragon hissed.

"Before you kill us," Rige said as he moved to the left, "I have a riddle for you."

The serpent hesitated. "Speak."

"Two eggs lay in a basket;
home to life and a casket.
One was white and one was brown,
one was up and one was down.
Only white goes in a flame.
Brown, though burnt, would yet remain.
What is the basket that holds these two?
If you can't answer, let us through."

The winged snake pulled back and curled a bit as it pondered. "If you win, I want the answer. If I win, I kill you both."

"If we win, we get a prize: to go free un-accosted. If we then have to give you the answer, then you're still winning. If we lose, however, you still win. I don't think we can agree to that. Instead, if we win, we still give you the answer, but if we lose, then you can attack us, but we will still defend ourselves. That's more than fair, is it not?" Rige asked as Garner slid right.

"In the worst-case, mighty one," added Garner as Rige moved farther left, "we're all no worse off than our present situation. This seems like you can only win while at least giving us a chance too."

"I am nooht interehsted in giving chaaances."

"So, I gather the riddle is too hard for you then?" Rige asked.

The serpent's head lifted higher from the ground. "I have heard something similar to thees behfore. Leht uhs seee. A whiite ehgg up high. Perhaaaps a clouuud."

Rige stiffened as the dragon chuckled.

"Yeeehs," it gloated, "I see thuh truhth of it."

Garner looked over and noted his brother had knelt and was running his finger around the inside of his boots. After a moment, he recalled the instructions to activate the magic in them and knelt to follow Rige's lead.

"Aaaand, so the hills are the brown ehggs." It expanded its wings outward as its tail twitched about. "Whhhich," it began to laugh in a sibilant hiss, "cahn ohnly mean ..."

Garner burst into a sprint of boot-enhanced speed and whipped his sword from its sheath.

Rige mirrored Garner.

The dragon snapped its wings outward and dropped into a crouch. As it launched itself up, the brothers reached the wings and slashed. Their swords cut deep, deeper than they would have expected, and Garner completely severed a large scale-covered tendon.

The dragon crashed back to the ground and released a gout of green flame at him.

Rige pressed in and drove his blade point-first into its side.

Garner fell back and whipped his cloak around him.

The serpent screamed as it spun about to face Rige.

Rige tore his sword from the dragon's side, and a fountain of blood followed it out. He saw the monster inhale, and then its mouth opened.

Garner took the moment of distraction to run at the tail with his magical speed, jump up, and ricochet himself off the scales onto its back.

The dragon seemed not to notice as it released a blast of green flame onto Rige.

Garner jumped up and slammed the point down into the scaly back.

It screamed and rolled away as Garner jumped off.

Rige charged toward it and saw his brother roll over onto his stomach.

"Go," cried the dragon. "Bother me no more."

Rige halted beside Garner and rolled him over to the protest of groans. Bone protruded from an arm, and burns were evident where the cloak hadn't covered him fully. He looked up at the serpent. "We never wanted your gem, great one. Only to pass unaided. Now we are all injured. And we need to get to the Samlin arch before the rest of your kind awake."

"Shall a pahct be mahde then?"

"Of what sort?" Rige asked as he helped Garner to his feet.

"You are strong. Only leave the gem for me ahnd, when dohne, I shall heeal you."

"And," Garner grated through his pain, "give us a riddle another dragon may not know."

They agreed. The dragon went forward and devoured the green rock. As it did so, its wounds healed.

"We may have made a huge mistake," muttered Garner.

At that moment, the unseen gloom and unfelt cold dissipated. The dragon healed them and gave them a riddle. They parted in peace.

Now sobered, the boys moved on as fast as they could

run until their boot's magical speed was used up. They stopped for a ten-minute rest to regain their wind and then completed the final hour at a slow jog.

The black arch stood out against the white of the grass, the word *Samlin* spelled out in white vines across its top. They clasped arms.

"We survived our first Chark," Garner said, squaring his shoulders and puffing up like a peacock.

"Against a dragon, at that."

"You know what that makes us, right?"

"Dragonslayers."

"Well, we didn't actually kill it," Garner pointed out.

"No. But this was our first time. Next time, we'll have more magic, and we'll be better."

"Maybe dragon speakers would be more appropriate."

"Dragon Riders."

"Dragand carriers."

"What?" asked Rige, pausing before his next suggestion.

"Dragand. Like 'drag and.' So drag and carry. Drag and carriers. Get it?"

Rige stopped just feet away from the arch. "That's pitiful, Garner. Nothing was being drug or carried. It makes no sense."

"But the words are clever."

"But it makes no sense. It needs to somehow fit with—"

"Okay, okay. I get it. So, what are we going to claim then?" demanded Garner.

Rige blew out a breath. "Okay, what about dragon

warriors? We did fight it, and we did do a pretty good job. That's why it suggested a pact."

Garner acquiesced with a tilt of his head. "After you then, dragon warrior."

Rige smiled and walked through.

VARIATIONS

She was ready. Merinda had spent the past week in Scrivenger Hall, one of the many dead-world rooms that had been converted to use as the local Inn library. The librarians had been very helpful, and she had read everything available about the Dream, how it worked, how it had begun, and the earliest accounts of Travelers. The library held hundreds of thousands of books collected from over ten thousand worlds.

There were some surprising stories of Hall myths, shadowy figures, and adventures within the confines of the endless building. But concerning subjects around sway, nudge, and twist, there was very little.

Sway is what the Dreamers cause. Usually minor, but not always. There's the odd case. She considered what she'd read about the other two. *We can affect the Dreams of our Dreamers, but it appears to be accidental; some sort of backflow through the Dream threads held by the Binder. There's no aspect of that which can be controlled.* "Useless to me. So, down to twist." She fingered the necklace she always wore in the Inn. She unclasped it and held it in her hand to study it closer.

A diamond shot through with veins of silver, it formed a hand holding a pen formed of black onyx. Merinda cast her thoughts back to that day she had turned Warrior. One of the local Hall Monitors—Inn police—had taken her aside to give her the new badge and this necklace.

"What is this?" she had asked, looking at it then.

"Something we give only to Warriors. This talisman, what we call here The Hand of Fate, can enable you to twist the Dream to your desire. You and your Binder agree on a short phrase. You take hold of the Hand and repeat the phrase three times in a row, concentrating on it and what you want to happen next. Those two actions will be sufficiently unique that the desire should flow back from you to your Binder, and then he will release the action into the Dream flow. Once that happens, you can expect things to happen in the Dream. It is a twist of the Dream reality, an immediate bending of its rules and structure in order to meet your desire. Do you understand?"

"That sounds like it might be dangerous."

There was no hint of a joke as the man replied, "Nine times out of ten, it ends in Dream collapse—death. There are cases where it has worked, but you can see why this would be a last resort."

Merinda's thoughts returned to the present. *But what if I used it, not in a moment of desperation to do something big, but in a moment of quiet to do something small?*

She arranged a meeting with her two Binders to warn them of her plans and request they keep her tests secret. After some argument, they had both agreed, and she now waited, near the end of her latest Crossing, near the Trailing Uptake.

The tube of light rose as always into the sky. She scanned about. An aspect of late winter dominated the brown landscape about her. Scraggly trees grasped at the sky in search of leaves lost months in the past. Squirrels and birds darted in and out of sight, and in the distance, low hills surrounded them like a furled up blanket.

She concentrated on the nearest tree.

What is the smallest change I could make to this that wouldn't roil the Dream?

Her gaze fell on a few brown, crackled leaves that yet managed to dangle from a branch.

"Okay, I'm seconds from the Uptake. Worst case, I jump through and I'm home."

Merinda closed her eyes and sought emptiness. After a moment, she opened them again.

No hint of Chark. The entire Crossing has been smooth.

She pulled the necklace out from her shirt and lay the Hand into her own.

Merinda released a breath and formed an image in her mind, willing it to happen, and began to speak.

"Maragathy, maragathy, maragathy."

Nothing happened.

She began again.

"Maragathy, maragathy, ma—"

The dead, brown leaves on the branch before her rejuvenated and became glossy green with renewed life.

She scanned around for any disruptions to the world about her. Nothing.

She smiled.

"Now for something larger."

Merinda imagined the entire tree filled with fresh leaves of summer. She focused and repeated her phrase.

"Maragathy, maragathy, maragathy."

Again, the pause, but this time she waited a few more seconds.

The tree changed before her.

"Yes," she exulted. "Yes, yes—"

A rumble in the ground cut her off. Her eyes popped wide as she watched the sky shimmer like ripples in a pond. Leaves appeared and disappeared on the trees in a pattern that followed the ripple across the landscape like a green brush sliding across a canvas whose tint lasted only a few moments.

The Trailing Uptake flickered and shifted a hundred feet away.

Merinda gasped and took off in a heart-pounding sprint as her fingers tingled from the shock of what had happened and the fear that the Uptake could disappear altogether, leaving her stranded. She leaped into the shaft of light and sighed in relief as the mist of the familiar Veil surrounded her.

On returning to the Inn, she collected herself, dropped off her pack, and left for real-world to take stock of her actions. Her housekeeper met her as always on her return.

"Glad to see you back safely, Ms. Davis. Your bath is prepared as always."

"Thank you. Bring me a glass of the shratelen wine, please. I need a little fortitude beyond the normal tonight."

"Of course. You had a rough Crossing tonight, then?"

Jennifer paused on the stairwell to reply, "No. The Crossing was very smooth. I tried something new tonight. It didn't go quite as I'd hoped."

"Well, I guess you've learned something not to do in the future then, right? That's also valuable."

Jennifer worried her lip over the response. "I've learned that I have more to learn before I can do what I must. A lost battle does not mean a lost cause."

"True. As long as you win the last battle."

Jennifer recalled an old quotation. "To the victor, the spoils."

She turned back and headed up.

BAD TO THE BONE

Hunger disturbed his journey into the past. He pulled out some cheese. He shook his head at the blandness of it. *Smell and taste; the two things in the Dream that are never as good as in real-world.* He shrugged as his thoughts returned to the journey that had brought him to this state. *And that's when I made my Ranger run; when I came here the first time. That's where it all really began. How could I have known?*

Clavin stared across a landscape twisted by gnarled boulders, baked dirt, sandpits, and the occasional cactus. A gray sky capped the scene like a moist, chilly blanket which deposited an unwelcome rain mixed with bits of snow. *This is all wrong. This whole trip. Now this mess.*

His Feening said this was the worst Chark in his memory and yet, nothing really bad had happened to him this whole time. It made no sense. *Something's wrong, somewhere.* The image of his Binders flashed in his head. *Could Mark or Alcot be sick?* Clavin took one more look around him. *Yep, this is a bad one.* He looked back the way he came, then into the distance toward his destination.

What did they call this? The Vast Desert? He scuffed his chin as he pondered the panorama before him. *Ten thousand miles across this thing.* "That's a long way. A very long way." *Three and a half days to cross. This Chark will blow over. Probably.* "Let's see if they told me the truth."

He drew out a blue vial from his pouch, uncorked it, placed a tiny drop on his forefinger, closed his left eye, and proceeded to rub the substance onto its lid. By the time he had re-corked the vial and put it away, he could see the fuzziness that betokened the action of the liquid.

Through his left eyelid, his vision penetrated the rain, mist, and snow, far out into the desert, much farther than he could with his other eye, and much differently too.

The desert sands that before had seemed all muddy brown were, by virtue of the potion, saturated with varying hues of reds, golds, browns, and blues, along with many other colors. It was the blues he sought.

At last prepared, he loped along, following the terrain, but he never climbed the buttes and dunes that lay about him. He made his way over to a blue patch to study it.

Wrong angle.

He scanned about again, found another of like shade, and made his way over.

Slightly off. He shrugged. *Close enough.* He stepped onto the patch, hopped up and down twice, and on the third bounce, leaped forward as high as he could.

As his feet left the ground, the world streaked into

a multi-hued blur, and then a moment later, as his feet touched down, the focus of the Dream Lands returned. He couldn't say for certain just how far he'd leaped, but he could guess.

About ten miles.

Without pausing, he scanned for the next splash of blue, and after two more attempts, found another angled to advance his progress across the vast desert. He repeated the process and jumped again.

The next two days would be long and exhausting, but if the Charkness didn't interfere, he'd make it with plenty of time to spare. He knew better than to hope for that, but he also had no choice. The desert had to be crossed in three and a half days. He settled into a routine and ate up the miles.

Clavin had made steady progress for an hour when he landed from his latest jump. Instead of scanning for the next blue patch, he paused, arrested by the sight before him.

A vast fortress sat, tall and menacing, behind a many-pointed wall that ran for miles in each direction. Formed of stone—mostly black, but some of red—it looked as if blood had dripped down onto a great obsidian mountain. Lightning crackled along its parapets.

Not good. Boy, would I like to go around this thing.

He shook his head. If he tried to avoid the fortress, it would likely just come looking for him.

Still, maybe I could go around. He pondered it. *No. It's a path blocker.* "Why else make it so large?" With a heavy sigh of resolve, he straightened his back and marched toward the imposing gatehouse.

The massive steel portcullis must have stood a hundred feet high and spanned twice that. The massive crossbars literally gleamed in the gloom, as if lit by some hidden source. It would have been impressive to any Walker or Runner and most Warriors.

He frowned at it. *Overdone.* He passed into the shadows between the towers. He pondered the extravagant dimensions of the castle. *I've seen better.*

A tremendous din shrieked at him as hidden chains retracted and drew the mass of steel upward, a clear invite to come in.

Why can't they ever be silent? He shook his head at the noise, almost disappointed.

Stopping, he drew from his wealth of experience in The Dream and called out in his most polite voice, "A Dream Warrior of Samlin begs humble entrance."

He waited but a moment. There was no answer, of course. With a Chark in full blow, he didn't expect one, but experience had often proved that courtesy could pay dividends later. With a shrug, he moved onward, passed under the giant grate and into the long tunnel on the other side. He was careful to scan for movement above.

He passed down the tunnel and came at length to another set of like gates that were, conveniently, already raised before him. Clavin paused as he approached. He glanced upward for any sign of movement and then quickstepped as he strode beneath them and into a vast courtyard perhaps half a mile on a side.

He slowed. *Across the middle gives more reaction time to*

attacks from the sides. "True." *But if I skirt to one side, I have a better chance of ducking into a building for cover.*

He compromised and trod across the space while staying far to the right.

In a place of darkness like this one, he always felt it best to stay on the *right* side of things. Clavin knew that many, if not most, of his Dreamers were religious, and subtle nuances and symbols could, therefore, have powerful effects in these situations.

Halfway across the vast space, he stopped as a woman came out of a building on the other side to meet him. A long, brilliant, white dress streamed off of her. Though it dragged on the ground, the garment of the beauty who approached took no mark from the soil it brushed. The cloud-shaded sun fell in shafts like cathedral beams into the courtyard and burned down upon her golden blonde hair, illuminating it like a pale flame.

He turned toward her. *Standard princess. What type? Let's see model one, held captive; model two, need of a knight; model three, sword-wielding princess; model four, time-wasting vixen; model-five, evil witch mirrored by model six, fairy godmother.*

"Two or four," he murmured to himself.

Clavin proceeded toward the woman while ever vigilant to potential dangers. After a minute or so, he stopped and gave her a full bow from the waist.

"Fair princess, I am a stranger in a strange land and seek thy guidance in furthering my travels."

They always like to be called princess.

"Thou art surely wearied from thy travels," she replied. "Follow thee along, Sir Knight, and I shall introduce thee to my father, the king. We shall see to thy recuperation."

Oh crap. Time-wasting vixen. He responded with a smile and a nod.

"Leadest thou on, fair one."

Turning, she strode away and led him up many stairways, down numberless corridors, through a series of great halls—each filled with beautiful adornments, but no people. It took almost half an hour of his valuable time to make the trek, but finally, they walked up to a series of doors, that seemed made more for giants than men, which swung back quietly. They entered into the dining hall.

There was a table, some hundred feet long and thirty broad, around which a great throng gathered, some seated, others standing. At one end sat a crowned man, beside who sat two huge dogs, and behind whom stood two huge, armored knights that made the dogs seem normal in size.

Just a minor quest for you, my boy, Clavin thought with a slight grimace as he imagined what the king would be asking him in a very short while.

Sorry, old bean, busy right now. I will, however, be taking that crown with me.

He smiled at the thought of actually saying that. *Someday ... maybe if there wasn't this Chark blowing ...*

"What brings the turns of happiness to your face, good sir?" asked the princess.

"Ah, my lady, naught but the joy of meeting your blessed father."

The princess stepped over to the king. "Father, this great warrior has come to us from the wastes of the Vast Desert. He is a Dream Warrior of Samlin."

A puzzled expression crossed the king's face at this.

"What, sir, is a Dream Warrior?"

"Great King, in my homeland, that is a type of knight."

"Ah." The king smiled. "Sit, sir, and refresh thyself at my table."

At this, the princess pulled back the empty chair and smiled at Clavin.

Enchanted chairs and wooden snares can clutch you tight and bind you, Clavin sing-songed to himself as he considered the invitation.

"Most heartily do I accept your kind offer. However, first, I must cleanse myself with ceremonial water from my homeland before eating or drinking. I beg your understanding, for it is a custom of my people."

To this, the king agreed, and Clavin had soon anointed himself with various liquids and doused some on the outer side of his cloak, which would contact the chair itself.

Clavin noted the patina of invisible magic on the food and drink set before his chair, so he also sprinkled them and, seeing the auras dissipate, settled down as a smug grin plastered his face. As he ate and drank, he studied the others who sat at the great table and ascertained a vacant look within their eyes excepting only the king and the princess.

Stupefaction enchantment. How did I classify that? Standard castle trick number nine? Well, no need to delay the inevitable.

"So, my lord and lady, I thank you for your generosity, but now, in truth, I must needs be off."

Or was it castle trick eight? No matter, I guess. I really should write all this down someday.

Clavin noted, as he had expected, that his declaration to depart had changed the expressions of his hosts. They both ceased smiling, and the king's face grew serious.

"You are he for whom we have searched these long years," said the king.

Or the past hour, in any case.

"Indeed, how then may I help you?"

"There is a task that only you may do for us. Our kingdom is enchanted, and only a great knight impervious to magic may break its spell. If you undertake this and succeed, you shall have my daughter to wife and my kingdom to rule. How say you?"

Run an errand, get a kingdom. Makes sense to me.

"Whatever I may do, I shall do so gladly for the king and his lady. However, whatever I do must be done quickly, for I have another task that I must soon accomplish. Tell on. What then is this?"

Clavin was quite pleased with how his reply had come out and was running it through his mind again for the next time he found himself in this situation when at last the king, having droned through the usual thanks, got to the meat of the matter.

He focused and, at the end, it struck him that it wasn't such a bad gig after all.

Okay, so there's a troll in the dungeon guarding a magic stone that I need to bring back here. I can't leave without bringing it back, and I'm sure I can't bring it back without killing the troll. Piece of cake.

"Very well, Great King, I shall descend to the depths of this mighty fortress and return with the stone or not at all. Who, though, shall guide me down?"

"Lords Rige and Garner," replied the king whereupon the two knights behind him presented their spears in sharp military fashion.

Fodder, he thought with a nod.

"I thank thee and these fair knights and welcome them to my side. Let us be off then?"

Surprised and pleased by his eagerness to be about the charge, the king agreed.

"Sir Garner, Sir Rige, lead him to the dungeons."

The two hesitated, as if they struggled with some internal conflict.

The king noticed. "Now, sirs. Do your duty."

They bowed and turned, arms locked in place at their sides, as if forced to obey, and the three were away—knight, Clavin, knight—armor squeaking as they unwound their path downward.

Squeak much? he mentally queried his two noisy companions.

After half an hour of descending and walking, Clavin asked how far they yet had to travel.

"We have but reached the ground floor. We have this far again to go to reach the very lowest levels of the fortress. It is there we shall find the troll," answered the knight behind him.

Always a half-hour. How long will this troll take to locate?

He anointed his eyes and ears with other oils from other vials and sniffed from a third. Next, he chanted some phrases with the result that both his leather outer clothing and his weapons glowed with energy visible only through his enhanced senses.

He took a few moments to contemplate Fodder One, who walked ahead of him under some obvious enchantment of his own.

I wonder if they're under a stupefaction spell? He shook his head. *What does it matter? They're not real.*

He glanced behind him at Fodder Two, then back to One as he considered how best to use the two of them. He nodded and settled on an old trick. Back into his pouch he went, drawing out another vial, and called a stop. He rehearsed the pitch he was about to give. *Yep, sounds good. Now, let's see if these two go for it.*

"Gentlemen, I have an elixir that will strengthen your already strong armor and give yet more power to your swords when striking at the troll. By your leave, I shall anoint you with it, having already prepared my own equipage, so that we may all be equally prepared." To this, they agreed, thankful tones in what had been strained voices. Soon it was done, and they were back on their way. As they moved onward, the light, the source of which was never clear before, was replaced by smoking torches emitting a pungent smell.

Gotta set the mood, of course, he thought eyeing the burning brands. *Why don't they ever put out the right amount of light? I guess we'll have moss and mold next.* On the next level down, water began seeping from the ceiling and dropping with an ominous *ping, plop* into the various inch-deep pools of water that splattered about the floor. *Dank puddles instead of moss and mold. Can't always guess right.* The moss and mold appeared soon after, and Clavin settled back into his satisfied dour mood, expectations met.

They stepped out from the final stairwell, and Fodder One announced, "Bottom floor" in a voice that sounded of both doom and desperation.

"Tell me," began Clavin, "don't you have any prisoners in this—" His question was cut off by the wailing sound of tortured souls held too long in captivity.

"Ah, never mind."

"Where shall we begin, Sir Clavin?" asked Fodder Two. "The dungeons are vast."

"No doubt. Bide a moment while I see if my magic can aide us."

He rummaged in his pouch, called forth the glasses he used at times like this, and put them on.

"De rattt," he spat, enunciating each syllable forcibly.

"What ho?" asked Fodder Two.

Shut up, squeak bucket.

"My apologies, good sir. An incantation that usually works well has failed me." *Man, how much of my stuff is going to fail on this Crossing? This is crazy.* "We must find another way to come to grips with the beast. Tell me of this place and its layout, if you would be so kind."

Clavin ignored the man's response, for he already knew the dungeon would be both enormous and a regular warren of twists and turns. As the man droned on, Clavin considered his next move. "I am sorry to interrupt, Sir Knight, but the thought suddenly besets me: Do you know perchance if the beast be intelligent or not?"

"For a troll, quite intelligent, for a man, far less so."

Clavin smiled as he nodded his thanks.

"Thank you, my friend. I have a trick I can try that, if successful, will likely lead the troll to us, saving us the trouble of hunting it down. With your consent, shall I attempt it?"

With their assent given, he begged them for total quiet for the next two minutes and, after seeing them follow his instructions, began to whisper a chant.

"Come to me, my scaly friend,
round the corner and the bend,
up and down the darkened hall,
come to me when I call."

Seven times, he repeated this verse. As he did so, he spun his hands about each other as if reeling in a length of hidden rope. On the final word of the seventh round, he tossed the pretend rope out from him down the hall. It was as if his echo ran before him, off into the darkness, in both directions. As it ran, they could hear it bouncing and calling.

He looked back at the two knights who remained quiet and thanked them for their patience. "Good sirs, if, as you say, our prey is intelligent, it will hear the call, and following it, be led back to us here. All we have to do now is wait."

An hour passed as they sat in silence and listened for the returning echoes that would presage the arrival of the troll. At last, they heard the ever so faint breath return in the long darkness, and they jumped to their feet and grabbed their weapons. Clavin, who'd long before recovered a ring from his pouch, now placed it onto his finger, knowing that the moment had arrived.

"What is that talisman you don?" asked Fodder One.

Cripes. He realized the invisibility ring had also failed to function. "Naught but a foolish hope. Prepare now. It comes," he said, somehow pleased that he yet managed to maintain the proper voice.

The troll had heard their voices, turned from the nagging whisper that had drawn it to them, sped to the sound of their voices, and leapt into their room. The monster was a blur of claws and teeth as it spun and slashed at the two knights.

Clavin, however, was untouched and un-assaulted. While the troll concentrated on Fodder One, Clavin managed to strike it through at least four times. Fodder One went down, and it turned on Fodder Two. The name of the potion he had placed on the two knights flashed through his mind as a brief smile quirked the corner of his mouth. *Attract hostile.* Clavin thrust the troll through four times more in the next minute as he enjoyed his protection. Fodder Two went down. With a mental salute to the fallen knights, he faced the troll alone.

The troll slashed and smashed and, had Clavin's armor not functioned so well, could have been sufficient to kill him. Clavin returned the favor and, after three more good thrusts, the troll fell before him. Clavin bought himself time for the next step in proper troll expunction and cut off its head.

Another vial from his amazing pouch enabled Clavin to dispense fully and permanently with the troll in the only way possible. As the fire roared up and the troll burnt down, Clavin drew forth what looked to be a tiny bullhorn from his magic pouch, placed it to his ear as if listening for something, and commanded the horn to its duty.

He paused for a brief moment as he considered the torn remains of Fodders One and Two. "Good sirs, thou hast done thy duty well, and thy king and kingdom thank thee. Good thee bye." *Good thee bye? I don't even know what that means.* With a small chuckle, he headed back the way the troll had come, listening intently to that which drew him on.

Though his magic that should have allowed him to see the troll's fading footsteps had failed, his horn that enabled him to hear them had not. Careful to keep his own movement quiet, he followed the distinct sounds of clawed steps ever careful of the possibility that other things might yet await him in the darkness. Moving along, half an hour passed, and he came across a room of lighted canisters in many colors. He stopped and turned in. *'Bout time. I haven't collected any good potion in the last eight Crossings.* He scanned the room, tested the floor for traps, and looked for magic. He entered and began to refill the various vials within his pouch. Picking up a huge beaker of bluish fluid, he poured and poured into his far-smaller vial until the huge beaker was emptied. He did the same with some others and then found one new to him, brownish with golden flecks within. All of the other flasks were open-topped containers that one could look down into. This one, though, was a bit different. Though constructed like the others, it was upside down. *Some sort of solid?*

He reached out and tilted the beaker a hair to the side. The liquid—for liquid it was—did indeed flow, but *up* and not down. He removed his finger from the top of the beaker after a few drops had spilled out and watched them race up to the ceiling. Understanding the mechanics at last, he recovered an empty vial from his pouch and stored the strange liquid. *Figure this out later.*

Off he went, and an hour later, found that for which he sought. A great green gem, set in a scepter of white gold, lay radiant in the center of a room atop a black plinth crowned by a red cushion. *Dramatic yet tasteful,* he silently approved. Around the chamber lay the bones and other remains of the troll's various victims. He scanned the walls and floors for traps. He strode across to the plinth and studied it carefully. *Probably one last trap here.*

Intense scrutiny revealed that no magic rested upon it and no pit lay beneath it. Clavin used his magic to probe the floor and found only solid bedrock reaching down deep into the earth. He looked up for enlightenment and noticed that, recessed into the ceiling above, was a great cupola of stained glass depicting a dragon crushed beneath a great rock. He probed with his magic up through the stone of the ceiling and found a clue as to the nature of the final trap. The entire structure above was formed like a massive cylinder of rock, held in place by vast pinions hidden from view. He imagined removing the scepter and then the entire ceiling crushing down upon him like a bug under a hammer or sealing him into the small space created by the cupola above. The stupidity of it irritated him.

If this trap ever were set off, resetting it would be an enormous amount of work. He shrugged. *Things in the Dream don't have to make sense. Like a desert with rain. They are because they are. But, like other things that make no sense, solutions are generally made possible before the problems appear. So, what is new and unusual on this Crossing that I might use?*

He strolled around the room and noticed a painting of a man holding a glass of liquid like the mystery vial from the previous room. *Ah.* Clavin recovered the vial from before and began experimenting. Moving out into the hallway, he poured a tiny amount that ran up onto a stone ceiling tile. As it struck the rock, it spread and absorbed into the stone, and he watched as the lines that separated it from adjacent stones disappeared. Nodding with satisfaction, he moved back into the room and, turning the bottle up toward the ceiling, watched as the fluid floated up and splashed against it, sinking into the stone. Clavin took care not to let the liquid touch his own fingers as he flipped the vial back over, and, after the final drops fell up, re-stoppered it.

After verifying that the lines that had once separated the vast ceiling piston from the wall no longer existed— that, in fact, they had fused together—he stepped down close to the plinth, said a quick prayer, and lifted the scepter from the pillow. The ceiling groaned but held, and Clavin hurtled himself from the room in a rush, lest the thing cave in anyway.

Bad to the bone, he thought with a self-satisfied smile.

In another two hours' time, through further use of his bag of tricks, Clavin managed to retrace his steps through the stupendous structure and into the dining hall where still the throng awaited him. Approaching the king, he presented the prize to him. Rising, the king insisted that he would make good on his earlier pledge: control of his kingdom and his daughter in marriage.

"Well and gladly do I accept your great generosity," replied Clavin, knowing that in the next passing, in a future Dream, it would be unlikely to find the king, his daughter, or even the castle in the present form. "However, as I explained earlier, I have a task that must be completed and an oath to fulfill. Though I must leave, I shall return within a fortnight, and then shall the marriage be consummated."

To this, the king agreed and, very soon, Warrior Clavin Roth was on his way, skipping ten-mile swaths across the great desert. Two days later, he found Cordis Castle, stepped through the Veil, and entered the Traveler's Inn, the portal to and from all the paths, to a grand reception of banners and cheering.

Dream Warrior Clavin Roth became a Dream Ranger in an elaborate ceremony after crossing a path and returning to the Traveler's Inn for the fourteen-hundredth time. After the celebration, he exited the Inn onto Cordis and visited a few friends who likewise congratulated him. That following night, he picked up a new load for his return trip to Samlin.

Before departing, as was the custom of most Travelers, he paused inside the Inn on his way to the Veil to talk with his friends. Staven brought the subject around to a pair of brothers, twins, that he'd gotten to know over the past few weeks and had fallen two nights before. "Yep, couple of good lads there. Nice and chatty with a fair wit about them," said Staven Drath. "It's a shame. You'd have liked them."

"What were they like?" asked Clavin.

"Twins. Two huge fellows. Hard to miss. Visions of grandeur still locked up in their heads. You know how that goes. Shiny, steel armor. Bright, pointy spears. Dragon slayers!" finished Drath with a dramatic roar and a raise of his glass.

"Yep, I remember those days. More fun, and a lot more dangerous. So, what were their names?" Clavin replied with a nod of his head and a lift of his own glass.

"Rige and Garner. They'll be missed."

Back once more on the Samlin-Cordis trail, Clavin found himself on an old path made new for him by recent events. Doubt and worry assailed him as they had not done for many a year. He had wondered, till that last conversation with Staven, why his Feening had revealed such a strong Chark when the task had seemed rather easy. After Staven's report, he knew.

It was rare for Travelers to share a trail, especially without knowing it—he would have said impossible. The Inn Routers organized things to prevent that from happening. Clavin didn't know how it had come about, but when he set out on the path two nights prior, Rige and Garner were still alive. The great Dream Ranger of Samlin-Cordis had shared his trail with Walkers Garner and Rige.

Dream Ranger, he thought as he shook his head in disgust. *You must have spent two whole hours with them. They were thick with magic, but all you could think was how lucky you were to have two patsies along.*

Bad to the bone? he wondered as he poured another drink. *Or just plain bad?*

FIRESTORM

The forests that surrounded Trailing City had burned for three weeks. Smoke strangled light and lung alike as dark clouds dropped a sooty shroud on man and beast. Jennifer insisted on short turnarounds so she could spend her spare time in the clean air of Wassel instead of coughing on the smoke of Trailing.

She made the trip to the Star and waited for Staven and Clavin to show up.

Clavin had a new table with the banner of a Ranger mounted on it. Only he and invited friends were allowed to sit there. She roamed out to scan the smasher pit for a few minutes. When he arrived, she went and joined him.

"Hello, Clavin. Smooth Crossing?"

"Fairly. A little trouble at the Blue Bog."

Memories from other recountings flashed. "That's near the end, right?"

"Right. Cestalanc showed up. The entire trip, smooth, and then it appears near the end."

"Cestalanc ... gold dragon?"

"Correct again. Big, powerful. Sometimes mean, sometimes reasonable."

"Chark, I presume?"

"Oh yeah. It started the previous day and grew. By the time I arrived at the bog, it was on fire."

"A bog on fire? Bogs are wet."

Clavin shrugged. "Right. And deserts are dry, but I've been through one in pouring rain. It's the Dream."

Merinda settled back and focused downward. "A Dream doesn't have to make sense; therefore, neither does a Crossing. But a bog on fire. It makes me think."

"About?"

She looked up and leaned forward, arms on the table. "Back on Trailing Prime—real-world—they're having a bunch of forest fires around the city these past weeks. My last four Crossings have all had aspects of flame and burning. There's been a Chark on every one."

"You think our Crossings are somehow connected? That's impossible. Different endpoints."

She shook her head. "Of course not. But your experience just triggered this thought. I think that my community of Dreamers on Trailing is carrying the effects of the fires with them and the images, the memories, of flame and fire are presenting on my Crossings. It makes sense."

After a moment, Clavin agreed. "Yeah. It does. Maybe you should lay off Traveling till the fires stop?"

She looked over as Staven Drath sauntered through the entrance. "Here's your twin."

Clavin waved him to a seat.

"So, what'd I miss?" Staven asked.

They caught him up.

"Okay, how'd you deal with Cestalanc? Fight or flight?"

"Obfuscation."

"Oh my," Staven exclaimed with widening eyes, "someone's been using his dictionary."

Clavin grinned. "I could have gone with onubliation."

"But that would be too much bloviation," suggested Staven.

"How so?" Merinda queried.

"Well," explained Staven, "it would have been an excessive use of unnecessary words."

"No," she cut him off and turned back to Clavin, "how did you use *hiding* to deal with the dragon? Details please."

"I sent a challenge to Cestalanc to meet me on the Desin plain, a barren wilderness of dried-out grass and dust during the summer. It showed up and tried to flame me. Everything caught fire. Like a giant tinderbox. I used a windstorm to blow it up faster, and it had the added advantage of whipping up the dust."

"Very nice," approved Merinda. "So, you hid from the dragon in the smoke and dust. Then what?"

Clavin shrugged. "Then I snuck off and rushed for the gate. Simple."

Staven slumped back. "Boring. The great Ranger ran from a dragon." He yawned.

Merinda addressed him. "You think he should have fought a dragon that he could avoid? Is that what you'd do?"

Staven grinned and shook his head. "Nope. Clave did the smart thing. But still boring."

"Clavin, weren't you choking on the soot?"

"Nope. Apparently, Mark, my Binder, imagines fire without soot. I didn't really have to deal with it."

"Good thing he didn't imagine soot as snow," Staven tossed out. "Then the snow might have extinguished the fire."

"Then I'd have been baked," agreed Clavin.

"Charred," rejoined Staven.

"Par-broiled."

Merinda couldn't help but grin as she shook her head. "You two."

Merinda spent three days in her home on Wassel as the conversation replayed on a loop and formed into a plan. She returned to the Inn early and spoke to some Merchants before leaving for Trailing. Other than an escape from a burning city, the Crossing was smooth. She requested a change in her schedule and waited three days on Trailing. Upon notice that her wishes from days before had been carried out, she returned to the Inn, collected her load, and passed through the Veil for her return to Wassel.

She was two days along the Crossing when the first fire began. Thick smoke billowed off the tops of the hills in the distance ahead as wolves and rabbits, lions and deer bounded from the woods as they rushed for the safety of the un-charred lowlands.

Merinda rode on even as the horse nickered and shied

sideways. An hour later, the soot began to fall about them as the air became thick and hard to breathe. She dismounted and stroked the horse's neck. "Okay, this is it then."

Turning, she focused on the sky and began to form an image in her mind, one that looked nearly identical to the skyscape before her. She withdrew the Hand of Fate and grasped it tight, digging the outline of it into her palm, as she began the chant to alert her Binder.

"Maragathy, maragathy, maragathy."

Tense, shoulders stiff, belly tight, she took a deep breath and blew it out slowly as she held the image in her mind.

A cool wind mussed her hair even as her cheek stung with the bight of a cold flake of snow. The world gave a tiny shimmer, like a mirage in a hot desert, and settled down. She stood frozen in dread at what could happen. *The Uptakes are days away. If this goes wrong ...*

She shook the thought from her head and stood still. After a full minute, she relaxed as the thrill of victory washed over her.

Visually, the world was little changed, but now snow fell in place of soot. The air was crisp and clean. She smiled.

It worked. It actually worked.

"Similarity and preparation."

Now, how can I leverage this to bring Clessy back?

"What looks like a Winder horse?"

She turned and looked at the mare behind her. She nodded. "Another horse." *Dye it blue, paint the hooves. Should I? This trip?*

Merinda shook her head. *Small steps. You've twisted this Crossing once already. How many can a single Crossing handle?*

"Besides, you have some artwork to send out. You have to prep first."

Next trip. And then ...

I get what's coming to me.

"I get what's mine."

BOTTLED UP

Why am I so cold? Clavin wondered. *And wet? Am I ...?*

He torqued his body around and pulled up out of the mud that he'd been lying in.

He scanned about while scraping mud from his face. Not a half-mile back was Samlin Castle. *I must be on the Path! How? I don't ...*

He turned the other direction; unfamiliar terrain stretched before him as far as he could see. Besides the castle that led to the veil and Traveler's Inn, nothing was familiar.

Which way am I going? Let's see, what was I doing?

His last memory placed him in Samlin, in his real-world home. *Ah, the bourbon. A couple of glasses before bed.* The memory of early morning drinks flashed. *So what?* Images followed that thought of the drinks before lunch and then dinner. "Whatever. Focus on now."

He looked down at his mud-buried feet. Just steps away was dry ground. His feet squelched as he made his way from the pit.

"So, how did I get here?"

Another look around provided no answers. He pulled off his pack and looked inside. *Ah, a cargo. Precious little more, but there IS a cargo. Okay, then how did I get here? Which way am I going?* He looked around again and fixed his gaze on Samlin Castle.

I'm in no condition to be making a Crossing. He took a step toward Samlin Castle. *I'm out of here. Better to play it safe than be the first Ranger to die on Samlin-Cordis.*

A voice behind him called out, "Hey, mister, where are you going?"

Clavin spun. His hand reached for his sword but found nothing. The voice had emerged from one of two—or both of two, Clavin wasn't sure—young boys who stood no more than a half-hearted stone's throw away.

They were young, closer to the womb than a beard. They wore unremarkable britches and tunics. Both carried in one hand a torch and in the other a ring with a large key on it—a key at least a foot in length.

Control! Clavin's experience commanded his reactions. *Control, now. One thing at a time!* He scanned down at his waist. *No sword.*

"Mister ..." Both boys *were* talking in unison. "You can't go back. You have to go forward."

Control! Stay in control! Clavin's experience was demanding, but he had learned to listen to it.

"Dear boys ..." *There, good start. Breathe.* "I assure you going back was far from my considerations. I was merely having a look around." *Which is always a good idea anyway.*

"You have to go forward. You have to take us with you. You are responsible for us."

Clavin noted they spoke in perfect unison. *That's going to get annoying.* "Indeed. Forward it is." *Roll with it. Sort things out first.* He looked at the two boys and smiled. He took a step toward them and was reminded of his very wet feet by the squeaking of his foot in his shoe. He drew near the boys, who noticed his dilemma and laughed.

"Squeak much?" they harmonized. They laughed loudly, almost a barking tone.

That was my joke. Clavin shook his head. *Not funny. Concentrate.* "Now, boys, I'd like a moment to think through our journey." He gestured toward Samlin Castle. "Since we are so close to Samlin Castle, we are either very nearly done with our journey or just beginning."

The boys nodded.

You're no help. "It seems I have come on this journey without my weapons. I'd like to propose that we go to Samlin Castle as quickly as possible."

"No!" they declared. "You can't go back. You have to take us with you, forward."

Well, at least I know the right direction now. "I have no weapon. How can I defend us?"

"We have these!" They held up their keys. "Here, take them."

Keys? Really? "Are these weapons?" Clavin asked, glancing back at Samlin Castle. As much as he wanted to turn around and run for it, experience had taught him that fighting against the Dream with too much vigor was dangerous. He was also Feening that going back was impossible, so he looked back at the two young boys.

They were holding out their keys. Clavin shook his head, not in rejection but disbelief. He turned to look once more at Samlin Castle. *Maybe ...*

"What in the world?" Nothing. From where he stood to the horizon was only the waving grasses, shin-high, for as far as he could see. There was no more Samlin Castle.

He turned to the boys, anguish burning inside him.

"You can't go back." They still spoke as one. "You have to take us forward."

Clavin shook his head again. "So you said. So you said."

He took a deep breath and exhaled. *How much did I drink to forget even going to the Sanctum? To forget passing the Veil? How did I get into this situation?* He looked down at his muddy feet. *No going back to Samlin? That's never happened before, either.* He turned to his two young companions. *Okay, time to start figuring some things out.*

But, instead of finding answers, he ended up with more questions. The keys had at least doubled in size. They had grown to two feet in length, hanging from six-inch diameter rings.

"Ah, the keys."

"Yes, you should have them."

"Weapons?"

They merely continued holding out the keys.

"How can a key be a weapon?"

"Oh, one of them is very dangerous," said the boy on the left.

"The other is safe," said the boy on the right.

"One is dangerous? So one is a weapon?" Clavin started sorting the details into what he hoped would soon be a solution. "The other is safe."

He looked at the boys again and noted once more their torches. "And those? Weapons?"

In unison, they answered, "No, of course not. Light is life."

At that second, as if some great lamp had been snuffed out, darkness fell all around. But for the torches of the two boys, all was blackness.

"Light is life," the one on the right declared.

"And," added the one on the left, "the light came into the darkness—"

More like darkness smothered the light, if you ask me.

"—and the darkness was no more in the world," they said together.

Clavin had heard enough. He snatched the keys from the boys abruptly.

"Okay, whatever. Let's move." Clavin stepped off in the direction he feened he should go. His shoes squeaked, and the boys laughed.

He ground his teeth. *Not funny.*

Clavin reached for his pouch and found it, too, missing. *Holy carp. No sword, no pouch.*

He looked at the two keys. They were, as far as Clavin could tell, identical. *One is dangerous, and one is safe. Maybe we'll be attacked by a lock.* He smiled at the image of that. *Okay, that was pretty good. I need to remember to save that* one for when I tell about this Crossing once I'm back in the Inn.

He glanced over his shoulder at the two boys padding behind him, torches held high. They looked at his feet and laughed. "Squeak, squeak." Clavin rolled his eyes and focused back on the trail ahead and came to an immediate halt.

Five paces away stood a large wall, black stone without seam, stretching as far in all directions as the light was able to reveal. *Now, where did ... okay, what do we have ... wall. Let me guess? There's going to be a door with a huge ol' keyhole. I'll have to figure out which key to use. So, left or right?*

He only paused for a moment before selecting right. *Staying on the right side of things is usually best.* "To the right." He turned to direct the boys forward, and his eyes popped open wide as he slightly recoiled. "What in the world?"

Their skin and clothing had disappeared, leaving behind two skeletons—not of bone, but of what looked like wrought iron. Where the boys had stood, Clavin looked at a complex network of metal pieces connected by wire and animated by ... Clavin couldn't guess.

"What?" asked the boys. They held their torches high, just as before.

Clavin regained control. *Looking a little thin, my lads.* "Nothing, young travelers. I was just surprised by your abandonment of your outer layers."

"Sometimes it is important to see beyond the outer

skin to know the true inner person," said the one on the left.

"It is the inner person that is true," said the one on the right.

"Right." *Whatever. Two skeletal philosophers. Great.* "So, this way, then." He shook his head. *I shouldn't, but ...* "Hold those lights high, now. You know light is life." His sarcasm didn't come off as funny as he had hoped.

They walked for a long time in silence, passing hundreds, maybe thousands, of yards of seamless, black stone. Clavin had much earlier given up on counting his paces when one of the boys declared, "Your shoes have stopped squeaking."

"Why, so they have!" *Things are looking up!*

"Too bad about the keys," said the other.

With that utterance, Clavin noted for the first time that the rings attached to the keys, as his steps caused them to swing, squeaked. It was a constant, grating squeak of metal on metal. *How long have they been squeaking? How could I have missed that until now? Or ... hmm ... or did his mention of it cause it? More likely ...*

Clavin tried for some time to walk in a way to keep the rings from swinging, but couldn't. He tried holding the rings in one hand and the keys in the other. That proved tiresome, and though the squeaking was somewhat controlled, in its place was the occasional clang and the continual annoyance of the effort required. Clavin was still battling with the two keys when the boys interrupted his efforts.

"Here we are."

Clavin looked up. Sure enough, within a few paces was the obvious next challenge. They faced not one door with a lock that would force a choice between the two keys, but ...

Well, well ... two doors. Two big ol' keyholes.

Clavin shook his head.

"What is the matter?" the boys asked.

"Just considering options."

"You can't go back," they said.

"Yes! I know!" Clavin snapped. *Oops. Don't anger the Dream.*

"You have to take us forward."

"Yes, yes." Clavin was now much more in control of his frustration. "Forward. Two doors."

He turned to the boys. "I don't suppose you know which door we should try?"

They shook their heads.

"And which key goes into which lock?"

"One is danger," said the one on the left.

"The other is safe," said the one on the right.

Funny how it seems to work like that. "But you don't know which?"

After checking for traps as best as he could, Clavin finally got around to trying one of the keys.

"Well, they look to be identical ... so ..."

He tried one of the keys, but it didn't go in the keyhole.

"Must be the other door."

"Or the other key," said the boys.

"No. The keys are identical."

"No," said the boys. "One is safe, the other is danger."

"Yes, but ..." Clavin decided not to argue. *I'll just show them.*

He switched the keys in his hands and, prepared that the key would not fit, attempted to insert it into the key-hole. To his surprise, it fit perfectly. He was so surprised that he tried something that he usually wouldn't have done—he removed the key and tried the other.

Blast it! No fit! Oh, I hope I haven't broken the trap.

To his relief, the original key fit the lock. *But what about ...?* He looked at the other key, then the other door. Trying it, he found that it fit. *So the identical keys fit different doors.*

The boys spoke again. "One is safe, the other dangerous."

Clavin nodded. *But which is which?* He stepped back and looked all around the doors for clues but found nothing different from one door to the other. They appeared to be exactly the same. *What to do?* The question had hardly faded from his thoughts when he heard new voices from the darkness.

"Ho there! Dream Ranger Clavin Roth!"

"Ho, friend!"

Clavin turned and peered into the darkness, straining to identify the sources. A moment passed before Clavin could make out two familiar faces coming into the light. Two of his friends were walking toward him. On the left was perhaps his best friend in all the worlds: Staven Drath. On the right was a man known around the Inn to be the life of any party: Happy Goround.

At least they look like Stave and Happy, but how ...

"Ho, friends."

The two drew near. Clavin appraised them intently.

"You two aren't really on Samlin-Cordis, are you?"

"Clavin, surely?" Staven shook his head. "You know Samlin-Cordis can only hold two Travelers."

"Three," Happy added, "if they match perfectly."

Clavin pointed to himself, then to each of them. "One, two, three."

"Oh, no," Staven replied. He swept his hand toward Clavin and the two boys. "Three, four, five. Naturally, we aren't on Samlin-Cordis at all."

Clavin looked at the two boys. *What? Are they real?*

"No, we are not on Samlin-Cordis at all," Happy replied. "We are just here to help."

"That's right," Staven answered. "You need us to help you move forward."

Move forward ... ah ... a Dream clue.

At that, Staven and Happy went each to one of the keys and turned them. They opened the doors. Clavin inched away, not sure what to expect.

"There you go," Staven declared, waving at the two openings.

Behind one was licking tongues of fire rising from the floor of the portal to the top. Clavin could feel the searing heat, despite the distance between him and the opening. Behind the other door ran a tunnel about ten yards long. A steady shower of water fell from the ceiling to the floor, like a perpetual deluge of some severe summer storm. Clavin compared the two passages and concluded that both were equal in distance and proportion.

"There you go," Happy repeated the words of Staven.

With a nod, the two apparitions walked past Clavin, fading in the darkness.

"The choice is yours," said Happy.

"It's all up to you," Staven added just before they disappeared.

Things just got a whole lot easier. He looked at himself and noted that much of the mud he had found himself in earlier still clung to his clothes and skin. *I need a bath, anyway.* "This way," Clavin called to the boys. "Looks like we'll be getting a little wet."

"The light is life," said the boys as a register of their complaint.

"Good point. It would be awful dark without the torches." Clavin examined the two lights and decided that if he held them with their flames down and ran, they would be able to handle the brief downpour.

He explained his plan to the two boys. They hesitated.

"The light is life. You want to carry the torches?"

"Well, yes. I think I'm going to be able to hold them down, away from the falling water. You're too short. You won't be able to keep the flame dry."

"So, life will depend on you, then? If the torches go out, all will be darkness, and we will surely die." The boys seemed reluctant but eventually agreed to the plan. They handed Clavin their torches.

"Okay, stick close to me. We can't get separated, and I can't wait in the tunnel for you. Stay close."

"You can't go back. We *will* go forward with you."

A chill ran up Clavin's spine, and all of his alarms went off at once. *What did they say?* Clavin noted the change in their wording. *New song? Or same song, new verse? Time to be very careful. What is the difference between 'You have to take us forward' and 'we will go forward with you?' Very subtle. In the first, I am doing the taking. In the second, they are going with me, regardless. Careful, now. I'm not sure I like the emphasis on will. Better take care.* Finding nothing in the wording to warrant a change of plan, Clavin decided to proceed.

"One, two, three, go!"

Clavin rushed through the deluge, cleared the other side, and looked back. The two boys were clanging their way right behind him and emerged just a breath after him.

"We made it!"

The boys said nothing. After a moment, Clavin shrugged. *Whatever. What's next?* "Okay, off we go, then." Clavin stepped off toward what he felt was the direction to Cordis. His once-again soggy shoes squeaked, and the boys laughed. There was something unusual about it. *Like metal grinding. But then, just look at them. Figures.*

They walked along in silence. A chill wind arose and danced the light from the torches that Clavin still carried, clutched together in one hand and held high. In time, Clavin noticed his shoes had stopped the infernal squeaking. *Better.* At the passing of the thought, the noise of the wind was drowned out by a squeak that eclipsed any sound Clavin had ever heard. He wheeled toward the boys. He shook his head in disbelief.

Rusted. Clavin shook his head again. They tried to move, and their efforts resulted in more squeaking. *Now, they squeak in unison.* "Come along, boys," Clavin urged. "You can do it."

"We'll go forward with you," the boys replied. "You can't leave us behind."

Another chill ran up Clavin's spine. *I can't? As in prohibited by some kind of rules or just a turn of phrase?* "Hurry, then, let's go." Clavin imagined the rust getting worse by the second. "Yes, let's hurry." He turned back toward Cordis, and his heart leapt in delight. In the not-to-far distance, the lights of Cordis Castle beckoned. "Come on! Hurry."

Though they tried mightily, the boys were losing the fight. The rust was taking over, and they were becoming immobilized. They followed Clavin as best they could, but in just minutes, they rusted to a stop.

I'll carry them. He turned back to the boys and wrapped his arms around one. Though he applied all his effort, he could not budge the wrought-iron skeleton boy. *Too heavy? Why?* He tried the other child with no better luck.

"We should have gone through the fire," the boy on the right said.

"The fire? No, it was too hot. It would have burned me up."

"We shouldn't have taken the same passage," the boy on the left replied.

Clavin's heart skipped a beat. *How could I have missed that? How could I? They are metal. The fire wouldn't have hurt them any more than the water hurt me, not for so short a run! How could I have missed that?*

Clavin tried again to lift one of the boys but couldn't. "What are we to do?" Clavin asked at last. "Do *you* know something? What can I do?"

"Light is life. We only have so long," the boys said, their voices now more a shrill sound of metal on metal than that of a child.

Clavin looked at the torches and realized they were burning out.

"You can't go back," came a metallic screech from the right.

"You must go forward," screeched the voice from the right.

"We *will* go forward with you," they screeched in unison again.

"You will?" Clavin's hope returned.

He turned toward Cordis Castle. "Come on then." He tried to lift his foot to take a step, but it would not budge. He tried again to no avail. He turned back to the boys.

"What's going on?"

"Go!" they screeched louder and more shrilly than before.

Clavin recoiled from them. One step, then another.

Wait! I'm moving again, he realized. Turning toward Cordis Castle, he tried again to take a step but couldn't. His foot would not lift from the ground.

"Oh, please!" he shouted.

The wind gusted suddenly, extinguishing one of the

torches. When its flame was gone, Clavin thought he heard a voice on the wind saying, "You must go forward."

"What? What!" Clavin shouted to the wind, turning toward the boys just in time to see the boy on the right crumple to the ground.

Clavin flinched away from the wreckage, again moving in his desired direction.

"We shouldn't have taken the same passage," the boy left standing squeaked.

"I made a mistake," Clavin answered. "I didn't do it on purpose!"

He backed away, yet another step. *Free again! Better move while I can!*

Clavin turned and prepared to run, but as soon as he turned away from the rusted boys, he was frozen in his tracks.

"Do you call this a mistake?" the standing boy screeched.

Clavin turned back and looked. He was gesturing to the pile that had been the other boy. "Yes, that is a mistake. It was my mistake. I'm sorry."

"You can't go forward without us," the boy groaned.

Clavin retreated another step. *Free again! Hurry!*

But as soon as he turned toward Cordis Castle, he was stuck once more. *What is this? What is going on?*

"We *will* go forward with you," the squeaking voice shrilled.

Clavin turned back again. "But you can't move!"

"*You'll* take us with you. You'll take us forward."

The wind gusted again, and the second torch went out.

Immediately, the second boy crumpled into a pile beside the first. Clavin thought he heard a voice on the wind call out, "Face your mistake."

Clavin turned to the two piles of crumpled metal but could see nothing. All was dark. He turned toward the light that was Cordis Castle. He could see nothing nearby, but he knew that if he could walk toward the light, he'd eventually find his way to safety.

Though he tried as hard as he could, he could not move. He was stuck, frozen in the darkness. He watched Cordis Castle for a few moments; then he began to have a strong feeling of dread. *A Chark is blowing in. I must get moving!*

He fixed his eyes on the goal and tried with all his might to take a step. The dread continued to grow as Clavin remained stuck. It was then that he noticed the light from Cordis Castle was fading. It was then that the sound of the wind changed to the sound of squeaking.

As the light faded, the squeaking became a roar. Then, in a blink, the light was gone, and utter darkness fell. Black ink surrounded Clavin, and he knew he was going to die.

Michael sat up in his bed on Samlin. "Nightmare. Another stupid nightmare."

He draped his legs over the edge of the plush mattress, letting his feet find the soft rug on which his bed sat. He looked at the bottle of bourbon and a glass sitting on his bedside table. There was just enough left in the clear crystal bottle to fill the glass one more time. So he did.

What a stupid nightmare. "You can't go forward. We're going with you! Woo hoo!" He shook his head. *Stupid dream.*

He drained the glass in a gulp and put it back on the table. He arose and walked to the window and drew back the curtains and lace sheers. In the garden below, he watched his gardener at work. After a few moments of distraction, his thoughts returned to the nightmare.

So I made a mistake? Big deal. Mistakes happen. It wasn't my fault. Not in last night's stupid dream either. That also wasn't my fault.

He returned to the bourbon bottle and confirmed that it was indeed empty. He shook his head. "I need a vacation." *Yep. I'm going to take me a nice, long vacation and forget all of this. I need to think about something other than Rige and Garner. I think I'll go to the ocean and do some sailing. Maybe go hiking. Some real-world exercise might do me some good, help me to unwind all of this.*

He picked up the bottle and the cork lying beside it. He crammed the stopper back in and nodded. *I'll bottle them up and put them back on the shelf. I'll label it sad and go on with my life. Someday, when I write my memoirs, I may take it down again and let them out while I pen a poignant line or two. But that's where they'll stay—nice and controlled.*

All bottled up.

FESTER

Michael sat on his balcony enjoying the play of wind and the sound of the birds. He took no thought for any danger which might fall upon him, unwarned, because this was real-world. He sat alone with his thoughts, the guilty suspicion that punishment was deserved and only delayed; this was his solitary companion.

He called for a drink, closed his eyes, and recalled to his mind the sound of the lapping waves on the water. A minute later, his servant, Corval, came with Michael's order and set it down on the table to his left.

"Sir, this Saturday is your mother's birthday. Shall I pick something up?"

Michael's eyes popped open. *Oh man ...*

Corval waited silently.

"Thanks for reminding me, Corval. No, I'll pick it up on Cordis. I'm due over tonight so I'll delay my return."

"Very good, sir."

"Corval?"

The man turned back from leaving. "Yes, sir?"

"What would you get her? I can't think of what she needs."

"You have provided all her physical wants, have you not?"

"I believe so. So what can I take her?"

"Something spiritual would be in order, I think."

"Spiritual? I can't capture an angel or anything. This isn't the Dream, and I'm not Clavin Roth in the waking world, after all. I'm just me."

Corval smiled. "No, sir, of course not. I was thinking of something a little less auspicious."

"What then?"

"A poem."

"What?"

"Write her a poem, sir. One you've really worked on. Not a one-minute effort."

Pretty clever. "Corval?"

"Yes, sir?"

"You're pretty smart. Thanks."

Corval nodded and left.

Michael sat and wrote. He'd write, and he'd think, read what he wrote, and start over again. After numerous starts, he found what he wanted and wrote out a very nice poem, in his opinion, for his mother, then lay down his pen.

"Corval."

The thump of footsteps announced Corval's reply to duty, and a moment later he appeared with a carafe.

Michael waved his hand as if shooing a fly. "No, no, no.

I don't need a drink. I took your advice, Corval." Michael picked up the paper. "I'd like this redone in calligraphy on some nice paper. Get a really nice envelope to put it in too."

Corval smiled as he set down the carafe and stepped over to take the paper.

"Of course, sir. I think that she'll like this very much."

"You haven't read it."

Corval shook his head. "A poem from a son to his mother can't help but be cherished. The words aren't important. The effort involved in it is."

"Okay, while you're at it, have some overpriced chocolates thrown in. With little bunnies or doves or some such, iced on their surfaces."

Corval smiled and left.

Yeah, it'll be a good touch.

Michael walked out the front and down to the stables. Down the long row he went and out the back where a man stood fixing a loose rail on the fence surrounding the paddock that held the eight horses.

The man stood when he saw Michael. "Shall I saddle a horse for you, sir?"

"No, thank you, Derrin. I'm just out strolling and thought I'd come here and rub down Gold-Dragon. Continue with your work."

Michael found a brush and went to work on the horse, which stood still and nickered for his touch. "You know, old boy, you've got a pretty good life here. You're fed and watered, have a nice barn to sleep in during winter and rain. And, when I'm not here, Derrin takes you for rides to keep you in shape."

Gold blew out a breath and bobbed his head up and down.

Michael laughed. "You know ..." He stopped and considered Derrin working nearby. *If this were a Crossing, I'd have to wonder if you'd really understood me after that nod.* He let his mind wander and followed the mane of the horse down to its proud tail. He enjoyed the bond he felt with the animal, felt its powerful strength under his hands and shared an empathetic bond of pride in their relative power.

I need to get over to Cordis for Mom's birthday. I've been putting it off. The trip to the ocean was nice but ... "I still need a couple weeks more." He shrugged. *I'll just take some more off when I get back. The birthday won't wait. I'll send a note to get into the docket for tomorrow night.*

He finished with Gold-Dragon, stepped back from the horse, and replaced the brush.

Derrin must consider it a bit odd that the mysterious nobleman likes to brush horses down. Once there was a time when owning a horse like this was just a dream to me.

He shook his head.

Now I have him, and I hardly ever ride him. Derrin rides him more than I do. The paradox of the rich: have everything, enjoy nothing.

Michael looked around the paddock at the horses. He noticed then that one walked with a limp, its foot wrapped in heavy bandages. "Derrin, what's wrong with Blue?"

"Well, sir, it looks like he developed a crack in a hoof.

Somehow, I missed a tiny stone that worked its way up. Don't know how long it was there, but by the time I got to it, there was a festering wound. I removed the stone, cleaned it out, and got him all bandaged up. It's going to be quite a few weeks before he's ready to ride again, but I expect he'll be good as new."

"I see. Well, good that you caught it and got him some help."

Perhaps it would be kinder if I sold Gold-Dragon to some- one who could really enjoy him?

He leaned against the fence as he considered it.

No. I like having him. Sometimes I still ride. And he is well taken care of. He's just lacking some freedom, enclosed by this fence I'm leaning on. Aren't we all? They're bound by this fence, and I'm bound by my guilt. None of us are really free, are we?

"No, we're not."

But he, at least, sleeps well at night.

Michael left and returned to the house.

The next afternoon, Michael climbed into a coach and headed into the city. Two hours passed before he stepped down from the coach with a packet under his left arm. Michael made his way through the Sanctum and into the Inn where he took on his identity of Clavin Roth.

He made his way through the typical looks of respect and awe that people gave him as the only Ranger extant, returned greetings given, and soon settled down at his special reserved table in the Star. He looked around and waited as others came in.

Eventually, Staven made his appearance, and Clavin waved him into a seat across from his own.

"So," began Staven, "a knight and a dragon are walking along ..."

Clavin smiled. "What color's the dragon?"

Staven gave him a look. "You want to hear this or not?"

"Okay, I couldn't resist. A knight and a dragon are walking along?"

"Good. A knight and a dragon are walking along. The knight asks the dragon, 'How do you think this is going to work out?' The dragon says, 'Beats you.' The knight replies, 'No, beats me.' The dragon replies, 'Okay,' picks up a huge boulder, and smashes the knight flat." Staven began to laugh.

"That's pitiful, Stave."

Staven laughed even more.

"No, no. See, the dragon says, 'Beats you,' and the knight ..."

Clavin had to smile at his friend's enthusiasm over the silly joke. "Yeah, I get it."

Clavin laughed at Staven's enjoyment.

"It's a killer," insisted Staven between chuckles.

Clavin nodded. "Crushing, you might say."

"Right."

They settled down after a minute.

"Enjoy your vacation?" Staven asked.

"Yes. I needed some time away. Went to the ocean. Did some sailing. No dragons, no five-headed beasts."

"No mermaids either."

"Nope, but I never take advantage of that kind of stuff anyway."

"Right. 'Ware the Passions."

Clavin nodded.

"So, Clave, anything new?"

Clavin paused. "Nope. Same stuff. There and back again. Turning the crank."

"And money pours out."

"Yep. Stave, what's the point of having a ton of coin in the real-world? We can't do anything there that matches what goes on here."

"Sure. Well, except for the Passions."

"Yeah. When I get ready to kill myself, I'll give it a try. Wonder how long it would take?"

Staven shrugged.

Merinda chose that moment to pull out a chair and drop down into it.

Clavin suppressed a flash of annoyance at the break in protocol, not waiting for his permission, but checked the words as he noted the wide smile pasted across her face. "Well, what's the word, sunshine?"

"What do you mean? I just got here. How're my two favorite characters?"

Staven broke off his own appraising. "Okay, spill. You aren't the most smiley person, and you're just beaming."

"Right," agreed Clavin. "And, by the way, it looks good on you." He framed her face in a square formed by his fingers. "Caption: Merinda, radiant. So?"

Her smile widened as she draped herself back in the chair and kicked her feet up to rest on the table. Clavin and Staven shared a glance before turning back to her.

"I might have had some recent success," she replied coyly.

"With?" Staven asked.

"I did it." She whipped her feet back off the table and leaned toward them. Her smile turned smug. "I brought Clessy back. I managed to control things and force an outcome of my own liking." She nodded. "And now that I know the secret, I can bring him back again if I should lose him in the future."

Wow. Clavin was impressed. "How'd you do it?"

"And how do you know you didn't just get lucky?" demanded Staven.

"Right," agreed Clavin, "it could be that your pet would have come back regardless of whatever you did. How can you be sure it was a result of your actions?"

A frown wiped the smile off her face. "Clessy is a friend, not a pet. "

"Okay, your friend then," replied Clavin. "The question is the same."

She paused.

"What?" demanded Staven. "You can't recall? Ten seconds ago, you looked like a cat in a milk pail, and now you have no memory of your great success?"

"The thing is," Merinda replied, "I'm not so sure that the authorities would approve of what I did. Maybe they wouldn't mind, but, given the nature of it, they might and, if they do ... well, they might prevent me from doing this again. I can't take that risk."

Clavin felt his eyebrows rising. "Well, that makes it all the more interesting. So, you think we'd share your secret? You don't trust us?"

"I do, but ... well, let's face it, you two do like to chat, right? In the heat of a moment, who knows what might come out? Plus, if you start using this method, it could leak out, and then I'm back to square one."

The idea that she didn't trust him jarred loose his usual composure. "You don't trust me to keep a secret?" He leaned away from her. "And what if something should happen to you? Something like this might be valuable to the greater community, but you're just going to hog it for yourself, and when you're gone, to hell with everyone else?"

Merinda stiffened at his change in tone. "I've made detailed notes on what I did. Someday I'll write them up and submit them to the community. But not now. It won't be lost, I promise that. And you'll be the first I tell when that day comes."

Clavin considered the reply and turned back to Staven. "What do you think, Staven?"

He shrugged. "On the one hand, I'm liking happy Meri. On the other, I don't like the evident lack of trust. If she doesn't trust us, then why should we trust her?"

Merinda rolled her eyes. "Oh, come on, it's not like ..."

"I agree," Clavin cut her off. "You're smart and clever, Warrior Swift. Smart enough to figure out whatever this is. Clever, but not clever enough to know better than to gloat over knowledge that you have no intention of sharing. I invited you to our little club here last year because I was impressed by your skills and professionalism. But our club has an underlying current of trust. I think you've just broken that."

Her eyes and mouth opened wide. "You're kicking me out? What does that mean?"

Staven nodded. "Merinda, this table is reserved for Rangers and those he explicitly invites to share it with him. I think you're smart enough to figure it out."

"Are you serious?" She focused on Clavin as she rose from the chair. "There is nothing you've ever concealed from Staven? You've never even had improper thoughts about the women here in the Inn? About this body I inhabit? You expect me to believe that? You have no secrets that you're hiding from us?"

Clavin's shoulders slumped. "You're right." He nodded. "You're right. Of course I do. I'm sure Staven does too. You got me. Sit down, Merinda. I would like to know, but I see your reasoning."

She sat and took a breath. "You tell me your secret, and I'll tell you mine. Is that fair?"

Clavin gave a wan smile. "More than fair. Instead, you *keep* your secret, and I'll keep mine. And we'll still be friends. Okay?"

She smiled and bobbed her head.

"You have a secret?" Staven asked. "I'm hurt, buddy, spill. You've been lusting after Merinda all this time and didn't tell me?" He shook his head, making tsking noises. "I thought you knew better than to let ideas like that get in your head?"

"I don't have that in my head, Staven. Well, I do—I'm a man—but I don't dwell on it. You know how it goes. Don't press it and get me to thinking about it."

Staven became serious. "Right. Sorry. Yep, those ideas stick with you. They fester. Something happens, you get an idea, and it refuses to go away. Let's focus on something else."

Clavin agreed. "Yep. Even after it's over, sometimes it's not really over. You have to change your focus. That's smart."

"I'm smarter than I look."

Clavin smiled. "That you are. Safe Crossing tonight, to you both."

They raised their glasses.

Clavin picked up his load, signed, and headed off. The trip was uneventful. The Blue Bog was, again, near the end, but again, the Cobbler was there to help him across. He came out of the Veil without a scratch. The drain of a sleepless night descended on him as he exited, and soon he was on his way to the estate of his parents, dozing in the carriage that carried him out. Hours went by before he arrived.

Michael stepped down from the carriage with a stretch and a yawn, package under his arm. The carriage clattered off, and Michael walked to the house. Before he reached the door, it opened, and Michael's mother, Gantiel, appeared.

"Buster, get on in here."

Michael ran up and hugged her. "Hey, Mom, how you feeling?"

"Good. Got my garden, got my friends, got your dad, and I've got the Lord."

Always that. The thought soured him. "I'm glad. Let's get inside."

"What's under your arm?"

"Something for you to open tomorrow."

"What do I need?"

"Not a thing."

"So why waste the coin?"

"Because I have it to waste, because you're my mother, and because it didn't hardly cost me a thing."

They walked into the house.

"Hardly a thing?" she said. "Do you know how long I was in labor with you?"

"Eighteen hours?"

"Eighteen hours! The night before," she began as she ignored his answer, "I woke up and told your dad, 'Hollen, get the midwife.'"

So, Dad runs out in his long johns down the street ...

"So, there he goes running, just in his long johns, down the street to get the midwife."

Michael listened to the whole story again as they went to sit down. One of the servants left to call for his father. Jase thundered in and demanded his attention, thereby delaying Gantiel finishing her story. By the time she finished, drinks and sandwiches were served to them, and Michael began to nod off from the effects of the lost night of sleep.

"Well, Buster, you go lay down and take a nap." She stood up, leaned over, and kissed him. "I love you."

"I'll get you something nice, Mom."

"Oh, tush. I don't need a thing. I'm glad you're home. Go to sleep."

They woke him a few hours later.

"Buster," said the voice of his father, Hollen, "need to get up for a while or you won't sleep a wink when you go to bed. And it's time for supper."

Michael wiped the gummy residue of sleep from eyes. "Okay, Dad." He rose and hugged him. "How you been?"

"If I were any better, there'd have to be two of me. And you?"

"Fine, Dad. Busy."

There was a pause, and Hollen nodded.

What's there to say? Don't want a lecture on morals or questions on girlfriends.

"Let's get down to dinner."

They went into a dining room decorated with ceramic plates matching the season and candle holders matching the plates. A large maple table with religious symbols inlaid in its top sat in the middle of the room. Plush chairs sat around it, each seat upholstered in soft glove leather with ornate carving in the backs. The curtains, pulled back, allowed the rays of the setting sun to blaze across the room, painting dark shadows on the opposite wall while bringing in warmth against the cooling air of the waning day.

Michael sat with his back to the sunlight, his parents on each end of the table.

His sister's family arrived. His brother-in-law, Kildain, sat across from him, as his nephew, Jase, pulled up a chair next to him. "What'd you do on your last Crossing, Uncle Mike? Did you fight a troll or an ogre? Did you find a treasure or some magic?"

Michael threw his arm around the boy and pulled him up in a hug. "Later, okay, Jase? I'm here for your granny's birthday."

"Awww."

"I might have brought something for my favorite nephew too."

"You're the best, Uncle Mike."

"That I am." Michael chuckled as he noted the disapproving frown on his sister's face.

Gantiel insisted on laying the meal out in serving dishes from which they drew the food out for themselves. The meal itself was of garden vegetables, sauced and seasoned according to Gantiel's experience. The smells and tastes took him back to the days of his childhood.

"Mom, it's delicious." *It really is*, he thought with a bit of surprise. *I guess you tend to like what you're raised on.*

"Good. I haven't yet lost my touch. So, Buster, have you been out fighting dragons? I know Jase wants to hear."

Yeah, Mom, I nearly got killed just a week or so back. Want to hear about it? He shook his head. "Nope. Been pretty quiet. Easy work, all in all."

His dad gave him a look that either said, "don't lie to your mother" or "I think there's more you're not saying, but I don't want to risk upsetting her."

Michael turned back to his plate.

"You know that Jase's birthday is coming up next month?" asked Hollen.

Michael shook his head. "Sorry. You know how bad I am with dates, Dad. The times and seasons on Samlin are different than they are here on Cordis. I know you think I'm just making excuses ever since I started Traveling, but it *really* is hard to keep track. But my servant should notify me. He's good with dates." He looked over at the boy next to him. "I won't forget you, buddy."

Hollen gave him a nod that said more to move on to another subject than it said he understood.

"Buster," began Gantiel, "you can be a great influence on Jase. How many little boys have an uncle that's actually fought dragons? He looks up to you, and you can help guide him into becoming a man."

"Who said that I fought dragons?"

"Michael," she said with a parental look.

"I don't know if Aline wants him to hear those kinds of stories. Might put ideas in his head. Ideas that might not go away. The kind that takes control of you and leads you down the wrong paths."

Hollen spoke. "Is that true for you, Buster? Are you

on a *wrong* path? Maybe you should think about coming home, spending some more time here?"

You don't like the Dream. I get it. We're arrogant know-it-alls because we don't believe in the Master.

Hollen continued to speak. "We'd love to have you; you know that we would. This house is yours, after all. You bought it for us. There's always a room kept empty for you, son."

"Dad, I'm a different person now than the boy you raised. I've seen and done things that would make a four-year-old squeal with delight, and others that would make him tremble in terror. You can't even imagine the things that I've been through. I can try my best to describe them, but the descriptions always fall short. I know that you and Mom are sincere in your beliefs. I know that you love me, and I love you too, but ... Dad, I don't believe anymore. I don't believe in the Master. There's no evidence."

"Nonsense. There's all the evidence you need. Michael, you choose to disbelieve because that is what you've decided to do, not because there is 'no evidence.' The statement is preposterous."

Michael took a breath to calm his anger.

Preposterous? I've seen more in my twenty-five years than you have in your entire life surrounded by other believers just like yourself. My breadth of knowledge is larger, my experiences greater. Go back to your pulpit and believing, leave the thinking to others.

Michael set his fork down and took another breath. Gantiel spoke up.

"Buster, sweetheart, we love you. We don't want to lose you. If you spent more time with us and your sister, and less with the other Travelers, it would help clear your thinking. It's easy to fall into the beliefs that others have when you're surrounded by them."

I'm out of here tomorrow after the party. Just get through 'till then.

"You and Dad aren't the only people to have strong beliefs. Many people believe differently," he said in his kindest voice.

"Those *other* people have no basis for their beliefs," Hollen insisted. "We do."

"You know, Dad, I'm just not going to argue with you. You haven't met the people I've met. You haven't seen much beyond your own small world. I understand why you believe what you do—you raised me on it, after all—but you're not able to understand me. Now, I'm going to bed. I'm tired."

"Michael," snapped his mother, "don't be rude to your father."

"I'm tired of hearing all this." The words burst out before he could bite them off. "I have my own problems, and this nonsense isn't going to help me. You're not capable of rational thought, so there is no use talking."

His mother looked like she'd been struck. There was an audible gasp from his sister, and Jase stared at him. A loud scrape of wood accompanied his father, who slid back his chair as he stood.

"Michael," Hollen said with a hard edge in his voice, "you need to apologize to your mother. Right now."

Michael turned back to him. "I'm going to bed."

His father's face reddened as he clenched his fist before he forced it to relax.

Oh, this is going to be a bad one.

Michael was surprised as his father's eyes began to water.

"Michael, if you can't respect us, then you have to go. It's your choice, but you can't stay here on any other condition."

Gantiel began, "Hollen ..." but was stopped by his father's raised hand.

Michael and his father stared at each other for a moment.

This is it. How could it have come to this over a simple meal? What does it matter?

Michael turned and walked back to his mother. He gave her a hug and a kiss on the cheek.

"Goodbye, Mom. I hope you enjoy your present."

As she began to cry earnest tears, he walked back across the room to the door and stopped by his father. "My life has given you everything you now have. This house, the horses, the servants. But you can't even listen to what I'm trying to tell you."

Hollen shook his head. "Sell it then. Sell it all. Take the money and waste it. The one thing that isn't for sale is our faith. We'll pray for you, Michael. We'll pray every night. But until your attitude changes, you'll not be welcome in our home, wherever that's going to be now. But if you change your heart, ours will be waiting to welcome you there."

An angry but sad Michael Envine stomped out and headed for the carriage house. His brother-in-law, Kildain, met him at the stable. "Mike, I'll drive you in."

Bitterness dripped in Michael's reply. "Well, Kil, that might get you kicked out of the house."

Kildain stepped in front of him and asked, "By who? Your dad or you?"

It took a second for the meaning to sink in. He raised a hand to forestall Kildan's worry and replied, "Kil, no, those were just words. I might consider kicking him out, but I wouldn't do that to the rest of you. It's okay."

"Thanks, Mike. I sort of figured. I'm sorry about this whole mess. I wish you two could get along. He loves you. I know it's not clear, but I'm here all the time, and I know it. I hope you know it too, somewhere deep down."

"Yeah, sure. Deep down. Deep, deep, deep down."

Kildain smiled. "Okay. Well, let's get that carriage hooked up."

They worked together, and Jase came out. "Uncle Mike, you aren't leaving, are you?"

"Hey, bud, yeah, I'm afraid so. I'm headed out early."

"When are you going to be back?" he demanded.

Michael looked over, held Kildain's glance for a moment, blew out a breath, and replied, "Well, Jase, that's a bit tricky. I'm not sure right now."

"Awww, okay."

Kildain hugged his son to him. "Okay, Jase. Run on, now. We're headed off."

"Can I come, Dad?"

233

After a moment of consideration, he affirmed it. "Okay. Run in and tell your mom, then meet us out front."

Jase did, and Kildain drove the wagon out to the front to wait, with Michael beside him. Michael's eyes traced the doorway as they waited for his nephew. *All the times I've dreaded coming here, and now I find I'm going to miss it. How strange.* He looked over at his brother-in-law. "Kil, I might not be back. You'll have to explain it to Jase sooner or later. I'm sorry to leave that on you but ..."

"It is what it is," Kildain replied to Michael's shrug. "But look, it's not the end of the road. We can still come see you wherever you're at. Right?"

Michael nodded. "Right. Of course."

Jase charged out the door, down the path, leaped onto the wagon, and they were on their way.

Hours later, as Michael lay down for bed, half-drunk from his wine, he thought about his dad's ultimatum. *It's been coming for a while now. He thinks he's right, and I know that I am. Like the crack in Blue's hoof, it has been working its way into the quick, festering, waiting to explode.*

And it finally has.

He turned to his bottle and drank himself drunk all the way.

GHOST STORY

Michael sat alone in his manor before a roaring fire. He sighed for the hundredth time and shook his head. *Rige and Garner. How could I have known?* He took another sip from the glass. He looked at his hands and forced back the urge to wash them.

Eventually, he set the glass aside, rose, and stepped over to study himself in a mirror. No heroic figure stared back. 5'10, twenty pounds overweight, eyes and hair both of brown. The real-world Micheal Envine. But on this world, people thought him the dispossessed son of a distant Earl, sent here to while away his days in humble repentance.

Repentance. Had I known how close that would be to the truth ...

A knock on the door drew his attention.

"Yes, Corval?"

"Sir," said the butler as he placed a silver tray on a walnut table next to the chair, "a note for you just arrived."

"Thank you, Corval," he replied with a nod, dismissing him from the room. He picked up the letter opener Corval had provided, slit open the envelope, and took out the contents: a sheet of paper and another envelope.

Wheels within wheels. He scanned the note:

Michael,

So sorry to intrude upon your privacy. Staven Drath was insistent that this be delivered to you without delay. Given your connection, I hoped you would not mind.

Kimberly Jones

Michael nodded and turned his attention to the inner envelope as he thought about his best friend.

I've been on a long hiatus. I can guess what's running through his mind. Has the old boy gone off his nut? Have a few more marbles gone missing? Is he still a dragon slayer? He shouted within as he brandished the opener.

He shook his head and opened the letter.

Clave,

Worried about you, old nut. If you don't make an appearance soon, I'm going to have to Travel over to see you on Samlin in Lorimen. If you're out of the business, at least come say goodbye.

Stave

Whacking and Cracking

This time his headshake was accompanied by a deep sigh. *See you in Lorimen.*

Michael had no doubt that Stave meant it. *Dangerous, hare-brained stunt just to drag an old badger out of his hole.*

"Corval," he shouted as he rose from his chair.

He stepped through the gate and paused to survey the familiar scene.

Midnight in the Traveler's Inn. The crowd is restless, and the drinks are many. All wonder who the mysterious stranger is suddenly stepping into their midst. Could this be the hero for whom they have searched for so long? Could this, they pondered, be ... the one?

With a shake of his head, he forced his mind to refocus.

Stop it. It's not midnight, the crowd's not restless, and no one's going to recognize you under this bloody cloak. That was the point, after all.

Clavin made his way through the Inn and to their usual venue. Staven sat with a couple other friends at a Warrior table close to the empty one reserved for Rangers. Clavin settled into a chair next to his friend.

"Whoa, ho," said Staven with a smile, "the prodigal returns."

"I think that would sound better with a *thus* in it ... thus the prodigal returns," he replied.

A serious look covered Staven's face as he nodded. "Absolutely. Drink?"

The other two at the table, Karen Dark and Kevin White, had sat quietly through this exchange, but it was Jennifer who broke their silence.

"You two need to catch up, so we'll run along. So good to have you back, Ranger Roth," she said with a slight nod to him.

"Thank you, Karen. Kevin," he replied politely.

As they left, Clavin looked over at his friend who had taken the liberty of calling up his favorite drink for him. Raising their glasses together, they spoke in unison.

"Whacking and Cracking!"

"How do they come up with names like that?" Clavin asked his friend as he nodded toward the retreating pair.

"Aw Clave, I think it's cute."

"Cute?" he asked with raised eyebrows.

"Sweet."

"Sweet?" monotoned Clavin.

"Nice. Romantic. Pleasingly appropriate. What would you call it, smarty?"

"An over-hyped juxtaposition of two word-concepts designed to highlight the attractive differences between two individuals who probably won't be together in three months."

After a pause to digest this, Staven replied, "Rough month?"

"Stave, you're my best friend, but I just don't want to discuss it. I came here to prevent you from doing something stupid. I'm alive and okay. Now you know."

Staven leaned back and contemplated his friend.

"Are you out?"

"I don't know," Clavin replied with a shrug. "This place is addictive. It makes the real-world look flat. Monochromatic. Dull. I can't imagine giving it up. You get it."

"Yep. We all do. I could retire back on Velickham, but I still Travel. That has to go many-fold for you."

"I want a change of pace. A change of scenery."

Staven rolled that over in his mind a bit.

"What," he asked in a slow measured tone, "do you mean by that?"

"I'm tired of Samlin-Cordis."

Staven stared at his friend with an expression on his face that made it clear he wondered if his friend really *had* slipped a cog.

"You're joking," he said flatly.

"Do I look like I'm joking?"

"Sheeesh," expelled Staven in a long breath.

They sat together for a moment and merely looked at each other as the sounds off the Inn washed around them.

Clavin, I don't know, maybe something in real world is eating you, maybe something else. But this isn't like you. Whatever happened to throw you off, you're unlikely ever to have to deal with it again. It clearly shook you up, but maybe you just need to take a few more months off and calm your nerves."

Clavin nodded. "You think I've gone jumpy. That makes sense."

"Haven't you?"

Clavin shrugged. "I won't deny it."

"Okay," replied a doubtful Staven. "Sooo ... catch you back here in a few months?"

Clavin shook his head. "No. No. You know what they say about falling off horses."

"That's my boy," Staven crescendoed. He raised his glass, waited for Clavin to respond, and they unisoned their personal motto once again.

"Whacking and Cracking!"

Three nights later, Dream Ranger Clavin Roth watched as the wagon train from Samlin rolled into Wagon Hall, the staging area of Traveler's Inn. He watched the compression magic done, then the box that now represented all of those goods was handed to him. He signed for it and tucked it under one arm.

"Thank you, Ranger Roth," the Merchant's representative declared. "And thanks for coming down to Wagon Hall. You spared me the trip."

"It's no problem. I am still fascinated by the magic." He held up the box.

One thousand golds' worth of various goods from the world of Samlin headed for the world of Cordis. Clavin inserted the box into his pouch and slung it on his back. He nodded across Wagon Hall to the Merchant, who seemed busy with some of those who performed the reduction magic. Clavin turned and headed for the exit of Wagon Hall. He ascended the stairs and emerged in Samlin Hall, to the gates to the veil.

Staven was there to see him off and wish him luck.

"See you on the other side."

With that, he performed his ritual. He opened the right gate, then once confirmed, he stepped through the door, down the short hallway beyond it, and into the veil. A deep whiteness surrounded him that, after a few moments, dispersed mid-step as he emerged from it.

Clavin stopped, looked down, and was satisfied that his pouch of wonders had appeared in the transfer about his waist. Over the next hour, he pulled one item after another from it and ran various tests. Finally having determined that about nine of every ten of his tricks were functional on this run, he set off.

He was on the trail. In seven days, he would step back through the veil, back into Traveler's Inn, and deliver his load on the Cordis side, an even richer rich man. He'd done it over a thousand times before and expected to do it again.

Every Dream trail was a place of logical inconsistencies. Clavin, being one of the most experienced Travelers in Samlin's Great Hall, knew about those inconsistencies better than anyone, and still, they puzzled, amused, and even annoyed him.

A Traveler could fight all day without tiring, but a ten-mile run could be totally exhausting. People could climb any height without breathing hard, but they still had to breathe—usually. *Well, there is that Runner who claims he can breathe water or something.* It was routine to spend hours upon hours thinking as hard as needed on any sort of problem without taking a break, but people still had to sleep.

And now it is time to sleep.

Clavin had been rolling along in a fine, horse-drawn carriage, properly proportioned yet improperly smooth, given the rough of the road, enjoying the calmness of the trail and the beauty of this Crossing, this manifestation of the Dream. Feeling the urge for sleep washing over him, he asked the driver if an inn were nearby.

"One mile ahead m' lord. The Three Ladies Inn. We shall stop there for the night."

Always one mile ahead. What a surprise.

Fifteen minutes on, true to his word, the white carriage whispered to a halt in front of a structure that resounded of elegance and grace, from the inside of which emanated the smell of fine breads.

Nice. Clavin approved.

He climbed the steps, looked up at a carving that hung above the entrance, and saw the image of two women, not three. The carving creaked on its hinge as it surrendered to a gust of wind.

Hmph? He shrugged. *Only two women? So much for consistency.*

Clavin entered and noticed right off that something was odd.

Every table with people had two young women and one man.

Okay, he thought as his alarms went off. *This has the feel of a Chark in the making. Let's just take it easy.*

As he stood at the door, two more young girls came through another door on the far side of the room and made their way over to him.

"Your table is this way," they said in unison. "Please follow us."

What have the Dreamers been up to lately? he wondered. *Where is all of this coming from? Why twos?*

Clavin was a normal man with all the normal responses of anyone from the waking world, but he was also a Dream Ranger, and he knew that unexpected surprises could quick-step into very unpleasant ones. Though no Chark was blowing, he didn't wish one to begin.

'Ware the Passions. Careful, now.

"Ladies, first I must see to my baggage and make arrangements for the night. If you would be so kind as to wait?"

"But that will not be necessary," they said as they lay their hands upon him, fingertips barely brushing his arms. "Your bags will be tended to, and your room is already prepared. Come."

Trap? Level two.

In his mind, a peg moved up on a board.

"No," he said in a rigid voice. "Though you doubtless mean well, I am a man of long habit, and I shall not break it today. I promise to return."

Ahhh! he scolded himself. *Rule number three! Never make promises if you can avoid them.*

Firmly but gently, he removed their hands, silently thankful that he *could* remove them. He left them with a bow and turned for the bar where he presumed to find the innkeeper.

As he walked, he dipped into his pouch and applied various enchanting ointments.

Ever vigilant. Stay sharp!

Approaching the bar, he spoke to the person who tended it.

"May I speak to the keeper of this fine establishment?"

"Of course. One moment please."

Clavin assumed he'd next meet a pair of innkeepers. *Billy and Bob, so nice to meet you,* he mused.

He was surprised and caught a bit off-guard when a single man came from the back and stopped in front of him.

"How may I help you?" he questioned.

So much for the twin motif. I thought I was on to something.

"I am wearied from my long journey and wish only to retire for the night and rest well till the morning. To that end, I beg you to show me my room, and I shall be of no further annoyance to you. How much is the room?"

"Two goldens. Is it well then?"

These places have gotten expensive here lately.

"Shall I pay now or upon leaving?"

"Oh, after, of course. Two-eleven," said the man as he held out two keys.

"What was that, then? Two-eleven?"

"Yes, your room number. And these are the keys."

The man held two silver keys, the teeth of which were whitest porcelain.

"I need but one key. I am by myself."

"Our doors are double locked," explained the man. "You shall need them both."

"Oh. I see. Where then are the stairs?"

With a pointed finger, the man replied, "Second hall on the right."

Something's odd about this. Out of kilter.

Clavin thanked the man, turned about, and saw that the room behind him, so full before, now stood empty and quiet but for a faint squeak which came from the doorway. No witty quip came to mind, but he tried anyway.

Something I said? he silently asked the missing crowd. He shook his head with a shrug. *Weak. That's really weak.*

He soon made his way to the door and into the hall. In a few steps, he passed the first side hallway to his right and came to the second. A short way down were the promised stairs. Up he strode to the second floor.

The door marked with the eleven was soon located. He produced one of his keys, placed it into the lock, and turned it. Hearing the satisfying clunk, he attempted to open it, but it held fast and, recalling the man's comments, he inserted the second, turned again, and entered the room.

Inside was an exterior window, a fireplace, a large bed, two chairs, and a cupboard. With the door pulled shut behind him, he turned the thumb locks and set about to make the place secure.

"Windows, floors, walls and doors, and check the ceiling too, hearth and bed, and what you're fed, and when you're done, you're through," he sing-songed to the room as he ran through his list.

As sleep weighed upon him, he settled in for a night of rest, eager to be gone on the morrow. He put the keys and coins upon a chair, set his armor next to him on the floor, and kept both sword and pouch beside him on the bed.

He tossed and turned as the squeaking from the sign over the porch managed to disturb him even through his earplugs.

Is there no bloody oil in this Dream? he wondered from beneath his pillow.

The night passed, otherwise, in Clavin's preferred manner: uneventfully. Letting out a great yawn, he woke as the sunbeams burned through the shuttered window.

"Good morning, fair sir," came the soft voice nearby.

Clavin shot straight up, as one only could in a dream, while hands grabbed for sword and vial. Next to his bed, in the two chairs, sat the two girls from the night before.

"What are you doing here?" he screamed in fright.

"Waiting on you, of course." They smiled.

He lowered his voice just a bit. "How in all the worlds did you get into my room?"

"You brought us in with you." They laughed.

"I did no such thing!" he shouted back, rattled, and brandished his sword for emphasis.

"Now that's not very nice," said girl number one.

"You made us wait for you on this chair," said girl number two.

"We split up," they both said.

Clavin was both quick and experienced. It struck him all at once.

Well, stew me alive, he thought.

"The keys?"

They gave him their largest, whitest smiles.

"Well, either way, you certainly have beautiful teeth. So, tell me, what's this about?"

"We have business that must be attended to before you leave us."

I'm definitely sending my Dreamers to chapel when I return.

"Ladies, I am from a far land, as I told you last night. In the place that I live, taking advantage of young girls is looked down upon and, given my profession, to do so while Traveling can have deadly consequences. I am afraid we will have to work something else out."

They began to laugh.

"Good sir ..." began girl number one.

"Or perhaps bad," interrupted girl number two.

More giggling.

"I am afraid you misunderstand us," said One.

"That is not what we want from you," finished Two.

Outright hilarity erupted from the girls.

Clavin, standing half-dressed on the bed, grew red-faced and stepped down. *Well, it's not so funny as all that.* Clavin kept one eye on the laughing girls while he finished dressing and equipping himself. Once finished, he turned back to them.

"Very well. What may I do for you?"

"It is not what you may do for us," said One.

"It is what we may do for you," said Two.

"That being?" he demanded dryly.

"We shall have a drink with you before you leave," they chorused.

"A drink?" he echoed back at them.

"In the commons. Downstairs. A drink shall be shared between you and we," said One.

"That should be *us*, not *we*," he said absently.

"Come. Let us go," said Two.

Clavin followed them down into the common room— girl, Clavin, girl. The girls strode over to a table, sat down, and beckoned Clavin to join them.

Clavin looked toward the door and, after a moment, sat with a heavy sigh.

I seem to sigh a lot. Might ought to check that. A matter for later.

The squeaking that had irritated him through the night continued to find its way in from the porch, and it grated on every nerve in his body. It seemed to reach down into his soul and prick at his most tender places.

"Why can't they fix that blasted squeaking?" he asked the girls directly.

"Some things cannot be fixed. They may only be accepted," they both replied seriously.

"Some things should not be accepted. Rather, they should be fixed," he replied smugly, resolved to ignore the squeaking.

"What if they cannot be fixed?" asked One.

"Then you must find some way to deal with them," he explained with a shrug.

"And can you deal with this?" asked Two.

"I can try," he replied. "Do you have any oil?"

"No, but here is our drink," said both.

With that, a waitress deposited a great cup before them, frothed and foaming and chill to the touch. With a swish of her skirt, she swept away.

Clavin was surprised to find one drink on the table and not three.

"Shouldn't there be two of her?" Clavin asked as he watched the departing waitress.

"Why? There are two of us," answered One.

Hmmm.

"Why is this so important to you?" he asked suspiciously.

"It is not. It is important to you," they replied.

"What if I do not drink?" he asked.

"You are going east, are you not?" asked One.

"Yes. To Cordis Castle. Why do you ask?"

"You have said you are from a land far away," said the other.

"Correct."

"The Castle Cordis connection can only be completed by circumventing the Campton Cusp," said One seriously.

You must be kidding, he thought with a smile. "You must be kidding." *Okay, I said it.*

"As a matter of fact, we are," said Two.

"We just like to say that," said both.

At this, Clavin laughed, and the girls joined in.

"You know, you're not like the other girls I've met," he replied as he wiped tears from his eyes.

"How many girls have you known before?" they asked.

"Depends on how you look at it. Not many and quite a few, both."

"We're not like most girls," said One.

"In fact, you might say that we're the *key* to the whole thing," said the other.

"Right," he said. "Back to business. So, what do I get by drinking with you? A clever story to tell some monster or some such?"

"Well, in truth, there is a forest that surrounds Cordis," said One.

"A dark forest full of monsters," said Two.

"But the monsters only bother people who aren't from here," they said together.

"So," injected Clavin, "by drinking with you, I am imbued with your essence, and I can then pass on through the dreaded forest with no thought of danger. Right?"

"He's pretty smart," said One to Two.

"Not bad," replied Two to One.

"Well, let us drink then," he said and reached for the cup.

"Ah, but wait," they said.

"What now? Must we stand on our heads while we do so?"

"No," said One. "But when we begin to drink, we must drink it to its dregs; else the magic shall not function."

"And we must all drink together," said Two.

"But there is only one cup. How then shall we all drink at once?"

"That," they said together, "is what you must now discern."

Right then, old bean. Bit of a puzzle, he thought as he warmed to the assignment.

He snapped his fingers with a crisp pop. "Got it. I'll sit here and wait for some other to come in and I'll watch what he does. Simple."

He settled back in his chair to watch their reaction.

"If you can wait that long," replied One.

"And if the next person knows," added Two.

"How much time do you have?" they both asked.

So much for trickery. "You're pretty clever yourselves, you know?"

"Of course we are. Otherwise, this whole thing would be silly, silly," said One.

"Silly, silly," said Two. "I like that."

"Fine. Give me a bit," he growled back.

With that, he removed various objects from his pouch and tried numerous things. No good. Careful to replace the lot, he leaned forward to study the cup.

"Can I touch it?" he asked.

"I don't know. How long are your arms?" they both asked and laughed.

Cute. See what's on the back of my hand? "If—IF—I touch it or move it, will anything bad occur to me or will the magic be spoiled?" he demanded.

"Of course not," said One.

"And you thought he was clever," said Two.

If I was your father ... he thought. "Thank you," he replied. He raised the cup from the table, one small space at a time, feeling for any resistance before lifting it above his head, and studied it from the bottom. He turned the vessel 'round to study it from every angle. Placing it back down, he stood up, leaned over the cup, and stared down into it. As he did so, from the corner of his eye, he saw One reach her hand over, wind up her finger and, with a quick thump, pop him on the ear.

Hysterical laughter followed as he turned and stared at her.

He waited for them to wind down and then asked, "Are you done?" which cranked them up again. *I'm in Hell, and these are my demons.* "Okay," he almost bellowed, "Goofy and Gaffy, there are no visible or invisible markings on this thing. There is some barely discernible magic, but nothing to suggest how it works. There is nothing in the room to suggest an answer. The table on which the cup sits is clean. What then is left?"

"Whatever's not right," they chorused in delight.

That took a moment to sink in before he got it. He forced himself to admit that he actually liked it. He made a half-shrug, half-nod. *Not bad.* He got down on his hands and knees to study the table from below. Nothing under there either. He got up and walked away from the table. Looking back at the pair who were getting out of their chairs, he barked two words at them. "Stay. Stay!" *Irritating puppies.* After a short stroll 'round the inn, he returned a few minutes later and pondered the problem again. Another elegant solution came to mind. *Surely not.*

"Ladies, would you be so kind as to grasp the cup with one hand?"

Without a sound, they acquiesced and reached forward.

Clavin did likewise and, pulling his hand back, it was as if a copy of the cup came with it. At that point, the other two knew he had solved the riddle and, pulling their hands back, they all sat pondering their now manifested, individual drinks.

Bad to the— he began before he cut it off. *Uh, uh. Need a new motto.* "Is there anything else you need to tell me?" he asked.

They both shook their heads without a word, almost as if they were sad.

"Very well. Down the hatch."

With that, they all drank.

They finished at the same time and, standing to his feet, he bowed to them. "Ladies, I thank you. Now, I must needs be away."

But they did not reply in return. He was about to remark on their silence when he noticed that the pair was now smaller than they had been. "Are you shrinking?"

They nodded back to him.

"This is the magic then. You shall fade and, in your fading, I am empowered to complete my journey?"

Again, they nodded.

When he turned away, he experienced an unfamiliar twinge of regret. Halfway to the bar, he turned and looked again at the two shrinking girls. "I am sorry." He strode to the bar and called to pay up his account. *Doesn't pay to leave without paying.* "Ho, innkeeper," he bellowed.

"Art thou ready to journey onward?" asked the man.

"Indeed. And now the accounting."

"Was thy night comfortable?"

"Except for that squeaking. Perhaps with this coinage, you can have it repaired?"

"Oh. I think that you'll find it is fading away."

Clavin stopped to listen and realized that the squeaks *were* growing softer. "Huh," was all he could muster. "Two goldens, correct?"

The innkeeper nodded.

He reached into his bag of coins, poured out a number into his free hand, and separated two of the gold coins revealed there. But their color was now red and on their faces was the image of two silver knights. As coin clattered on counter, he spun to look back at his table. Where each girl had sat, there was now a great silver helmet. Some things, he knew, could be neither fixed nor accepted. Instead, they had to be dealt with.

FOUR CHARK

Clavin stood and pondered the grass of the field that lay before him. The soft, vibrant green invited him to lay down in it. It was a plush, velvet ocean which beckoned him as the cool breeze caressed the grass while glints of sunlight interspersed throughout. He shook his head and chewed the inside of his bottom lip. *There's something not right. Something is wrong.*

He found a stick and tossed it into the grass. *Nothing.* Next, he drew a knife and probed into the veldt and drew it back again. *'Kay, no grabby grass at least.* He replaced his knife and pulled out his sword. He knelt and made a bold scythe-like sweep, reaping the green and bringing the smell of fresh hewn grass to his nose. *You're an idiot. It's just grass, after all.* He stepped into the hewn grass and paused again. *What are those glints from?*

"Dewdrops." He nodded. *Sure, dew goes on grass. It's dew. You're due to move on. Do you get it?* "Stop that!" he barked. He clamped down on his thoughts, took three more steps forward into the grass, and sighed relief. "See? It's just grass."

255

Shouldn't reflections change as you move? He stopped again. "Yeah, they should." Clavin focused on the nearest lit grass, made his way over, and knelt to study it. The shoots didn't shine just because of the sunlight; they also shone because their tips appeared dipped in silver. He reached out a finger but stopped short of a touch.

Let's not do that.

He stood up and stepped back a long pace, careful that no silver-tipped grass lay in wait behind him. He opened his pouch and thought of ... *bread.* Soon he drew a doll-sized loaf of it out, which immediately expanded into a normal loaf. He broke it in four parts and tossed one at the grass. He missed that time and the next, but not the third.

As the bread chunk touched down, two green spears blasted up and shredded the bread with a sharp whoosh of air. Tracking the spears, Clavin watched them sail up, maybe four hundred feet, and fall back down to land not five feet away. They sunk into the ground, turning back into grass, silver points up. His first blind steps he had taken in the grass came to mind along with a short lived knot in his stomach. *Holy Carp.* He shook it off. *You're alive; don't dwell on the could-haves.* He looked around. *Where are all the dead animals?*

With a shrug, he stepped over to the shoots and reached into his pouch. He pulled out a shovel then stopped with a shake of his head. *How am I going to store them? If these things 'go off' in my pouch, they could kill me.* After a while, he put away his shovel and pulled out a vial in its place. *Darn, those could've been really handy.* He closed his left eye and rubbed a drop on his eyelid. Replacing the vial, he could already see the contrast in the grass through his left lid. All about the field lay pairs of silver shoots that now blazed in his magic sight. "Always in pairs."

He shrugged and moved on till the end of day, which came one hour later and within sight of an inn. Entering, he turned right to the bar of polished oak wood. "Ho, innkeep."

A man came out and smiled at him. "A room for the night?"

"Yes, please. One with a door and lock if you have it."

"That we do. It will be two golds."

Expensive. Clavin fished the coins out of his pouch.

"My son will guide you up and carry your gear."

"I'll carry it, but thank you anyway. Where is the lad?"

"Rige," called out the innkeep, "lead this man to his room."

Rige. He sighed. *They've been on my mind ever since ...* He shook his head and held his breath as he waited for the boy.

It was just a young boy that entered.

He released his held breath and followed him to his room. *Coincidence.*

He rose with the sunrise and the name of the innkeeper's boy nagging on his brain. Two hours later, the road ran into a garden-like area dotted with carved stones, words engraved upon them. Out in the center sat two women, red eyed and tearful.

He paused at the gate. *A road through a graveyard?* He shook his head. *Me not like this.* He turned his horse to go 'round to the right. The fence grew longer in response. And that's when he first noticed the Chark—very low-grade, no more than a three. *Ewwww.* He dismounted, stepped to the gate, and pushed it open. It screeched as it gave way. Clavin led his mount as he walked to the ladies. *Questing time.* When he grew close, the women looked up, dried their tears, and stood to greet him. *Sir, there's a terrible "bad-thing" up ahead.*

"Tell us, good sir, where be-ist thou bound?" they asked him instead.

He considered their speech. *Fluid. I like it.* "Dear ladies, I am headed for Samlin. I'm told I'll reach it by the end of this day. Is this the way?"

"Yes, sir, it is. But thou art blocked in thy journey by the Tunnel of Grief."

"Can I not go around?"

"Thou *canst*, but thy *may-ent*."

What? "I'm sorry, fair ladies, but I do not understand what you mean."

"Thou hast the ability, but thou shan't be allowed."

He nodded. "Who then does the allowing?"

"The dragon, none other."

In Clavin's mind, a peg moved up a notch on a board. "The tunnel is guarded by a dragon?"

"That is so. None pass to Samlin unless they pass it."

"Does the dragon ask riddles in return for safe passage?"

"We do not know. We simply mourn for the lost."

He paused on that note. *Let's try directing the Dream to do what I want.* "This is the graveyard of those who have fallen?"

They nodded.

"So those who have fallen attempting the passage are interred here?"

"Yes, that is so."

Here goes. "Then people have gathered the fallen and brought them back to be buried here, is that not correct?" *Yes?*

They shook their heads in the negative.

So much for interviewing the bearers.

"No, sir, it is the magic of the graveyard, bound to the Tunnel, that sendeth them here."

He sighed. *Of course.* "So, what then must I do to pass the dragon?" *Don't say I have to fight him.*

"Thou must slay-eth the beast. What else wouldst thou expect?"

He repressed a scowl. *What did I just say?* He considered the women. "So, if I don't pass, you two will stand here, mourning for me, and a new grave will appear?"

"No. Only one shall be here."

His eyebrows squinched together as he paused his reply. "Why is that? Lack of funding?"

It was their turn to squinch before answering. "No. There is always a mourner for each combatant from the previous try. Last time there were two. Thus, there are now two of us."

His face relaxed as he breathed out an "Ah." He continued, "And if I succeed?"

"The dragon shall die. We and the graveyard shall disappear with it."

"I understand. Can you tell me, does the dragon live inside the Tunnel and, if so, is it very far back inside its confines?"

"An hour's walk in, the Tunnel grows wide, and there thou shalt meet the dragon for battle."

"What if I try to flee from the beast? Will it allow me? Perhaps the Tunnel constricts it?"

They shook their heads. "We do not know. We only mourn."

He cut off an eye roll at this. *Useless.* "Okay. Thank you. I'll return in the morning." Clavin went back the way he came, mounted his horse, and rode away. *I've got a lot of work to do to get ready. Going to be a long night.*

About the same time the next morning, Clavin arrived back at the picket fence. *I can't wait to see their reactions. They better not change any of the rules they gave me yesterday.* Clavin opened the gate and proceeded toward the same crying women who knew him from yesterday's meeting. He paused to relish the confused expressions that washed over their faces.

"Good sir, what, pray tell, do you have in the wagon?"

FOUR CHARK

Clavin looked back at the two tethered horses that followed behind him pulling a large wagon covered with a larger canvas tarp. *I knew that would get you curious!* "Ladies, I fear that too much information may not be good for my health. Suffice to say I have a plan in mind. I believe that you shall not weep after the end of this day."

"We wishest thou well, good sir, though many have tried this deed before."

But they weren't Clavin Roth. "Good day and goodbye." He moved to the other side of the graveyard, squealed open the gate, and moved on in anticipation.

Four hours passed, and Clavin came to a tunnel carved into a large hill with a sign beside it that read only, "Grief." The horses began nickering—eyes wide, noses flared open. *Dragon stench.* "Whoaa," he whispered as he dismounted. "Steady there, boys. You're not going into the nasty tunnel. Steady, steady." Clavin unsaddled his horse and unhitched the others. Stepping back to the wagon, he unleashed the tarp. He took care to not let it settle back into the wagon, then, in a quick movement, whipped up the tarp and yanked it completely off the wagon. He opened his pouch and drew forth a tiny rectangle of fabric. He dropped it on the ground, and it snapped out into a large rug that he then stretched out. One at a time, with steady movements, he unloaded the wagon contents onto the rug. With a short command, the rug floated up to waist high, and Clavin strode forth, pulling the carpet along behind him. An hour's walk in the cavern, and it opened out. Clavin called magic into his sword, his armor, and onto himself. Next, he walked back down the tunnel to where it constricted and lay the carpet down on the floor. With a smile, he strode back up the tunnel and cried out a challenge.

The dragon answered immediately; from the depths of the cave, light blazed forth on the left. Clavin both felt and heard the drumming of large legs.

Little fire-breather on the way. He backed down the tunnel. The beast came into sight. Sixty feet long, it was a two-headed dragon, and one of the heads was a match for Clavin's own. *What the devil?*

The dragon charged toward him, and Clavin modified his position in an attempt to halt the beast over his dirt-covered carpet. It worked perfectly. But the dragon didn't lie down.

Clavin leaped forward and swung his sword.

The dragon struck back with a claw.

Clavin jumped high and struck down. The sword cut a groove along the red scales, but the impact spun Clavin around, and with a *woof*, he slammed down on his back.

The dragon felt the sword score its under flesh as scales fell away, broken and sliced.

ROLL OUT, Clavin mentally screamed. He rolled, but *toward* the beast and not away.

The dragon leaped left and back to try and get Clavin out from under its body. It made a quick strike to crush Clavin flat.

In the last second, Clavin rolled to his feet and darted

forward. A great talon tore the cloak from his back. Clavin struck out and grooved the talon to the quick; green syrup oozed out like maple sap from a tree.

The beast shifted its mass to make another strike, and its right claw came down on the dirty rug.

Four spears blasted up: two into the foot, two others between the talons and deep into the muscle of its upper leg. The dragon screamed as it leaped away, stumbling in pain.

Clavin rolled cape-less to the rug and snatched onto two clods.

The dragon inhaled.

Clavin ran for a boulder.

The gout of flame lit up the cave as Clavin dove for cover, tunic now blazing.

When things go wrong ...

The flame subsided, and Clavin felt the floor shake as the beast shifted about for a better angle.

An agonized Clavin rolled on his back. He extinguished the fire and tossed the clods under the bulk of the dragon. He came to his feet in a run as his hand reached into his pouch and he thought of ...

WATER!

He could hear the woosh of a mighty breath being drawn.

He yanked forth a blue vial from his pouch, spun around and, with a short pause, released the contents at just the right instant. A torrent of water battled with onrushing flame. Clavin moved left, and the dragon shifted its weight, one side crippled by the embedded spears. He couldn't quite tease it over the rug. *Move your arse over.*

The dragon cut off its fire.

Clavin likewise cut off his water as he charged forward, vial still in hand.

The dragon roared defiance, and Clavin gave it a mouthful of liquid, shutting it off. Shaking its head, it coughed up the water, leaped backward from Clavin, and its hind parts at last landed square on the carpet. The dragon screamed as it thrashed and twisted in its final agony as sixteen more spears blasted into its groin and legs.

Now that's gotta hurt, Clavin thought with a painful half-smile.

Clavin had to retreat from the thrashing mass of scales as it worked out its own time to die. He struggled to remove his pack without rubbing his back and grimaced at the pain of his own charred skin. He reached up to the back of his head. Hairless. *What'd you expect?* He waited an hour till the beast settled down. Grabbing his gear, he made his way around it, careful lest it raise itself. "You nearly got me," he said to the hulk.

One eye from the Clavin head opened.

Darn, not dead. Clavin grasped his sword and prepared for another assault.

The Clavin head spoke in a language that sounded like rusted metal screeching.

What? What's this all about? He shook his head and made his way on down the tunnel. Soon he came to an archway filled with white smoke, engraved with the word "Samlin." He stepped through. As he did so, the wounds and pain of the Path dropped away from him, and Clavin Roth emerged back into the Inn as unscathed as he'd left. *Ahhhhh*, he sighed in relief. *It's good to be back at the Inn ...*

Clavin made his way to the Night Star and seated himself at his usual table, reserved for Rangers, which of course meant him alone. He flagged down a Caller and gave him instructions. "When Warrior Staven Drath arrives, have him come by please." Clavin waited an hour. People came by and said hello, but he didn't invite any to sit, and none requested; it wasn't Inn protocol. Finally, Staven came into Samlin Hall and over to Clavin, who waved at an empty chair.

Staven sat.

"Easy run?" Staven asked with a smile as he gestured to a waiter.

Clavin shook his head.

"Actually, no. I did something stupid and nearly got killed."

Staven donned his serious face and leaned forward.

"Really? You look golden to me."

Clavin shrugged.

"We all have near misses. You've had 'em. But this one was a little weird."

"Yeah? So? Out with it."

Clavin set his glass down.

"Okay. So here I am, rolling along, doing my thing, not messing with people, not letting them mess with me. Four days in, I come up to a graveyard straddling the road. Right? It's a *through* and not 'round sort of deal and, right in the middle, these two women are sitting there crying. So what do you think I'd do?"

Staven gave a shrug as he scrunched up his face.

"Go 'round?"

"Of course I do. But the fence—oh, yeah, it's all enclosed by a nice, white, picket fence—decides to *extend* itself and cut me off. So, I'm off through the graveyard and up to the women." He paused.

"Chark?" Staven guessed.

"Yeah, but not bad. Low-grade. No big deal. So, up to the girls, and we have our little chat."

"So, it's off on a quest, I presume?"

"Nope, it's just that I have this tiny, little obstacle to overcome in order to pass to my gate."

"And the tiny obstacle was?"

"A dragon."

Staven whistled.

"Well, the Chark was low-grade so I presume the dragon was too?"

Clavin shook his head.

"Not really, he was pretty decent. I'd give him a six on the scale. Nothing I couldn't usually handle."

Staven's eyebrows went up. "But?"

"But, at the moment, I'm still thinking the dragon will be smaller, not larger. It's probably a four Chark. In retrospect, I should have considered that the full graveyard of his defeated foes would have suggested something stronger. But I didn't. I was too concerned about how to use these grass-spear thingies I'd come across the day before. They were pretty interesting, and I really wanted to use them."

Staven nodded.

"So you've got some spears you can use to wipe out the dragon, and you want to use them. Sure. But, I presume, it's tricky to use them? Otherwise, why all the thought?"

"Right. The spears are actually blades of grass with silver tips. Touch a tip, and it becomes a real spear firing up from the ground as if from a ballista. Nasty. Hard to haul. Very temperamental."

"Ah. So you don't have any with you. You go back and get some for this little effort."

Clavin nodded.

"I go back and collect the grass spears and head off to meet Mr. Scaly. I'm in the tunnel, and I get to where I'm due to encounter him. I back off and lay my trap. This is when I get stupid."

Staven cocked his head in anticipation.

"I'm figuring, 'Hey, why waste my most powerful stuff on this fellow? He's probably small.' Weak Chark, remember?"

Staven nodded.

"So, I do my basic spells: sharpen blade, blow deflection, stutter-step. None of the big potion stuff like cleave stone, twin self, air-shield, fireproof. And with that, I walk out and give a yell."

Staven smiled.

"Then, I see the fire."

"So you start with the potions?"

Clavin shook his head.

"Nope. Genius here still thinks, 'Oh, it's a small fire-breather. No biggie.'"

"What shows up instead?"

Clavin leaned forward.

"A two-headed dragon, sixty feet long, and one of the heads ..."

"Yeah? What?"

"Is mine!"

Staven sat back with a shock.

"Yours? Your head on the dragon?"

Clavin nodded.

"What do you make of that?"

Clavin flipped his hands open with a shrug.

"I don't know, Stave. It's weird."

Staven nodded.

"'Kay, so then what?"

Clavin described the rest of the battle to a very appreciative crowd that counted, by then, more than Staven. A dozen others had gathered and stood in quiet attention behind Clavin's friend.

"Whew," whistled Staven. "That was a close one."

Others murmured agreement.

"Ranger Roth," asked a woman of Runner status, "may I ask how many dragons you have fought?"

Clavin looked at her.

"That one was thirty-seven. But, to be fair, nine have been rather small. I'd say only twenty-eight that count. Five were really bad. Two I fled from. Now, ladies and gentlemen, I'll need a private moment with Staven here, if you please."

The crowd moved off and left them alone once again.

"Something more?" Staven asked.

"The Clavin-head spoke to me, just before I left."

Staven's eyes opened wide. "And?"

"It asked me a question."

"'Kay."

"It asked me, 'Who is the monster?'"

"What does that mean?"

Clavin pondered his friend for a moment and then shook his head. "I can't really say, Stave. I can't really say."

269

SILVER CORD

Clavin yawned and rocked his chair back on two legs. He looked over at his companion. "Well, Stave, it's getting late. I think I'm about to wrap it up here and head out."

Staven twisted his neck, and it gave a pop. "Yeah, I'm thinking the same."

They pushed back their chairs and headed for the exit.

A man they both knew strode through the hall in their direction, gaze locked on the pair.

Staven spoke first. "Hey, Sash, you looking for one of us?"

Sash nodded. "Both, actually. Warrior Swift is overdue. I thought you'd want to know."

Clavin shared a glance with Staven. *Uh oh.* "Thanks, Sash. We'll head over immediately. Gate?"

"Trailing, twenty-two."

Clavin nodded and started walking, Staven glued to his right. Neither spoke a word. A fast walk past numerous unacknowledged salutations took them to gate twenty-two in Merinda's hall. There were four others there. Staven barked out to a woman, "Glitz, what's the situation?"

"She's over eight and a half. Some of the Dreamers are starting to wake. The Wardens have sent in the docs to medicate the rest."

Clavin relaxed a hair and released a breath. *Protocol; extra measures to help out us higher ranked Travelers in an emergency.* "Great. She'll make it."

Staven agreed. "Yep. Mer is the smartest Traveler we know. She'll pop out any moment now."

Glitz shook her head and tossed her oil-black hair about. "No word that any Dreamers woke on a nightmare. Gotta be a Chark though, right? Why else would she be late? Nothing else could keep her in the Dream, right?"

The image of a blue horse flashed through Clavin's mind, and a weight of depression clawed down on his shoulders. He shook it off. "No. She'll be out any moment. How long have you known her, Glitz?"

"About six months. She's a hard one to get to know, but we sort of connected a while back."

Staven scuffed the toe of a boot across the floor and then looked up at them. "Yep, we know. She's a hard nut to crack but worth it. Clever, thoughtful. Great analysis on a bad Crossing. But ... not a lot of friends."

Clavin's eyes scanned about, and he nodded. *Overdue and only six people here.* He shook his head.

They stood and chatted stories about Merinda, the Hall, and each other. As time passed, their glances flicked more and more often to the return gate behind which lay Merinda's returning Veil. A woman nearby stroked the wood and whispered to the door. Everyone began to fidget and pace.

"She's eleven in," whispered Glitz.

"Three hours late," mumbled another of the waiters.

Come on, Merinda. No Chark, what's going on in there? Clavin looked up to the ceiling and forced his tensed muscles to relax for the twentieth time.

Everyone was quiet. Conversation had ceased. Only the sounds of boots pacing stone or fingers tapping leather could be heard. Minutes drug by as their small group crowded closer to the gate, as if trying to pull their friend through the mist by sheer will and closeness of presence.

The gate door and the number above it wavered, lost color, and vanished. Nothing was left but a blank, stone wall.

Clavin staggered. His inner cry was mirrored by the voices of others who cried out, "No. No, Merinda, no."

Clavin clenched his fists and grit his teeth. He turned to look at Staven, who looked back.

Two sad-faced men shook their heads in unison.

Staven turned back to the gate. "We'll keep a spot open for you, back at the Star. Goodbye, Merinda. It was fun sparring with you."

Clavin nodded. *Words. Say something. Speak.* He took a breath and addressed the wall too. "Meri, the silver cord has broken; find rest now in the Dream that gave you the life you always yearned for. Perhaps there, I hope, you'll see your dad again and be the woman outwardly that we got to know." After a short pause, he shook his head. "It was a privilege calling you friend. Goodbye."

Staven and Clavin shared another look and nodded.

They went their separate ways and left the Hall and their friend in the past.

TREND MAKER

Clavin stepped from the Inn to find himself in a place of cold stone and dim light from the veil that twisted behind him. *Different.* He closed his eyes for a few seconds. He stood in a carved tunnel which canted upward, ran twenty feet forward, and ended in a great slab of stone. He walked the length of the corridor and saw that a shovel hung on the wall to the right. The hall-ending slab was split down the middle and bound together by a great metal bolt shot into a latch whose match might be found on a castle entrance or other such fortress. Underneath the bolt and latch assembly was a metal handle.

Big, stone double doors. How many of these, in my years ...

On the left door, a long metal bar, curved at the end, hung off a hook. On the right door, a thick metal band was bound to the door face. He shrugged, grasped the handle, and paused. *What if outside is some nasty beast?* He glanced back at the veil. *Just twenty feet.* He unlatched the bolt and pulled on the door. It didn't budge. He tried harder with the same result. *Okay. Hinge check. Yep, there are hinges, apparently. Definitely a pull operation. Well, as definite as the Dream can be. Hmm …*

Clavin stepped back and inspected the obstacle again. *Let's see …*

He took down the bar, placed an end under the band, and leveraged open the door. A crackling sound accompanied its movement as light poured in along with frigid cold and the white fluff of snow that blocked the way out. He retrieved the shovel which hung from the wall and attacked the snowdrift. He shoveled the snow ahead back, deeper into the tunnel behind him. He soon found himself outside the tunnel on a wide, frozen landing, but in clearing his exit, he had blocked the tunnel behind him and cut himself off from the veil. *Inconvenient. Oh, well.* He stood and scanned about him.

Clavin stood near the top of a mountain, buried in deep, winter snow. A frigid wind blasted unceasingly and blew a white mist off to the east. *Whoa, this is new.* Clavin stopped to admire the view of the valley and lakes dotted far below him, green in their summer, away from the cold. He shivered. *Four miles, maybe five*, he estimated the height of his perch. *Mountains are hard to climb in the snow—up or down.* He looked back at the cave.

Maybe I bail out on this one. He chewed his lip. *Well, I've only started. No rush. Let's look around first.* That took but a moment. The area he had cleared of snow was not very large, and nothing about it was remarkable. *Nothing. Just the way I came in.* He turned, shoveled the snow to the sides of the passage, and walked back into the tunnel. He lit a torch and studied the walls and the floor. The tunnel was a perfect eight-by-eight square, obviously carved into the mountain. The walls, floor, and ceiling were all smooth except where the carvers had grooved the floor and the walls.

What are those for?

Two parallel lines ran down the hall from the veil, four feet apart, eight feet in length. In front of these grooves, perhaps four feet out, were the carvings of hooves, enough for two beasts. On each wall above these prints in the stone, a line marked the walls about two feet up from the floor. He rubbed his face as he pondered the grooves. *I have a bar and a shovel, not one thing more.*

He shrugged.

There's nothing to do here, no way down this mountain. Well, I could try some potions to see if there's anything more. He shook his head. *That's valuable stuff. Don't want to waste it, not ten feet from the Veil.* Clavin walked back up to the door and re-hung the bar. Taking the shovel, he cleared out the snow from the passage to allow him to close it again. *What are you doing? Just leave.* "I can't bail this quickly." He ran his finger along the groove in the wall next to him. "I'd be embarrassed to go back so soon." *Then try the ointment.*

"Shut up and shovel."

I'm going to move all this snow and then jump through the Veil back home. "Wait." *I do have something else. I have the snow.* He paused and scrubbed his chin. "I'm in a tunnel on top of a mountain. The tunnel slopes down from the entrance to the Veil." *That's why the doors are needed, to prevent the snow from filling the passage up in the first place.* "But why doesn't the tunnel just slope *up* to the Veil instead of *down* to it? Then they wouldn't have even needed the doors. That'd make a lot more sense." Clavin opened the doors once more, then began to shovel the snow into the tunnel, pushing it onward until he covered the floor, its grooves, and the eight hoof marks. He piled it up until the lines in the walls disappeared.

And then he stepped back and collected his breath.

Well, that was fun. Now what? "Take me to Samlin," he cried. *Nothing.* "Rise to my bidding." *Nada.* He pondered it. *Maybe a poem? Sometimes I get pieces of verbal magic— worth a try.* He made up a poem and then called it out.

"Two white horses, icy white,
pulling sleigh through day and night,
carry me safely o'er snowy drift,
guarantee passage, one sure and swift."

He recited this seven times and waved his hands about him in what he thought would be a magical manner. The snow in the tunnel began to churn and roil, creating a whiteout that blocked any view of what was going on within. *Okay, progress.* Clavin braced and waited. It cleared after a minute and revealed two horses of snow in frosty traces bound to a sleigh also made of white.

The steeds turned their heads toward him with no hint of breath.

Clavin smiled as he mounted the sleigh. With a quick "haw," they were off down the mountain. They raced down the cliffs at impossible angles, sure-footed stallions holding their place as they went. In thirty short minutes, the snow thinned and gave way to rocky paths, but they kept moving downward. In thirty more minutes, the horses began to melt as cold, mountain air bowed to lowland summer. At long last, the stallions squished to a stop, unable to take him any farther. Clavin dismounted and nodded his thanks. With that, they collapsed into a pile of slush.

He headed down the trail and, an hour later, he walked into a town marked with a sign. *Samlin.* Down the main street, his feet took him in search of the stable that was usually there. It was, and Clavin turned in to buy a horse and ask for directions as he always did.

"Ho, the stable," he called to the darkness.

Not a sound answered. No groomsman or stable boy stepped forth. *Where is he?* Clavin strode the length of the stable and peered into each stall, both left and right, as he moved along. He continued out the back and into a paddock swept clean of dung and trash but empty of people and horses. *Empty. The stable is here, but no people—no horses to buy, either. Maybe the town's having a party?* Clavin retraced his steps through the stable and back out to the street. A woman passed by, and he approached her with a warm smile.

"Madam," he said to capture her attention.

"Hello. Are you new in town?"

"That I am. I was wondering if you could help me?"

"Please. Any way that I can."

"I came to buy a horse, but the stable is empty. Can you tell me where the horses have gone?"

She glanced at the stable, then back to him.

"The stable has been abandoned for a week. Two knights came along and bought all the horses. It was the talk of the town. I don't believe that any new horses are due for a while. I am sorry."

Two knights?

"Fair lady," he said, and earned a smile in response, "could you describe them? The two knights with the horses?"

"Oh, yes. Unforgettable. They were even taller than you. They wore silver plate armor that shined in the sunlight. They bore spears gleaming like lightning in their gauntlets, and when they removed their helmets, they were identical twins. Nearly as handsome as you. But not quite."

Clavin grew somber at this discourse.

"Is something wrong? Do you know those two knights? Are you, perhaps, a knight yourself?"

"Did these two knights, perchance, give out their names?"

"Oh, yes. Sir Garner and Sir Rige. It is not often you meet men like them. Or one like you, for that matter."

"Well then, having taken all the mounts, I suppose I must walk till I can find another."

"I am Badti, good sir," she said as she placed a dainty hand on his arm. "Please, what is your name?"

No Chark, it's fine, he thought as he resisted the urge to yank his arm away.

"Lady, I am Sir Clavin Roth, Knight of Cordis, on a return journey to thence. Perhaps you know the way?"

"Yes. Do you need me as a guide perhaps, Sir Clavin?"

'Ware the Passions, he admonished himself.

"No, my lady, the way is dangerous, and I must travel it alone."

"Oh, no," she insisted, "the way is not dangerous. Besides, you would be with me."

Level two, make it plainer.

"No, my lady. I shall travel alone as is my wont, lest my lady fair have reason for jealousy."

He marked the change in her demeanor at this. *Checkmate.*

"Well, Sir Clavin, the way to Cordis is down this west road. It is, perhaps, five days to Cordis when made by horse."

"Five? I was told it was four. Are you quite certain?"

"Well, near the end is a bog of blue peat that takes a full day to compass. If you could travel across it, the journey would be but four days in the making."

He nodded. "I'm told that one lives in the bog who can make such a journey quite simple. I shall contact him and elicit his aid in the matter. I need to complete this journey quickly."

"On foot it will take you many more days."

"No matter. I feel certain I shall make the journey in the needed time." He bowed. "Farewell, my lady. Enjoy your day as I begin mine."

"Shall we speak when next we meet? Or will that too trigger your love's jealousy?"

Clavin paused. *Don't make promises ... but what can it hurt? I'll never meet this woman again. Or at least this incarnation of her.* "Indeed, we shall. Till then."

He set off on the road to Cordis.

If these ghosts have stolen my horses, they likely mean to encounter me. I'm sure they'll have the horses with them.

Clavin walked, stride steady and measured, along the rutted dirt road that cut through the grasslands. The hours passed in a rush and, as the sun stood high above him, a woodland appeared in the distance ahead, and the road ran straight as an arrow into it. Where the path penetrated the woodland, a marker stood near, words carved into stone:

The Bramble Wood

Two miles straight through,
ten miles around.
Don't talk to strangers,
they'll just delay you.

Be through by night,
and all is all right.
Pass in the dark,
get lain in the park.

Clavin re-read the last line. *Graveyard?* He shrugged. *Two miles.* "Forty minutes, perhaps fifty if I tarry somewhere."

Six hours till dark. Clavin walked forward into the wood. As he walked on, he noted the path was well cleared and the sun-hungry shrubs did not press in close on the trail. Birds chirped in the trees as squirrels played mad games of tag in the higher-up branches. He walked on, enjoying the trip and the shade of the trees. Ten minutes in, he spotted a deer hidden in the brush, resting, legs akimbo. *Hmm ...* Thirty feet from the path, among the deep shadows, he saw hooves and legs that jutted out at the wrong angles. *Bear?* Clavin didn't break step but strode along, refusing to be side-tracked. Over the next five minutes, he sighted more such mangled carcasses, always in bushes, always in shadows. *This place must get nasty long about dark.*

A few minutes later, he heard a girl's cry with a Chark undertone that rumbled through the earth. *Dead ahead.* Clavin ran through his routine. He applied all of his base magic, checked his weapons, and took off for the sound. A minute later, he burst into a clearing.

They stood there waiting, in their shining armor, spears at the ready. Horses stood bunched in a long picket line, and in a wagon, bound, lay a woman.

"Somebody help," she cried.

As the two knights spread out, Clavin charged straight at them. They were huge and well armored, but they were just wraiths, and Clavin was not. His sword bit deep, and he dodged their parries. First he cut off their spears, and soon after cut them down too. He turned to the wagon and the lady bound there. As she rolled over, he saw the woman from back in the town. *Disconnect! Warning.*

"Thank you, good sir, for rescuing me."

Uhhmmm. He paused. *Don't talk to strangers.*

"Sir, will you not speak? Am I not worthy of your condescension?"

He blew out a breath as he considered her. *To speak or not to speak, that is the question.*

"You did promise that next time we met, we would speak again. Would you now go back on your word?"

Bound and pegged. Either way, this could go bad. "It is true that I did," he answered as he measured out his words in a slow metronome. The light faded as shadows ran across the glade like wild rabbits chased by hawks. "Oh crap!" *Oh crap, I said that aloud.*

The girl now laughed a strange sort of sound, like a soft blowing wind that rustled the leaves of an oak. She began to change as he watched her.

Clavin took off for the horses like a shot as his hand reached into his pouch and his mind called forth ... *Fire!* A vial of red flame came into his hand. He struck the picket line of horses loose with his sword and sheathed the blade in one very smooth motion. With no more adieu, he leaped into the saddle of one of the mounts and kicked the beast into a run. He thundered onto the path. The limbs and briars pressed in near to him. He glanced at the sky as he held to the course. Where there had been hours of daylight just minutes before, the sun was now setting. *Ten minutes left, maybe fifteen.* As darkness fell, Clavin drew forth another vial and anointed his left eyelid. Others came forth for use on sword and armor. All vials replaced, except for the red flame, he soon had to dismount as the bushes closed into the path and cut off his progress. With his enhanced sight, he lay into the bushes, hewed them down, and sprinkled fire about him.

The wood recoiled from Clavin, and he ran along, leading his horse. When he broke from the trees, the dark was full on him like a great blanket which stifled the light and groped for his life. He shuddered, relieved. *Don't talk to strangers.* "I could have walked 'round and been here by now." He shook his head. *But I did get a horse out of the bargain. Who's the man? Eh?* Clavin made camp well away from the wood and settled in for the evening. The night passed in peace, and at dawn, he was back on his way.

Clavin rolled along, enjoying the ride and foot-soreness avoided. He made good time as he pondered the previous day. *Rige and Garner are hounding me. It could be a problem.* He shrugged. "They went down easily enough." *If they reappear ...* "I'll smash 'em again." *I didn't even have to use my hard stuff—nothing to lose sleep over.* "O'course, I wasted some time escaping the wood." *Stupid. Don't talk to strangers. The sign made it clear.* "Idiot." *Last time they were just helmets in a chair. They didn't interfere, just laid a guilt trip on me. This time they changed the entire system.* "Or, rather, I did. I brought them with me." *I changed the Dream. They did. I did through them, because of them, because of my guilt—yada, yada. It's a mess. One thing's for certain ...* "I hope I'm not making a new trend."

The rest of the Crossing finished without irregularity, but worries and doubts about Garner and Rige weighed on Clavin. When he passed through the veil into Cordis Hall, it was a frustrated Dream Ranger who emerged.

GHOST HUNTER

Staven Drath sauntered along the Travel Hall toward Cordis. He greeted several people and turned into Chance Hall. From there, he walked over to a cordoned off area with the words *Shifty Dice* emblazoned in dancing letters over the entrance. A woman greeted him.

"Staven, back again? Business or pleasure?"

"Lucky, it's always a pleasure with you. What's the word? Any new blood to bet on?"

"Gotta recoup that loss on Clavin, right?" Lucky Break shook her head. "You make the craziest bets, you know that? Betting against the Ranger like that, and him your friend."

"Still is. We laugh about it now. Lucky, I'm betting you can't take no for an answer."

Her eyebrows collided as she pondered that.

Staven grinned.

She shook her head. "Did I miss something? What are you talking about?"

"Flirting."

Lucky shook her head. "No, you got that messed up, backward. I'd have to be hitting on you, and you respond *no* to me. But I'm not hitting on you, so it doesn't make sense."

Staven squinched his eyes closer to shut and shook his head. "I'm not so sure about that."

"What? It's obvious. Look. Hey, stud, why don't we go check out the Raven, just you and I? See, then you could say no and it would make sense."

Staven stepped up next to her. "Looks like I'm lucky now."

"No," she insisted, "that's not how it goes. You tell me *no*, and then I try again and ..."

He cut her off. "But I didn't say no."

"Wait, what? I didn't mean ..." Her face brightened, and she laughed as she stepped back from him. "Oh my, how long have you been planning that? You got me."

"Can I tell everyone I got Lucky Break to ask me to go to the Raven with her?"

She sighed and looked up to the ceiling. "Yes, yes, technically, you did. I won't deny it if asked, but I will explain how you got me to do it. Okay?"

Staven chuckled. He looked over her shoulder to a man dressed in a suit with polished nails, delicate fingers, and two neatly stacked piles of paper in front of him. A pen and ink well stood evenly above the papers while some books stood sentinel between bookends on his left. To his right, on the floor, sat a small wooden chest. "Hey, Roulette, guess what? Lucky just asked me to go the Raven with her."

Lucky spun around to face the man who registered surprise on his face.

"What? No way. Lucky, tell me it's a lie."

She raised a hand to calm him. "Technically, yes, but practically no; he tricked me."

Staven walked past her, over to where Roulette sat now chewing his lip, and flipped out a hand, palm up.

Roulette slapped a token into his palm. "Half a gold, as stated." Then he flipped open a book and made a notation.

Staven heard her call out behind him.

"Wait. You mean you bet on that?"

Staven bobbed his head up and down and laughed again. "And not just with Roulette, either. I just made five gold."

Lucky's mouth fell open as she focused off across the hallway. Finally, she chewed her lip and laughed. "I'll get you back, Staven Drath, mark my words."

"Get me back where? In the Raven?"

Lucky raised both hands as if she would scratch him, hissed like an angry cat, then turned about and fled the scene.

Staven pulled out a chair and plopped down beside Roulette. "Victory."

Roulette shook his head in dismay. "I warned her too. How the heck? I should know better with you."

Staven leaned to his left with a crooked smile. "'Cause you never imagined I could get your girlfriend to say it to me." He nudged Roulette with his elbow. "Come on; you know you're impressed. Say it. Say it."

Roulette shook his head. "I'd say that was more dumb

luck. Why should I be impressed? I'm impressed by your luck. I can say that for sure."

A nonchalant Staven slumped back in his chair and studied his fingernails. "I've been dropping by here every night to chat with you two for the last month. I've talked about family and friends but never the Raven or people hooking up. It's almost like Lucky got lulled into a sense of false security. Accident?"

Roulette looked up from his ledger and lay the book down as he turned to face him, his eyes wide. "Nooo."

Staven's lips pulled back from his teeth like a piano cover raised from its keys. The twinkle in his eyes put a period on his thoughts.

"You mean ...?"

"Yep."

Roulette sighed. "I should have put a tighter time limit on it." His head wobbled back and forth in forced admiration. "Okay, I admit it. I'm impressed."

"That I got your girl to ask me to the Raven or that I'm really lucky?"

"I said I'm impressed. Get on with yourself."

"Will you admit to the other bookies that you said you were impressed that I made that happen?"

Roulette's mouth fell open. "No. You didn't. You couldn't have."

More teeth appeared as Staven's smile grew wider.

"I tell you what, Rou. It'll cost me almost three gold with them if I lose the bet. If you pay me, I'll keep my mouth shut."

"All I have to do is deny it."

Staven pursed his lips. "True. But I do have a pretty good reputation for being truthful on my bets. You want to put your rep up against mine?"

Roulette thought it over and lay three more tokens down.

Staven looked at them. "That'll cover my losses, sure, but I won't be making anything. What about me? How will I eat? Think of the children."

Rou scowled and slapped two more down.

Staven raked the tokens off the table. "Thanks, Rou. So, what have we got tonight? Anyone new or interesting?"

"As a matter of fact, smart guy, there is. Older man. All business. Running the Samlin-Cordis trail."

Staven shrugged. "So? Doesn't sound too interesting."

"He took on the aspect of a fifty-year-old."

Staven leaned back in his chair. "Yeah. I see what you mean. Who does that? It must mean something." He nodded at the ledger. "What are the odds?"

"Even money he makes it past five."

Staven shook his head. "Nah. Not interested in that." He drummed his fingers on the table. "Well, not yet. Samlin-Cordis?"

"Yep. Same as your buddy. You going to check it out?"

Staven took on a mock surprise. "What? Me look for an advantage?"

"Course not." Roulette nodded toward the exit. "Go. He's probably in already. Gets in early, I believe."

Staven pushed back. "Name?"

"How many fifty-year-old men do you think are roaming Samlin-Cordis tonight?"

"Name."

"Ghost Hunter. I'm sure you can't miss him."

Staven ducked into Cordis, the first of the two along his route, and nosed about. The key man looked up Ghost Hunter and sent Staven on to Samlin Hall where he found a rugged, fit man, early fifties, the image every guy imagined being at that age, staring down into the Smasher's Pit.

"Hey, you Ghost Hunter?"

The sandy-haired man looked over, straightened up, and held out his hand. "I am."

Staven smiled at the faux pax and swiped his hand through the other man's. "We can't shake, remember? We're ghosts to each other here in the Inn."

"Oh, right. Old dogs, new tricks."

Staven leaned back against the railing. "Speaking of. Why fifty? Most people go between twenty and thirty."

Ghost paused. "Well, let's just say I'm not much into pretension. I did go with the ultimate fifty-year-old though. Still want to be in top shape for facing any troubles on the Path."

"Hmmm." Staven studied the man before him a second. The man waited him out. "So, that's it? No other reason? If you just wanted to stick out, there's other ways, you know. There's a guy named Pale Master; he's the extreme, but a good example. If you're still in the kindergarten, this would be the time to make any changes."

Ghost shook his head. "Nope. I'm good. Thanks

though. Is that what brought you here? To ask me that? You already knew my name when you walked up."

"Substantially. I like to get the scoop on the newbies who come in on the Halls near my own. I run Peael-Seeg."

Ghost focused on Staven's pin. "Warrior. You've been at this a while, I see. Got any tips for a new guy?"

The words of Merinda floated into his head, and he sighed before nodding. "Sure. Let's pull up some chairs and chat. An old friend of mine would have wanted me to."

They headed over to the kindergarten.

"Sounds like a nice fellow," Ghost replied. "What's his run?"

"Her. She ran Trailing-Wassel and was a Warrior too. Merinda Swift."

"Ran? I hope she's retired?"

Staven shook his head. "From life, not from here."

"Oh. I'm sorry to hear that. I know something ..."

They took their seats.

"You know something about what? Loss? Well, I guess most people do. No big surprise."

"So, what can you tell me about this place that I might not already have been told? I plan to write a book. Not just about my own travels, but about the people here and this place, how it works."

"You should hang out in the nearest Keeper Hall. It's like the library of the Inn. There might be a million books in there. I bet everything you want to know could be found there."

"Maybe I will. They didn't mention that in training.

Yes, definitely. I suppose they'll have writings on my own trail, Samlin-Cordis?"

"Sure. They'll have notes on everyone who has ever walked it, how many trips they made, when they made them, the size of any Charks encountered, the Binder, and probably even something on the Dreamer Groups. Lots and lots of useless info."

"Has anyone ever survived Dream collapse? Are there any rumors of such a thing?"

"No, no one survives that. In one sense, the Trail isn't real. It is created by the Dream energy of all the Dreamers and woven into an actual world by the Binder. When they wake up, the Dream world disappears."

Ghost focused back down into the Smasher's Pit below. "Thus, the terms Dreamworld, Dream Gates, Dream Warriors, etc. And in another sense?"

"In another sense," Staven continued, "it's totally real. People like us, Dream Travelers—or just Travelers for short—can enter those worlds and cross them from one gate to another. Real people go in, and real people come out."

"So why can't someone just come out on another night if they don't make it out on the first one?"

Staven nodded at a woman who sauntered by. "Well, Ghost, it's one of the oldest questions. The world the Traveler is *in* disappears when the Dreamers wake up. See? The entire world, not just a piece of it. There is no place for the Traveler to wait because, well, there is no world for a *place* to exist in. The world disappears, and so do they."

A sorrowful look brush-stroked age lines across the tanned features of Ghost.

"Ghost? Did you lose someone?"

Ghost snapped back into the moment. "No. I mean, yes, I've lost friends in real-world, but not here of course. I'm brand new to Dream Walking. Anyway, about those tips?"

"I'm guessing you're older in real life, so this might not be as big a deal but, then again, considering how my uncle was, it could be; first, avoid relationships with women on a Crossing. You probably got the condensed version in training, but I'm reiterating it. There's a lot to suggest that men hop in the sack with some astounding beauty and then wake up in the arms of a monster, unprotected."

Staven drew a finger across his throat.

"I can do that. Anything else?"

"Remember, nothing you do on a Crossing is real. The people aren't real, the dogs aren't real, the money isn't real."

"Right, they told us that."

"Yep, they told you. Let's go back over it. You meet someone, girl or guy, cat or dog ... or horse, that you really like. They're kind and helpful and all that stuff. Something happens and you're faced with a choice; abandon them, maybe even kill them, or stay and fight for them. It's hard, but you have to remind yourself: They are not real. You are. They cannot die because they are not really alive. You are alive, so you can die. Get it? Do whatever you have to and get back to the Veil."

"I think so. "

Staven shook his head. "You won't really feel it till the time comes, and when it does—and it will—it will feel real. It will be a lot harder than you think right now. But there is an upside that you need to focus on."

Ghost nodded. "Which is?"

"You can't really get hurt. If you get burnt, lose an arm, take a sword through the gut, etc., it doesn't matter. So long as you make it back to the Veil. Once you step through, all your wounds and hurts will disappear."

"Right, I recall that. That seems particularly strange to me. What if you actually got killed? You wouldn't really die?"

Staven shook his head. "It's happened. There have been cases where two Travelers co-walked a Trail before. One of them got killed, but the other carried the body out. Soon as it hit the Veil, the guy healed and woke up."

There was a pause. Staven squinted as he studied the man. "Ghost? You with me?"

Ghost nodded and cleared his throat. "That's why we can't modify goods in the Dream, right?"

"Exactly. Otherwise, people would carry stuff into a Dream-world, find a wizard, and let him cast some magic on it. They'd turn lead into gold or heal real-world wounds and then just step back through."

"So, the only thing that is truly real is entering and exiting. How strange."

"It is. But it makes all of us willing to take the risks very wealthy."

A voice called out behind them, "Ghost Hunter?"

Staven turned to see the green-capped Caller looking at them. "Well, Ghost, that's you. Good luck. I'll see you in a couple nights."

Ghost nodded, collected his key, and moved off.

Staven returned to Roulette and leaned down against the table. "Half a gold Ghost Hunter doesn't make ten."

Roulette shook his head. "I don't know enough about him to guess if that's a good bet or not. I suspect you do. No bet."

"Smart. There's something in his past. I don't know. On the flip side, I've given him some pretty solid advice tonight. Maybe it'll help."

Roulette considered it. "Tell you what. I'll bet *you* Ghost doesn't make ten. It's a gold to me if I win and one to you if you do."

Staven looked around in an exaggerated manner. He settled his gaze back on Roulette. "Do you have a mirror?"

"Mirror? No. Why?"

"I'm just wondering if someone managed to write the word 'sucker' across my forehead while we've been talking."

Roulette smiled. "Look at it this way; in effect, I'm betting you that your advice can't keep Ghost alive more than ten Crossings."

Staven straightened up and worked his fingers across his closed lips before nodding. "Oh, man, that's good. That's a challenge. And it's interesting. It's like a project. Okay, odds?"

"One to one, like I said."

"No way. I just told you I didn't think he'd make it. Now you want one-to-one on this bet? Where's that mirror again?"

"Staven, you just took me for five gold tonight. That's a chunk of money. You can afford to risk some of that back to me, right?"

Staven threw up his hands in surrender and stepped back. "Okay, Rou. Mark it down. One gold."

"Why not make it five?"

"One gold, Rou. I'm not giving away my whole stack tonight. I'm being generous as it is."

"Okay, one on Ghost Hunter to make ten Crossings."

"And now, I need to get ready to make my own."

Staven left the man writing in his book.

BLAME GAME

How, he wondered for the hundredth time, *could Rige and Garner have got on his path that night?* Michael Envine sat on the marbled balcony of his countryside mansion and stared over the grounds that led down to the river. He'd been doing a lot more of this since the Two Sisters Inn. The knights had reappeared again since that Crossing. *They're not going to go away. They'll keep coming back. My guilt is resuscitating them. I need to find out who's to blame. Who screwed up and let this happen? How could I have known or been expected to know? Or even to guess?* "No way." He shook his head. "No. It's not my fault."

Into his mind, though, came the images of Rige and Garner, glowing under the aegis of some visible enchantment. *I could have tried the potion.* He shook his head again. "How does the mercantile side of the Gate system work?" he murmured, clearing the last thought from his mind. *I've been doing this for six years, and I've never bothered to look into it. Time that I did.*

"Corval," he called out into the hall, "bring my food to

the study." He pushed back from his table, arose, turned, walked into the mansion across the parquet flooring to the second hall, and veered left. He strode into the study and over to the bookshelves. He scanned over them, pulled three books off the shelves, and laid two of them on the desk where he then sat down. He read the cover. *Protocols and Procedures of the Dream Gate Commerce System.* With a slight groan, he opened the book and began to read.

Still, quiet hours passed, accompanied by the syncopation of turned pages, rolled eyes, deep sighs, and paced floors. Corval attended to his master's needs, bringing food and drink, sweeping away the detritus from the previous round of deposit.

Finished, Michael pushed back for the final time and swept out to the patio from whence he'd begun. *The Merchant wouldn't agree to let a Traveler onto the Path without a proper way-ticket. The ticket comes from the ticketer who, in turn, receives requests from the Merchant. It has to be the Merchant or the ticketer. Let's think it through.*

The Caller gives Rige and Garner the signal and their gate key. They get up, read their ticket, and go to the listed gate. But, for some reason, it's the wrong gate. Which means what? Rige and Garner didn't read their number right. Michael nodded at the sense of that.

So, Rige or Garner scans the ticket, misreads it, and they end up at the wrong gate. Normally not a big deal. The Merchant would stop them, and they'd figure it out. But they went to the wrong gate. So, there they are. No Merchant with a cargo pack. What then? They go stupid and step through the

Veil anyway? That would be incredible, suicidal. "No way," he said aloud, shaking his head. "Besides, their key wouldn't fit the wrong gate. So it's the Merchant's fault then?"

The Merchant comes in the day before. I get picked for one route and Rige-Garner for another. The ticketer makes up the way-tickets. Rige and Garner show up early, get their call, and go to the gate. Tickets match, and they're on their way. "It's perfect. If it weren't for the fact that they're dead, I'd say it couldn't miss."

He pondered it for a while.

Try it this way. The Merchant comes in the day before and picks me for one route and Rige-Garner for another. He takes the information to the ticketer who makes up the way-tickets. The ticketer puts the **wrong** *gate number down on Rige-Garner's way-tickets. Rige and Garner show up early, get their call, and go to the wrong gate. Tickets match, and they're off, on a path they know nothing about.* "They're screwed. And it makes perfect sense. The ticketer's carelessness killed them, not me. Nope, not me. Now I'm going to find out who that idiot was and have him fired. Corval, get my carriage ready to head in."

Michael Envine arrived at the Sanctum and into the business wing. He made his way to a door whose carved words notified him he had arrived.

Personnel.

He pushed through the door to see a young clerk seated behind a desk. "May I help you, sir?"

"Yes. I need to have a search done. About two months

ago, specifically the Inn night of Drenin 26, I believe that a grievous error was made by one of the ticketers. We need to identify the individual. Can you help me with that?"

The clerk's disinterested face changed expression as he stood and came 'round the desk.

"What details can you give me on this issue?"

"I believe that two Walkers, Rige and Garner, died by improperly being assigned to the Samlin-Cordis trail that night. I'd like to know who wrote their way-tickets."

"Oh my."

A pause.

"How certain are you about this? It's a rather serious charge."

"Certain enough," Michael dryly replied.

"And you are?"

"I'd rather remain anonymous, if possible. At least for now. If it comes to a trial then, of course, I'll have to come forward."

"Very well. I'll have a records search done. Can you come back tomorrow?"

"Gladly."

With a nod, Michael turned on his heel and left the room.

The next day, he had his answer.

"Sir," said the clerk, "Mr. Johnson from Records is waiting with your information. They would not release it to me in my position. Do you know where it is?"

"No. Sorry."

"Quite alright. Go down the hall to your right."

"Rige and Garner Lossenfell were slated for the Samlin-Cordis trail the Inn night of Drenin 26. They never returned. The Merchant, Caller, and ticketer are all being questioned about the incident, but given the work and the time that has lapsed, I doubt they will recall anything."

"Wait, they were, in fact, slated for Samlin-Cordis and not some other trail? Are you certain?"

"As certain as the records can be."

"Well, that's not what I expected. I thought you were going to tell me they were due to Travel another path that night. So, Samlin-Cordis was the right Veil."

"It seems that there were three instantiations of Samlin-Cordis that night. Two going to Cordis, one coming back. Do you need more of the particulars for the other Paths?"

Michael looked back at the man.

"I'm very sorry for having disturbed you, sir. I appear to have been mistaken."

"I suppose you are a family friend or some such," replied the man, trying for a sympathetic voice. "On the Paths, things happen. Often, they are tragic. I am so sorry."

Michael nodded.

"As am I. More than you know. Good day."

Days passed before Clavin Roth re-entered the Inn.

"Well, old nut," Staven asked him over a drink, "how's it been?"

"On and off, off and on," he replied with a yawn. "You?"

"Same ole," replied Staven as he slumped back. "Want to meet some new kids?"

Clavin shook his head. "Last time, that didn't work out so well. I don't think I need a repeat performance."

"What? Last time?"

"Those two twins. Remember? Dragon slayers! You thought I should meet them. Never made it back."

Staven thought a moment. "Yeah, right. Night of your Ranger run." Staven shrugged. "Happens. You know. Can't stop you from having fun, can it?"

Clavin stared into his glass a moment, and his shoulders slumped. *If you only knew.* "You're right, of course. But let's do it another time."

"Sure thing, Mighty One."

"Hey, Staven ..."

"Yo?"

"Ever wondered about the system? Can it mess up somehow? Send one of us off onto the wrong Path without us ever knowing? Maybe cross them, scramble them?"

Staven stared back for a second before shaking his head. "No. Not the sort of thing I want to think about. Stuff like that ... well, I don't need things to muddy the waters, so to speak."

Clavin nodded.

"Why, what's up?"

Clavin shook his head. "Never mind. Just pondering the infinite, you know?"

"'Kay," replied Staven doubtfully.

Just then, a green capped Caller walked by. Clavin stood up and waved him down even as he moved off from the table and away from Staven.

"'Scuse me. Where do you store the keys?"

"Well, sir, the key locker is kept behind the Map Room."

"So a Merchant asks you to flag, say, John Smith to his gate, and you do what?"

"I go to the key locker, find the name John Smith on the board, read the gate number beside it, and ask for the key to that gate. The lockmaster retrieves the key, and then, using the location note on the board, I find the Traveler and give him the key. That's all there is to it."

"Can the keys get mixed up?"

"Sure. If they do, though, it won't match the paperwork."

"And the keys are marked anyway." *I've seen enough of them to know that.*

The Caller nodded.

"Thank you." Clavin looked back at his friend at the table. "Gotta run, Stave. Check you later."

Staven nodded, and Clavin headed off. He arrived at the key locker mere minutes later.

It was simply a long bar sporting a wall full of keys in the background, hung on a row of hooks that marched like soldiers down the wall and each marked with a large number. Behind the bar, but in front of the keys, stood a man taking orders from several green-capped men taking and returning keys.

Large tablets of paper were laid out down the bar, which sported no drinks or food of any kind, nothing but the tablets and a large sign.

No food or drink on the bar.

Clavin approached and looked down. The tablet in front of him sat underneath a large letter, M. The tablet to the left sat under an L and the one to the right under an N. There was writing on the tablet he faced:

Parden Mei	Phoenix Lounge	283
Deern Masher	The Eagle & Chick	821
Ferden Maul	Washbasin	173
Slaver Mange	Hardluck	532
Eric Mist	Fool's Quest	329

So, if I were to change 283 to 999, Parden would go the wrong gate. So what? When he and the Merchant crosschecked their way-tickets, they'd see the problem, right?

He nodded.

And that's presuming that 999 was extant on that night. But, if I were going to do this on purpose, I'd pick one that was. So what else? What if he skimmed it? What if I changed this to 238 instead? Parden gets a key to 238 and goes there. He glances at his ticket, and it looks like a quick match.

No. No Merchant to meet him. That'd be a giveaway.

Clavin wandered away from the key locker.

What if someone wanted to kill Rige and Garner? How hard would it be to put on a green Caller-cap and give someone the wrong key?

Another head shake.

"No. Still, no Merchant to meet him."

Clavin noted the look from a girl who overheard him.

"Just getting senile."

She smiled and moved on.

But what if I changed the number back there and then pretended to be the Merchant? Of course, to do that, I'd have to forge a document and I'd have to know the confirmation code on Rige and Garner's way-tickets.

Forget it.

Clavin stopped and watched as a young man very nearly fell on his face while staring at a passing woman. Everyone burst into laughter as the embarrassed young man beat a hasty retreat.

Newbie, he snorted. *Hasn't yet clued in. We're all stunners here. Even himself if he'd look in the mirror. Always fun to watch 'em make fools of themselves. Getting distracted like that can get you killed on a Path.*

"Wait!"

Garner and Rige, though not green, were still relatively fresh. What if they got distracted? What if the Merchant was a Merchantess and, in turn, distracted by them? Staven said they were fun to hang out with.

Garner and Rige are hanging out in their favorite spot. They've done this before and have made a splash. A junior Merchant, female, has worked with them before and is taken by one or both. Instead of tasking a Caller, she goes and gets the key herself. But she calls for the wrong key. She skims the way-tickets she has and gets the wrong key.

"Yep."

She finds our two studs and offers to walk them to the gate personally. Slight break of protocol but, hey, what's the difference, right? So our two oxen follow her like sheep to the slaughter. Why check their tickets too carefully? She's already done it.

"You poor schmuks," he whispered. "No doubt, one of you did a quick skim of the number before pushing on and missed the mismatch. Let's look this girl up."

And say what? You killed Rige and Garner by flirting so well? Where's the fault? A break in protocol, a little distraction and, poof, you're dead. We know better on the Path, but here in the Inn?

Clavin shrugged.

He went to Hall-Records; it was a ten-minute stroll.

"Hello," he said to a man, and he got right to the point, "I'd like to see the records for Drenin 26, Samlin outbound runs. I'd like to know three things. First, what was the gate number for me that night? Second, what was the gate number for Walkers Rige and Garner? And, lastly, what is the name of the Merchant who contracted their loads?"

"Certainly. One moment."

The man went back down a shelf, pulled off a large book, brought it back, and lay it out on a large table sized to hold it. He soon had the answers.

"You ran Gate 943. Rige and Garner Lossenfell ran Gate 948. The Merchant was Liallen Shades."

Clavin nodded. "Thank you."

Clavin returned to the main concourse and asked around for Liallen. He found her without much trouble.

Liallen Shades was a Merchant who stood out distinctly in a place characterized by people distinct in their beauty. Like most in Traveler's Inn, she was beautiful, yes. But at 5'6", Liallen was short for an Inner woman. Since female Travelers tended to contrive their ideals somewhat taller, it was the habit of all who entered the Inn to do so as well. Liallen was, thus, quite outstanding in her selection of 5'6" for her height. Otherwise, she matched any Inner in fitting an ideal—beautiful appearance, though hers bore somehow a unique quality.

Her hair ran in jet-black rivulets midway down her back. It framed a narrow aquiline face set off by cat-green eyes. Aside from her choice of height—and teeth that weren't brilliantly white as was the Inn norm—she was beautiful in every other way.

"Liallen Shades?"

"Yes?"

"I'm Clavin Roth. May I ask you a question?"

She arched her eyes, cocked her head sideways, and returned an alluring smile.

"Ranger Roth. Of course. What may I do for you?"

Little Vixen, this one.

"Do you recall a couple of months ago, two twins by the name of Rige and Garner?"

She straightened, and her eyebrows wrinkled as she thought for a second.

"Why, yes. Very nice fellows. I liked them a lot."

"Do you, by any chance, recall the last time you saw them?"

Her eyes appeared to focus elsewhere for a minute, and then her smile faded. She nodded. "Yes, I do. It was their final Crossing. What a shame."

"Did you walk them to their gate?"

She looked surprised at the question. "It's not protocol."

"I know. Sometimes people break protocol, though."

"Well, I'm fairly certain I didn't. I certainly don't recall doing so. Why are you asking?"

Clavin paused as he scuffed the toe of his boot across the floor.

Do I tell her I think that she killed them?

"Is something wrong?" she demanded.

And if I am wrong?

He made his decision. "No, not really. I knew them," he lied, "and was trying to make sense of the final details of their lives. Someone told me you had walked them to their gate."

"I see. For what purpose?"

Now what?

He blew out a breath. "I don't know why you'd have walked them to their gate. I was ... I just ..." *Um! What do I say?*

She saved him. "No, what is your reason for trying to make sense of their last Crossing?"

Ah! So ... say what? Um ...

"I was thinking of writing a letter and sending the account of their last Crossing to their parents. Perhaps it would give them some closure."

Her voice softened. "Oh. That is a lovely thought. But, Clavin, don't you think that something like that would be best delivered in person? A letter would be a little impersonal, don't you think?"

The thought of that meeting made his stomach queasy.

God, no.

"Of course, you're right."

Another pause followed.

"Well," she broke into the silence, "good luck, Ranger Roth. It's a fine thought. For my part, I only met them at the transfer of the cargo to them. They came down to Wagon Hall, and I checked all the paperwork, gave them the goods, and bid them on their way. I believe I had other shipments going out that date too." She paused, smiled, and touched his sleeve. "And I'm sorry for your grief."

"Bad or good?" he mumbled, more to himself than to her.

"What? I'm sorry? What was that?"

Idiot. Keep your mouth shut.

He shook his head. "Nothing. But ..."

Shut up! Shut up and move on!

"But what? Is there something you want to ask me?"

Clavin sighed. "What do you think? Is grief good, or is it bad?"

Liallen paused. She wrinkled one corner of her mouth and let her eyes drift up and away. Clavin waited it out. It was like they were bound together by awkward conversation, neither wanted to be rude and simply walk away.

"I guess," she began slowly, "it depends on what the source of the grief is? If you're sad because of a sad situation, then it can be good. If you're sad because of something you did, it depends on whether or not you're trying to fix it. If you are, then it's good grief. If you're not, then it's bad."

She shrugged. "Does that make sense?"

He nodded as she continued to explain her view.

"I believe grief that comes because of something we do is really guilt in disguise. I think God gives us ... or if you don't believe in God for some reason, guilt somehow all by itself serves the very useful purpose of calling our attention to things we have done wrong. But once we have realized that wrong, grief is no longer needed. It's done its job. Once we take steps to correct the wrong, then we don't need the guilt anymore. That's when we need to let go of the guilt, and when we do that, the grief will pass too. As long as we refuse to do what's right, I think guilt has the right to hang onto us. We've not let it do its job of correcting how we live. We go on doing whatever we were doing before, and the guilt never goes away."

Clavin nodded again.

"Does that make sense?"

"Unfortunately, it does."

"Unfortunately?"

Clavin Roth, shut up! New topic. Change the subject.

"Liallen, can I ask you something else?" He barely

waited for her to nod. "Why did you contrive your-self short?"

"Excuse me?" A confused look crossed her face.

"All the other women in the Dream make themselves at least four inches taller. You chose to be short. Why is that?"

She smiled her smile again. Clavin could see that she was put off by his sudden departure from the serious conversation, but he didn't care. He was relieved.

"I'm unattractive?"

"Of course not. Every girl here is a knockout. But they all went tall. You went short. Why?"

Her smile widened. "Because," she leaned forward and whispered, "this is the real me."

"What? You mean ...?"

She nodded.

"You look like this in the real-world?"

"You're shocked."

"I'm amazed. Wow."

"And you?"

"Me? Me what?"

"How do you look in the real-world?"

"Uhmm, that's sort of personal, you know."

"You asked me why I was short."

Bound and pegged.

"Liallen, in waking-world, I'm completely average. Just a regular, average guy. Five-ten, short brown hair, twenty pounds overweight. You'd scan right over me in a crowd and never notice I was there."

She paused. "You don't know that. There's more to you than just looks, you know."

Clavin smiled. "I *am* a witty fellow."

"At least *half* of one," she joked.

Clavin laughed in reply to the barb.

"Ouch. Not bad yourself. Look, Liallen, I need to be going. It's been a pleasure talking to you. If I can ever do anything for you, let me know. Okay?"

She smiled. "I will, Ranger Roth. I think what you're doing is very sweet. Let me know how it goes, will you?"

He nodded, reluctant to even appear to agree to the request, then left.

Clavin should have felt lighter as he stepped through the Veil onto the Path, now that he thought the mystery was solved. He was sure it wasn't his fault. Liallen had doubtless forgotten the details of that night. It had been a while after all. Why would she remember flirting with them? He was sure it was her. Yet something still nagged. He chose to ignore it.

Before him lay this Crossing's version of the golden wheat fields of Samlin in spring. Workers scythed the fields down and bunched the wheat into bundles. Wagons came down the rows to collect them. Harvest time was in full swing. At his back was the door of Samlin tower. He checked his gear and headed out. *Pretty blasé, but it's nice and quiet.* He crested the hill that had risen before him and looked down at the town. A half-hour later, he came to its outskirts. A sign there was posted:

Welcome to South Orrow

No hyphen. He shrugged and walked on till he found a stable where he turned in. "Hello there, any horses for sale?" he called to the stalls.

A man popped out. "Righto, we have a few. What are you looking for?"

"A fast horse to carry me to Cordis and directions on how best to get there."

"Yaw. Simple. Ride out the north road, and you'll be there in five days. I've got three or four horses that will make the ride easy enough. Two goldens."

"Excellent," said Clavin as he pulled out the coins. "Tack and harness?"

"One more."

Clavin handed him three large gold coins.

"Any problems along the way? Issues that may slow me down? Deserts, bogs, such as that?"

"Aye, toward the end is a right large bog of blue peat and silver ghosts, they say. Don't know much about it though."

Silver ghosts? Why couldn't he have said "misty," or "spooky?" He shook himself. *Just another Blue Bog crossing this time.*

"Summat wrong, yung master?" asked the man.

"Not a bit. Just a chill. Saddle me up, if you'd be so kind, and I'll be on my way." Clavin rode to the north end of town, verified with a local that the road led to Cordis, and rode out on a path formed solely of red brick, so dark in its hue that it could almost be black. He found it disturbing. A subliminal Chark began to play in his bones. *Dreamer headache?* He shrugged and rode on. *It'll pass. Five days to Cordis.*

It was on the second day that the terrain took a dramatic change. Clavin rode out of a forest to behold a rainstorm like none he had ever seen which drummed the ground an arrow-flight onward. Melon-sized raindrops fell from the sky, *ker-thump*ing the earth, throwing up mud slicks which burst upward and out, pocking the water-soaked ground in their fury.

"Cripes." He pulled his horse to a stop and dismounted. *Can't ride through that.* "Well, boy, time to say goodbye." He strode down the path to study it closer. After just a few paces, the rain began to fall on him in normal-sized drops that expanded as he forged on. By the time they reached fist-sized, he had stopped and retreated. *That's quite a pounding.* He mulled it over. *Go 'round, under, or over?* He pondered the vials that he carried, the spells that he knew, the tricks and the rhymes. None seemed to help. *I am not going to be stopped by rain. There's nearly always a way. But what? What have I missed? Wait. What is that?* He closed his eyes and listened. He was sure he heard something else besides the drumming, but it was so soft it was easy to miss under the beat of the rain.

He called forth a little horn from his pouch and placed it against his ear. Then he heard it. Music. An old dirge of a boy going off to war, maybe never to return. One of Clavin's favorites. Clavin began to hum. And then he began to sing. "Oh, Danny Boy ..." As he sang, the drops grew smaller, but the rain did not lessen. "Ah," he said, stopping his song.

The large rain returned immediately.

Clavin went back to the horse, remounted, and began to sing. He rode into the rain—now nothing more than a light, weeping shower. Clavin sang till he was hoarse and tired of his own voice. He had tried other songs, but it was only the first that did the trick on the rain. After five hours, he rode out of it and stopped for a much-needed rest.

It was on the fifth day that he arrived at a place where the ground fell away, but the path continued. A bridge— an extension of the road, really—hung from nothing and was supported by nothing, yet it extended across the vast gorge and disappeared into the distance. It was easily wide enough for one to walk, but the absence of any side railing intimidated.

He peeked over the edge of the precipice and could not see a bottom even though the sun shone down from its noonday position. *That's a fall.* He looked again for the other side of the ravine but couldn't see it. *Long walk on a narrow bridge. I think I'll leave the horse.* He tested the bridge to be sure that it was real and would hold him. All his magic said that it was. *As real as anything else in the Dream, so far as the magics can say. Off then.* He walked for an hour at a brisk, determined march when he came to a tall frame of darkest black marble which straddled the bridge. The frame held two silver doors locked in the middle.

Geez. He stared at the marble. *Why does this bother me? It's just a silly doorway on a bridge. Geez.* He paused to take stock and a breath. *Okay, so it is a bridge over a bottomless gorge. With no side rails. And with no apparent means of being held up. So, okay, still. They're just doors.*

"Silver doors," he muttered.

Shut it.

He took a deep breath and held it as he pushed on the doors with a staff drawn from his pouch. They squealed in protest but opened before him. On the other side stood a man with a book, and beside him a huge knight in black armor.

Here we go.

"Ah," said the man to the knight, "someone has opened the door. Protocol met. Now you can go onward."

Clavin watched the pair approach. *Interesting.*

"Nay," replied the deep-voiced knight. "But be my companion here and beyond."

"I should not do so," said the man brandishing the book, "the book does not allow it."

"Nevertheless, come."

"Very well."

So the two came toward Clavin, who was then forced to call out, "Sirs, the path is too narrow for three. Please let me pass on your right."

"No," replied the black knight. "We must go on together. You must go back."

Irrational bolt bucket.

"It is an hour's walk to return and but a moment to pass. Please, good knight, allow me to pass."

The knight paused.

"Lay thee down, and we shall pass over you."

Yeah, right.

"You could lay down and let *me* pass over *you*."

The knight drew forth his sword. "Go back or lay down. That is all I shall allow."

Clavin shrugged and drew his own blade. The fight was brief; it ended when Clavin managed to trip the knight and tumble him headfirst off the bridge. Clavin fixed the other with a look and demanded his name.

"Rotocol. Peter Rotocol. I attended Sir Slaine on many a trip. I shall do so no more. Had I left him at the door, as the book commanded, he'd be with us now," he lamented.

"I bear you no ill, Peter, but I cannot trust you will let me pass in peace. Lay face down on the path and let me cross peacefully or go back ahead of me. It is your choice."

Peter lay down; Clavin stepped over and was again on his way.

The next day, just before noon, he arrived at a forested bog over which steam drifted in the colors of red, orange, and green. The road dipped into the water of the bog in which blue vines floated in thick, choking mats. Beside the road stood a sign which pointed left.

Cradeiss, 2 Miles

He tried on his boots and tried out his flute, both magics he'd used on previous Crossings. Neither one worked. *Hmmm. What's new this time? Danny Boy?* He began to sing even as he took a step forward. His foot sank into the water, and he stepped back, stopping his song. *Nope.* He pondered a moment. *Maybe the bread this time around?* He shrugged. *Out of bread. Time to find Pictu.*

He turned left and headed for Cradeiss. A half-hour later, he entered the town and asked a man about crossing the bog.

"Yai, crossing the bog is what yer wanting tuh do, is it now? Cheaper to go 'round. But if it's a crossing yer set on, you'll be needing the Frost Archer to do it."

"How long to go around?"

"Aww, three days, mayhap four."

Clavin shook his head.

"Too long, I'm afraid. Where can I find this Frost Archer? And what is his name?"

"Pictu, he's called. Take the Woodsman's Way road two miles to his cottage. You'll find him there. Unless, of course, he's here in the town."

"If he is here, where then would I find him? I'll make a quick check before setting off."

Fifteen minutes later, Clavin set off on the Woodsman's Way road. He walked along with a careful eye out for dragons and anything else that could ruin his day. Nothing did, and he soon arrived in a glade adorned by a cottage, framed by a stream, and home to a man who sat working on arrows.

Clavin knew him immediately and walked straight up to him. The man stood in greeting, and Clavin spoke first. "Hello, are you the Frost Archer of the Blue Bog, by any chance?"

"Indeed. How can I help you? Do you have need of crossing the bog this day?"

"Correct. How long will it take? Four or five hours?"

"Four, if we leave now. I know it's expensive, but the charge is two golden sovereigns."

Clavin pulled out two golden coins and handed them over.

Pictu squinted at them and then bit on the metal. He pocketed the money and reached for a large quiver of arrows along with two of his bows.

"Very well, let us be off."

Clavin followed the man down a path, over a footbridge spanning the water, and down a deer trail that ended in the bog waters, blued from the stain of the grasses that grew there.

Pictu stopped, drew forth an arrow, and launched it at a tree in the distance. It flew true and stuck, but what was most interesting was that the water beneath the flight of the arrow froze solid and steamed in the dappled sunlight.

"Quickly now," said Pictu as he strode forward onto the ice and over the bog.

Nice. I'll buy some before we part ways.

"How long will the ice last?"

"It will hold the weight of two men, fully equipped, for a time of near on two minutes. Past that, you risk breaking through the melting ice."

Pictu arrived at the tree and fired another arrow ahead but, before setting off, pulled out the one embedded next to him.

"So, you only need two arrows then to cross the bog? The others are in case of breakage or loss?"

"Close. Breakage and loss are issues as you have cleverly surmised. But each arrow is only good for ten flights. After that, they have no more power. So it will require many arrows. My quiver holds thirty, which is more than sufficient. But at times we will follow some paths that exist inside the bog and conserve the arrows lest chance requires them later."

"Very wise. Lead on."

They walked for two hours and then, onto the ice path ahead of them from behind the tree of Pictu's latest shot, stepped out a knight, black in his armor, very much like the one from the bridge.

Pictu paused.

Clavin's internal alarms went off.

"What shall we do?" Pictu asked. "The ice will hold only two. It cannot bear the weight of all three. Shall I use another arrow? We have plenty."

And probably have to fight him anyway on this slippery slope?

Clavin shook his head as he looked for another tree. He saw one off to the left.

"Shoot that one there, if you can."

Pictu looked at it, nodded, drew the arrow and shot the tree. A new path formed, and they headed off on it.

The dark knight stopped and stared at them without speaking. He took off at a run.

He's coming for me.

Clavin reached into his pouch and pulled forth a large hammer. He stopped and smashed at the ice over which they had just crossed. He backed away and continued to widen the gap. The knight reached the tree they had just left and turned up the ice on the path they now trod. He rushed at them like an un-tethered oxcart.

Clavin stood up and stepped back, replaced his hammer, and drew his sword.

The rushing knight leaped to cross the gap.

He smashed through the thinning ice on Clavin's side, disappeared with a slurp, and didn't come up again.

Who's the man?

"Who was that poor knight? Did you know him?" asked Pictu behind him.

Clavin turned around. "No. But he clearly meant to do us harm. Let's keep moving."

Pictu turned and headed off.

"He'd have taken more care if he'd known that the path could only support two," said Pictu ahead.

It could only support two. Just like the bridge was only two wide. He pondered that as he walked along behind Pictu. *It could only support two.* He kept returning to the thought. And, finally, an hour later, it hit him. *My Path could only have supported two. They double up for leeway. There's no way Garner, Rige, and I could have walked my Path together for even a bit. Which means what?*

His eyes flared open. "Oh my god."

Garner and Rige weren't on the wrong path.

I was.

HARD TIMES

Clavin had dreamed of Rige and Garner the night before, and that was not a good thing. Thus, as he paused for a moment in front of the Veil, an uncommon discord warred with his natural calm.

You're the man. Go on and prove it.

He stepped in. After three strides, he cleared the fog and found himself upon a sunlit path.

He took in a clean breath as he glanced about him.

Sunny and Charkless.

He stepped off of the path and ran his *pouch* test. He was pleased with the results, finding the things he expected, and set out on his Crossing. He descended from the castle, 'round a soft wooded trail, bedded down in brown pine needles, which allowed peeks at the lake that surrounded the isle.

Soon he arrived at the boat dock where he stepped into a boat and cast off its mooring. As he sat down, the boat surged as it moved off, away from the pier. Clavin stoppered his ears and waited for the mermaids' appearance. A half-minute later, he saw them coming. He waved at the girls and waited for their men, but none appeared, and he left the girls in his wake.

The boat soon arrived at the usual landing where he jumped out and moored the craft. *I like Crossings that start with the lake. Soothing. What I need.* Clavin strolled up the path and into the wood that abutted the boathouse. The path was equally pleasant, and he came out the other side in a matter of minutes to see a town a long bowshot away. Where the path left the wood, another joined it, running left to right. A sign stood on a post five feet away. He stopped to glance at it.

Samlintown   <

Ragtown, 30 miles   ^

Noway, 80 miles   v

Samlin Castle   >

He walked into the town, down the regular street, and found the stable that usually sold him his horses. The horses were there, as was the owner, who sold him a mount and answered some questions.

"So, what is the terrain like between here and Cordis? Any obstacles or monsters or armies or such?"

"Cordis? Ay've naver hard of it," replied the man as he saddled Clavin's new mount.

Clavin didn't worry; this had happened before. "Where can I find a map of the lands? Is there a sage nearby I can talk with?"

"Thaat der is," agreed the man.

Clavin got the directions and walked through the town, turned down a street, and into a door surrounded with glyphs. Beyond the door was a large room filled with books and with scrolls ordered on shelves on the left wall. The wall on the right held cabinets which housed bottles of liquids, and the wall on the back held instruments and other items. *Is this what I think it is?*

"Hello," he called out.

Through a door in the back came a woman whose face he knew from a previous Crossing. But he knew many that way, so it caused him no alarm.

"Hello, good sir, how may I help you?"

"Madame, I came in today in search of a map, but now that I'm here, I see that you sell much more than those. What are these cordials locked up in the cabinets?"

She appraised him. "You have the look of a warrior, but there is something about you that suggests you are more." She stepped to one of the cabinets and pointed at a blue vial. "This is a vial of compression. In it, you can store one thousand gallons of liquid. Many Merchants use it when entering the desert. The cost of this one vial is two hundred golds. Do you have such sums? If not, I need not continue. The others cost even more."

Holy smokes. It's like the hoard of a dragon-mage, but without the fight.

Clavin opened his pouch and thought of ... *diamonds.* He pulled out a bag and opened it onto a counter. Brilliant stones poured out onto it.

The woman's eyes widened at this, and she leaned over to inspect them.

"May I test them?" she asked.

"Please do."

"Shandra," she called to the back room, "come out here, please."

A moment later, a younger woman came out to meet them.

"Shandra, could you test these, please?"

The young lady waved her hands over the stones as she spoke some words.

She nodded to herself, then pulled out a vial and sprinkled the stones with some powder. She looked up at Clavin.

"This is quite a fortune you have here, good sir."

She looked at the first woman.

"Badti, I would estimate their value at eight thousand golds."

"Thank you, Shandra."

Badti looked back at Clavin with a smile and a nod.

"What would you like to see?"

Clavin spent an hour in an attempt to buy out the store. The large weapons and armor he left. He preferred to travel light and trust to his quickness, rather than trod heavy, asking plate to defend him.

It took all of his diamonds and some of his gold.

Not too much left. May have to plunder some hoards when the opportunity arises.

"Now, lady Badti, I must return to the task that brought me first to this wondrous shop. My original task was mundane; I simply needed advice concerning the Crossing to Cordis."

"I think we can throw that in for free," she said with

a smile as she dropped the gold in her purse. Badti moved to the wall with the books and drew one down and opened it up. It was soon replaced, and another drawn down. After numerous books, she turned to her maps.

"Cordis, you say? I'm having trouble locating any such place."

What? "Castle Cordis is typically found beyond a blue bog or, perhaps, outside of a great desert. Could I see a map of the area?"

"Of course. Here is a map of the kingdom, and we are here," she said, pointing, "in Samlin Town."

The dot of Samlin was drawn against a large lake; Samlin Castle was depicted on the one island that lay in the lake's middle. The map showed the Kingdom of Garfall bounded on the north by the Vast Desert waste.

Vast Desert this time.

"My lady, do you have a map of what lies across the Vast Desert?"

She shook her head.

"Good sir, the desert is aptly named, for none have crossed." She scrunched her eyebrows as she reconsidered. "Or, rather, none have returned from attempting to cross it."

I'm sure Cordis is there. But if I'm wrong and try to cross? I'm dead.

Seeing him hesitate, Badti spoke again. "I'm sorry, good sir. In this, I cannot help you."

He nodded. "I must consider this. Perhaps I shall return again."

"You shall be most welcome."

Clavin roamed about the town and asked various people if they had ever heard of Castle Cordis. No one had.

He paused for a drink in a nearby tavern marked by two doves, pierced with one shaft.

"Water and wine, if you please," Clavin requested.

The bartender nodded and soon set them down in front of Clavin.

"Two silver," said the man.

Clavin handed him a gold and waited for change.

"So, have you ever heard of a place called Cordis?" Clavin asked.

"Nuuph, 'fraid not."

"No one else has either."

"What about it?"

"Cordis? I need to get there, and to get there, I need to know where it is."

"Aww. Quest or sumwat?"

Clavin nodded.

"Well, ye could try the Well."

"What? The Well?"

"Yaah, the Quesson Well."

"The Questing Well?"

"Well, it could well be that too, I suppose."

Too many wells *in this conversation.*

"Are you telling me that there is a well, as in a source of water—a hole in the ground with a bucket above it—that I can go to and get questions answered?"

"Shar."

Okay, we're rolling again.

"Marvelous, where is it?"

"Well, now, I reckon that depends."

Ah, crap.

"On what?" he asked politely.

"On the saker a curse."

"You're placing a 'curse on the seeker' or do you mean 'on the seeker, of course'?"

"Right."

Ahhhhhhhhhhhhhhhh.

"Which. One?"

"On thu seaker, o course."

Of course I can ask for more directions, but I might go insane deciphering the answers. Clavin sighed. *But he's the first one to know anything.* "Alright, good man, please tell me, how do I find this Well of Questions that you speak of?"

The man raised a finger and signaled Clavin to wait as he walked off down the bar and soon came back with a towel, words stitched into the fabric.

Words of a riddle on a dirty bar towel. Clavin shrugged and studied the lines stitched into it.

> *The Quesson Well that you would find*
> *is out of sight and out of mind.*
> *In a cave of burning black,*
> *the letters here keep you on track.*

I just want to know where Cordis is. What's the deal with all this hassle? "Are there some black caves around here?"

"Shar. Yuh go out dis her dur ..."

Clavin focused on the slurred speech and questioned the man on the bad parts to be sure he had it correct. He thanked the bartender and left, with towel in hand, glad to be free of bartender slur. He rode out of the east gate where he spied a sign that read, "Black Caves, two miles." He rode on, determined to solve his little puzzle without losing the day. After five minutes, he saw black smoke in the distance. He rode another five minutes and stopped as his horse crested a hill. In the pause he could hear, off to his left, the soft squeak of metal. Soft fingers of trepidation ran up his spine. *What is that?* He shook his head. *Ignore it and keep going.* But, after a short inward struggle, he turned his horse, rode toward the sound, downhill, back up, and paused at the scene beneath him.

There at the bottom, sitting 'round a campfire, sat two silver knights, spears laying by them. Between them sat a gleaming, silver bucket with a short tail of rope attached to its handle. They looked up at him and rose to their feet, grasping their spears and speaking words over them.

He sighed. *Leave 'em be. Ghosts of your mind. No need to kill them again.* Clavin turned his horse back to the original trail and rode on. After ten minutes more, the ground changed from pleasant forest to rough, quarry-like stone. Over the next five, the path drove in between two cliffs that rose higher on each side as he rode onward. The gray rock walls at his side turned black by slow demarcations. The black smoke called him on like a dirty beacon, and soon he dismounted in front of the mineshaft from which the smoke rose.

Like a dirty, black dragon. Let's hope there's not one.

His horse did not shy from the mouth of the cave, so hidden dragons seemed to be unlikely. Clavin tendered a light and headed into the cave. Thirty feet in, he came to the first split. Over each entrance was a single letter: T over one, J over another.

Clavin looked back at his towel. "Reveal," he commanded. Nothing happened. "Explain," he requested. Same response. "Which way to the Quesson Well, if you please?" he plead of the towel. *I'm pleading with a dirty bar towel. Yeez.* He studied the letters and shook his head. *Not a clue. Poem?*

He arranged one in his mind and spoke it seven times.

> "Dirty bar towel in my hand,
> by the Well help me to stand.
> Show me now the way to there,
> where I can ask my question fair."

He stared at the towel for a minute before he looked back up.

Nope.

Clavin stepped back and studied the walls. He took a vial and rubbed a drop onto his left eyelid, but nothing changed to his sight. Next, he pulled out some bread and tossed it before him into the right and left tunnels. Still, nothing happened. He drew his sword with his right hand and slowly extended his left pinky finger before him, down the right hall, under the J. He pulled the finger back with no effort and sighed in the throes of mixed relief and annoyance.

Somehow the letters tell me the right turn. "Correct turn," *I should say in this case.* Clavin turned right and stepped into the tunnel. Thirty feet down, the tunnel it split again into two. Over the tunnels, letters were carved, an L and a G. He redid his tests and took the rightmost and walked another thirty feet down where it split yet again. *K and S this time. Let's go back.*

Clavin turned 'round and, after a thirty-foot backtrack, he came to a place where the tunnel split ten different ways. *Holy Carp! The tunnel is magic.* He smacked himself on the head. *What do you expect when hunting magic wells?* "Idiot." But Clavin's viewing ointment was still fresh, so he could see the footsteps he had made, and they led him safely out of the tunnels back to where he began. *Let's try going left.*

The next two tunnels sported the letters H, and M. Clavin began to work in and out of the first two levels gathering all the combinations. He pulled out some paper and a quill pen and began to write:

```
        T               J
    H       M       L       G
    N   E   B   A   Z   A   K   S
```

Left, left, left spells THN. Left, left, right spells THE. "Possibility." *Left, right, left spells TMB, Left, right, right spells TMA.* Clavin shook his head. He worked out the rest, and none of them looked any better to his eyes. *Okay, let's push on down the THE trail and see what is next.*

When he arrived at the next split, the letters were a Q and an F. He looked at the towel again and looked up with a smile. *I'll go down the Q and see if one tunnel has a U over it.* Stepping along, he found the U and finished his way to the tunnel's end using the bar towel as his guide. A little more than half a mile down, he came to the final K and entered a large room.

Dots of flame adorned the walls, but Clavin left his own light source on. In the center of the room, a pit punctured the earth. Clavin approached, each step punctuated by a pause as he probed for a trap. Above the Well sat a stone and timber structure which supported a rope hanging slack from a wheel. Attached to the wheel was a handle, but nothing was attached to the rope. Up near the top, four simple words gave Clavin pause: "Draw up your answer." Into Clavin's mind came the image of the silver bucket which sat between the two knights he'd avoided. *Hell's bells.* Clavin stomped back the way he had come and made his way out and up the black ravine. He rode back to where he'd seen them and dismounted short of their location, wary of traps.

I could potion myself silent and sneak upon them. He shook his head. *Why? They're waiting for me. I'll just go smash them down again and be on my way.* So Clavin walked down the hill to the knights, and they rose to meet him, bucket behind them. They spoke words to their armor even as Clavin spoke the same ones to his own. *Now they have spell-magic?* He shrugged. "Sir Knights, is that the bucket from the Quesson Well behind you?"

In reply, they moved toward him and leveled their spears at his heart.

I guess that's a yes. Clavin charged at the nearest one and struck at the spear with a resounding blow. The spear did not shatter, and Clavin dodged back, surprised. *Cripes.* Clavin struck twice more, his sword denting armor both times but not destroying any. One of the knights slammed him into a backward somersault. Clavin retreated, cast his stutter-step spell, and returned to the fight.

Clavin found it far easier to dodge from the knights' blows while he managed to strike them over and over. After some minutes, and having taken a few more hard strikes, he struck into a gap, punched through the mail, and killed one of the knights. A moment later, Clavin put him down too. Clavin leaned on his sword and caught his breath. *That was a darned hard-fought battle. Much harder than last time. What happened to my magic?*

Clavin walked over to a tree and struck into it. His sword sank four inches deep. *Magic works fine. Just not on their armor.* "They have their own magic, as effective as mine." *Cripes. Maybe it IS mine. Maybe they learned it from me the last time.* "Oh, crap. That would mean ..." He shook his head. "Oh, crap." *If they start learning my magic each time I use it on them, then they'll get continuously stronger, which means that someday ...* "Oh, crap."

Calm down. They aren't real people. They cannot learn.

It is all in your head. You are calling them up. Just shut them down. Stop thinking about them, and you'll be back on track. "Right," he said, taking a breath to calm down. *But you did kill them.* "Shut up."

Clavin retrieved the bucket, rode back to the tunnel, relocated the Well, and tied the bucket back on. He lowered it down, then asked his question. "What is the way to Castle Cordis?" He then cranked the bucket up and sat it down. Nothing happened. He had a pail full of clear water. "So?" Still nothing. Clavin poured a little of the water upon the floor to see if perchance it would spell out an answer. It didn't. *Here goes.* He raised the bucket to his lips and took a drink. He sat the bucket down again and heard the words in his mind. *Cordis lies ten thousand miles across the Vast Desert.* He was pleased. *As expected.*

He paused. *Long trip with them on your tail.* He shook his head. *No. You finished them this round. It is doubtful that they'd resurrect.* He shrugged. *But it could happen. From now on, you've got to hoard your magic like never before. Like a miser with gold, you've got to protect it. Don't bring it out unless you really need to. At least, not when they are around. You may be in for some really rough waters. Hard times are ahead.*

He nodded.

"Hard times."

335

RATCHET

Clavin arrived at the Night Star and took his privileged seat early and waited. He didn't know whether to scowl or to laugh. *Staven and his hair-brained bets. Why do I care? How'd I let him overrule my policy on meeting newbies? 'Cause you're a kind and considerate person?*

That thought did make him scowl. "Please."

'Cause you think a few good deeds might lighten your guilt.

That ejected a scoffing bark from his lips.

Lighten? How do you lighten something like that? His hair swished as his head rejected the idea. He glanced at the entrance. *"Where are you?"* Clavin returned the pleasant hellos directed at him by various passersby and then released a sigh of relief, or perhaps annoyance, as he saw Staven escorting a man, much older than normal, past the entrance guard and over to his table. Clavin stood. He noted that the man exhibited no glow and reached out a hand.

"Ranger Clavin Roth. Nice to meet you."

They shook, and Clavin gestured to a chair.

"Have a seat." Clavin took his own position and slouched back into his chair. "So, Hunter, what can I do for you?"

Ghost leaned over and propped his elbows on the table. "First, Ranger Roth, thank you so much for granting this meeting. I have heard that you make it a practice to avoid getting to know new people. I understand. I have no intention of trying to make your personal acquaintance or developing a friendship that could bring you pain later. This is strictly business. I just have some questions that you might be able to shed some light on. May I proceed?"

Clavin glanced over at his friend. "Go place your bets, Stave. I think I'm safe." He turned back to Ghost. "So, Hunter, lead on."

Ghost proceeded to pull out a writing quill, ink, and some paper.

Clavin straightened in his chair a little. "You come prepared. I'm impressed. I like to be impressed. So? First question?"

"Sir, you are the most experienced Traveler presently known. Is it possible that, in your Crossings, you have met a person that appeared to be real?"

Clavin's heart jumped a beat as he stiffened. "Real? What do you mean, Hunter? The people on the Paths are merely images constructed by the imaginings of the Dream Group. You know that. What a strange question. What are you getting at?"

Ghost nodded. "Yes, sir, I do know that. But, no one

truly understands the Dream, the Gates, the Crossings. People disappear in Dream collapse and are never seen again. Their bodies are destroyed and can never return. But is it possible that their essence—their souls, I would say—still exist and can re-instantiate on a Path?"

I'm liking you less by the second.

Clavin's response came slow and measured. "That does not seem likely, Hunter. That is more the realm of miracles than magic. You would say their souls, but I have no belief in souls." *Not anymore.*

Hunter paused to make a note before he looked back up. "I have talked to people who insist they have met others on their Crossings that responded like actual people. They talked about their previous lives, about the very Crossing they were in and about how they died. Have you ever heard of such things?"

After a shallow sigh of relief, Clavin replied, "I have. In the cases I know of, the people were known to them before. You know the Paths are formed by the Binder weaving together the Dreams of the Dream Group in interaction with the Traveler himself, correct?"

"I do. I believe I know your thought, but I don't want to taint it by my guessing. Please, continue."

"What is more likely? That the soul of a friend would reappear on a Crossing or that the Traveler himself, unconsciously, recreates the person using his knowledge of their personality to form them so adroitly as to make them seem real? One is akin to resurrection, the other simply Dream-amplified imagination. Which is simpler?"

"The answer, Ranger Roth, depends on your answer to the ultimate question: Is there a God?"

Clavin blinked. "Is there a God? How so?"

Ghost lay his pen down. "If there is a God, then He is spiritual. If He is spiritual, then He lives and rules from a spiritual realm. If there is a spiritual realm, then there is a place for other beings to go to when they die if they too have a spiritual aspect. I believe that we all have a spiritual component and therefore when we die, we go to that place. If there is a place that we can go to then, it is feasible that we, or that eternal part of we that I call the soul, can return from it. If we return on a Path, then we can take on a physical body again and there, in the Dream, experience a resurrection."

Clavin focused down at the table and contemplated the words. A minute passed while Ghost waited quietly. Clavin looked up. "Why does God have to be spiritual?"

Ghost leaned back and steepled his fingers. "If there is a God, then He is the creator of our worlds and therefore of us. If He created our world, He must have been somewhere else since He clearly could not be inside the world He is about to create. That place is what we call the spiritual realm."

"Okay, granted, but why do we have to imagine that this being created our world? Can he not be a God and yet be part of it?"

"Such a being is not God; it is merely a very powerful being. It had a beginning and will have an end. If people can obtain enough power, they could capture or kill such a being, and any being that can be captured or killed by people is not God."

Clavin shrugged. "Sounds like we're talking about definitions."

"We are. But, since I am the searcher, I am the one who gets to apply his definitions. To me, God is the creator and stands outside of our world."

Clavin nodded. "Okay, stipulated. But, unfortunately, I don't believe in God. So, for me, the simpler answer is the other—a figment of our imaginations made solid in the Dream."

"Of course. Now, what if one of these figments told you something that neither you, your Binder, or any member of your Dream Group had knowledge of? What if, later, you validated the facts of it and it was true. What then?"

Clavin shrugged and leaned forward. "You'd have a difficult time proving to me that no one knew, even subconsciously, those details. But, if you could do it, then I'd have to reconsider my stance."

"So, you would agree that, if a Traveler encountered, say, an old friend on a Crossing who knew some information that later turned out to be fact, the Traveler would have reason to believe the person was real."

Clavin squirmed about in his chair. "Or it could be another person from real-world with knowledge of those facts who had somehow made it onto the Traveler's path that night."

Hunter's mouth opened and closed as the idea settled in his mind. "Well, okay, yes, that would be possible." Ghost opened his notebook and made a short annotation in it before replying, "Thank you. I had not considered that.

For now, if we presume that did not happen, are there any other possibilities?"

Clavin mulled it over and shook his head. "No. It would have to be one of those two. Hunter, I was of the impression that you were looking for advice on your Crossings. My friend, Staven, suggested he had an interest in you, so I agreed to meet with you. Yet, you have not asked me anything remotely related to advice on making a Crossing. What is this about?"

Hunter squinted at Clavin before his eyes took on a faraway look. "Ranger Roth, I am willing to confide in you a secret I have vigorously guarded these past two months. You have a very impressive reputation here in the Inn. Can I trust you to keep my secret?"

Clavin's eyes opened a bit wider. *Well, this just got interesting.* "Hunter, so long as your secret isn't covering something illegal or immoral, then yes, I can keep it."

Ghost glanced back at him. "You *can* keep it, but will you?"

"Now, that is a fine splitting of hairs. My dad used to call me on that. You two would have been peas in a pod."

"Will you?"

Clavin lay his hand over his heart. "I, Ranger Clavin Roth, promise to keep your secret to myself only, so long as it does not involve actual crimes or moral failings. Sufficient?"

Ghost Hunter leaned over the table and lowered his voice. "I understand that the Merchants are opposed to allowing people to Travel who enter with a personal vendetta or mission of any sort that could jeopardize the delivery of their goods. But that is not a law, so far as I understand. Is that correct?"

"So far as I know, that is correct. Do you have a vendetta? That might skirt moral failing if you intend to hurt someone, you understand?"

"I do, and I have no such intent. My purpose is simple. I want to know if I can see those who have fallen. Months ago, my two sons fell one night—the same night you made your Ranger run, in fact. I want to see them again, and I don't care what that takes."

Clavin's eyes blew open wide as his breath ran short and his heart pounded like a grinder's water wheel. *No, god, no.* He pushed back from the table to separate himself from the man before him.

Surprise registered on Hunter's face. "Ranger Roth? Are you okay?"

Clavin shook his head. "Ghost Hunter. God. No. Don't do this. Please. Baggage like that ... no, it'll kill you. I should report you. Save your life."

"No one takes my life, but I lay it down. Do not worry for me. I only ask you keep this secret between us."

The sons and now the father. I'll have killed them all. God, no. "Hunter," Clavin pled, "do you not have any family who will miss you? Anyone else to live for?"

"I just want to see them once. One more time. That's all. Then I'll leave." Hunter's eyes misted over and spoke through a tight voice. "Just once more."

Clavin bit the inside of his cheek, hard, and regained

control. He stood, and Ghost followed him up. "Then I pray you see them tonight." *And that I do not.* "Good luck, Ghost. Time for you to go."

Ghost reached out. Clavin forced himself to respond in kind and shake the hand, as he imagined his own dripping red on the floor. After Ghost left, Clavin dropped back down into his seat and covered his face with hands curled into fists while a quiet groan leaked out underneath them.

COVER UP

How do you say something without saying it? Michael wondered as he pondered the lines in his palm.

"Cheat notes?" asked the other.

Michael looked back, confused by the question. "What?"

"I asked you why you are here, and now you are staring at your hand. I just wondered if you were reading the answer?"

Not bad. Michael nodded. *We just might get along.*

"Well, if anything *is* written there, it's too subtle for me."

"Perhaps I can see something then."

Without a word, Michael thrust out his arm, extending his hand for inspection.

"Hmmm. I see the marks of a soft life, much wealth, and of a man with too much time on his hands."

So much for getting along, he decided as he took back his hand. "I'm paying *you*. Remember?"

"So you are. So why the waste of money? I can be of no use whatsoever if you refuse to speak."

"How do I know I can trust you to keep my thoughts secret?"

"I think that is a fair and excellent question. I believe the simplest explanation relates directly to economics. I am a professional counselor to those of wealth and power. You, and others like you, pay me as well as you do because I have an excellent reputation—not only for being able to help people, but also for keeping what secrets I know absolutely secret. Should you leave me and proceed to noise it about that I have been revealing your private secrets, then my business, which relies so heavily upon my reputation, would all but dry up. Unless I want to bring a quick end to my very enjoyable lifestyle, it only makes sense for me to stay altogether quiet. Satisfied?"

Michael thought it over before he responded with a nod. "Okay, I'll buy that."

"Excellent. So, what brings you to my parlor on a fine Lorimen night?"

"Tell me, Counselor, what do you know of the Dream Paths?"

"If we're going to have a personal discussion, you should feel free to speak to me more informally. Please call me Godfrey. Now, as to the Dream Paths, I know more than you might suspect because I have had clients who were Dream Travelers. Beyond what is commonly known, however, I am not at leisure to reveal details from other clients."

"Really? You've had other Travelers here?"

"How is this germane?"

"I, too, am a Traveler."

345

"Clearly not a Walker, for you are known to be an extremely wealthy man in the city. For that same reason, I would guess you to be either a highly seasoned Runner or possibly even a Warrior."

"Reasonable guesswork. But incorrect nevertheless."

"Hmmm, from what I know about Travelers, your apparent wealth tells me that you are neither a Dreamer nor a Router. A Binder or a Merchant then?"

Michael smiled and settled back into his chair. "Nope, but not bad."

Godfrey shrugged. "Very well, I am officially stumped. Are you going to tell me, or is it even something that I need to know?"

"You're giving up, just like that?"

"Plainly, you enjoy being in control of things. I, however, don't have that same need. I am here to help you work out your problems or to provide limited counsel. As you said before, 'you pay me.'"

"True. I'm sorry to be arrogant, but in my profession, some of that is required to survive. Do you know what a Dream Ranger is?"

"Sorry. I must confess that is a new term for me."

"It is the next rank beyond Warrior. That is what I am, newly promoted."

"Ah. Just out of curiosity, how many trips does that take?"

"Fourteen hundred."

"Impressive. Tell me, is there by any chance another title at three thousand?"

"At forty-four hundred. Master."

"And another at ten?"

"Close enough. You would be called Lord should you ever reach that. There are, to my knowledge, no Lords extant, nor have there ever been. Same for Master. You would have to Travel every night for ten years to do it. It can't be done."

"I see. So, Dream Ranger, what brings you here? Something to do with your profession else you would not have revealed this to me, I suspect."

"You are quite right. On both counts." Michael leaned toward his counterpart. "Godfrey, I'm being haunted."

"I presume you mean that in more than just the figurative sense?"

"Exactly so. Two figures have stalked me on my last six trips. Sooner or later, I'm going to run into another bad Chark and, if they're there when that happens, the outcome could be devastating for me. I need to get rid of them. I need to deal with this."

"My understanding of your profession leads me to believe that, for this to happen, these apparitions must be arising from one of four sources: the Dreamer Group, the Dream Binder, the Path itself, or from you."

"Correct. I can save you some guesswork on this point. They are coming from me."

"Well, that eliminates the easy solutions then."

"Changing Dreamer Groups or my Binder?"

"Right."

"Actually, those could be solutions too, but before

taking such a drastic step, I want to try to fix it at the source."

"I agree. So then, what can you tell me about these two figures?"

"I ran into them the first time on my Ranger run, the fourteen hundredth. Their names were Rige and Garner."

"Hmmm. Do these figures match anyone you know?"

"I didn't know it at the time, but they were real people, two other Travelers who had been trapped by magic within the Dream. Garner and Rige. I'm told they were nice fellows."

"Were?"

Michael glanced away. "Dead. They died when my Dream-self met them."

"Ah. I see. Something you did or didn't do led to their deaths, and you blame yourself. Misplaced guilt."

"Misplaced? Maybe you don't get it. I cast a spell upon them, causing a troll that we later fought to only attack them. It worked like a charm. Of course, since they were ensnared, they couldn't use whatever magics they may have had, and so they were doomed. *I killed them.*"

"Well, that's not strictly true, of course. It was the troll who killed them, not you. In any case, we are talking about a Dream, and you cannot be held accountable for things that you do in your Dreams. It would be preposterous. You have stated that you did not know that they were real. So then, are you now to second-guess your every move, when to do so could cause you to hesitate when split-second decisions are necessary? No. It is regrettable.

It is sad. It is not your fault. But, even if it were, feelings of guilt are foolish."

"You really believe that? It's okay? It just seems that, if I made a mistake of some sort in the real-world that caused someone else great harm, it would be equivalent to this situation."

Godfrey took a sip from his glass. "Let us suppose that very thing. Through some accident of yours, another person ends up dead. Why respond with guilt? I will tell you why. Religious theology ingrained into you at an early age is causing you to transfer fear into an emotion that we know as guilt. We who are trained in these matters know better. Michael, the solution to your problem is simple: There is no god. Once you understand that, believe that, know that, then these feelings will disappear."

Michael's eyebrows scrunched. "I'm afraid I don't track your logic."

"Do you have any children?"

"No. I have a nephew, though."

"Excellent. When a small child does something that he has been told is wrong, what do you suppose that he feels?"

"Fear of getting caught for whatever he has done."

"Exactly. The fear of getting caught. In this case, caught by whom?"

"His mom or dad."

"Right. The fear of getting caught is real because there is a real person who has set rules for him to abide by, and he has broken one of them. So children, as they grow, are trained into patterns of behavior by their well-meaning parents to experience fear whenever they do something that has been classified for them as being wrong. Does that make sense?"

"Okay. I suppose. Go on."

"As we grow into adulthood, we take charge of our own lives and actions and cease to rely upon our parents. However, those patterns of childhood are still there. When we do something of which they would have disapproved, we feel a twinge of that old fear. Now, since we know that neither Mom nor Dad is going to *catch* us, we must attribute that fear to something else. But to what? In the depths of our minds, we recall what they told us long ago. About a mythic character who watches us all the time, who knows our thoughts and who, one day, hands out rewards and punishments. Ah. So there is still yet someone to fear. There is god. But imagine this, Michael. What if you could expunge from yourself the concept of god? What happens to the fear? What then, happens to the guilt?"

"I begin to see what you mean. But how can I do this?"

"You must cast off your old chains. You must learn that the past behind has no power over the future ahead. You must learn to accept and depend upon yourself."

Since taking Godfrey's advice, months had passed, and Dream Ranger Clavin Roth had made twenty-four runs on Samlin-Cordis with no more armored ghosts. He found that his personal life back in Lorimen had improved, and he experienced added comfort in his reliance on self. His meetings with Godfrey had proved to be life-changing. No bad manifestation of the chilly darkness, known to the Travelers as the Chark, had blown up since and he looked forward to the next one to prove that the old Clavin was back, better than ever.

Though Michael's personal life on Samlin had made a turn for the better, his relational life on Cordis had taken a decided turn for the worse. His Sister and Mother no longer bothered trying to come see him in the city. Only Kildain and Jase reached out to him anymore.

Michael regretted that he had chosen his particular Dreamer Group based on his dad's recommendations. Those cards, however, were dealt and best not reshuffled, he knew. The only variable that he could safely alter was that of himself, and that, he felt, should be quite enough. No doubt he could have had a lot more fun on the Trails with another, less restrictive, Dreamer Group, but he had what he had.

Clavin stepped through the veil onto the Dream Path with an air of routine expectancy. Every Crossing was different in some ways. Generally, however, the starting and ending points were the same—two castles, one named for each endpoint. Outside of each castle would be a small township in which information about the route could be collected. Today, as there often was, a forest seperated the castle from the town. Clavin, ever the professional, went about his usual routine, rose to his feet, headed into the woods, and left Castle Samlin behind him.

Clavin made his way through the wood, as he wondered what he would find on the path this time, and out the other side to the village of Samlinsk. He entered into the local tavern, the Three Pitchers Inn, and collected directions to Cordis Castle.

"You be headed to Cordis then?" replied the barkeeper. "Well, you've got a right nice little trip ahead of you, my friend. Some two-hundred miles over many a dusty road."

Clavin absorbed what little the barkeeper could tell and, after making more inquiries, pieced together a mental list of the potential dangers while he purchased a local map for reference.

Seven days to Cordis.

Clavin made steady progress for four days before the Chark began to blow. Softly at first, it blew hard against him by the fifth dawn. When he saw the high mountain range rise before him, he could almost feel his hands itch in anticipation.

Just on the other side of this pile of rock is Cordis Castle and journey's end. One more day, he thought as he stroked his sword hilt and a smug grin quirked up the left side of his face.

With that in mind, he found the trailhead, dismounted his horse and, after he'd run through his usual preparations, started his ascent.

Some hours up the mountain, he came across the first signs of trouble. On the trail before him lay the half-eaten remains of three unfortunates.

Always half-eaten. You just can't get good help anymore.
With a shrug and a kick, he cleared the body from his path and moved on. It wasn't long before he came across more such scenes. As he stepped over one body missing its arms, he looked down for a moment.

Need a hand?

He chuckled and moved on.

He climbed for two more hours and came to a mountain village where he paused before a stone gate that stood ajar before him.

"Hello, the gate," he called out grandly.

Out stepped four young men with spears in their hands and fearful looks in their eyes.

Besieged village, act one. "What passes in your fair village?"

"Who are you?" demanded one of the youths.

Blunt.

"I am a Dream Ranger of Samlin trying to pass over this mountain. What village is this then?"

"Nevig," answered another boy.

"Who wants to know?" demanded a third.

"Please call me Traveler," replied Clavin.

"Don't sound like no real name to me," spat the fourth.

Aren't you slack-jawed idiots supposed to be asking for my help right about now? "My mother thought otherwise," answered Clavin in a steady voice. "Now, my friends, it appears that you're having a spot of trouble in this area. I saw the fallen remains of others on the trail. Perhaps I could help you?" *Get the hint?*

"What's a Dream Ranger?" demanded another.

"A type of knight."

The four looked back and forth at each other and shuffled their feet in the dirt, before one gave a response. "Right. Come this way and talk to old Ben."

Finally.

In short order, they had passed through the gate and across the courtyard wherein lay the clear evidence of an encounter with some creature or creatures. Human remains lay about, and blood pooled in sticky puddles.

At least there are no flies. That's one for the Binders.

The boys led Clavin before an older man who sat amidst various articles of clothing atop some steps, which led into a building. Dirty and ragged, he lounged there eating an apple, taking his rest.

"Who's this?" he asked as he looked down at Clavin.

"Ben, this here fellow calls himself Traveler. Says he's a knight and wants to help us out," said a boy beside Clavin.

"Is that so?" He tossed his apple aside and rose to his feet. "How interesting. How fortunate. You have come at our point of need. You are most welcome, but nevertheless, I have a question."

First, you wash under one arm. Then you wash under the other. "What would you ask, wise, Sir?" Clavin replied.

"Why have you come here? Why would you help us? What, indeed, can we do to earn the strength of your arm in battle?"

That's three questions, you ignorant bag of dirt. "I needs must traverse this mountain as quickly as may be. To that end, I seek a guide to help me avoid any unnecessary pitfalls. If I can aid you, then you can aid me."

"Our need is simple yet great. 'Round the other side of this valley, four hours from here, is another village. In it live the sons of our enemies. Every day they come and attack us, seeking to slay those of us who remain. We, on the other hand, being weaker, require the cover of night to return the favor. If you were to aid us, we could break through their gate and bring an end to this ongoing conflict."

What if I just kill all of you and torch this place instead? "Why then do they attack you?"

"The temple you see behind me is the heart of our village. Within lies the source of our strength. They wish to have it, and we wish to keep it."

"Is this treasure theirs?" Clavin asked pointedly.

"Nay, it is not so. The treasure is ours and must not be revealed."

Sure it is. But really what difference does it make? It's just a Dream. "Very well. Night is but five hours off. If we leave now, we can rest ourselves along the way and be ready for battle come nightfall."

They moved along the wall of the great valley as the sun sank to its invisible mooring lost behind the ancient peaks that rose about them. From high above could be heard the faint screech of an eagle-like bird in flight as it swooped and dove, looking for prey. Prey, he felt, would be difficult to find, for in the area about them, the plant life was stunted. No other sign of life, be it beetle or berry, was to be found.

"So, what are those birds that call out to us?" he asked Ben, who walked behind him.

"We call those White Stalkers," replied Ben with a tremor of fear. "Once they were a source of great danger to us but, thankfully, no more."

"Why is that? What changed?"

"We grew up and grew strong. Now *they* fear to approach *us*. It is well."

"Alrighty. Tell me of these peaks 'round which we travel. What are they called?"

"We call them the 'Ribs of the Master.'"

"Nice," he replied wryly. "That puts us where? In his stomach?"

"No, not at all. Just above, I would say."

"Right," said Clavin as he pictured a giant, red ruby in the confines of the temple he had recently left. "How much farther then? Do you have a place in mind at which to rest?"

"Little past an hour from now, we know of a cave wherein we can stop."

Clavin nodded. *No trailside inn today.*

Some three hours later, they found the cave and took a rest. They returned to their trek along the twisting trail and found themselves looking upon the gates of the village they had come to attack.

Clavin could see evidence of burn marks and pounding upon the gate, but it appeared the gate was yet in good shape. He scanned the top of the walls and could see that it was well patrolled too. He looked back at the group and saw their eyes glowing an unnatural red in the dark but remained calm and ignored them. Clavin prepared again for the coming assault and reapplied some of the potions that had worn off on the long walk. He looked back and saw a group of people represented in double image; the greater image overlaid a lesser one of giant rats. *Rats!* "Well, Ben, you ready to chew into them?"

"Yes," chittered the excited rat-man. "Let us do exactly that. But first, how will you handle the gate?"

"Give me a bit."

An hour later, Clavin reached the gate, masked in invisibility. There, he applied various potions, amplified them with spells, and made his way back to the rat-men.

"Alright, when I break this stick, the gate will crack open, and we can push in. Are you ready?"

"Aye, that we are," gibbered Ben whose teeth had now sharpened. "Lead us in, and we follow behind. One thing, however."

Why is there always 'one thing?' he groaned. "Yes?" he growled.

"The Temple Priest is a great warrior. It would take many of us to bring him down. If you can deal with him, we can deal with the others."

"Okay. Any more surprises? No?" he said rapid-fire. "Then let's get this done." With that, he stood, called out some words, smashed the stick across his knee, and broke it in half. The gate split down the middle and blew inward. He ran forward and glanced behind to be sure that the rat-men followed. Satisfied, he charged into the court-yard, toward the temple, and ignored the men who rushed, shouting, about him. He noticed, abstractedly, this was a far cleaner place and well organized too. He felt a twinge of doubt about his actions but forced it down. *It's just a Dream, you idiot. Finish the job and get out.*

Clavin rushed up the steps and threw the doors open where he saw a man run for an exit on the other side. He bounded after him and caught the man just outside the temple. He thrust his sword into the man's back. As he struck, Clavin heard, as well as felt, the peaks of the mountains about him crack with a resounding boom that knocked him to the ground. He looked upward and could see, through his enchanted vision, clouds rushing over and darkening the already blackened moonlit sky. Where some few stars yet peeped through, he could see they dimmed and, down the sides of the cliffs, massive boulders bounced toward them. Just then, he gasped from a pain in his chest. He looked back down at the priest and was shocked as he realized it was himself who gazed back. His *real* face, the face of Michael Envine, was now plastered upon the dying priest. *I'm killing myself. I'm helping these rats to eat me alive.*

Frantic, he dove into his bag of tricks, found the potion for which he searched, and poured the ointment onto the priest. The wound healed immediately, and the tremoring rock settled down, but a scar remained. The pain in his chest subsided; he drew forth a ring and placed it on his finger, whereupon he disappeared. *Time to get whacking,* he thought grimly. A minute later, Clavin snuck up on Ben, who stood stabbing a man repeatedly, and slid a cold knife up on the rat-man's neck. "Call your men over here, rat-boy. Right now," Clavin ordered.

"Won't do you no good," Ben cackled. "We'll just open the temple if you make us. You don't want that, I think. Click, clack, click, clack. Ha, ha, ha, ha."

"Call them, you rat!"

"Click, clack, click, clack."

With a quick jerk, Clavin cut him off.

For the next ten minutes, Clavin raged through the village and killed the rat-men. Soon it was over, and he proceeded to heal those defenders who could be helped. *Waste of good potion on fake people.* As he finished, the Temple Priest made his way to him.

"I am Covern, High Priest of Rofnu. I thank you for your help. But why did you do it? What caused you to turn on them?"

"I realized that I had been a fool to help them. I realized that I was connected to this place and to you. In helping you, I help myself. I am sorry for the harm that I have done. All that I wanted was to cross the mountains. I must be in Castle Cordis in less than two days."

"As you have said, you have done much harm," replied his double. "Will you help undo it?"

It's a double helping day. "I must be away and over the mountains by midnight tomorrow, or I shall be cutting my journey too close."

"There will be time."

Of course. He nodded wearily.

The morning was still hours off as Clavin and his new party made their way back to the village of the rat-men of Nevig. With an hour to go, they saw clear signs that the quaking of the previous day had forced a rent in the earth. Now, a new path led away from them, down and out of the mountains. He pondered the change in topography. *Things are looking up. We finish the rats; I run back here, and in another few hours, I'm down this rock and on my way to Cordis. Four hours later, I'm home.*

Soon the defenders became the attackers. As the sun rose, the rat-men returned to normal strength. Clavin charged through the open gate, and they smote a terrible slaughter upon the rat-folk. Near the end, the rat-men regrouped and fell back toward the temple. As they backed their way up the steps, Clavin was reminded of Ben's last words. *Well, carve me a new one. You better get back on your game before they open that thing.*

Clavin dove into the fight with renewed vigor. He broke through their line, rushed to the entrance of the temple, and stood to guard the doors. Clavin noticed that when the rat-man pressed into the shadow of the temple, they grew stronger. When pushed back out into the light, they grew weaker. But it made no difference in the end. The rat-men were destroyed. Clavin turned to the doors and threw them open. As light poured into the temple, the last rat-men shrank down into oversized vermin and scattered in every direction.

The clank and squeal of metal armor yanked his

attention back to the interior of the temple. Two silver knights now strode toward him. Clavin turned and ran for his life.

Many hours later, Clavin Roth burst out of his returning gate into the Traveler's Inn. His furious entrance was no cause for alarm. The Trail Head doors were thick with the constant traffic and, without recognition of who he was, those who stood close by merely presumed that some newbie Walker had managed to survive yet another close encounter with the unknown.

He threw his hood up, pushed his way from the reception hall, and rushed away in search of a quiet place to sit down and collect himself. For nearly forty-five minutes, he strode down halls and upstairs and past the ever-thinning foot-traffic. Finally, he reached a place of silent stairs and clear passages whereupon he turned into a hollow chamber. Pausing just a moment before the door, he glanced at the plate affixed to the outer wall.

Harven's Portal.

He made his way to a back corner and took a seat. Clavin leaned back in the chair, propped his feet on the table, and closed his eyes. After a while, he heard footsteps. A man, surprising by his average looks, stood before him.

The Inn was not known for average-looking people.

"We don't get many visitors here," said the man. "Mind if I sit?"

Clavin waved at a chair beside him.

"Name's Justinus. Yours?"

Clavin paused as he considered what to tell the man.

"Tell you what," continued the man before Clavin could answer, "how about I just call you Traveler for now?"

Clavin nodded, grateful the man understood. "Thanks. So, Justinus, what brings you to this lonely outpost here in the Traveler's Inn?"

"My feet." He grinned.

I should find that funny, he thought flatly.

"What about you? And mind you can't use the same joke as me. It's in the rules."

"I'm afraid I'm really not equipped for snappy comebacks today in any case. I came here to be alone. To think."

"It's a good place for that. Mind, of course, that you don't think too long. Sooner or later, action is required."

Clavin pondered the words. "Well, I've always been good at taking action. I imagine I'll figure out something."

"No doubt. But for any fork, there are many tines. Just be sure to take the right turn."

Clavin pondered that statement too.

"Well, could I bring you something to eat?" Justinus prodded.

"Hmmm? Oh, sorry. Yes. Bring me whatever you suggest. I'm not that picky."

Justinus walked away and left Clavin to his thoughts.

I wonder what Godfrey would say? Michael, you're still adhering to the old patterns of guilt impressed upon you by your parents and teachers. The answer is within you. You must take charge; throw out the old and replace it with the new.

Clavin nodded.

Soon after, Justinus returned and deposited a meal of simple vegetables and delicious bread upon his table, along with one pitcher and two glasses. Noting the extra glass, Clavin looked up at Justinus.

"Please have a seat."

"Thank you. I felt you might be ready for some conversation," he replied as he slid into the chair. "In any case, I know that I am."

Taking up the pitcher that Clavin reached for, Justinus said, "Please allow me." As Justinus poured, he continued, "So, you seem to be feeling much better already. That didn't take long."

"No. It pays to be quick in our profession. Is that water?" Clavin nodded at the clear stream pouring into his glass.

"Quite so. I thought you might need it."

"Actually, yes. It's somewhat surprising here in the Inn though. Tell me, Justinus, how long has it been since you've walked a Path?"

"I walked my Path long ago. I need walk no others. I enjoy meeting people and helping them."

"What Path did you walk?"

"I'll make you a deal. You tell me your name and your path, and I'll answer your question. Fair?"

"Hmmm. Yes, that's more than fair. Perhaps another time?"

"At your convenience. So, Traveler, tell me, did you learn anything on your last Crossing?"

"I think so. I learned that you cannot do things by

halves. You must go the whole way or not go at all. You must be committed."

"Committed. I like that. But what, may I ask, are you committed to?"

"Freedom."

"From what?"

"Guilt. Freedom from guilt."

"Are you guilty?"

"Guilt is foolish," Clavin exclaimed. "What is the point of holding onto it? I cannot change the past."

"No, but the past can change you."

"I don't need to be changed," Clavin insisted as he waved some bread about.

"Don't need to be or don't want to be?"

"Either way. What's the difference?"

"Oh, my friend, it makes a great deal of difference."

"How so?" Clavin challenged.

"Listen, please. There are two kinds of people: those who are willing to change, and those who are not. Those who aren't willing can cover their mistakes and ignore them. But for the others, no amount of effort can forever seal up the pain of past mistakes. Sooner or later, like festering wounds, the memories erupt, breaking back to the surface worse than they were before and, like rats, can eat you alive."

Clavin slammed his glass down, soaking his white-knuckled hand in the process, and rocked the table beneath as he leaned forward against it. "Who are you?" he demanded.

"Whatever is wrong, my friend? Have I hit too close to home?"

"Do you know me?"

"You're the Traveler. Do you know yourself?" Justinus calmly soaked up the water with his towel.

Clavin leaned back in his chair and slid his hands across the rough tabletop as he went.

"Does anyone?" He shrugged. "Does anyone *really* know who they are?"

"Some do," said Justinus as he finished drying the table.

Noticing a sudden grimace on Justinus' face, Clavin asked, "What's wrong?"

"Splinter. Old beaten furniture, you know. Chock full of them. They pain me from time to time."

Clavin, who had already noted the poor condition of the furnishings, asked, "Why don't you just reset all this junk?"

"I thought I'd restore them."

"By hand?"

"Yes. There's no other way."

"Why bother?"

"Then they'd lose their individuality, and I wouldn't want that."

"To each his own." Clavin leaned back in. "Would you like to know why I'm here?"

"Please," prompted Justinus, as he tossed the splinter away.

"I did a bad thing, and I've been trying to cover it up. To ignore it. To make it go away."

"Some things, my friend, can be neither covered nor ignored."

"That's certainly the case here. What, then, should I do?"

"First, you must recognize what you are."

"What do you mean by that?"

"You, my friend, may be the best Traveler in the Dream, the best man in the worlds, yet you are still a man, one who relies on his self, his own inner strength, his wit and his courage."

"Your point?" asked a confused Clavin.

"It isn't enough. It has never been enough. For anyone."

"You sound like my dad."

"Your dad is a wise man."

"You two could have a great conversation."

"Maybe we have."

Clavin smiled. "Are you a believer?"

"No," Justinus replied, "I am a knower."

"You're enigmatic, you know?"

"Some things take time to grow in the soil of doubt. I believe that your field is still being plowed. Come back for another talk soon. Then, perhaps, you'll be ready to do what needs to be done." Justinus rose to his feet.

"Where are you going? You're leaving?"

"No, you are."

Clavin realized that he was, in fact, ready to leave.

"So you have no advice for me then?" Clavin rose from the table and turned to the door.

"You must do as I did with the splinter."

"What? What do you mean?"

"You must get rid of it."

"Oh, really? Is that all? 'Just get rid of it.' Why, then, didn't I think of that? Another man told me the same thing. Not long ago. His advice has been no better than yours."

"His advice was different."

"How would you know? His advice *was* the same. I told you."

"I would say it is a difference of direction."

"What? What do you mean?"

"Your friend was talking about North and South. I'm talking about East and West."

"'Scuse me?"

"The future you long for requires the elimination of the deeds of your past."

"We've covered that. It isn't possible."

"Is it not?" Justinus asked.

Clavin shook his head. "Any more words for a poor, weary traveler?"

"If you can neither fix nor accept your guilt, and covering it up has likewise failed, what else can you do?"

Clavin stared at Justinus intently. "Leave it. I can leave it behind me."

"And how would you do that in this case?"

Clavin shrugged. "I'm not exactly certain. I'm pretty sure there is a way though."

"Will you walk a new trail, take a new Path?"

Clavin paused. *A new trail? A new Dream Path? Now*

367

that would be dangerous. But maybe not as dangerous as Rige and Garner. Hmmm. "You know, you may have hit on something there. Pretty extreme, but it may do the trick. I'm going to keep that in my back pocket for a bit while I think on it. Thanks, Justinus, that's an interesting idea."

"Till the next time."

"Till then."

EIGHT CHARK

DAVID JONES:
DREAMER IN CLAVIN ROTH'S DREAM GROUP

It had been a bad day for David—actually, a bad month. He dragged himself in a listless routine toward his "night" job, dodged traffic, and nodded back to the greetings given him as a recognized Dreamer of Clavin Roth's prestigious Dreamer group.

I should take a few days off, but I need the coin.

He did need the money. His wife, Molly, had begun a total redecoration of their home months ago. Their kids were tutored in art and fencing, and that cost. Then his brother had begged for some help. That's when the purse strings began to strain. Next Molly came down with the flu; doctor's bills, and now the medicine.

He looked down at his fine clothing.

That's another part of the problem. There was a time when I never imagined having a suit like this, let alone five.

On the street ahead of him came three people draped

in black from head to toe, reminding David of what really bothered him that day. He released a sigh and stopped in his tracks to stare at the group.

Why, Mike, why would you do that?

The three approached and passed him.

I spent the whole day next to you. You never said a word. Never let on a thing. Why? Why?

David wrenched himself back to his journey.

You don't need to go to sleep like this.

"But I need the coin," he muttered to himself, resenting the need to work when he knew that he should not on this night. "There's a thousand of us for a reason. And I sleep like a rock anyway. It won't matter."

He saw another passerby's reaction to his personal conversation, stopped his muttering, and continued to walk.

Closing on the wall that surrounded the Sanctum, he stepped off the main path where hundreds of tourists were buying their tickets to visit the Dreamer Complex and made his way to a simple doorway of onyx stone embossed with the carving "J3."

"Papers please," asked the guard politely even as David handed them over.

"Here you are."

The guard scanned them and spoke to another that stood farther back with a J-embossed book.

"David Jones," read the first guard to the second. "Ranger Clavin Roth's Dream Group."

The other guard nodded and began turning pages in his book.

"You're an early shifter then," stated the first man as he moved his attention back to David. "Early to bed, early to rise, eh?"

David recovered his papers. "Just this week. Next week, I'll be in three hours later with the bulk of the others, standing at a J gate."

The guard in the back found the information about David, compared the bare description to that of the man who stood there, and then spoke up.

"Your code, sir?"

"Goshawk," replied David absently.

"Correct. Have a good night."

David continued down the tunnel and came out in the greeting area. He tried to relax, enjoyed the luxuries, paid for a massage, and tried to lose himself in the music played in the auditorium. At seven, he made his way to one of the "early" chambers and lay down to sleep.

MARK HASTINGS:
BINDER FOR CLAVIN ROTH'S DREAM GROUP

In the Binder's room, Mark Hastings prepared to form the gate to allow the Merchants, Keepers, Routers, and early Travelers access to the Inn.

It would be a night to remember.

CLAVIN ROTH

Clavin rolled into the Inn as his own ghosts weighed him down. His last five Crossings had been thankfully untarnished by the appearances of Rige and Garner, and he hoped tonight would be the same. He stopped off for a drink and waited for Staven to show.

While time passed in the Night Star, he sat in state and replied magnanimously to those who greeted him. He invited one or two for a quick drink. After a bit, a Runner named Bone Stripper stopped at his table.

Clavin looked up. "Bone, how are you, my friend?"

"Good, thanks. I was asked to deliver a message." He held out a sealed envelope.

Clavin took it. "Thanks, Bone. Have a safe Crossing."

"You too, Ranger Roth."

Clavin opened the envelope.

Clavin, could you meet me in the Aviary? Liallen Shades.

Oh man, what has she found out? I don't want to rehash this. I'd like to hang out with you, Liallen, but I don't want to talk about Rige and Garner.

He pondered a moment.

I owe her. No matter how you slice it, I owe her. So, here I go.

With that, he left his haven behind, made his way out of the Night Star, and into the hall for a trip to the Aviary; a darkened out-of-the-way place decorated in bird motif hung with curtains that looked like wings. He pushed in through the dove-wings that fronted the restaurant, looked about him, and grabbed the waiter.

"Liallen Shades?"

"Right this way." The man led him to a back space where a tearful Liallen sat waiting.

"Liallen?"

She stood up, wrapped her arms around him, and started to cry.

Not Rige and Garner then. Something else, thank god.

"Oh, hey, okay," he mumbled awkwardly and patted her on the back. "What's wrong?"

"Diamond Anne," she cried. "I just heard that she got hurt today. Really bad. She's with the doctors. She's my best friend, and she's on another world. I can't even go see her."

"Oh, I'm sorry, Liallen, I'm so sorry."

He felt Liallen nodding. "I just needed to talk to someone. I'm sorry to be snuffling all over you like this."

"You go right ahead. At least I'm useful for something." He thought about it. "So, where is she? What's her world? We can at least get something delivered."

Liallen pushed back and looked up at him and wiped her eyes.

"Yes. Actually, she's on your world. Samlin. If you could take her something, I'd really appreciate that."

Clavin smiled. "Okay, now we're talking. I'd be delighted to take her anything you want."

Liallen gave him a weak smile in return.

"You're the great Ranger. I know that you can deliver

anything. But I don't really have anything physical to send. I just want her to know how much I miss her and how badly I'd like to see her again. That's about all."

Clavin stared at her. "That's it?"

"Well," she stiffened, "I don't know what to say in a note. It couldn't carry the weight of my feelings. I want to see her and talk to her, not send a few words on a piece of paper. You can do that in person better than I can do it on paper. That's the next best thing to my being there."

Clavin nodded.

"Liallen, I know that you have a lot of friends here in the Inn. I suspect you have quite a few back in real-world. Why did you choose me to come to?"

"None of them have had to deal with their own problems like you have. I didn't know if they would really hear me out. I knew that you would."

"Yep, I know all about Inn-related problems," he muttered.

"Still?"

"We're here to talk about you tonight," he said as he shook his head and cut her off, "not me."

"But ..."

He placed a finger on her lips.

"Now, we're going to sit here, and you're going to tell me about all the things that make Diamond Anne such a wonderful person. Then, when I talk to her, she'll tell me about what makes you so wonderful, and I'll know everything about you."

He smiled and waved at her chair.

As she sat, he continued, "Then I'll have you over a barrel, and you'll have to give me better rates on my Crossings."

"You already have the best rates now," she replied as she settled into the chair.

Clavin shrugged. "When you're right ..."

"You could take me over with you, you know."

There was a pause as she studied him.

I think she's serious! That could be a disaster.

"Oh, Liallen, I'd love to do that, but it's a one-person class five path. We could get killed real easy trying something like that."

She nodded.

"Maybe I could find a wider and safer route to ride over?"

Clavin chewed his lip.

"Liallen, if you have to make four or five Crossings, the total danger could be greater. And then you'd probably want to come back. Don't do it. Okay?"

Liallen nodded. "Okay. The first time I met Diamond, she was screaming at the Smashers down in Torgen's Wagon Hall ..."

An hour later, Clavin rose from his chair at the cry of a Caller: "Ranger Roth, way ticket for Cordis."

Clavin looked down at Liallen. "See you tomorrow."

"Safe Crossing, Clavin."

He met the Merchant, compared their tickets, signed for the load, put the pack on his back, opened the door, walked down the short hallway behind it, and stepped through the Veil. Clavin thought he heard voices in the fog but was through before he could be sure.

"Odd."

He rifled through his pack, checked on some magics, and, satisfied, headed down the wooded path to the dock. There he took a boat across the lake, avoided the mer-folk, and soon found himself in Samlin-town.

Clavin wasted no time, purchased a strong horse, and was on his way.

Three days passed uneventfully.

ROBERT MULDOON:
DREAM TENDER TO SLEEP ROOM 12

David Jones slept with eleven other early shifters in a cool, dark, hexagonal room with a sleep tender named Robert Muldoon assigned to watch over them all. Robert's job was fairly routine with Clavin's Dream Group, and he sat reading by candlelight *The Kings of the Hall*. Robert had been on duty for five hours and reached the part where the prince would morph into a ravaging dragon—an engrossing page-turning read. It was completely understandable that he didn't see the first twitch from David's face.

CLAVIN ROTH

Clavin approached a hill and stopped to read a sign: "Michael's Deep." A chill ran throughout him that had nothing to do with the weather.

Uh oh.

He rode up the path to the top of the hill and looked

down on the town. It was an unusual place formed of a ring of attractive buildings that surrounded a core of dilapidated others with a dark, stone tower right in the center.

Does a troll named Michael run this place? Or maybe it's some sort of moral about the real me?

He rode down with a shrug.

He stopped at the Inn and walked inside to behold a group of people who sat quietly, eating with vacant stares.

Stupefaction magic?

A figure moved to his right; he turned and found himself speechless at the soiled image of Liallen Shades dressed in a barmaid's attire.

She absorbed his gaze with hollow, black eyes that frosted his heart and made him long for the sunlight just outside the door. He felt the Chark strengthen as she stood there, silent before him, not saying a word.

The hairs rose on his neck as the seated people turned around to stare, silent, at him; all except two huge figures who sat, backs toward him, cloaked in the corners.

Clavin lay a hand lightly on his sword hilt as he spoke to the girl.

"I can leave if you would prefer that?"

Her mouth smiled in a way that touched not her eyes, and she gave a reply. "Noot ah tall. We're noot very used tuh stlangers roond here. Noot manny visit tuh Michael's Deep. Playes coome in an seet. Yahll be eaten in justa minute."

Clavin's palm itched to draw his sword. *Eaten or eating?* "Very well."

He walked to the one empty table in the far corner and drew out potions as he made his way over. The two non-responsive figures sat frozen like statues, and he relaxed just a little. The people turned back to their tables in silence, and Clavin sat down after he validated that it was safe per his magic-sight potion.

As he sat there tingling, fear gnawed upon him, and he applied still more of his potions. He muttered the first few of his spells on himself, and then the Chark ratcheted up once again. The sunlight from the doorways and windows disappeared. The room darkened, lit now by only the candles that sat on the tables. A feeling of hopeless depression washed over him.

What's the point, Clavin? You don't have any friends; no one really cares about you. If you died here right now, some words would be spoken back in the Hall, Staven would say something clever over your empty casket. The Merchants would regret the loss of the Ranger. But not you. You're just a number to them—just a statistical probability of success. Back in real-world, you're not much of anything, and that is the truth.

Clavin stared at the table before him without actually seeing it, and he sighed at the solitary life he had made for himself. He saw movement nearby and raised his eyes.

The Chark wound up tighter.

The barmaid stood there in a form-fitting dress; she leaned down cat-like, forearms on the table, and looked up at him. Taking on a sultry, seductive pose, she asked, "Wat whood ju lake?"

Clavin studied her face as she opened her mouth and licked her bottom lip. The depression of his mind dampened the typical response of his body, and he stared back at her, numb and quiet.

She gave a mirthless smile, and he saw her teeth were now sharp and pointed. The Chark wailed as it climbed in power, and rain began to fall on the roof.

Clavin pushed back a hair from the table.

"Just some bread and water please," he replied dully.

She stared at him for a moment, like a hungry tiger, and then began to pull up slowly from the table. She stretched out a hand toward the single candle which burned there.

"Maaybe yood pefer thu tweens," she said.

With that, she snuffed out the flame, and the entire bar plunged into darkness.

Clavin clenched up and stifled a gasp.

Just two candles inside the room remained lit. The barmaid and all the patrons were gone, and Clavin was left with the two silent cloaked figures, backs still turned toward him.

As Clavin sat in shocked despair, the figures began to turn, ever so slowly, in a smooth, steady motion that whispered to him of a wrongness occurring as the chairs that they sat on squealed in rusty protest.

Oh god, no. Not now, not here.

The Chark screamed in power as the wind moaned just outside and slashed the building in a torrential downpour. Despair battled fear. Clavin slumped in his chair while he waited for death to come round to face him.

In the deadly murk of the room, he heard a bare whisper from somewhere: "Michael, your parents love you."

And with those words came his past.

There was his dad, throwing him up in the air and catching him while he laughed. Next, he saw his mother; she stood holding a boy who'd broken her favorite vase, and she whispered words into his ear. "I love you, Buster. I love you more than the vase and more than this house. I love you more than my life. Do you know that, little man? Do you know how much I love you?"

Michael Envine awoke in the heart of Clavin Roth, and with a groaning cry, the Ranger tossed aside his table with his magic-enhanced strength and burst from his chair. He ran for the door and drew his sword while casting his Twin Self spell; it was two Clavin Roths who exited the Inn.

The sky, so pure blue three minutes before, now raged in indigo darkness that roiled the heavens above him and cast everything about him into early night.

Twin lightning bolts split the storm into three parts with such incandescent blaze that it left a bright after-image burned on his eyes for a few seconds following. Rain sliced through the air and stung his face like tiny, wet pebbles.

Wails poured from the clouds and the buildings about him as if from the heart of a sad, lonely man.

But it was none of these things that froze Clavin in

his tracks; it was the sight of more buildings and streets lying before him in the stygian gloom where minutes before had been only the green grass of the hillside. People stood frozen along the road where they stared at him and his double in silence through the downpouring torrent.

Death maze.

DAVID

David thrashed on his bed in the Early Dream Chamber unheeded by Robert who, engrossed in his book, turned the next page.

MARK

Mark Hastings also slept, but his sleep was different. He lay at the focal point of a Dreamstone spoke system that conducted the Dream force of all of the Dreamers to the couch where he lay. He could feel the flow of the Dreams coming in. He blended and smoothed them as they flowed outward and down toward the Dream Gates that formed the bridges into the Inn.

He could tell when a nightmare entered the stream by the change in the color that flowed in his mind. The darker the Dream, the sooner he'd find it.

Mark saw this one instantly; a deep, black emptiness that ran like a vein of dried blood out from one of the Early rooms.

DREAM LORD

He probed backward, touched each couch in the room, and, reaching thirteen, felt a numb despair strike him so hard that a reverberation ran out from him and throughout the Dream Group.

MARILYN

Marilyn Stillhaven dreamed of her mother, who had passed away three years before. She was a little girl once again in the kitchen with her mother who stood at the cutting board slicing up chicken breasts to mix with onions and peppers and many good things.

When the reverberation struck her, Marilyn found herself lying on the cutting board. A demonic caricature of her mother stood above her and held a knife. With a laugh, it struck down into her stomach.

She awoke with a scream.

Twenty others woke on the first wave of the nightmare.

MARK

Mark felt the secondary impact as fifty lesser nightmares struck all in an instant; twenty Dreams snapped off as Dreamers awoke in shock. Another reverberation rolled out from him.

CLAVIN

Clavin felt the shock also and fell to one knee, weighed down by the knowledge that certain death now awaited. Grabbing again onto his memories, he pushed himself up and ran through the deluge, using his hand to ward off the rain that stung his eyes. Clavin glanced back to see the emergence of two obsidian figures, cloaks now discarded, who dripped acidic darkness.

They wore silver helmets.

They glanced right at him and began to chase while the frozen people started to walk in unison toward him. Some slashed at his double image, clawed fingers finding nothing but air.

Vampires.

Clavin pulled on his ring of deflection and ducked down an alleyway only to find a shut door at the end. He slammed hard into it, but it was solid and locked.

Damn it to hell!

He rebounded off of the door enough for a swing of his sword; the wood door burst open, and he rushed into a dark room with trash on the floor where four waiting vampires came straight toward him. He charged to the back door and outran the four, but then he heard the drumming of heavy claws on the roof above.

Cutting me off.

He spun around to run back to the front; the hollow-eyed vampires had him blocked. With a quick slice of his blade, the vampires separated, and Clavin charged through the offal and guts that spilled out around him. With a small jump, he smashed through a window and rolled back to his feet in the maelstrom that raged outside the building.

Thankful that neither creature awaited him there, he ran down the street searching for anything he could leverage for aid and dodged the vampires whose claws reached for him. His stutter-step and deflection spells kept them from making any contact.

He saw the stone tower ahead.

Make a stand there.

A glance behind revealed the vampires in full pursuit, hair slicked down by rain that ran down their faces like tiny snakes hunting prey.

Watchers.

Clavin pulled two tiny boots from his pouch which quickly expanded out to full size. He reached the vestibule of a building where he ducked in for cover. There, he promptly drew on the boots, followed by his invisibility ring. With the wind at his back, Clavin ran into the street to head for the tower, leaving no tracks behind him.

They'll search that building first.

A hundred feet back, one of the things made its way down the street, plainly following the tracks he had made to the building he had just left. Nine feet tall, dark as onyx stone, claws for hands, and talons for feet. Steam rose from its body as the rain burned off it. Its eyes glowed out red from inside the helmet.

To look at it froze the blood in Clavin's veins. He knew, from the Chark, the thing was the most dangerous monster he'd ever met in all of his travels. He hesitated to think it, but his mind couldn't stop: *Demon.*

MARK

So strong was the nightmare, Mark knew he would never reach the man who had created it, but he could reach another who slept in the same room in quiet repose. the Dream Tender should be shaking the man awake who, Mark presumed, was probably screaming in terror. But in case he wasn't, he'd make doubly sure.

Mark pulsed couch twelve with an urgent message to wake and a directive to yank thirteen from his sleep.

DAVID

David slept like the dead. As a lad, he had slept through the burning of a neighboring building one night. He never knew a thing till he woke the next day. It was a great blessing that, in this case, had turned into a curse.

His dream was terrible and, blended with Clavin's nightmare, had become a monstrous thing. Where nearly any other would wake, David slept on.

But he moaned on his couch and twisted his sheets.

CLAVIN

For one heart-stopping moment, Clavin thought the demon saw him; he froze in a shadow and hoped that if his invisibility didn't work, normal dark might.

He gave a huge exhale in relief when it turned to follow his tracks, and when he did, it snapped around to look in his direction.

Damn the Dream, screamed Clavin's thought. *That's impossible.*

He ran for the tower.

With a glance back, Clavin saw that it was making up distance as it ran through the drench like a boar through tall grass. Its eyes now glowed silver instead of red.

It can see me now.

He looked back at the tower at the far end of the street; so close and so far.

I'm not going to make it. I'm not going to make it!

ROBERT

Robert Muldoon froze as the girl on couch twelve woke up and cried out, "Thirteen. Couch thirteen, couch thirteen!" Luckily, Robert's surprise lasted barely two seconds, after which he jumped to David's side and roughly yanked him from his bed, breaking his contact with the Dreamstone and his damming input into the Dream.

386

EIGHT CHARK

CLAVIN

The oppressive dread of the Chark let off so abruptly that the demon slowed even as the vampires temporarily halted. The rain lightened as the wind dropped back from a howl.

Clavin's ability to think returned in full force; his mind focused on the rain which poured off the roofs in cascading waterfalls. A sluice of water ran out from an alley ahead in a torrential stream, and the thought of a bug trapped in amber entered his mind.

Maybe.

He called forth his water vial and raced into the alley. Rain poured down in sheets from the non-guttered roofs and formed the stream that he ran through. Geysers of water blasted up with each step. Fifty feet down, the passage dead-ended. Clavin spun about, two arrows notched on the bow in his right hand, water vial held in his left.

Clavin's magic-enhanced sight cut through the gloom of the downpouring drench and allowed him to see the thing stopped at the end of the alley. Rather than charge directly in after him, it paused and let out a victory scream and revealed a double row of red teeth.

That's right; take your time. A bit narrow in here for you, after all.

Clavin stepped up onto a crate to bring his feet clear of the water that flooded the alley.

The demon started in, taloned feet hidden beneath the outflowing water.

The corridor was no more than five feet across. Clavin

387

made a left-handed throw of his vial even as he formed the thought, *Burst all in one.* As the vial took flight, his left hand grasped onto the bow that his right swung up by the string. The pull and the aim left him no time to wait before a thousand gallons of water exploded around the demon in the alley's confined space.

The two Frost Arrows flashed on their way into the water and froze it solid with the demon inside. The alley-way water iced in a flash all about him, and sleet fell in sheets. The walls next to the demon caved away from the expanding ice on either side, bringing down a cascade of brick, rain, and mortar.

Clavin dropped his bow as he drew out his sword and charged forward. He levered himself off of some crates and, aided by his super-strength potion, leaped high with his blade that could cleave stone like butter.

In just those few seconds, the demon's massive power had already shot cracks through the ice, and Clavin could see the thing's claws tearing free.

Sword angled down, with all his weight behind it, the blade speared through the ice into the monster's neck where it was stopped by a resistance like iron. The sword hilt slammed up into Clavin's chin and nearly broke his jaw as the demon twisted so hard that Clavin felt ice and demon both crack under the strain.

Shards of white rock blew all about him as he rolled away from the thing without his sword, now stuck in the demon.

It staggered upright and turned to stare at him, now

back on the side of the alleyway's entrance. The sword stood embedded a full twelve inches deep in the neck, and the monster moved much slower now. Tiny scales covered the demon, and silver blood flowed out from the wound in its neck.

With a lurch, it started toward him.

Clavin turned and ran into the street.

Where is it? Where is it? Frantic, Clavin scanned the darkness for the second demon.

A roar gave him the clue, and he glanced up into the soaking sky to see the other demon running across a roof, splintered tiles flying away from its feet. Twin lightning bolts blasted the gloom into whiteness which framed the demon and blinded Clavin for a second.

I'm dead.

MARK

Mark Hastings saw the contact had broken. However, the Dream was created and couldn't be stopped in an instant without the potential of cracking the world. He injected peace and tranquility into the Dream, poured an image of power into his view of Clavin, and clamped down on the threads; the reverberations dampened.

CLAVIN

Clavin hurtled down the street and felt Mark's tranquility hit. Three of every four vampires appeared to turn back into men; they, in turn, saw the demons and other vampires and ran for the buildings. Many of the vampires chased after them; the ones that remained began to stalk Clavin again.

He drew forth fire and released a stream of it at the stalkers. The torrential rain and soaked clothes prevented the fire from doing much damage, but the vampires fell back to protect their faces, and Clavin ran past them as the alleyway demon came from behind. Hurt as it was, he could outrun it.

He felt the thud as something massive struck the ground; he glanced back again. The second demon had leapt off the roof and landed solid, cracking stones under its talons; it would overtake him within twenty seconds.

With his sword, he might have fought it for a bit. If it were large, like a dragon, he could have tried to hide in the buildings and escape it. But there was no time, no tools, and no strategy that he could fathom to fight this thing in the seconds he had left. Desperate, his mind clawed for any possible method by which to survive.

And the image of Merinda Swift burst into his mind.

Twist.

Clavin concentrated all his will on a medioxumate god's lost sword of such power that no being could stand before it. He grabbed the Hand of Fate and rattled out his keyword repeatedly as he continued to run. In his mind, he saw it fall from heaven to land before him in a blaze of lightning.

A scintillating bolt rent the dark veil above in two, leaving a split in the sky and a bright, glowing object buried in stone fifty yards on.

YES.

The earth shook beneath while buildings to each side of him ran cracks through their stonework.

MARK

Mark saw, to his horror, the current of threads contort from a pulse that came up from the Dream Gate. At the same moment, the image of a great sword burned in his mind, and he knew what Clavin had done.

Oh my god. Did the Dream just collapse?

But the knot of Dream energy soon smoothed itself out. Mark breathed in relief until he saw the crack in the flow. He held his breath, and it began to widen.

No. Oh no.

The Dream energy had split itself into two separate flows. For the moment, they still ran smoothly together, but soon they'd begin to vibrate in dissonant motion as two different versions of the Dream battled with each other for the same space.

CLAVIN

Clavin ran for the sword and salvation.

The demon behind him wasn't fooled, like the vampires, by Clavin's double image and ran after Clavin like a hound for a fox. Clavin felt the ground vibrate under the hammer blows from the thing's heavy, scaled talons.

Scales.

His hand dove into his pouch, shoved the fire vial in, and drew another one out with golden flakes in brown liquid. As the demon closed the final few yards, he unstopped the jar—that he held upside down—grabbed onto a storefront post which helped him to spin about, and then tucked into a roll at the demon's feet.

The liquid poured up through the down-falling rain to splatter the creature's lower torso. Clavin rolled on past, but the demon's snakelike speed made up for his Stutter Step spell. The crushing impact from a claw broke two of Clavin's ribs, sending him rolling like a little girl's doll through the puddles and muck of the street. Had it not been for the magic on his leather armor, he would have been dead.

The first demon lurched toward him from the other direction and sandwiched Clavin between it and the second. But the second demon's legs now moved in much shorter steps due to the action of the Fusing potion.

Clavin levered himself up, grit his teeth against the pain of his ribs, and rushed back past the fused demon toward the glowing object. He reached it and found there a sword buried in stone. He placed his hand on the hilt and pulled with all of his might.

The sword didn't budge, and Clavin nearly screamed in frustration but chose brain over mouth. His eyes fell on an engraved word that glowed on the blade of the sword.

Peccavi.

He heard the two demons coming, not thirty feet back, the first having awaited the second.

He cried, "Peccavi," aloud.

With that, the burning sword leaped out from the stone and lay free in his hand. Clavin spun to meet the demons.

The fused demon had torn itself in numerous places which now formed a netting of wounds that bled silver from its lower half. The demons could no longer out-run Clavin, but that didn't matter; the cloying despair of nightmare had evaporated, and Clavin wasn't in the mood to run anymore. Items formed in Charks were the most powerful of all, and this was the most potent Chark he had ever known or heard of.

The blade in his hand blazed like a sunbeam hungry for shadows.

Showtime.

Clavin charged right, ducked beneath the first blow, and struck the thing under its armpit. The blade sliced a gash six inches deep clear across the chest, and silver blood sprayed in a long, splattering arc.

The demon tripped Clavin with a back talon which sent him into a dive on the cobblestones. Clavin rolled into a ball and back to his feet, but a broken rib punctured a lung as he did it. Blood came to his mouth as he spun around and separated the head from the first demon while slicing his embedded sword in half too.

Fast, he thought, as he regarded the creature's response which had almost disarmed him.

The other struck.

Clavin ducked, ducked again, rolled forward, and sliced the taloned foot that nearly caught him in a tripping attack like the first demon had done.

The thing limped back, now shy two of four talons.

They circled each other and, with a hiss, it released a black gas that blinded Clavin's magic sight; he struck out by memory even as he ducked underneath an imagined blow.

The blow came anyway. It backflipped him away, and Peccavi spun from his grasp.

Clavin rolled to a stop. Still blinded, he rose and ran hard in a direction he hoped was away from the demon. After ten seconds, he slammed into something face first, breaking his nose and smashing some teeth; his vision narrowed to a tunnel as black spots clouded his sight, but this wasn't the time for a nap. He pushed back the blackness by force of will. In the haze of his tear-filled eyes, his vision began to return.

Hands latched onto him. They were strong and grasped him tight, but Clavin's super-strength potion made him even stronger. He allowed the creature behind to hold his body, and he swung up his legs and scissored them onto the head of the nearest vampire just before him. With a hard twist, he flipped it to the left while the assailant who held him up was thrown to the right, and both dropped down onto the wet stones.

As they fell, a knife from the third one licked out and scored down Clavin's left forearm. The vampire paused just for a moment and then leapt onto them both. The pause, however, cost the thing its life as Clavin's own drawn knife punched between ribs and burst the heart. The one behind released his grasp to grab for Clavin's knife-hand.

Clavin rolled free, back up to his feet, and tried to spit blood from his lungs into the vampire's eyes. He missed but couldn't pause to mourn the failure. The creature he had thrown with his legs had risen and now rushed upon him. Clavin's knife whipped out, and it returned a red smile below the chin as its head tilted back for a look at the sky.

The thing which had fallen with Clavin now hit his legs from behind even as the last demon closed in upon them. But this wasn't Clavin's first dance, and in an acrobatic move, he tucked in, rolled backward, and came up to his feet.

Clavin's thrown knife lodged into the final vampire's chest even as he drew out a white-filled vial from his pouch. *Good for the gander*, he thought, recalling the demon's blinding breath from before. He slung the vial at the face of the beast and grit his teeth against the pain in his body. Clavin noticed the demon was short an arm and realized his blindly struck blow had connected after all.

The demon disappeared from his smile in a burst of white flour that blinded the monster for two crucial seconds. In just three seconds more, the rain cleared the air and left behind a pasty, white monster which followed the sound of Clavin's stumbling feet. It roared a screech of tearing metal even as Clavin made a beeline for Peccavi. Vampires moved to block Clavin's path, but he used fire to scatter them once again.

Sides heaving, face and ribs broken, Clavin reached the sword and swung around with it as the demon came at him for another pass. He saw it inhale and timed his blow to intercept its neck as it blew forth its breath. Clavin allowed the thing to blind him again as Peccavi licked out to slice off its head.

Unable to see, Clavin began to spin Peccavi in an arc around himself while he backed away from where he felt the demon had fallen. After some seconds, one of his feet caught up in something that felt like a pile of slick rope. He fell to a knee and heard a victory shout from behind; he fell to the ground and brought Peccavi about in an arc.

Something heavy fell against him as he rolled in his blindness and made it back to his feet even as a knife sliced into his leg from behind.

Peccavi came around once again.

Clavin's sight cleared enough to reveal dim shapes about him. With his skill and Peccavi, that was enough. A single swing arced around and killed two more creatures; the rest fled.

Five split corpses lay on the street along with the wreck of the final demon.

What did I trip on?

His eye caught a torso whose entrails had been pulled out by something, and he had his answer.

No guts, no glory.

Able to rest, he could finally gasp out a word.

"Wow."

Who's the man?

He shook his head.

You were darn, near the corpse. Don't get too cocky.

Clavin looked up and saw the sky clear, like leaves

in a wind, and settle into a strange double image which reminded him of a watermark done on paper; one clear and solid, another barely perceptible. Above him, it was blue with an under image of stormy and rain. It made him uneasy.

Clavin began to call forth his potions and healed his multiple wounds from the fight. That done and potions replaced into the pouch, he picked up Peccavi and admired the sword he had earned from such a fierce trial.

"Girl, you've just made my life a lot easier from here on."

The earth quaked beneath him.

MARK

Mark could feel the disturbance in the Dream strands as the entire group tried to settle down from the shock of sudden nightmares and Dreamers blasted awake on their couches. He studied the discordant threads and pondered removing them right away—which would risk another round of dissonance—or to wait and see if they settled out on their own. He could feel the two strands as they strove to break free from each other, and he struggled to hold them together lest they begin to whip about and destroy one or both.

CLAVIN

Clavin looked up and saw the effect in the sky above was now manifested on the earth as city buildings superimposed themselves with the ghostly image of demons and dragons.

Not good.

Clavin rose to his feet and began to run.

Three days back and four days ahead. The nightmare came from behind, which means the contagion is in the Samlin group. It's closer to Samlin, but the Cordis group is unwounded. I can make it in two days if I go all out.

As Clavin pushed beyond the damaged town, a massive tremor struck, and he glanced back to see a crevasse open beneath the town as the buildings dropped in. He crested the hill and continued to run.

After a few minutes, he looked back again and saw to his horror the crevasse now ran across the land in both directions, growing wider as it went and dropping the ground and hills into oblivion.

Dream collapse. Oh my god. Oh my god.

Clavin ran. He drew on his potions to keep him running; every hour, he downed some more and ate up the miles. After three hours, he ran into the town of Chistleheim.

Rushing up to the first man he saw with a good horse, he stopped.

"How much for your horse?" he demanded.

The man looked over the bedraggled, bloodied, filthy sight of Clavin and sneered at him, "You can't afford him."

The ground shook.

Clavin pulled out a handful of gold coins worth twenty times the value of the horse and shoved it at the man.

"Enough?"

The man's eyes bulged at the sight of so much money, and he nodded without a word.

Clavin dumped the coins into the man's hands, leaped on the horse, and took off without another word.

Another tremor shook the ground.

When the chasm gets deep enough, the world will start to crumble everywhere.

Clavin pushed his horse without mercy, dousing it with potions instead of himself. Night fell, and he rode. The earth shook at regular intervals. He rode through villages where people met and prayed and cried out to him as he passed through like the wind.

"Stranger, do you know what's going on? Have you heard any news?" they would beg.

He rode without answer, knowing the answer, and that the answer was beyond their comprehension.

Just before morning, the earth heaved so hard that both he and his horse fell. Both suffered broken bones, but he still had healing potions. As he applied them, he looked back at the pre-dawn night. The sky glowed red across the horizon, lit by the fires of the earth from below. His stomach clenched, and fear ran through him.

A demon could be fought. Dream collapse simply had to be outrun. At his present speed, he had six hours left until reaching Cordis.

He rode.

MARK

Mark could feel the vibrations as they cascaded through the Dream Group. Too many Dreamers had awoken already. Mark estimated that if five more people awoke—the right five—Clavin's world would collapse immediately. That could happen on the next antipodal wave between the two worlds. On the other hand, ten could awake if they were the right ones, and Clavin could still survive.

Two specific sleep chambers appeared to power the second Dream. He could tell that Clavin was alive but not where on the path or in which world he moved. He could send an order and have chambers cut off, but he couldn't know which world Clavin was in.

To guess wrong was an execution.

If he sent the order and Clavin died, then Mark would be known as the Binder who had killed the Ranger of Samlin-Cordis, and his career would be over. Standard protocol insisted that the best course was to depend upon the Traveler to make it out in time. No one could debate that, and he would probably continue to find Binder work.

But the threads that powered the second Dream were so erratic he couldn't imagine Clavin surviving in it for over a day. Besides, the other world didn't appear to have enough Dreamer threads to support a person, which meant that Clavin couldn't be on it.

He couldn't be sure, though.

From within his own special dream, he shrugged. He was already a wealthy man because of Clavin Roth.

He sent the order.

A Dreamer awoke in room nine and called to her Tender.

"The Binder says to cut off rooms eight and twenty. Go. Eight and twenty."

The Tender stared at the woman in disbelief. He'd never imagined he'd hear such a directive in his life.

"What are you waiting for?"

With that admonition, his training took over.

"Binder code?"

"Ravenhurst," she said, recalling the code word from her dream.

He tore open an envelope, read the contents, and then ran from the room.

CLAVIN

Clavin blew out a sigh of relief; the world stopped shaking, and the southern sky turned back to blue. The ground stopped shimmering, and the half-formed illusion of beach-lined ocean overlain by verdant green forest solidified at last into bark and green leaves.

Mark's working it for me. You're going to get one big, fat bonus and hug from me, buddy.

Clavin was nearing the point of the Blue Bog and felt confident that he would soon be home.

Three hours for me, seven minutes for Mark. Hold it together, buddy, hold it.

He rode into the forest and began to contemplate what would be his final obstacle—the Blue Bog.

Okay, I've got Frost Arrows, boots, and bread. With Peccavi, I can chop Cestilanc into dragon-steak if he shows. I don't think anything is really going to slow me except the bog itself. I'll need two hours to get through, and then I'm home. I'll be through this forest in another hour, so three hours from now, it's all over.

Reassured, he rode out from the forest an hour later, and his stomach twisted up. A hundred feet down the path, where the bog usually began, there was no bog to cross—in fact, there was nothing at all.

He dismounted his exhausted horse and approached the end of the world. Ahead of him, his view was blanketed by a thin mist. Clavin extended his knife out into the mist and watched as the end of his weapon disappeared. When he drew it back, the tip was missing.

Oh god. This isn't just some misty chasm. There isn't any Dream support for this piece of the world. I'm dead. I'm DEAD!

"Stop it."

Okay. Okay. I'll just ... uhmm ... okay.

"Stop saying 'okay' and think of something useful."

Okay, Mark halted the collapse. How? He must have wakened the bad eggs to settle things down. That worked like a champ, but entire pieces of the world are now gone too, like this little bit of land between me and Cordis. Minor puzzle to solve and, if I don't solve it, I'm dead. No pressure.

"Why isn't the air pouring into this breach?"

Clavin felt the wind begin to blow toward the chasm.

You and your mouth. Now you've done it.

"Well, that's just dandy."

If I try another Twist, that'll probably kill me. So I've got what?

He shook his head.

"Days? Hours?"

How long does it take to drain the air from a world? More importantly, how long does Mark think it takes?

Clavin stood and stared at the end of the world. There was no way home. Samlin was seven days regular travel back the other way—if there was land to travel over—and he was cut off from Cordis, if it still existed.

I think I'm going to have to try to Twist it again and just cross my fingers. Cordis and Samlin still exist, of course. The endpoints are always the very last places to collapse, and I'm close. So Cordis is out there, maybe five miles away. If I try anything extravagant, I'm dead. What is the minimal Twist I can do and still make this thing passable?

"I can't climb down and walk across because there is no world there to cross, nothing to rappel down. Even if I had a flying spell, it wouldn't work for the same reason. Magic won't work because there is no Dream support in which to work."

I'm dead.

"Shut. It!"

If this were a real chasm, what would I do then? I have the carpet.

He shook his head as he tried to ignore the steady breeze.

I can float up and down on my carpet, but I can't really fly because it doesn't move horizontally on its own.

He imagined the nothingness as a mist-filled canyon

filled with birds and air. In his mind's eye, an eagle flew there, flapped hard in the currents as it rose up high, and then, closing its wings, dove at an angle into the mists where it disappeared from his vision.

"Wait. That could work."

Clavin called out his magic carpet. A tiny piece of cloth rapidly expanded into an eight by ten square rug with tassels on the corners. He bound the tassels to his feet and gripped onto two others. He crouched at the edge of the gulf and concentrated upon a simple replacement image of mist-filled air which filled a giant canyon. His concentration built as he slowly filled in details of soaring birds. He added nothing but that and prayed it would be enough.

He took hold of the Hand of Fate and began to chant his keyword.

MARK

Mark Hastings felt the disturbance run back up from the gates.

NO, Clavin, no!

Mark came close to waking himself as he clamped down hard as he could in his exhaustion. He wouldn't be able to hold it for long.

CLAVIN

The world tremored as Clavin felt and heard a massive, groaning crack from deep in the earth. Fear tingled him even as hope rose in his heart at the change in the noth-ingness before him. He glanced back to the south and saw the collapsing edge of the world as it rushed toward him.

He jumped.

Clavin let out a whoop of victory as he realized that he was still alive and able to realize anything. He fell through a rush of air and held himself at what he felt was an angle. Minutes passed as the wind whistled in his ears. And then, no more than a quarter mile ahead through the mists, he saw the edge of the cliffs on the far side as they rushed toward him. Relief washed through him like a cold wave, and he gave a command: "Carpet, rise." His fall stopped, and he began to ascend.

What felt like an hour passed, and Clavin worried that he might not have enough time. Ten minutes later, he cursed himself for a fool. *You knew this thing didn't climb fast. God, how far can a man fall in a minute anyway? How many minutes did I fall?*

Clavin shrugged.

There was no other way to cross the abyss.

The mists swirled about him.

Twist again?

He shook his head as he muttered, "Don't even think it. Don't you dare say it."

Five minutes later, the mists began to thicken around him and roiled with wind gusts that snapped him back and forth. It soon settled out, and his lungs labored for air as he came up to see a sky whose color was shifted to black.

The chasm filled in, but the air is pouring out now to the other side. There's almost no air left up here now.

Clavin dove again. The air was so thin, he made little progress toward the canyon wall. Only down inside the canyon, where the air was still thick for some strange Dream-reason, would his trick work. He stopped himself just a foot away from the wall and drew out his water vial. He aimed it behind him and uncorked it. The force of blasting water pushed him across the cliff edge and over solid land. The carpet settled gently to the ground.

Clavin despaired as he saw the walls of the city a half mile away. *I can't make it that far.* But he wasn't a quitter, and he'd go down walking, if not fighting. He began to unbind his feet when words in his mind urged, "Keep using the water." Clavin glanced back in a brain-fogged stupor and began to unbind the carpet again when the words sunk in. He ordered the carpet to rise, pulled the water vial out again, and cracked it open at full force. The carpet leaped forward and shot like a javelin across the landscape below. After a full minute, the vial emptied and the carpet drifted to a halt almost at the city wall. He released his bindings, staggered to his feet, and began to walk as the image of Cordis Tower flashed through his mind.

Please be close.

He made it to the gates where he slumped against the wall and heaved for air. Clavin pushed off and began to stumble through the city. Minutes later, his vision closed as black spots dotted his sight.

Consciousness returned to the pain of some sharp

object that dug into his skin underneath him. He struggled back to his feet and looked down to see the six-inch splinter that had forced him back to the land of the living. Pushing on, he paused every few steps to gasp in enough air to force the blackness out again. His head pounded as if an angry blacksmith had chosen him for an anvil. Birds and other animals lay about the streets as they too gasped for air or lay silent, already dead. People lay strewn about as if some crazed dollmaker had gone on a rampage tossing out the work of his hands in every direction.

He looked up and saw, in the near distance, the top of Cordis Tower, and a wave of despair struck him again. *It's too far.* He shook his head.

Walk. NOW. WALK.

But somehow the sight of the tower undercut, rather than buoyed, his will, and after ten more steps, he fell to his knees in a desperate struggle against his failing sight. Clavin then did something he had never done before; he dropped the pack which carried the load bound for Cordis and his reason for being there in the first place. He then unbuckled his armor and dropped that on the path too along with his bow and knife.

Peccavi?

He shook his head, too short of air to waste any on speech.

No.

He pushed himself on through an eerie quiet broken only by the gasps that came from his own lungs. Clavin staggered through the city, like a midnight drunk, street after street. He saw piles of bodies at the various sanctuaries where people had met in desperation to pray to their false gods. Other groups could be seen splayed around the homes of mages who lived in Cordis. All about him, the city smoldered, unable to burn in the absence of air.

The worst of the horror was the sight of the children. Those he staggered past had no strength left for anything but to whimper and cry as they clutched onto their little, stuffed toys. There was nothing he could do for any of them. Clavin steeled his heart and kept going.

Clavin made the final turn and saw the tower come into view less than a hundred yards before him; his willpower failed. He fell to the ground, unable to pull himself back to his feet, and began to crawl. Bodies blocked the way. Some he drug himself over and drove out their last bits of air. Most he could, thankfully, crawl around.

Cordis Tower beckoned. He was shocked to see that a moat surrounded the tower, and his stomach tightened as he imagined the drawbridge being up to deny him access at the very last. But it wasn't so; the great, wooden bridge to safety was down, and relief washed through him. He staggered by a gray, metal gatehouse at the foot of the bridge. Bodies lay everywhere, but these had died in combat, not from suffocation; the wood was soaked with red blood. Almost two thirds of the way across, he slipped and fell while navigating over a corpse. He lay there for a moment and gasped for air to regain strength to crawl the final thirty feet. He noted an absence of bodies and saw, out in the moat to his left and right, were short, metal guard shacks which joined the main span at this point, and he realized what had happened.

The people fought to get into the tower.

As he approached the open gate, a bloodied Clavin saw that it was filled with the white smoke of the Veil. Just feet away from safety, the earth heaved as if the Dream knew its quarry was about to escape, and half the city collapsed around the tower. Ricocheting stone slashed and lacerated his skin, one large shard of granite tearing into his left side. But the pain was surmounted by the agony of his lungs as he gasped for air. The ground cracked, and heat shot up from deep rents in the earth. The city was unable to fire—nevertheless, the inferno burnt his skin.

As his hands entered the mist, the sun flared, incinerating the clothes on his back and creating pain that supplanted that of his lungs for a moment. With no air to scream, he simply pressed forward the final few feet into the mist as the world collapsed behind him.

Fresh air filled his lungs.

Thank god, thank god. He pushed to his feet, stepped forward, and all his wounds fell away, leaving him healthy as he stepped back into the Inn.

A raucous cheer greeted Clavin as people who'd heard of his plight had gathered to wait and see if the great Ranger could pull it out once again. They quieted, and a hush ran through the crowd as they watched him. Clavin stretched out a hand that shook like a palsied, old man toward Staven who leaped to place an arm around him.

"Where to, buddy?" Staven asked.

"Star," Clavin whispered back.

Clavin's Merchant stepped forward, ready to sign for his load.

Clavin shook his head at the man.

The Merchant couldn't completely hide his disappointment, but nevertheless, he nodded and stepped aside.

Clavin felt a strong desire to kick in his teeth.

Staven waved people out of the way and led him back to his place and his seat in the Night Star. A crowd gathered around the two of them, and Clavin nodded at his friend.

"I'm good now, Staven. I'm good. Thanks."

"How did it begin, Clavin?"

"It was all very calm and normal up to the point at which it began. There wasn't the typical slow buildup. It was one of those scenes in which you're talking to a group of nice people in a room and, ten seconds later, they've all become vampires or something. It came on so fast. From the first moment of, 'oh, it's a Chark,' to the terror of 'I'm going to die,' was maybe three minutes."

"So the demons were rough."

Clavin shook his head in disbelief.

"Stave, I've fought my share of dragons. Two or three of them were as bad as these fellows. But I could hide from them or take cover or something else. I could use their bulk against them. None of that applied to these things. They were faster, quicker, and stronger than me in every way. They had countering magic to at least some of my spells. The sheer terror of their presence had me locked up. After all the dragons I've fought, these things had me frozen."

"How'd you survive then?"

Clavin's eyes focused somewhere far away for a moment.

"I remembered the love of my parents and knew how'd they'd grieve if I died there. That's what got me moving again. That's how I survived."

"You being you once again," replied Staven.

Clavin stared at his friend for a moment. "Maybe. In any case, I don't mind telling you that I don't ever want to experience that again."

"Well, I guess it's no wonder. The Keepers and your Binder have already conferred; it was an eight, a solid eight. No one has ever survived an eight Chark before unless they were minutes from a gate to escape by or the Dreamer woke fast and shut it down. Those few who have survived one did so mostly by luck. You did it by wit and strength. You survived two days in it. You're the man, Clavin Roth, you really are."

Clavin's eyes took on a vacant look. "Staven, I wouldn't have lasted another five minutes. The end ..." Clavin shook his head as he laid his hands on the table in an effort to still them. "The end was a real nightmare. A Charkless nightmare by then. You can stand to see warriors die by the thousands, but the women and children ..." He shook his head again. "I'm afraid that I'll have nightmares for years about that."

Staven raised his glass. "Ranger Clavin Roth, Bad to the Bone."

Clavin groaned at the phrase he used to use and Staven

meant in respect. His glass raised slowly in a quivering hand, as if he lifted a great weight instead of a light glass.

"Thanks, Staven. I may be 'bad to the bone,' but when you're fighting demons, it's probably better to be pure at heart. I don't know."

Staven studied his friend for a moment, aware of the crowd. They too had noted the shake in his hands.

"You okay, Clavin?"

Clavin took his turn to pause. "No, not really. I'm kinda at the end of a rope."

The attendant people showed sympathy to the great Ranger, understanding that they looked now, not upon an Inn-god, but a man who'd just been shaken to his very core.

"Maybe you need to take some time off. Some real-time off. Not just a week, but a few months or more? What else is there to do at the end of a rope?"

Clavin stared back at his friend. "Find a new one?"

"What?"

Clavin shook his head and said nothing but leaned back in his chair.

Find a new one, of course. Like that guy ... Justinus ... suggested.

It's time for a new Path.

RUNAWAY

Staven's mouth dropped open even as he shook his head. "Changing Dream Paths? Did you actually just say that? I couldn't have heard that right."

Clavin chewed the inside of lip and forced a grin he didn't feel. "I am, old nut. I know it sounds crazy, but I'm going to run Samlin-Kakel. I wanted you to be the first to know. Now you can go make your bets."

Staven just stared back at him. "Uhm ..."

Clavin barked a short laugh. "Staven Roth at a loss for words. I finally did it. I shut you up."

Staven relaxed a hair. "So, this is a joke? You just wanted to rattle me?"

"No, no joke. I'm switching."

Staven leaned over the table. "Why? Are you mad? Have you lost it? Are you still mourning Merinda? Are you still shook from that eight Chark? What the hell? 'Scuse my language, old nut, but really, what the hell?"

"That eight Chark shook me, Staven. I can't deny that.

It took a while to get my confidence back. That might be part of it. But that's not all of it."

"So, what's the rest? Merinda?"

Clavin denied it with a firm shake of the head. "No. I was sad about Merinda, yes, but this isn't about her. Merinda was tortured by her feelings of inadequacy due to her looks in real-world. But I didn't assign any of that to myself. If anything, I think I was always supportive of her."

Staven settled back into his chair. "Well, you don't know that."

"Oh no, I do. She had arranged to have an entire set of diaries delivered to me after her death. I've been reading them. Some of them are heartbreaking. I feel honored to have known her here in the Inn, where her looks were never an issue. We learned the beauty of the Inner woman and weren't affected by the outward appearance."

Staven waved it off. "Yeah, okay, that's sad, I agree, but back to you. You just said those journals are sad. How do you know they aren't affecting you? In fact, what good can come of reading them anyway?"

Clavin's mind flashed over previous internal discussions he'd had with himself which concerned the need to keep what Merinda had learned about controlling Twist secret. *Gonna keep that quiet for now.* "Staven, Merinda was a good friend, and she had no one. Reading her diary keeps her alive in a sense. I feel like it is the least I can do."

"Okay, I'll take your word for it. Then why? If you start a new Path, you're starting over. You're going to lose a ton of the magic that you've collected on Samlin-Cordis. You'll have to come up to speed on the new Path. And money. They won't pay you Ranger rates anymore. You'll be starting over. It doesn't make any sense."

Clavin steeled himself to put out the lie he had rehearsed for this moment. "Staven, do you recall how it was in the beginning? How fun and exciting it was? Samlin-Cordis isn't that fresh anymore. It pretty much the same things, rehashed over and over. I'm ready to see something new, experience a different type of world."

"Well, your Dreamers and Binder will still give you a lot of what you had before." Staven waved a hand. "You know that, right?"

"That's why I'm changing them too."

Staven's mouth fell open yet again.

"Ha," Clavin barked. "Twice in one day."

Over the next week, the Inn buzzed with talk about Clavin's change of Path. Some was positive, and a lot was negative. All of it served to enhance his reputation. But none of that mattered to him. He was doing his utmost to leave Rige and Garner behind for good. Three months and thirty-eight Crossings passed, and he was well on his way to Runner status on his new Path.

"Well, it's certainly different," he murmured as he studied the giant treetops of the forest that lay before him. "I kinda like it."

Two miles and more in height they stood, and the base

of each, so he'd been told, was four hundred feet in width. The leaves were nearly black, and the bark almost white. The lowest limbs began a thousand feet up, and the fallen leaves that carpeted the dim caverns of the forest floor were lost to his sight over the horizon.

The Tall Forest appeared to be normal in other respects, and for that, he was thankful.

Wouldn't do to encounter a colony of giant ants, he thought. *Course that doesn't mean it won't happen.*

With that note of caution in his mind, he continued to walk toward the distant forest that rose before him like a mountain range. He drew forth his map and consulted it carefully for any clues.

He could see the path he trod clearly entered the Tall Forest, plainly labeled as such, and wound its way through it and out the other side. Kakel was drawn as a castle buried amid that massive wood, directly on the path.

The town ahead of him was also shown, labeled in generous script: "Woodstock."

The only real problem that presented itself was the sheer length of the journey. The Tall Forest, if his map could be trusted, ran two thousand miles in one direction and another thousand in the other. Clavin knew from long experience that there would be some way to make the long journey to Kakel in the five days that remained before the Dream collapsed.

However, if he didn't find it very quickly, he would need to turn about and make the four-day return trip to Samlin before time ran out. He had been on the lookout for tricks that could speed him on his way but, as yet, had found none. Clavin stopped and gave the situation a professional evaluation. Time had become a real issue. If he pressed on and didn't unravel the mystery of traversing the Tall Forest, he would be dead. If, however, he turned about and headed back, his pride would take a beating, and his reputation would suffer among the Travelers.

Five days to travel five hundred miles through a mile-high forest.

"How?"

Carriage line or swift-moving river.

"Right."

A flying horse or one that can run without tiring. Anything's possible. There's just no way to know at this point.

"Okay, I need another half day to make it to Woodstock," he said to the wind. "Let's say I walk on in and then find that those things don't exist. What then? I'll have all of, what, four hours tops to discover some trick to make the trip possible. And if I don't figure it out by then?"

I'm running flat out back to Samlin with a narrow margin.

"I don't think so."

How long has it been since you've done that? Everyone is going to hear that the ex-Ranger had to bail on his run. "How the mighty have fallen" will be the phrase of the day.

Clavin stood frozen by indecision for a few seconds.

Mistake number one. I'm no fresh Walker, and I've got enough rep to last me a lifetime. Time to pack it in.

He turned his back on the Tall Forest and retraced

his steps toward Samlin as he moved away from the giant treetops that taunted him in the receding distance. Clavin walked for half an hour when, far ahead, he saw a glimmer of light. He raised the farsight tube to his eye and focused in on the flashes. Two armored knights camped on the trail miles in the distance. Clavin snapped the tube closed, turned 'round, and began to head back toward Woodstock at a trot.

For the love of ...

The ghosts of his past, thrown off for a while, had found him at last on the trails of Samlin-Kakel.

Clavin jogged into Woodstock a few hours later. He wasted none of his remaining time and got right to business. He hailed the first person he saw.

"Hello, sir, have I come at last to the town of Woodstock?"

"Aye, that you have. And where be you from?" asked the old man in return.

"I am a Knight of Samlin, newly made with miles to travel until I reach Castle Kakel. I'm told that it lies deep within the Tall Forest. Do you know if that's true?"

"Kakel ... aye, it's a long piece of travel, and few travel there. Long in the saddle, but more on the feet. I suppose you'll be trying the latter."

"That depends on this town, my good man. If there's no better way, then yes, I'll set off on foot. I was hoping, however, a horse and a carriage might exist here to take me."

"Well, there is if you have the right stack of coin. I'm thinking, perhaps, you don't have the look."

"Never fear about that; my looks are deceiving. If transportation can be bought, I should have coin enough. Where shall I inquire?"

"In the middle of town meet two major streets. Take the one off to the right, and you'll come to the Carriage and Coach, a quarter mile down."

With those simple instructions, Clavin thanked the man heartily and took off at a run. Five minutes later, he bounded up on a porch attached to a stable with many coaches and a carriage outside. He pushed through the doors, entered the office, and turned to the man who called out.

"Hello, good sir, how may we help you?"

"I'm looking for transport to Kakel. It needs to be both fast and soon on its way. A man in town directed me here."

"The next coach leaves tomorrow morning. It is one gold in advance. You'll be there in four days."

Clavin imagined the two knights coming behind reaching the town later that night. *I don't think so.* "Why the delay? I need to be going. Sooner than soon."

"We must fill the coach to match income to cost. A line such as this is quite expensive to run."

"If that is the reason, I can pay for the lot. The coach will not hold more than six people, so six gold would seem to have me on my way."

The man raised an eyebrow. "Correct, sir, but there is cargo involved. The total for the carriage is nine. Do you have such a sum?"

"That I do."

Both eyebrows climbed over his glasses as he appraised Clavin's clothes. "This will be in advance, you understand?"

Clavin reached into his pouch and drew forth the coins, setting them down and stacking them up.

"It is rare, indeed, to encounter a rich man in Woodstock, but not beyond question. I will need to check the coin that you offer, and if it does pass, then you'll be on your way. You do understand that I have to be cautious?"

"Of course, sir. Only, I beg you to be quick about it. Time is now dear to me as my offer should prove."

The man *was* quick, and forty minutes later, carriage hitched and horses watered, Clavin clattered toward the Tall Forest.

They rolled through wood caverns in the permanent twilight at the base of the trees. The trail was well kept but twisted and turned as it wound 'round through the night, broken only by the light from the carriage's post lamps.

There was little to see, but once in a while, eyes glowed back from the dark. Now and again, a great fallen leaf, browned in its age, poked out from the blackness, revealing a glimpse of what Clavin supposed lay hidden from sight.

From time to time, over the clip and clop of the horses' hooves, above the clatter of carriage wheels, Clavin would hear a flutter, as of some mighty bird was winging 'round in the dark. He asked the driver about this, but in typical Dream fashion, the driver knew nothing but the way of the path.

Every ten miles, and on every hour, the carriage pulled up at a forest waystation. The team of six horses was soon changed for six fresh ones and, with no delay, they'd set out once more. Eleven such changes were made that first day, and on the twelfth and last change, they stopped for the night.

Four days passed in this manner until at last, the carriage stopped amid the road beside a great marker of moss-covered stone. Dismounting, the driver came 'round and opened wide the carriage door.

"All out for Kakel," the driver said.

"What are you talking about? There's nothing out there but silent dark. Where's the city?"

"What? Don't you know? It's up there."

Clavin's eyes followed the man's arm, pointing straight up.

"Up there?" echoed Clavin hollowly.

"Yes, sir. In the top of the forest. Kakel is the tree-top city of the Tall Forest."

"Oh. I see. Very well, then. That wasn't clear to me from my map. So tell me, how do I get up there?"

"I'm sure I don't know. You could always try the stair, but it's supposed to be right dangerous, it is."

"What stair?"

"There's said to be a stair that winds 'round the Kakel Oak and takes you to the very top. But there are also many dangerous beasts that roam there as you go higher. It's too dark for the really bad ones down here, they say, and for that I am thankful."

Forget giant ants, he thought as he imagined a battle with a giant squirrel.

"I have to make Kakel by end of day. Have you no other information? Haven't you dropped others here before?"

"No, sir, you're the first. However, there's an old rhyme that I've heard about this place:

If you want to go to Kakel, you must learn how to fly,

for taking stair 'round wood and tree is a goodly way

to die."

Crap, Clavin thought. *I've got four hours—time's a-wasting.*

Clavin stepped forth from the carriage, climbed up its frame, and took down a lantern. He pulled forth a golden coin from his pouch and forestalled the driver's protests.

"Wait here for a bit. I may have more questions."

He walked to the marker stone, read its directions, and took off to the right. Pressing out into the dark, Clavin stepped from the paved path and onto one of unkempt dirt lined with whitened rock. From out of the dark, just off the trail, appeared a tremendous giant leaf, browned and curled up in its death, perhaps forty feet long. He stepped over to it, reached forth a fist, and tested its shell.

A hollow thud echoed from the paper-dry hull.

Onward he walked until the trail passed through a tunnel bored through a root that could have been an average tree fallen down. With great caution, he walked through, and soon after that came to a vast wall of bark that was doubtless the trunk of the Kakel Oak. Grown into its side was a stairway that wound into the dark in an upward right spiral.

I need some more light. This magical torch doesn't put out enough.

Back to the carriage, Clavin asked the driver if the torch could be made to emit greater brightness.

"That it can. The lantern uses fuel but doesn't burn it with a flame. If you turn the base about, the light will shine forth brighter. That, however, will cause the fuel, like any other, to be used a great deal faster. The lanterns have enough to last a ten-day journey."

Clavin turned back to the darkness. With a sharp turn of the base, light blazed forth from the lantern and blasted a vast swath of light all about them.

Scattered all about the forest floor, leaves lay random and sparse. Clavin was quick both of wit and of mind. He knew in an instant that something was strange. He stared and pondered the view while he puzzled it out.

Not enough leaves. The whole place should be covered—stupid Dream logic.

But something yet nagged at him, a restless thought that tickled in the black dark of his mind.

"Something's not right about this," he spoke to the driver.

"What would that be?"

"There's not enough leaves, for one. But there's something more beyond."

"Huh. I wouldn't have thought of that. Hey, they're in various colors. Some are quite fresh and others quite old."

He's right.

"You're right. The wind might snap off a new leaf or two, but they generally fall when they're dried up and old. I'm going to check out that green one over there. Wait here."

As he made his way over, Clavin heard another loud flutter, and down from above wafted a dried out oak leaf curled up at the edges. It floated down gently, three or more hundred feet from his vantage as Clavin considered the difference between old leaf and new. He examined the green leaf around which he walked and bent down to inspect the side to the ground.

A cobweb-ish material ran thick underneath it, and Clavin took care lest something come out.

Wonder if it's super sticky?

He thrust in a glove and pulled it back out. The web he touched had stretched taut and resisted, but none of it stuck in the least to his glove. Next, he took his sword and swept the blade underneath, removing the webs, and smiled at the result; the side of the leaf bent upward before him as it reached for the sky.

I'll be darned. This ought to be fun.

Clavin stepped onto the leaf and cut through some holes. With rope from the driver, he rigged up a harness. With a sweep of sword under leaf, Clavin leaped to his harness but soon stepped back off as nothing more happened.

Not enough, I suppose.

Three times more he tried, and on the last, he succeeded. Having swept clear the underside of the leaf, it tore itself free and shot up from the ground into the darkness above. It twisted and turned as it rose through the night. Clavin, however, had ridden magic carpets many times on Samlin-Cordis and knew how to handle himself in the air.

With guide ropes attached to the leaf, front and side, he'd soon mastered his vessel and rode calmly upward. Mighty branches appeared. Clavin dodged 'round them like a dancer in a troupe and, after fifteen long minutes, spied light from above. As he rose on still farther, he noticed the branches, so barren before, bore leaves now upon them.

His job became harder as he rose to the light, dodging tree-branch and leaf, but also easier as light brought to his vision paths he could chase that once had been hidden. As he approached the canopy, the upward thrust weakened, and the leaf fought to approach each limb that it passed, but Clavin was smart and would not allow that.

When it touches a limb, it will likely attach, and when it does that, I'm stuck going on foot.

At last, near the very top of the tree, the leaf would rise no more, and Clavin fought to stay in control while it swooped and bucked as it dodged side to side.

This is as high as it'll take me.

With all of his skill and strength, he steered the leaf in and made for the trunk. After his leaf had attached, Clavin jumped off and onto the limb, a twig for this tree, not two feet across. Rope bridges ran all through the treetop, and Clavin was soon on his way up.

On the roof of the world, under a white cotton cloud-bank, the bridge he was on ran up into the mist to the city that lay on top of the clouds which billowed above him. Clavin climbed upward and left the treetops below. Soon he had passed through the cloud to come out onto a blue path that led to a castle a half-mile beyond.

Who's the man? he thought happily. *Who is the man?*

Then, up through the mist between him and the castle, rose the sight he felt should still be far behind him. Two silver knights came squeaking toward him.

Clavin gave a full-on curse in his mind.

He spun about and ran back down the path to the rope bridge that descended through the clouds. Halfway down to the treetop, he turned and prepared an audacious and desperate maneuver. There on the bridge, swaying, he waited, sword in his right hand, left arm wound in the roping. The knights approached, single file. As they closed the final distance, Clavin chopped on the right hawser and snapped it cleanly in two.

The knight behind never saw what he had done and tumbled off without a sound to disappear in the mist.

The knight in the front had seen just in time and grabbed the near rope with both hands, dropping his sword.

Clavin twisted about, sheathed his blade, and worked his way forward till he stood near the knight whose armor plate weighed him down. He drew his sword and sent the knight on his way with a single quick thrust, after which Clavin clawed his way back to the sky-path above.

Shaken sick with the shock of his fright, he ran through the Veil, out through the returning gate just ahead, and into the Inn where, without further ado, he retched on the floor. Looking up, he saw surprised recognition in the faces about him. In some, he saw pity.

Pride crushed, he ran from the room. He made his way, slowly and surely, but without truly planning, back to a place he'd been not long before. Only as he reached the last hallway did he understand that somehow his feet had managed to bring his aimless wandering back to this empty chamber.

Harven's Portal.

He stepped in, looked over to the left, and waved at the man who sat behind the bar. The man smiled at him and, with a quick nod in reply, Clavin headed to the back corner where he had occupied the last time. He sat down at the rough table and gave passing notice to its poor condition as he leaned elbows upon it and buried his face in his hands.

He heard Justinus approach, looked up, and sank back into his chair.

Justinus deposited the bread and water on the coarse tabletop and then appraised Clavin for a quiet moment before speaking. "No one is perfect you know."

Clavin absorbed these words and shook his head. *Man, I must look bad.*

"Justinus, I can't fix the past, I can't ignore it, and I can't bury it."

"No man can do those things, Traveler."

He recalled that he had never told Justinus his name. *Right. Traveler.* "There's no hope then. There's no hope for any of us."

"Oh no. With me there is always hope."

A soured look covered Clavin's face. *Lucky you.* "Well, I wish I could say that. I wish you could give *me* some of that hope."

Justinus smiled and replied, "I will if you ask."

"Isn't that what I just did?"

"Many people wish for things but refuse to ask," Justinus explained.

Hairsplitting.

"Alright. Justinus, would you please share your hope with me?"

Justinus reached under his shirt and drew forth a rough, wooden talisman. He handed it over. "Ask, and you shall receive."

"Magic?" Clavin asked sardonically as he reached out to take the token.

Justinus shook his head as he laid the object into Clavin's hand. "No. A gift. A free gift from me to you."

"Well, it's a nice gesture, but I don't know how it helps. Thanks, anyway."

"You need to deal with your problem. You need to get rid of it."

"You said that before but offered no practical method."

"You need to find something else to lean on. Something besides yourself. Something greater than you."

"Like this?" Clavin replied as he fingered the talisman he now held.

"Why not?"

"I know that you mean well, and I do appreciate that. But I can deal with this in my own way."

"I will not see you here again."

"How do you know that?"

"You'll find that I'm an excellent judge of both character and thought."

"You know, I really think that you are. I'm leaving the Dream for good. There's no other way now."

"There is one," replied Justinus as he nodded at Clavin's hand.

"No," Clavin replied as he shook his head. "Not for me."

Stuck on the world of Kakel, cut off and friendless, Clavin generated yet another round of Traveler gossip; he hired Venif Crush, the most experienced Warrior on Samlin-Kakel to take him back to Samlin.

This would be, Clavin felt, his last Crossing, and wherever he landed, he would live and die there. He had wrestled with where to finish his days, Samlin or Cordis. Clavin was no longer close to his parents, and he feared his notoriety would follow him down onto Cordis making him, there, the butt of many a joke. So Samlin it was.

As he set out that night, Clavin considered what Venif must think about him.

How the mighty have fallen. The sting was tremendous, and little was said between the two men as they traveled the trail onward to Samlin. When they met the two knights, Venif the Warrior had little difficulty with them, whereas Clavin the Walker would likely have died. With their dispatch, Clavin and Venif made it on in with no further trouble.

Humbled in spirit, Clavin made his way 'round to

where his friend Staven waited. Those who sat with him said not a word, but got up and left as Clavin sat down.

"Embarrassed to be near me," Clavin said bitterly.

"Clavin, I've got to ask you, as a friend, just what in the hell is going on with you?"

"I think you've hit it on the nose."

"I'm sure that's somehow very clever, but frankly I don't get it. Plain speaking. What's up?"

"Hell. I'm going through—have been going through, in fact—my own personal hell. It tracks me in the Dream Lands now, and I can't shake it, can't bury it, and can't run from it. So, I'm going now where it can't go. I'm leaving."

"A year ago, I would have thought you nuts to say that. Really, I would have. But now, the way you've been acting, I think perhaps it's for the best. Sorry, old nut, but that's the plain truth."

"Old nut. Appropriate for final salutations I think."

"Clavin, I don't think that you're nuts, just ..."

"What? Broken? Burned out? In need of a little rest, perhaps?" Clavin shook his head at his friend before he spoke again. "Never you mind, old bean. I know what you meant. Now, I've had time to consider my final toast words, and they are these."

He raised his glass and waited for Staven to do the same.

"You do the Whacking, and I'll do the Cracking."

Staven smiled in reply. "No, here's to the wittiest man that I've ever known. May your life be happy and your road be smooth."

Clavin nodded. "Thanks, Stave, and right back at you."

As he left the Traveler's Inn, Clavin paused at the portal and considered his life, his fortune, and his fame. Finally, he turned away, stepped onto Samlin, and said goodbye to a lifetime of glory.

Days would pass, and a restless Michael Envine, young of age and fat of purse, grew increasingly bored with life and yearned for adventure. Though he tried many things, he found that none could compare with the fantastic sights offered up by the Dream Lands.

So he drank.

He drank in the morning to relieve the pain of the evening, and he drank in the evening to quench the guilt of the past. For the most part, this worked, but it had one basic flaw: He could not drink when passed out in bed. And, waking in the early hours, the flaw presented itself in nightmare fashion as tormenting dreams broke down his walls of alcoholic numbness.

Michael woke again, having dreamed of Garner and Rige. They taunted and challenged him even outside of the Dream Lands, in the routine dreams of his natural slumber. A month or more passed in this unpleasant manner with no rest in sight. A defeated Michael came to the realization that he'd have to take care of his problem or the problem, un-dealt with, would take care of him.

Michael sent for his lawyers and made out his will. He spoke to his head servant, Corval, and informed him that he was about to return to the Dream and might not be back.

"Sir," asked a sympathetic Corval, "why is this necessary? You are a very rich man. You can retire in wealth and live in peace for the rest of your life."

Michael laughed at that.

"Corval, my friend, I don't mean to insult you, but the simple fact is you have no idea what you're talking about."

"Perhaps not, sir. You would understand better than I. It is clear that something has been bothering you for quite a long time now. I hope you can find a way to put it behind you."

Michael sighed. "Oh, I've tried that. Yes, indeed. I have humiliated and debased myself trying to do that very thing. People who once looked up to me as a giant and a mentor, who hung on my every word, now laugh at me behind my back and can barely stand to sit at my table. How the mighty have fallen."

"Sir, may I suggest something?"

"Of course, Corval. Suggest away."

"Sir, sooner or later, even the mighty fall but the great ones, the *truly* great ones, are great for one simple reason."

"Let me guess. They get up?"

"Oh, no, sir. Even the strongest can reach the point where he can no longer get up."

"Huh. Okay, what then?"

"They ask for some help."

Makes sense. "What if there is no one to ask?"

Corval had to pause before replying. "Then, I suppose they find something else to lean on."

Michael rolled that around in his mind for a moment

before nodding. "You know, Corval, someone else told me the same thing."

"Perhaps he was right."

Michael shrugged. "I'll tell you when I get back."

FINAL CROSSING

Who's the man? he thought as he stomped through the hallways of the Traveler's Inn with a sour look on his face. *I'm going to kill 'em. Next time they show up, I'm going to kill 'em and kill 'em and kill 'em. I'll cut 'em down, pick 'em up, and cut 'em down again. I'm going to smash 'em and slash 'em. I'm going to put such a hurting on them that they'll never darken my trail again. I'm the man, and I'm going to show them what that means.*

Mess with this bull, you get the horns.

Some minutes later, he was seated in his usual place across from his friend.

"Clavin, what's going on?" Staven demanded. "You roll in here a couple months ago, tell me that you're switching Paths. Last month, you were quitting altogether. Now you're back and returning to Samlin-Cordis. I think that's a good move, a smart move, but clearly something is wrong. Something's been wrong for a while now."

"I've got some unfinished business that has to be taken care of. I thought I could ignore it. I tried to deal with it, and then I tried to avoid it, make it go away, but now I know that I can't. I've got to deal with it, and to deal with it, I've got to return to Samlin-Cordis."

"Are you going to be able to close the books on this business? Will you finish this time?"

Clavin ground his teeth together. "One way or another. One way or another."

Staven pondered the words. "There's a certain tone of finality about that. Almost fatalistic. I'm not too sure that's the right attitude to take in there with you."

Clavin snorted a mirthless laugh. "Confidence, power, strength. That's the right attitude, correct?"

Staven cocked an eyebrow back at him. "You know better than I."

"No. It won't work. I've tried it."

"Then what? What's left?"

Clavin's fingernails dug across the tabletop. "Commitment. I'm going in fully committed."

When the Caller came, Staven followed him to his gate and met the Merchant who stood waiting with paperwork and a backpack.

Clavin signed for the load, took the backpack, and inserted his key into the gate. Hearing it click, he pulled the door open. A short hall, maybe eight feet long, ran down to the twisting opaque whiteness of the Veil that now taunted him. He took a deep breath as he prepared to step in.

Before he could, Staven spoke. "Good luck, old nut."

Clavin turned and raised his right hand. Though they

could not touch, Staven raised his own in response and held it up next to Clavin's.

A fake grin pulled up the corner of Clavin's mouth. "I put down ten gold against my return tonight in your name. Well, I paid someone to do it. A hundred to one."

Staven's mouth dropped open, and his hand dropped away. "Clavin, don't go. Go home."

"I can't, Staven. I can't go home again. That door is closed against me. It's forward or nothing now."

Staven's hand jerked out to grab him, but it passed through Clavin's arm to no effect. "Clavin, stop."

Clavin backed into the hallway toward the Veil.

Staven looked around and cried out, "Stop Clavin. Someone stop him. Quick." He looked back, and they locked gazes.

"I'll see you on the other side, Staven." He turned and took three steps. The mist enveloped him, and he was gone.

Clavin Roth would never be seen in the Traveler's Inn again.

Clavin passed through the narrow band of white and appeared outside of a gate in Samlin. He sat down in the grass to run through his usual routine of checking and prepping. Satisfied, he repacked his gear, rose to his feet, and set off down the hill toward the crystal-blue lake laid out below.

The lake peeked in and out of view as he made his way down through the pine forest that covered the mountain.

It was a beautiful day of warm sunlight and singing birds, and soon he found himself on level ground as he approached a boathouse. He looked around for a keeper but, seeing none, stepped down into the one boat he saw, cast off the ropes, and sat down. He was unsurprised when the boat began to move through the clear water and make its way toward the distant shores of the surrounding hills.

Clavin had seen all this before.

He reached into his pouch, drew forth some wax, and stoppered his ears. Just a few minutes later, the reason became clear. Mermaids rose from the crystal-liquid blue about him and began to call out to him.

Clavin smiled back and waved in response.

No go, fish girls.

The girls disappeared with a flip of their tails, and Clavin chanted words that usually worked magic and was pleased to find that they worked well again; the boat doubled in speed. He glanced behind and chuckled as mermen, who had followed up on the mermaids, fell astern as they shouted silent curses and brandished spears at him.

He waved back at their furious gestures. *Be glad you didn't catch me.*

A hundred feet out from the bank, the vessel gave a slight lurch as it slowed until, with a soft thump and a bump, it docked and sat still. Clavin stepped out of the boat, onto the dock, and headed up the path and into the woods.

The woods were thin and allowed the sun to dapple the floor of the forest with leaf-filtered light. Clavin passed through the wood and, rounding a bend, stopped at the edge of a clearing and next to a sign.

Samlinsk Village.

He moved onward and addressed the first person who happened nearby him. "Excuse me, young man, have you ever heard of the Castle of Cordis?"

"No, sir. Never been far. Janey might know. She's traveled a lot."

"Where may I find her?"

"Fourth building down, ahead on the right. Painted in pink. No way to miss it."

A short minute later, he knocked on the door and stood back to wait.

"Come in," came a voice.

He worked the latch and entered the room in the middle of which sat a fair woman of youngish middle-aged years threading a shawl.

"A young man up the street directed me here. He thought you might know of a castle called Cordis."

"Once, years ago, I traveled a bit," she replied with a smile. "I've seen some and heard some. Cordis, is it? Now that's a far piece indeed."

"Do you by chance have a map? Could you please show me?"

"I don't have a map but, had I some paper, I could sketch you a rough one."

"That will do nicely." Clavin recovered the items from his magic pouch and handed them to her. While she worked, he recovered the Hand of Fate and held onto it as he muttered his keyword just over a whisper. She glanced up at his whispering.

"Sorry, I'll be quiet."

She smiled and went back to work even as he focused on his desire.

Let the Dark Castle exist as it existed before.

When she finished, he took a small breath, picked up the map, and peered down at it intently. An image of the Dark Castle now lay in plain sight.

He smiled and released the breath he'd taken. His mind flashed through the preparations he'd undertaken using the notes he'd read that Merinda had left him. Drawings from his nightmare, images of Rige and Garner trapped in their armor, the king's hall, the troll, the princess. Copies sent to all of the members of his Dream Group with instructions to study them nightly and commit them to memory.

Thanks, Meri. Here at the end, I needed your help.

Tonight, it would all pay off.

Elated, he paid the woman, thanked her profusely, and left.

Clavin strode down the street until he found a stable, then walked over and in. "Hello. Is anyone home?"

"Just a minute," came a voice lost in the back.

A man stepped out of a stall, turned toward him, and shortened the distance between them. Callused hands brushed up dusty clouds against the sides of brown pants worn thin. The man got straight to business.

"So then, sir, how can I help you?"

"A horse. I need a horse, both strong and fast."

"Well now, we have strong ones and fast ones but few that are both. Some can be bought, and others cannot."

"May I take a look?"

"Please."

Clavin walked along the aisle and peered into stalls until he found what he wanted.

"This one. Is this stallion for sale?"

He was not, it turned out, for sale at all, being the mount of some local celebrity. Clavin, however, had soon worked around that and was off on his way with five fewer golds.

As he thundered from Samlinsk, he had but one thought on his mind.

Three days to the Vast Desert.

Clavin reached the edge of the desert with naught but the usual collection of nuisance distractions which he'd quickly dispatched on the edge of his sword. On the third day, he had ridden into the town of Edgewater, the very last before the Vast Desert, past which no civilization existed. He left the horse, refilled three of his vials with an impossibly large quantity of water, and headed outward to force a last showdown.

He drew upon his vast storehouse of knowledge, gathered from years of Traveling this trail, and was able to find and use the blue sands of jumping to move him along at ten miles a leap. Ten thousand miles, one side to another, stretched the sands and the buttes of a snake-ridden land. The weather was strange in the Vast Desert, alternatively pouring down heat and cool water, cloudy by day and moonlit by night. The wolf and the jackal were frequent companions, calling at times across the vast, sandy land. Yet water was there in sufficient abundance that, in the real-world, grass would have grown and covered the dirt.

The desert was desert for one simple reason: This was a Dream, and in the Dream it was so.

Clavin's stated goal was to cross this desert and get to Castle Cordis with his load of goods. Clavin's personal goal, for once in his long career, was different.

He had a castle to find, that was true, but not Cordis. Not yet.

He inspected the crude map drawn for him in Samlinsk. Clavin concentrated on that small image in the desert depiction and willed it to exist, to stay put and wait for him.

If this works, all I need to do is move toward where I think it should be, and it will be there. It has to work.

Clavin moved on, diverting from Cordis, in search of the other. Hours passed and, after yet another jump, Clavin's blood rushed as he saw, rising before him, the miniature mountain of the Dark Castle for which he searched.

He froze.

A violent, shrieking Chark began to howl about him where moments before all had been calm. The chilly darkness had come for him as he had come for it. His Feening

441

told him a gale roared about him but, to his natural senses, all was as it had been before—calm and peaceful.

Just like last time. Maybe even worse. But this time, it's all me.

Clavin stalked toward the stupendous gatehouse.

Who's the man? he demanded as he worked himself up. *Who's the man?*

He approached the great portcullis, and it began to rise. Clavin paced back and forth as it clattered its way upward and left a twelve-foot gap. As he passed under it, it dropped.

He dove forward, rolled back to his feet, and glared about him.

Want to play rough? Fine by me.

He drew his sword, cast various spells, and stalked down the dark passage. A minute later, he passed under the other massive gate that, this time, didn't try to kill him. He stared at the gates and dared them to move. He glared out across the giant courtyard and took off on a leftward tangent. *Let's shake it up a bit.*

Halfway across, out from a passage on the other side of the courtyard, came the princess figure. He turned toward her and prepared for the worst. Two minutes later, they closed the gap between them and stopped.

Though dressed in black, her eyes shone an eerie white which matched the hair that adorned her. She was alto-gether beautiful but in a bizarre way.

Okay, standard wizardess, witch, princess model number who-the-hell-cares.

"Who are you, and what is this place?" he demanded gruffly.

She raised her eyes to capture his. "Not a very elegant salutation."

Still testy from the gate, he replied, "Your gate quite nearly killed me back there. You might say I'm on edge."

Better not kill her. Might not find my two boys.

"For that, I am sorry. What may we do to put you at your ease?"

Last time it was the banquet hall next.

"I am quite famished from my long journey. Perhaps some refreshment?"

"An excellent thought. Even now, my father sits at his table."

No kidding.

"Please follow me." She turned and began to walk away.

A half-hour passed and half again more.

He frowned. *Timing is off. Everything is off.*

Just as before, the castle was vast beyond reason, and they walked through rooms that seemed to have no end. Up they went, stair after stair, landing after landing until, at last, he walked into a room at least a hundred feet tall. Deep shadows draped the ceiling while the far wall of white marble outlined two blackwood doors forty feet high and adorned with blood red stones.

His guide stepped toward the massive doors, stopped, and waved toward them.

"The throne room of his Majesty, King Finis the Last, of the Dark Castle. Be welcome."

Clavin took a breath and looked at the imposing slabs of darkness.

Afraid of a couple of doors?

He snorted at the thought as he potioned himself with super strength, then stepped up to the portal and shoved.

Clavin snapped back to the present.

I guess that brings the story up to date. Here, in this room, the final chapter will write itself. No one will know what happened. Just like Merinda—pop, I'll be gone. His thoughts shifted again. *I hope Mom likes the poem. I want her to know—for both of them to know—that at the end, I loved them. All of them. How did it go?*

Take me to an alpine valley and there let me lie,
listen to the whispering wind soft upon the land,
walk through sunlit flowers dancing under clear blue sky
and circling back at last to me gently take my hand.

Squandered treasures from my birth; your hand a satin glove,
arms circled around me shielding; a disregarded band,
childhood dreams and tragedies you smoothed out with your love,
reach down to me one last time and gently take my hand.

Remembered now the times we spent together on the lake,
you showed me how to cook the fish later on the sand,
though I drifted far from you, those memories cannot shake,
feel my sorrow as you reach and gently take my hand.

A sister ever testing, strong, determined to be seen,
and yet later, we grew close as foolish youth was banned.
I should have told you that I thought you clever and so keen,
forgive me now for words unsaid and gently take my hand.

Let flowered valley in your minds now fill the empty space,
and we shall meet and laugh again in that magic land,
waiting now I can dream these words will find their place,
I reach out in my mind to you and gently take your hands.

An hour had passed, and they heard the beast coming. His heart thundered as his body stood and reached for the spear. He heard the beast as it turned and charged down their corridor. Clavin pictured his parents one last time in his mind.

Bye.

Clavin raised the spear and braced for the fight. He glanced up and thought, *God, help me.*

As he did so, a splinter pricked painfully under his armor, and control returned to him in a burst.

Clavin had been stuck in this room with the ghosts of his victims for hours. Besides recounting his life, he'd imagined what things he could do if he could just do anything, if he could get hold of his sword, Peccavi, which lay sheathed on Rige-ghost's left hip.

He already knew that Rige haunted the left corner.

Clavin leaped to the far wall to get between the two men, but closer to Rige. Their helmets spun around to face him. Clavin turned and made as if to face the coming fight. They followed suit.

Clavin sidled left, closer to Rige, and the man looked over at him and shouted, "Stay."

The troll burst into the room, spun right, and headed straight for Clavin.

The monster delivered a massive blow against Clavin's breastplate that he, in turn, used to amplify his own leap backward.

Directly at Rige.

The Rige-ghost, already in the left corner, dodged with a leap to the right.

Clavin rolled up, levered off the wall, and came up behind a surprised Rige.

The troll, attracted by the spell Rige and Garner had placed on him earlier to focus its attacks on Clavin first, found an obstacle in its way: namely, Rige. The monster struck out to remove it even as Clavin's hand latched onto the pommel of Peccavi in Rige's sheath.

As Rige flew rightward, toward his brother ghost, Garner, Clavin cried out, "Peccavi," and the sword blazed into power. One blow later, from an overhand swing, the troll went its separate way and stopped bothering anyone.

Clavin turned to face the two ghosts that had tormented him for so long.

So, we *got here after all.*

"You're supposed to go back to the king now," said Rige.

"Get moving," Garner ordered.

Clavin grinned.

Their fight came to an immediate end as Peccavi licked out, sliced through armor, skin, and bone alike, leaving them two feet shorter and four feet shy. Clavin then proceeded to brutally torture the helpless specters, ignoring their screams of pain and agony. To keep them alive, he used his potions liberally again and again. An hour passed in this horrific manner. Finally, burned out, blood soaked, and even disgusted at what he'd just done, he stopped cutting on them.

"Now," he said to the dying men, "I really don't ever want to see you again. I don't want to hear you, smell you, or anything-else-you ever again. If I do, then this little party will be just the beginning. Do you understand me?"

All that the wrecks of flesh and bone could do was to moan in response and, as they did so, they melted away before him.

Clavin nodded and turned to prepare his exit from the Dark Castle when a terrible screech from the armor set his teeth on edge. During the bloodletting he'd just done, his armor had rusted to the extent that it was now more brown than silver and every move caused an earsplitting shriek. Clavin was forced to plug his ears with wax that reduced the sound only a bit. He tried many oils and potions, but none of them helped to quiet the sickening racket.

God, this is worse than before. I can hardly think.

Unable to remove the armor or quiet it, even with the silence spells at his disposal, Clavin was forced to go onward as the armor emitted a perpetual squeal. He made it to the desert floor and began to move east again, toward Cordis. Within an hour, he had a splitting headache.

I can't take this for two more days.

But with no other good options available, he was forced to keep moving.

The hours crawled past; his headache increased till he couldn't bear the sunlight and his stomach regurgitated through the slats in his helmet, making his nightmare all the worse. Night came and went, and Clavin pushed on. As noon of the next day approached, he arrived at the edge of the Vast Desert and knew that he was but an hour from Cordis.

He staggered on through the blistering heat until he came upon an obstacle new on this journey. Where before the Blue Bog had often acted as a final hurdle, now a mighty river, a mile or more in width and black as sin, flowed ahead of him.

Clavin stumbled forward to the bank of the river and came to a halt. He dipped in the tip of his left pinky. A stab of pain shot clear to his elbow, more like fire than ice, and he yanked his hand back with a scream. His left pinky shattered off his hand at the second knuckle, oozing blood from the stump.

He goggled at the ruined finger for a moment.

He rummaged through his pouch as he tried various things and found, to his despair, that nothing helped to make this river crossable.

I've got to swim this thing, he realized, weak now in both body and mind. *But it can't be swum.*

I've got to get this bloody armor off, but it's now part of me, bound to my guilt.

Clavin sank to his knees in the tall river grasses which ribboned the desert from the water and shook his head in pure, hopeless despair.

It can't be done. It can't be.

Clavin rolled onto his back and closed his eyes. *The final resting place of Clavin Roth. There ought to be a sign posted.* He considered how tantalizingly close he was to Cordis. *So close. But it may as well be a million miles. Instead of dying in terror or glorious combat, I'll die here, exhausted, on my back, waiting for the world to collapse.*

He thought of Rige and Garner again. *In the end, they won after all.*

He thought again of his parents. He was too drained to even feel sad.

I tried, Mom. And Uncle Antik, I didn't give up. I think you'd have been proud of that, at least. At the end, there was just nothing left to do.

Through his closed eyes, he saw the light darken as something threw shadow across him.

"Hello, sir, are you okay?"

Clavin cracked his lids open to see two young faces above him: a girl and a boy. He struggled to sit up, and they reached down to help him.

He shook his head. "No. Who are you? From where?"

The boy replied, "I'm Lohlen, and this is Lientag. We're from Crosstown, just over that hill." He pointed upriver at a hill round which the river snaked.

Hope blossomed, and he found a trickle of new energy. *Ferry. They're sure to have a ferry.* "Ferry," he wheezed. "Have one?"

"Oh no, sir, I'm sorry. Crosstown doesn't have a ferry. There's no way to cross the river."

"Kidding?"

"No, sir. I'm very sorry. Why do you need a ferry?"

"Cordis. Going to Cordis," he almost whimpered.

"Oh, I see. Yes, then you must cross the river. Can you swim it?"

"Armor. Too heavy. Can't swim in it."

"Why won't it come off?"

"Rust," he said sickly.

"Maybe we could remove it."

"No." His head barely wobbled in a shake. "Won't work. Won't come off. Part of me now."

"I've seen others with armor like that. Same problem. Very loud."

Clavin paused as he pondered her words.

"'Kay," he gasped. "Try your way. What's to lose?"

"That armor."

Clavin replied with a short cough meant to be a laugh. "What do I do?"

"It's really quite simple. All you need is oil from the Oil Tree. It can remove anything, including rust. It never fails."

"Where?" he begged.

"On the other side of the village is another hill. Up on top is the Oil Tree. Collect some oil and rub, rub, rub. That's all."

"'Kay. Thanks." He struggled to rise to his feet, and they helped. He leaned on them as he staggered around the hill to the small village on the other side. They blocked their own ears against the noise yet continued to help him.

Clavin wobbled his way through the small village as both people and dogs alike ran away from the squeal of his armor. He passed on through the tiny town and came to the base of another, larger, hill on the other side. He looked up, saw a long, winding trail high above the top of a huge tree.

The children stopped. "I'm sorry, sir. Our father won't let us go farther than this with you. I hope you make it."

He looked back at them, took a large breath, and nodded. "Got me this far. Thanks." With that said, he turned to begin the ascent. As he climbed, he staggered, fell, and crawled as he made his torturous way up the hill until, with trembling muscles and nearly too exhausted to move, he flipped on his back for a rest at the summit.

There was just one single tree on the top of the hill, but it was gigantic indeed. The great tree was filled with life as numerous birds, chipmunks, and squirrels frolicked in its branches high above. In the trunk of the tree, some six feet off the ground, Clavin could see an object embedded that looked like a spigot.

The oil.

After ten minutes, he rolled over, levered himself up, and crawled to the trunk. Leaning on the tree itself for support, he managed to get to his feet to work the tap and found he could not turn it.

Now what?

Clavin struggled with the tap for a while as he tried to force it. He turned back to his pouch and again found nothing to aid him. Exhausted once more from his meager effort, he leaned back on the tree and slid to the ground. Finally defeated, he looked up into the leaves above him and said with disgust, "God, I need help."

With that, the tap above him began to turn on its own, and the brown oil ran down the trunk of the tree behind him.

Too tired to nod, he understood. *The oil is free, but you still have to ask.* He slumped his helmeted head down to wait. Soon he felt the dark, flowing oil touch his neck, having worked its way down over wood and past armor. When it did, the great limbs above him disappeared, and the grass-topped hill became a white, rocky knoll. A wave of refreshment rushed through Clavin. He glanced upward, and in place of the tree, he now saw a great wooden post. Up where the spigot had been in the tree, there was now an iron metal spike, and in place of brown oil, red blood flowed instead. Farther up still was a single crossbeam in each end of which one bleeding spike was driven as well.

Stories from his past rushed through him, and Clavin nodded. He held back tears as he stripped off his armor, which no longer squealed and came away clean. Only the rough, wooden cross, given to him by Justinus, remained— old and worn.

As Clavin stepped back from the post, his avatar fell away, and he became Michael Envine, the man he'd been born. There, in the Dream, Michael knelt and prayed to the God of his father, after which he went down to the river.

He gingerly tested the water with another left-handed finger and found he could not press it into the water at all. He next tested using a foot, which also refused to sink into the black river. Michael laughed as he ran back to the Veil over the deathly water that no longer threatened him.

Clavin Roth never returned to the Traveler's Inn, but Michael Envine did.

As he pushed open the door to reenter the Inn, he heard the thunderous roar from a huge crowd of people erupt. He heard his name being shouted in a chant, and as he stepped out, the huge throng of people before him faltered and ceased as they stared at him.

Staven stood waiting, not ten feet away, mouth open as arms, that had been raised to greet him, fell to his sides. "Who are you?" he demanded.

Michael smiled, understanding their confusion. He raised both hands as he replied. "It's me, Stave, Clavin. I know you'll think I've really lost it this time, but it's me, the real me, Michael Envine. I've had, well, what you might call an *experience*; I'm a changed man. From now on, this is going to be me."

Michael could hear others speaking to each other and caught some of the conversations.

"Is that Clavin?"

"Did he change aspect?"

"Why would he change?"

"What's going on?"

Staven stepped closer to him. "Tell me, who was Merinda's best friend?"

Michael gave a wan half-smile as he nodded. "I understand. It was a blue horse she called Clessy."

Staven's eyes opened a bit as his tense shoulders relaxed. His head bobbed in return. "Okay, Clave, you've got a story to tell, that's clear. Let's head back to the Star so we can hear it all, right?"

"Sure thing. I want to explain it. We'll do that. But there's something I have to do first. It might have to wait till tomorrow night." He looked over at the Merchant who had also moved up. Michael's mood was too good to be soured, and he smiled at the man. "I'm sorry, Coinmar. It was taken from me. I couldn't bring it back."

The man's face fell, but he nodded and turned to leave.

Michael froze him with his next words. "Come see me tomorrow night. I'll stand good for your loss."

Many people gasped.

Coinmar stopped and stared at Clavin/Michael for a moment before replying, "I don't know what happened in there, but I'll be here tomorrow night, and not for the money."

Michael smiled and began to push into the crowd. They parted before him, leaving a wake of whispers as he exited Cordis Hall. He then made his way through thinning hallways, down empty corridors, up many a lonely stair and, in the vastness of the Inn, wandered about till finally he located Harven's Portal again.

Michael stepped in and looked around.

"Justinus? Is anyone home?"

No answer called out in reply.

The room was not large, and Michael made a quick circuit of it. Coming 'round to the corner where they had sat, something strange caught his eye. The table, so rough and worn not long before, was polished to a shining gleam. On the top in its center lay a plain, wooden box.

He stepped to the table and tested its surface with the palm of his hand.

"You're good, Justinus, very good."

Clavin picked up the box, opened it, and looked within.

A tiny wooden splinter, red from drawn blood, lay on a sheet of white satin.

Clavin stared at it for some time as his hand involuntarily rose to rub his own chest, and then he replaced the lid. *Who's the man?* "You are, Lord," he said to the bar and the man who had once worked there.

"You are."

PRODIGAL SON

His carriage clattered back to his mansion, and Michael dismounted. He dismissed the driver who rolled off to the stable and left him at the foot of the staircase.

Michael stood and stared around him for a while, taking it in, and enjoyed the feeling of being alive. Not much went through his mind; he stored the scene of the rising sun's glow, casting long shadows away from the lake and toward him.

Finally, he walked up the steps and took in the sensation of smooth marble sliding beneath his hand on the balustrade. The door opened, and Corval came out to meet him, carafe in hand, glass on a tray.

Clavin smiled. "Corval, you don't approve of my drinking, do you?"

"Sir, it is not my place to say."

"No. But I'm asking, so say what you want."

Corval paused.

"You're not going to get fired for telling me I'm a drunken, lazy lout who should behave better because I was raised better than this."

Corval's face registered surprise. "Sir, you are certainly not lazy. But drinking so much isn't good for you. I wish you would take better care of yourself."

"Corval, you are very tactful. Have you ever considered leaving me to spend more time with your kids?"

Corval's face dropped a little.

"No, no, no," said Michael as he took the glass and carafe from his servant. "You don't understand. I'm not firing you." Michael set the containers down on the top of the flat railing and reached over to take the older man's arm.

Corval's face now registered surprise as Michael steered him back into the mansion.

"My friend, I am going to sell this place, horses and all. I am moving back to Cordis to live near my folks. I want to see that you are taken care of."

The servant stopped in the hall, which forced Michael to stop also. It warmed Michael's heart to see the smile on the man's face.

"Sir, I am so glad to hear that. I think it will do you great good."

Michael smiled. "I've already had some *great good* done for me. Now, it's time I did some of my own. Starting with you. You have a choice: cross with me to Cordis or allow me to pay you a severance."

"Sir, my family is here. I shall remain."

"I thought so."

"Sir, when will you leave?"

"Tomorrow. I have to get back to Cordis immediately. I have some apologies to make, fences to mend."

"No, sir, I meant when shall you leave Samlin? When do you intend to sell the estate? This way, I can inform the others."

Michael nodded. "Corval, I shall leave it to you to sell everything. Your severance shall be a tenth of the proceeds. Get the best price that you can. After tonight, I'm not planning to return. Get my lawyer out here today so that I can wrap this up before I leave tomorrow."

Corval looked stunned by the statement. "Tomorrow?"

"Yes, Corval, tomorrow shall be my last time here. If I have my way."

Corval nodded. "Very well, sir … but, sir, a tenth of this entire estate is a considerable amount to give away to a servant."

"Corval, I'm in a generous mood. I'm not drunk or drugged. I'm tired, but not loopy, from loss of sleep. I know what I'm saying. Call the lawyer. Have him here by noon, and wake me when he arrives."

Corval bowed. "Yes, sir. Thank you, sir. Thank you so very much. It has been a pleasure to serve you."

Michael smiled, patted Corval's arm, then went to his room.

He slept like a baby.

Michael rose, met his Samlin lawyer, and signed various papers. The next morning, he left for Cordis. He had one stop to make before going to the Sanctum and, not knowing how long it might take, set out early to make it.

The carriage deposited him before the farm an hour after noon. At the end of a long gravel road, sat a small farmhouse. Two gables and three windows faced the road, painted white and edged in gray stone. His stomach knotted as he walked down the path and focused on the door as if he approached a dangerous snake rather than an inviting portal. He stepped to the door and took a deep breath to calm his thundering pulse. Strength drained from his arm as it refused to knock. He took another breath and forced his knuckles to their duty.

The wooden panel swung back to reveal a woman of fifty-odd years.

"Yes, young man? How may I help you?"

His knees tremored. "Madam, my name is Michael Envine. I need to tell you and your husband a story. May I come in?"

"A story? About what?"

Michael's throat tightened, and his eyes began to water. He coughed hard and forced a pause.

A worried look crossed her face.

"About Rollen and Garth, Madam," he managed to choke out, "but I knew them as Rige and Garner."

Her eyes teared enough for the both of them as she drew the door open wide.

"Come in, please."

She led him into the den and called out back for her husband to come in from the field. While they waited, the woman brought some tea.

Michael's leg jerked while his knee bounced up and down even as his hands sweated and his pulse raced. It seemed like an eternity passed before her husband arrived.

Michael could see the resemblance between him and his Inn image. The perfected version of the man at his age. Michael got to his feet, wanting to run but determined to stay.

"Hello?" greeted the man as he held out a hand. "Graif Lossenfell. Pleased to meet you."

Michael shook it and blew out another large breath. "Well, I'll let you withhold judgment on that for a few minutes. My name is Michael Envine, but we have already met. Ghost Hunter, meet Clavin Roth."

Graif's eyes opened wide. "Well, well, this is a surprise. And an honor." He turned to his wife. "Alona, this man is the most famous Traveler in the Inn. Clavin Roth, Dream Ranger of Samlin-Cordis."

She looked back at Michael. "So, you said you knew something about our boys?"

Michael opened his mouth to speak and gave a small choke as he struggled to control the tears and the strain in the back of his throat.

"Sit. Take your time."

They all did, and Michael began again. "There is no easy way to say this." He struggled with himself and shook his head. "Your sons, Rollen and Garth, are dead because of me. It was my careless ineptitude, my callous disregard for the pain of others that led directly to it." He looked over at Graif. "Sir, now you understand my shock when you confronted me that night with your secret. I have been through a living nightmare with the guilt. I am here, now, to accept any punishment you would choose to levy."

Alona turned her face away and bit on a knuckle as she wept anew.

Graif stared at Michael for a moment as his hands gripped his chair. "Could you tell us what happened?"

"Yes, sir, of course. It was the night of my Ranger run. There was a huge party at the gate. Over a thousand people were chanting and hooping, and then they started calling for me to make a speech. You, sir, understand that such a scene basically never happens in the Inn. I had never experienced anything like it and, frankly, I lost focus."

Clavin's lips pressed together for a moment as he shook his head. He continued.

"I got caught up in the moment like some newbie fool and made the simplest mistake imaginable. You'll understand this; I had already cross-checked my ticket with the Merchant and opened the door. It was then that everyone demanded a speech and I stepped away. I had never done that before. Not once. But that night, I did. I said some stupid words, and the crowd went wild. A band started playing and I ..."

He shook his head before finishing the sentence. "I did a dance." Michael closed his eyes and ground his teeth as his jaw muscles jumped. He forced out the next words. "A dance." He shook his head, opened his eyes, and focused on Graif. "And that stupid dance killed your sons."

Graif's chin wagged back and forth as he replied, "I don't understand."

Michael sighed.

"I had moved away from my gate. Without thinking,

caught up in all the noise and excitement, I moved down to the next gate. It turned out that the next gate over was where Rige and Garner had already left through. Thus, the door was open and, not rechecking the gate number, I walked through, not realizing what I'd done. For a long time, I insisted on thinking they had made the mistake but, eventually, the obvious truth hit me that it was me, not them. I ended up walking their Path with them, not the reverse."

Enel came into the room, and Michael stopped. "Missus Lossenfell, do you want me to tell this in front of your daughter?"

Alona shook her head, wiped her eyes, and reached out a hand to the little girl. "Come here, Enie. You and Mommy need to go for a walk while Daddy talks to this man, okay?"

But Enel didn't move, didn't even turn her head to look at her mother. She stared at Michael, eyebrows scrunching.

"Enel?"

Enel moved closer to Michael.

A confused Michael looked to Graif for guidance.

"Our daughter, Enel, cannot speak. She never has. It was why our sons became Travelers. They thought that maybe a cure could be found, somewhere, out there."

Guilt stabbed him yet again. He wanted to run for the door. *God, why would you let this happen?* Michael dropped to a knee to look Enel in the eye. "Your brothers were the best of us. I am so, so sorry. They loved you, Enel, and I promise that I will do anything in my power to help you. I will not let their sacrifice pass in vain."

Enel reached out a hand to touch his face.

"I dreamed of you last night," she replied in a hesitant whisper.

Graif and Alona gasped even as Michael's eyes widened in surprise.

Enel's fingers jumped to caress her own lips as she, too, gasped and a huge smile covered her face. She continued, louder and confident. "You were there with Rolly and Gar and the other man."

Michael knelt frozen as he hung on her every syllable.

"They told me to tell you ..."

Michael leaned in as she reached out and took his face in her hands.

"You're forgiven."

Enel's statement shattered him, and he wept the tears of a boy at the grave of his best friend. He saw her parents kneel beside their daughter and wrap her in a great hug as they wept unbelieving tears of their own.

Michael's fingers covered his face as he shook with the flood that now rolled down his cheeks and, some moments later, felt Graif's hand fall gently onto his shoulder. It was two hours later that an exhausted and wept-out Michael left the house and headed for the Sanctum. He was soon on his way and onto the Path.

He was halfway along his journey when he came across the campfire of two men, twins, camped beside a lake. A fire crackled before them, warming their faces as they ate from a large loaf of bread while cooking their food.

He walked down to them, and they stood up, arms opening wide, mouths turned up in smiles.

He'd thought he was done crying.

"I'm sooo sorry."

They offered him fish.

They sat around the fire. They had no words but sang songs of redemption and friendship to him as he cried and then cried some more. When the meal was over, they reached for their packs and drawing their swords, saluted Michael.

Honored by this final action, Michael drew forth his own sword and saluted them back. As he stood there staring at them across his blade, he noticed the engraving begin to twist on the metal and, as it did so, Rige and Garner faded before him. When they were entirely gone, Michael noted a new word that now replaced Peccavi on the blade.

Tetelestai.

He shrugged in bemusement and continued on his way.

Michael stepped back down to Cordis. He passed through the Sanctum and out to where carriages waited to take people back to their homes. Rain poured from a gray sky, and Michael waited as a carriage was brought under the portico for him to enter without a soaking. He gave the man his directions, and then Michael sat back in his seat and stared out the window as his mind revisited the past few nights.

As the carriage approached his destination, Michael felt a strong desire to walk the last little bit, to enjoy the squish of his boots in the mud, to splash in the puddles and feel the rain on his face.

He laughed at himself but called out to the driver anyway, "Ho, driver, stop here."

The carriage pulled to a stop, and Michael stepped out into the rain.

"Thank you, good man. I'm walking the last bit. Have a good day."

He was less than a half-mile from the house but, in very short order, was soaked clear through his cloak and his clothes underneath; he could feel beaded water running along his skin and into his boots.

He looked down and laughed at the mess he'd made of himself. With a whoop, he took off at a run, kicking the puddles into great sheets of water. As he approached the house, Michael stopped, stared at the door, recalled the last time he had seen it, and the last time he had desperately wanted to see it again.

I made it, after all.

His rain-soaked reverie was interrupted as the door slammed open. His father rushed out and down the steps yelling out, "It's Buster. Gantiel, it's Buster." By the time he reached the bottom stair, a servant came at a run behind him, carrying cloaks in his arms with his mother in tow.

Michael met his dad in the rain. "Dad …"

His father cut him off as he gripped onto his forearms. "Two nights ago, we awoke from the same dream. Our boy was dying in the sand beside a black river."

What? "Dad, I *was* dying. You saw me? You're telling me you and Mom had a vision?"

His father nodded his head. Michael could see his tears as they mixed with the rain.

"We prayed and plead for you and, after a few minutes,

suddenly, we both felt like we could stop praying. But, for two days, we have wondered if we'd ever see you again." His dad's shoulders now shook with emotion. "And here you are." He pulled Michael to him and wrapped him up in a huge hug.

By now, the servant and his mother had caught up, and she latched onto him like a mamma bear.

As his own eyes began to run, he said, "Mom, Dad, you prayed me all the way home. I'm sorry for the way I've been acting. I want to come home to stay."

Hollen took the robe from his own shoulders, covered his son, and together they walked up the steps and back home through the door.

ACKNOWLEDGEMENT

A few decades back my friend, Bill Snodgrass, got me interested in writing. So, I blame him for all the work I put into it subsequently. He helped me write this but, in a drastic edit some years ago, I ended up cutting all of his chapters—and a few of mine—except one, not because they were bad, but because I realized I was letting the book spiral out of its original scope too much. So, I want to make sure to thank him for his work and his help on this project.

www.ingramcontent.com/pod-product-compliance
Lightning Source LLC
Chambersburg PA
CBHW011339010726
47493CB00009B/2877